Copyright © 2024 by Adrian R. Hale
All rights reserved.

Edited by Lawrence Editing
https://www.lawrenceediting.com/

THE *Southern* SUBMISSION

ADRIAN R. HALE

Playlist

Coffee - Miguel
Just Pretend - Bad Omens
Big Energy - Lato
Lonely If You Are - Chase Rice
Fall For Me - Sleep Token
Mind Games - Sickick
Water - Kehlani
Bad For You - Chappell Roan
Play With Me - Rendezvous At Two
What's Your Fantasy - Ludacris, Shawna
Heartbroken - Diplo, Jessie Murph, Polo G
Mastermind - Taylor Swift
Comfort - Pour Vous
Latch - Disclosure, Sam Smith
Freaky - Bryce Savage
Alone With You - Ashlee
Home - Good Neighbors
Nasty - Tinashe
Ocean Eyes - Unsecret String Quartet
Never Let Me Go - Florence + The Machine

Dedication

For those who have been hurt in the past and don't trust easily – there is a golden retriever stern brunch daddy out there who will patiently learn just what you need and give you everything you want. Don't settle for anything less than someone who sees all of your vices, flaws, and failures, yet builds you up and shows you unconditional love despite it all.

Never think you're too much.

You're just right exactly as you are.

Content Warning

This story contains elements of cyberstalking, sexual and non-sexual degradation, light somnophilia, verbal, emotional, and physical abuse on and off page, gaslighting, physical violence, and aggression. Your mental health is important. Please consider if these themes are triggering for you in any way before you decide to pursue reading this story. Some topics may be sensitive to readers. This story is best suited for readers 18+.

The Dom/sub relationship and elements of BDSM and kink in this story are one example of the many ways a personal relationship can look based on my research and consultation with other members of the kink community. Establishing clear communication and determining the boundaries required to safely explore your kinks with a trusted partner is of vital importance.

One

Payton

"**F**ucking finally!"

I turn toward my sister-in-law's husky, feminine voice and give her a teasing smile.

"Harlowe," I acknowledge. "What's the deal? I'm not late."

She reaches for the bright pink box with the oversized bow I'm carrying, places it on a table behind her, and wraps me in a quick hug. Her growing baby bump presses against me uncomfortably as I pat her back.

"You're supposed to be the buffer, but you've failed. Get your ass in there and buff. There's only so much Paige and Zander can do to make Hayes and me play nice for very long. I need more allies," she grumbles, releasing me from her grasp.

I laugh. There's bad blood between them and it doesn't matter how many apologies Paige forces out of Hayes, or how long they've been family, the two may never be friends. They begrudgingly ended their feud following her reconciliation with my younger brother six months ago. Since then, they've barely tolerated each other without coming to blows. It started as a slight Hayes served Harlowe five years ago when he tried to pay her off to stay away from Zander. Treating her like one of the hundreds of other women Zander had slept with didn't go over well, and it still stings Harlowe's pride even now.

"You could always fight it out. See which lion wins. My money's on you," I joke. She narrows her dark eyes on me, looking like a lioness ready to attack, and I put up my hands to warn off her claws. "Okay, fine, relax."

Harlowe drags me deeper into the Buckhead mansion Hayes and Paige live in. Soon, the squawking cries of my newborn niece, Madelyn can be heard. Paige is reclined with the tiny baby in her arms, tired but happy. Harlowe and Zander's son, Hendricks, is next to her, peering at the baby with interest. Hayes hovers nearby, watching his wife and newborn intently as if they'll need something in the next second. Zander sits on the other end of the sofa, observing his son with a smile.

Zander missed out on the first four years of Hendricks's life because he didn't know he had a son. Once he found out about his kid, he became the most enthusiastic father and loves that little boy with a fervor I haven't seen from him since he discovered skydiving.

This little scene of domestic bliss is a touching sight. My brothers now have wives and children, settling into a new era where our company, Olympus International, is no longer the prime directive in their lives. It's still my top priority, and I'll continue that way. I have no intention of settling down or letting myself fall prey to whatever's in the water they're drinking. There's no chance of that happening because I don't date. At most, I have play partners who let me take out my desires and urges, and that more than satisfies any need I have for companionship and sex. But...I have to admit, seeing my brothers like this makes me happy for them, even if it's not for me.

"Hi!" Paige calls with a smile. "Come hold Maddie. She's waiting to meet her other favorite uncle."

My eyes grow wide as I tentatively sit next to Paige, holding out my hands for the pink-wrapped bundle she hands me. The little thing inside has dark hair and a tiny, squashed face that blinks at me sleepily and cries as I take her in my arms. I've never held a baby before. She feels fragile. Her cries grow louder as I hold her close.

"I'm doing this wrong. She doesn't like me." I try to give her back to Paige as the bundle squirms.

"She cries at everything right now. Let her get used to you. My arms need a break and yours are strong from all that swimming you do. Stand up and walk around. She likes that," Paige instructs. I do as the Southern belle tells me, rising carefully and walking the length of the room while my older brother keeps staring like the brooding, protective father he is.

"I'm not going to drop her, Hater. You can stop eyeing me like that." I use his childhood nickname that always riles him up, making him grimace.

I laugh and the tiny baby settles in my arms, her cries growing quieter as I pace. I catch sight of Cerberus, Hayes's hulking black Cane Corso guard dog, watching me with shrewd whiskey-colored eyes from his bed in the corner. He's not a typical dog that'll love on you or happily take treats from guests. He's only a snuggly pet for Paige. With the rest of us, he's a menacing presence protecting his people, and apparently, I'm holding his newest charge and could be here to hurt them.

"Hey, tell your demon spawn I'm not a threat," I say, glancing over my shoulder at Paige, who has more sway with the dog than Hayes does now.

"Cerberus, Uncle Payton is our friend. We love him, okay, big guy? I have yummy treats if you behave yourself," she coos in a baby voice that instantly has the big dog's stubby tail wagging. He lowers his head to his paws and lets out a chuff of air as he finally relaxes his bulky shoulders. That dog is too fucking smart and scary. I breathe a little easier now that he no longer appears to want to jump over the couch and take me down for holding Madelyn.

"You look so natural with a baby," Harlowe says in a singsong voice. She's curled in Zander's lap, glancing over at Paige for confirmation.

Paige nods when I catch her eye, looking a little too dreamy herself.

"She's right, Payton. Seeing you with my baby is making my heart burst with happiness. Hayes, you better get over here and hold me before I cry. My hormones are all over the place." Paige dabs at her eyes.

"When will you start dating seriously so you can have a family of your own? Don't you want this for yourself?" Harlowe asks, a gleam in her eye.

"Oh, no, you don't," I warn, ready to hand the baby back and get the hell out of this trap my sisters-in-law are setting for me. "You're both hormonal and crazy if you think I need a wife and babies."

"It's like what Jane Austen wrote in *Pride and Prejudice*," Paige says. "*It is a truth universally acknowledged, that a single man in possession of a good fortune, must be in want of a wife."*

I scowl at them both. I don't want a wife. I don't want to date. I just like to fuck petite blonde women who call me Daddy on occasion.

"I know the sweetest woman you should meet," Harlowe says with a calculating look as if this was her plan all along. "She's hot as shit. She's a friend from my old modeling days, so I think you'd like her. Consider it a favor to me since she's new to Atlanta and needs a tour guide. You're just the man to do it because I'm too busy."

I look around the room. Paige is beaming up at me, fully on board with this idea, Hayes is smirking, and Zander is openly laughing as he listens to his wife bait her trap. Fuck no. I'm stuck here holding a baby, without an easy escape. What fresh hell is this? At least Hendricks is ignoring the conversation, rolling his Hot Wheels cars along the couch between Paige and Zander, oblivious to the snare being set.

"I respectfully pass. I'm sure she's wonderful, but I don't want to be set up with one of your friends. Or with anyone, for that matter."

Maddie makes a gurgling noise in my arms, drawing my attention to her tiny face, and I wonder if I did something to upset her. Is she on Harlowe's side, too? *Women.* They can't all be against me.

Harlowe gives me a disbelieving look and fishes her phone from her purse. She quickly opens it, then flashes the phone toward me with a stunning redhead's Instagram account on display.

"This is Jillian. She's adorable, funny as hell, and loves the water, like you. You should really meet her before you make that decision." She swipes through the photos and videos for me to see what I'm turning down as I rock back and forth in front of her with the baby in my arms.

Harlowe's not wrong. Jillian is hot and fit, and from her carefully curated Insta feed, seems like a lot of fun. But I'm not looking for the relationship Harlowe wants to saddle on me.

"I believe you. I'm just not interested. Don't waste your time trying to set me up." Jesus, my hands are getting sweaty at the thought of being tied down to one of Harlowe's friends when all I want is to work to my heart's content and focus on my job. I *like* being a workaholic. It suits me.

Hayes lets out a bark of a laugh at my discomfort and stands, not wanting me to hold his child anymore. He relieves me of my burden and cradles the tiny baby in his huge arms like it's nothing.

"This is fucking great. You're in for it now. Glad her sights are set on you and I can finally relax," he says in a low voice with his back to the sofa. I raise an eyebrow at him but smile in challenge at Harlowe, ready for whatever she thinks she can throw at me. I settle on a chair across from her as Hayes moves around the room, soothing the fussy baby.

"Okay, maybe not a model, then," Harlowe says, intent on her Instagram as she quickly searches and turns the phone to show me another account. "This is Libby. She's a single mom friend that I know from Hendricks's school. She's a total MILF, with the sweetest little boy that Hendricks is obsessed with. They're in the same class, and Theo's smart, too." She shows me a photo of a stunning brunette with huge blue eyes and a gorgeous smile, holding the hand of a cute little boy on a playground.

"Harlowe," I warn as she scrolls through Libby's Instagram, showing me more photos of Theo and her mom friend, an apparently down-to-earth and smoking-hot woman who knows how to take a killer photo.

"The father's totally out of the picture, so no baby daddy drama, either. Ready-made family, win-win for company PR! She's a total sweetheart who I like, which is rare, but I've heard what she likes in bed and it's hot. Not at all saying she's easy, but if you hit it off, I could see it being mutually beneficial."

Paige chokes out an embarrassed laugh and claps a hand over her mouth, scandalized by Harlowe's brazen words. She's young and innocent, completely sheltered until she met Hayes, who has likely corrupted her thoroughly at this point, but it's hard to remove the impeccable Southern manners forced into her. Harlowe is unapologetically herself and can be a bit much, especially for a prim and proper debutante like Paige. The fact they get along so well is still shocking, but everyone likes Paige.

"Damn, Harlowe. You're shameless. Do you even hear yourself? Libby's hot and that kid's super cute, but I'm not interested in dating anyone. Find her a good guy who will do her justice as a boyfriend because it's not going to be me."

"You're impossible. You can't be the only Olsen brother without a partner. It's indecent."

"Indecent?" I scoff, my smile slipping as Harlowe grows more insistent. I point at my younger brother. "Zander being a player for ten years was indecent. Not wanting to date your friends is far from that. Let me live my life on my terms and enjoy my work. I'll be fine." I'm keeping my words family-friendly due to the little ears around me, but I want to let her know how irritated I am with her insistence.

"Fine." She rolls her eyes. "I think it's bad for business. You're the PR guy. You know better than anyone that being in a relationship would show the world that the men of Olympus are calming down, becoming more serious than ever, and committing to the stability of their company. Isn't that what Zander being married did? It's done wonders for your subsidiary stock prices. You're the lone holdout. We need to wife you up."

She wraps Zander's arm around her belly and laces her fingers with his. He pulls her back into his lap, fully on board with whatever she says. He's a stupid, besotted fool. I swear he loses his ability to think with his big brain whenever she's around.

"My love life's never been a problem for the company, like Zander's was, so you can't use that against me," I point out, gesturing at Zander, who makes a face at me like he doesn't want me bringing up his past indiscretions in front of his wife, who is all too aware of them. "As for being committed to the company's stability, there's a hacker I need to track down, and all the operations to run. I'm putting in more time than ever to ensure the company's success, so obviously I'm already doing my part. I don't need a wife or a girlfriend to do that."

Harlowe's shoulders slump as I refute her arguments with ease, but she straightens and gets a gleam in her eyes I don't like the look of. "Just let me introduce you to a few people. Give them a shot and see what you think in person," she persists. "You need a girlfriend."

"Uncle Payton, do you want to borrow my girlfriend?"

I look over, surprised at the small voice chiming in, and catch Hendricks looking up at me from the rug where he's playing with more of his toy cars. "That's a nice offer, buddy, but I don't want to take your girlfriend," I say with an easy smile. "Your momma is playing around. I don't actually need a girlfriend, but thank you."

"It's okay. It's just pretend. Taylor and I play boyfriend and girlfriend on the playground, but it's not real. You could pretend to have a girlfriend and Momma would be happy."

I chuckle at his suggestion. "That's very nice of you. I'm sure

Taylor likes playing with you more than she'd want to be my girlfriend."

He shrugs and goes back to his cars satisfied that he no longer has to be a part of the conversation. I turn back to Harlowe and give her a look.

"You see what your antics are doing? Your kid is trying to save me now. How about we leave this subject and get back to the cute baby and new mom we're supposed to be celebrating? I'm good on my own. There's no need for you to meddle in my love life."

Harlowe pouts for a moment before leaning forward and pinning me with her most calculating stare. "Mark my words, Payton, a woman is going to come along and turn your world upside down and have you eating your words. I'm going to laugh my ass off when it happens."

Her words sound more like a curse and a tingle of unease runs down my spine. "If that's the case, I'll laugh with you." My smile feels a little more apprehensive than usual after what she said. I need to plan for a future assault where Harlowe is concerned. She doesn't give up easily. I'm going to be an ongoing target for her machinations if that look is anything to go by.

Two

Payton

I'm going to kill Harlowe. She's asked me to meet her at a place called the fucking Unicorn Café on a Saturday morning in June. I *should* be at the coast escaping the oppressive heat and humidity of Atlanta, but she won't take no for an answer.

My phone vibrates in my pocket as I open the door and get a welcome blast of icy air conditioning in the face. My eyes adjust from the blazing sunshine outside and aqua blue immediately assaults my senses. Blue and white flowers decorate the ceiling and cascade down the walls above the aqua bench seating, with marble tables set at intervals along the periphery. I blink back my surprise as a giant carousel unicorn greets me at the entrance, a bemused smile on my lips.

"Fucking Harlowe." I laugh to myself as I scan the packed

café for her.

She picked the girliest shit imaginable for whatever she has planned, which I suspect is devious. I don't see Harlowe's tall stature and supermodel face anywhere as I walk up to the pastry counter and scan the menu on the back wall. Every item is called something *enchanted, magical, whimsical,* or some shit that makes you wonder what they could possibly put in it. Sprinkles and rainbows, most likely. It'll be a slow death for Harlowe, I decide. Something befitting the lack of normal coffee on the menu. I don't care if she's married to my brother or the mother of his children. This is a serious offense.

My pocket vibrates again and I pull out my phone to see a few texts from my brothers.

Zander: RUN. Harlowe's scheming. This meetup is a trap. She's going to ambush you.

Hayes: HAHA! I love this for you, Pay. You're fucked.

Zander: I tried to stall, to give you time to escape. I fucked her into a puddle of submission, but she's still intent on whatever plan she has to wife you up.

Hayes: This is the group chat, Zand. We don't want to hear about your sex life.

Zander: It's inspo, Hater. Pay, you have thirty minutes. Make up an excuse to leave. Save yourself before it's too late.

Yeah, no shit. I type out a quick reply as I chuckle quietly. His wife's a scheming woman intent on seeing my single days end because she's enjoying matrimonial bliss and thinks me being unattached is an atrocity to the family name. But I'm just as stubborn as she is.

> Me: She's been trying to set me up for two weeks and I've managed to evade her attempts. If I can maintain our company image through a mine collapse, having our asses handed to us through public smear campaigns and cyber attacks, I think I'll hold my own against your wife.

I snap a photo of the gold filigree menu board with the frou-frou drink names and the flowers dripping around it and send it to the chat.

> Me: Your wife has horrible taste in cafés. This place sucks.

My phone vibrates a moment later.

> Zander: That's her favorite café. Don't say it sucks or she'll cut you. Again, RUN.

> Hayes: Paige loves their high tea. I refuse to go in. You're a braver man than me, brother.

I pocket my phone, head to the counter, and smile disarmingly. "Do you make a drink that's not enchanted? Maybe something befitting an ogre who drinks regular old swamp water or something rather than a pretty princess who wants rainbow sprinkles in their coffee?" I ask the woman in an emerald green dress and—no shit, a sparkly tiara—behind the counter.

She blinks at me and blushes. "Everything on the menu is magical. I can help you pick something if you tell me what you like. To drink, that is," she says, looking away quickly, flustered by her innocent slipup.

I smile wider and lean toward her, wanting to play with her, but she's already flustered because she finds me attractive and I should go easy on her. "How about a plain iced Americano," I say to put her out of her misery.

"We have an enchanted Americano. It has cinnamon and nutmeg with a golden cold foam topper."

I suppress a grimace at her description of the bastardized drink and smile again to keep from showing my bad luck. Harlowe owes me for this. "Why not? I'll live on the magical side and try something new."

I hand over my black AMEX as more customers line up behind me, waiting to order their drinks. No surprise, it's mostly women and girls. I'm one of the only males in the place, and the others are clearly here by force of their partners or daughters.

I give my name before turning away from the counter and discovering my next issue. This café is packed. Groups of women are having tea parties, or taking photos of their aesthetic food and drinks on the tables to post on their socials before they take their first sip or bite. Making pretty drinks and food that customers take photos of and post to their feeds is a great PR move by the café. No wonder Harlowe loves it, being a social media foodie and chef herself.

"Enchanted Americano for Payton."

I look back at the counter where the barista placed my drink. It's in a tall glass with a gold-tinted foam at the top sprinkled with cinnamon. I suppress a gag. I take it with trepidation and walk to a table I spotted earlier.

I slide in next to a woman wearing a pink Yankees baseball cap pulled low over her face. Her blonde hair is in a low bun held up by a pen in a way that strikes me as too sexy for how casual it is. It shows off the graceful slope of her neck, looking perfect to stroke a finger along as a reminder for her to relax. She has earbuds in, intently focused, and furiously typing on a laptop. She's been here for a while, evidenced by the debris of a half-eaten chocolate chip muffin, two glasses—one empty, the other half-full of an iced coffee—and a few crumpled napkins around her computer.

She stands out as the only person working on a computer. This place is obviously a photo op, not used for work, and seeing her with a laptop out on a Saturday while other patrons are here for aesthetic reasons intrigues me. That and it's the only available spot. Maybe her intense work vibes scared off anyone from taking the table. She doesn't scare me. I work more Saturdays than not myself.

I take a small sip of the Americano and suppress the urge to make a face when I taste the additions that earned it the enchanted moniker. I sigh. It's the only caffeine I'm getting that won't come in a teacup or covered in sprinkles. This place is fucking ridiculous. I'll give Harlowe such a hard time when she gets here. I take another sip of the abomination and shudder. It's a travesty to coffee.

A frustrated grunt catches my attention. I look over at the blonde who's staring in frustration at her laptop, face set in a scowl as the screen displays a page of frozen code instead of whatever she was working on. She taps her fingers on her trackpad, looking for a way to remove it, but can't get the code to go away. She rubs her face and blows out an angry breath. I watch curiously as she inhales deeply and balls her fists. I can almost hear the silent conversation she has with herself to calm down and approach the situation with patience while she slowly blows out her breath. When her eyes snap open, I know her internal pep talk did nothing to quell the storm of violence she wants to rain down on the misbehaving laptop.

I smile to myself as she quietly starts to lose her shit, smacking the keyboard, clicking on the trackpad, and even hitting the power button, to no avail. The code has frozen her screen, keeping her from her work.

"Come on, you piece of crap," she mutters, clearly vexed, seeming ready to throw the laptop on the floor at this point. Maybe with the amount of caffeine she's had, she will.

I could fix this for her. It would be so easy. I saw the solution the moment I looked over at her screen. My smile slides off as she wraps her small hands around the laptop and lifts it. Fuck, she's about to hurl it onto the floor. I quickly place my hand over one of hers to stop the motion, forcing the laptop safely back onto the table.

"I can help," I say gently, holding back my grin, not wanting to laugh at her tantrum over her tech issue.

She looks up, pretty hazel eyes widening as they lock on mine, plump pink lips that were just set in an angry snarl parting in shock. Something flares behind her assessing gaze, whether in recognition or maybe interest, I'm not sure. She's difficult to decipher at the moment, and that's intriguing since I typically read others at a glance. Her eyes roam over my face quickly, taking me in and gauging whatever threat I may present. She lets go of the laptop with the hand not caught under mine and pulls the earbuds out of her ears.

"What did you say?" Her words are clipped. Her attitude meant to end the conversation as she stares me down, unafraid of offending me by not capitulating to the expected niceties of the situation.

"I can help," I repeat, smiling in earnest at her frigid response. I like a challenge, and, oh boy, is this woman a fucking challenge.

Warily, she unclenches her hand from the laptop and slides it out from under my palm. I liked the warmth of her smaller fingers under mine, so I kept my hand over hers under the guise of preventing a technological travesty. I do hate when people blame a computer for what amounts to user error, but it was nice. It's also been a while since I've touched someone like that. Maybe too long if I'm getting off on manipulating a situation like this.

"Why would you do that?" she drawls, clearly from the South, but not Atlanta, and she's certainly not charmed by me. She's wary of my offer and unafraid to question it. She frowns at the laptop, giving the screen of code a dirty look, her fuller bottom lip pouting a bit. I suppress my smile at her hatred. She doesn't have a great relationship with this machine.

"You're clearly working and need a functional laptop. I can fix your issue and get you back on task. If you *have* to work on a Saturday, you might as well get it done as quickly as possible so you can continue with the rest of your weekend." I attempt to keep the humor out of my tone as I gesture at her laptop. "Mind if I borrow this?"

"If you can get this stupid thing to work and get me back to my story so I can meet my deadline, go ahead. Whatever you do, don't lose my work. I need everything that was on that screen before this piece of crap wanted to act a fool. It's been janky since I got it," she grumbles, confirming my theory that she's not a fan of the laptop. She huffs and flops back against the seat, crossing her arms over her chest, her tan skin standing out against her white tank top.

"Story and deadline. I'm going to take a guess and say journalist or marketing job of some sort?" I ask, picking up her laptop and setting it in front of me.

"The former. My editor assigned me a story last minute that needs to be in today because of course he'd give the youngest reporter the shittiest story with the quickest turnaround time over the weekend along with the oldest laptop that hates me."

I stifle my laugh at her explanation as I type in a series of keystrokes and pop up a command prompt box. "It's not the worst computer I've used," I offer to soothe her worries.

My fingers fly over the keyboard, typing in familiar code sequences and prompts and quickly scanning the returning messages for errors. This is a piece of cake. She has nothing to worry about. Her laptop has plenty of life left for her to continue a long, dysfunctional relationship with it.

"I didn't realize you're so tech-savvy," she says, then snaps her mouth shut and straightens up as if she didn't mean to say the thought out loud.

I glance over quickly. She sits rigidly, tension radiating from her as I work on her computer. I smile politely, hoping to disarm her, but I'm quickly assessing the situation, figuring out what she knows. She's a journalist and I'm a person of interest. A billionaire. A high-profile businessman who's well-known in this city.

"I guess I'm at a disadvantage here. It sounds like you know more about me than I do about you, despite just sitting down next to you and offering to help when I noticed you were in computer-related distress. How about you put us on even footing while I fix your laptop?" I still my fingers to show her

I can just as easily stop my attempt at fixing her problem and leave her to it, or I can save the day and get her back to making her deadline.

Panic crosses her features as she quickly understands my meaning. Her eyes dart to the laptop and back to my face before she gives me a look of resignation, her mouth settling into a line of grim determination and a pink tint rising in her cheeks. The rosy flush sets off her smooth skin, hazel eyes flashing at me, and those damn alluring lips that she's twisting together under my appraisal. She rolls her eyes and huffs, making a motion for me to continue my ministrations with her laptop.

"I'm Ainsley Montgomery, a staff reporter for the Gazette, a small community paper. I know you're Payton Olsen of Olympus International fame because I occasionally write articles for the business section, and Olympus comes up often. Well, I write whatever my editor tells me to, which is basically everything because he dumps extra work on me due to the paper being underfunded and understaffed."

As soon as she starts talking I begin writing code for a program that will initiate anytime she types my name and continue until she stops. "That wasn't so hard, was it, Ainsley Montgomery?" I drawl, liking the sound of her name in my mouth. "Now, where are you from? Doesn't sound like Atlanta by your accent." I hold my fingers over the keyboard again, prompting her to continue before I free her laptop from the clutches of her code issue.

She bites her lip and stares at my fingers. I want to reach out and free that soft lip from her teeth, but I keep my hands just out of reach of the keyboard she wants me so desperately to type on. Her eyes narrow like she's willing my fingers to move without having to give more away than necessary about herself. Tricky girl. I wiggle my fingers at her as a taunt. She brings her gaze up to mine and I smile at the frustration I see snapping in her amber depths. She's a prickly one. It's adorably at odds with her pretty pink pout and hat.

"Charleston, South Carolina." She sighs. No extra information. Just the bare bones provided in resignation. I only have time to type one line of code this time. I'm thankful for my quick typing skills to manage even that.

"Come on, if I'm fixing your computer and you're putting us on even footing given you know way more about me, you're going to have to give me more than that. Why are you working in a café where people prefer to take photos of their magical lattes than drink them?" I prompt.

Her shoulders lower a fraction at the simple question. Her eyes meet mine again but with less hostility this time. "I like the chaos. It drowns out the noise in my brain and helps me think. This place is always busy on the weekends, and I can get lost in the people and shuffle."

I complete more code while she speaks and stop when she does. "What do you like to write about most?"

"I like human interest stories. Things that give insight into who someone is behind the facade and public persona." She inhales deeply and lets out a sigh as she looks around the café. "This is pointless. If that laptop is dead, just say so and stop wasting your time. I'll call my editor and tell him this shitty hand-me-down kicked the bucket and cost him my story, and I'll go home."

"Don't count this dinosaur out just yet," I tell her playfully, typing in my final series of code that will complete my hastily created—but brilliant if I do say so myself—program and issue commands to finish the sequence, watching as a series of pages flash across the screen, replacing the code.

She leans toward me, gaping at the laptop as her document finally appears, just as it was when the code originally popped up. "You fixed it!" she quietly exclaims, her face lighting up with a brilliant smile that should be seen more often because it's absolutely stunning. She could get people to do anything she wanted just by flashing that gorgeous grin. It'd be a dangerous asset if deployed correctly, yet she chooses hostility and contention. Interesting.

Ainsley Montgomery just became a puzzle I want to solve.

I don't tell her I had the issue fixed with the second command I typed on her laptop and was using the rest of the time to create a program that will initiate if she types my name. I type a final command and close the prompt box before handing the laptop back to her, regretting having finished the task and likely ending our interaction. There's no reason for someone young, beautiful, and busy like her to talk to me now. But she'll certainly be reminded of this interaction should I come up in her writing in the future, and that makes me unreasonably happy.

She takes the laptop reverently and sets it back on her table, still smiling as she scrolls through her document, checking to be sure everything she wrote is still there. She hits the save button three times, her eyes narrowed like she doesn't trust it to do as she asks.

"You only need to save it once, but if it makes you feel better to do it multiple times, you can." I laugh.

"Better safe than swearing," she replies seriously. She looks over at me, and her cheeks stain pink once again as she fidgets against the aqua velvet of the banquette. "Um, thanks for the help. I don't know what I would've done if this laptop had died on me and taken my story with it. I would've missed my deadline for sure. Maybe given up completely." She rolls her lip with her teeth and looks down.

"You would have been fine," I assure her. "You strike me as the industrious sort and would have come up with a solution to your problem that didn't involve throwing the laptop on the ground in a fit of anger." I can't help the laugh that breaks out of me this time, remembering how cute she was as she lost her shit and lifted the laptop to do just that. She has so much personality and I've barely broken the surface.

"I was about to before you intervened," she admits, propping her elbows on the table and hiding her face in her hands.

I restrain myself from reaching out and tugging her hands away from her gorgeous face. That would be something a more familiar person would do, not a perfect stranger like me should. Instead, I lean back and silently watch her, waiting to see if she'll look over again, or if she'll take this as her out and get back to work on her story.

A moment later, she drops her hands and glances over at me, her face a mask of anger I wasn't expecting to see. She sees my casual posture and leans back to match me.

"How am I supposed to repay this act of generosity?" she snaps.

I raise an eyebrow at her tone and resist the urge to bring out more of the brat in her for fun. "That's assuming I was expecting you to repay it in the first place instead of helping because I could without any ulterior motives."

"People don't do nice things for strangers. There's always some kind of expectation, insidious or blatant."

She's sassy and I like it. I want more of her.

"Look at you, pulling out your fancy journalist vocabulary trying to figure out my motives. I helped you when you needed it because I have the skills to do so. That's it."

I run a hand through my hair and give her a look I hope

conveys I purely wanted to help. She narrows her eyes, so I roll mine at her and laugh. She huffs in indignation.

"Just take the help when someone offers. Why question everything?" I straighten abruptly. She sits up quickly, mirroring my movements while appearing uneasy. "Unless you want to owe me a favor, Ainsley Montgomery." I pin her with a calculating stare, knowing it's far more intense than anything I've sent her way this entire exchange. She squirms under the scrutiny.

"That sounds like a motive to me, Payton," she fires back.

Fuck, she's feisty. I like the roiling energy she matches to my easy enthusiasm. I lean my arm on the back of the banquette, entering her space. She refuses to give up an inch of her position, allowing me closer. I breathe in the sweet scent of vanilla and coffee coming from her that smells better than the blasphemous Americano I was drinking. I should start every morning with a hit of her.

"What'll it be?" I ask softly, instead of letting my mind wander to the what-ifs and remote possibilities. "Take it as something nice a person did for you, or you're now beholden to me for an unspecified favor of my choosing."

Her choice will say a lot about how she views the world. She's already told me plenty just by insisting that strangers don't do nice things for others out of the goodness of their hearts. She expects there to always be a catch. Despite her assumptions, I had no ulterior motives when I offered to help her. But if she willingly chooses to owe me a favor when given the option to accept that it was good luck that I happened to sit down next to her and could fix her tech issue, well then, that seems to be my own good luck. If fate wants to tie Ainsley Montgomery to me so easily, why the hell would I turn that down? I'm an opportunist to my core, and I like the idea of more time with her for some reason.

"Why would I agree to an unspecified favor of your choosing? There are too many uncertain terms in that phrase. I'd be stupid to agree to that."

She crosses her arms over her chest, drawing my attention to her perky tits that are now straining under the white cotton of her tank top. I look away at the busy café. I have no business checking out the chest of a beautiful woman who has to be a decade younger than me. I'm usually better than that, but I'm unreasonably attracted to her. There's no denying that she's my physical ideal from top to bottom, and her attitude has me itching to teach her a lesson on what bratting this hard will get her with me. Apparently, it's been too long since I've exercised my desires thoroughly to ignore the spike of *want* for her that's risen in me. I return my gaze once I'm back in control.

"I didn't say you have to. The choice is yours." I reach out and playfully tip the bill of her hat up, and she swats at my hand.

"It's not much of a choice," she says, adjusting the hat on her head. "I owe you for fixing my computer. I just don't like your terms. I need them defined in order to agree. Or at least to understand the level of the favor that's required."

"I saved your ass today," I point out as I tip my head at her.

I'm arguing a point I hadn't even wanted to originally, but now think is hilarious as she takes us down this route when she could have avoided it altogether. I have no problem stirring the pot when presented with the opportunity. Ainsley just happened to give me a very tempting pot.

She bites her lip and narrows her eyes at me, and this time, I can't stop myself from reaching out to grab her chin gently, using my thumb to pull her lip from between her teeth. Her eyes grow wide as I tap the plump pink softness once before releasing her face.

"You abuse that poor lip when you're thinking. It's not nice to do that to something so pretty." I smile and lace my fingers in my lap to keep them to myself. The last thing I need to be doing is touching a stranger, flirty banter or not. *Especially* not a journalist who writes about my company. She'll likely use this interaction against me the next time she's given an assignment on Olympus. I can see the headlines now, *Olympus COO manhandles strangers in cafés off the clock*. Just what Olympus needs. I have to rein in my desire to flirt with her for the hell of it. Flirting with everyone may be my go-to and ingrained in my personality, but it doesn't have to get me into trouble when I need it the least.

Her cheeks flush, but she doesn't look away, her gaze fierce and determined. "Fine. I owe you a favor. I hate that you're being super vague on purpose and seem to enjoy my displeasure about not knowing your terms of what that means. I don't like the idea of you fixing my computer and not expecting anything from it even more. I'd feel worse about that."

My brows rise at her agreement and my heart soars as I study her for a moment. "You're an enigma, Ainsley Montgomery. Most would've taken the help and moved on without another thought. You choose to owe me an unspecified favor. What's wrong with you?" I chuckle at her look of rebuke at my question.

"Nothing's wrong with me. I just know the world always expects its pound of flesh. If I didn't pay you back for this, there would be something far worse waiting for me. Why do you keep saying my full name like that?"

"That's such a morbid way of looking at life. I say your full name because that's how you introduced yourself and I like the way it sounds."

"Do you always say everything you think?" she growls, pressing her arms tighter against her chest as she grows exasperated, closing herself in more.

I suppress another smile. She has no fucking idea. I haven't said even a quarter of what I've been thinking. "Are you surprised that people can be honest and unfiltered when you keep yourself guarded with this prickly persona for whatever reason?" I challenge back.

She drops her arms to her sides, her hands in fists. "I'm *not* prickly."

I grin at her with amusement until she drops her gaze.

"I'm just annoyed by you," she admits quietly.

I raise my eyebrows in mock surprise. "How very annoying of me to offer help when you needed it the most. If there were even one other free table in this café, I'd take my annoying self away and let you brood in peace over your work that you seem intent on ignoring."

She glares at me. "I'm *not* ignoring my work. You're distracting me." She narrows her eyes at me. "Why are *you* here, anyway? This doesn't seem like your type of place unless you're a secret unicorn and magical coffee lover."

I shudder, shaking my head. "Definitely not. This place is horrible. I'm meeting my sister-in-law here. She picked the spot and has terrible taste, but she's running late, so I get to annoy you by fixing your laptop while I wait. I'm going to need your contact details. Your phone number and email. Probably your address as well."

"What, why?" she sputters, her hazel eyes widening in horror, making me laugh at her disproportionate reaction.

"For my unspecified favor that I can call in at any time. I need to be able to contact you somehow. Texting or calling is the obvious option, but if you don't reply, I'd email. If you don't respond to that, I'd take it upon myself to show up where you live to cash in on that favor. You've already told me where you work, so I could just show up there if you're extra tricky."

She gapes at me. "You're insane. You'd stalk me just to call in a *favor*?"

"It's not stalking if I tell you my plans in advance. Besides, you're the one who chose to owe me the favor and made it that much more appealing. I just want to make sure you'll hold up your end of the bargain when it comes time to pay up. And don't get any ideas about going back on it now."

"I would *never*." She leans toward me, her eyes flashing with contempt that I would even insinuate that she would back out.

I fish my phone out of my pocket and open my contacts before holding it out for her to fill in her information. "We're going to be good friends, Ainsley Montgomery. You're going to love having me in your life," I promise with enthusiasm. This is so much fun. I like getting under her skin. It's so easy.

She takes the phone warily and stares at me. "You're not at all like I expected." She types in her contact details and hands the phone back to me with a scowl.

"Oh, Ainsley, you can't say something like that and not elaborate. What did you expect of me, exactly?" I lean forward eagerly, ready to hear what she has to say.

Three

Ainsley

Payton Olsen is not at all what I expected. He stares at me like he can see right into my soul with those vivid, ocean-blue eyes, and I'm stripped of all my defenses under his piercing gaze. It was a surprise to look up from my work daze and realize the well-known and revered middle Olsen brother was sitting next to me, offering to help with my laptop.

Even more complicated was the fact that I happened to be writing a story about Payton's company, Olympus International, at that very moment. Having one of the men who run the company I was writing about appear and offer to help with the laptop holding a story that mentions him by name made me wildly uncomfortable. It was even more shocking to find him flirting unabashedly with me while he fixed the dang thing. Payton, a billionaire, and one of the most powerful businessmen in the South, was flirting with *me*, a young, grumpy reporter, in this busy, unicorn-themed café where he's so out of place, it's comical.

However, I can't help thinking that this meeting is fortuitous, and I need to take full advantage of it. I've been looking for an inside route to the Olsen men since moving to Atlanta two years ago when I received my first story assignment covering their business dealings. They're enigmatic, ruthless, and for some reason, have bought up untold businesses and dismantled family legacies without any oversight. While some of their subsidiary companies are public, the brothers privately hold Olympus, so they don't even have investors to answer to, making the man in front of me a formidable opponent of a magnitude I've never come up against. I'd love to know him better, for the sake of journalistic curiosity. He could be the key to my big-ticket story and to finally earning my way into a bigger paper and stepping out of obscurity at the Gazette.

Only now *I* owe him a favor, and he's demanding *my* contact details and threatening to show up at the Gazette to get me to repay it. Stalker vibes and red flags never looked so good as they're delivered with that beautiful smile he's so free with, despite every attempt I've made to dissuade him from deploying it. I'm willing to override every one of my self-preservation instincts to run in the opposite direction from his charming, effervescent personality just to have a shot at learning more about the way his business runs, and, if I'm being honest, who he is beneath the public appearance he puts on as the businessman who spins all the PR for Olympus.

"Oh, Ainsley, you can't say something like that and not elaborate. What did you expect of me, exactly?" He reaches out and brushes a strand of hair off my cheek so quickly it's like it didn't happen, but I feel the burn of his finger against my skin even after it's gone. I swat at his hand again to keep up the pretense, and he smiles like it's a new game now that he knows I don't want him touching me.

Dammit. My big, fat mouth lacking a filter just got me into a less-than-ideal position because I was thinking about him being charming and wondering who he is behind the smiley mask instead of focusing on what I'm saying. I cringe. I'm usually so much better than this, but twice now I've managed to say something that should have stayed inside my head as an intrusive thought and he's called me out both times.

I close my eyes and breathe in, looking for anything that will get me out of this conversation with my dignity intact and without embarrassing myself. When I open my eyes, Payton is still staring at me intently, his chin propped on his hand while he leans his elbow on the banquette behind us, and it doesn't help me find any sort of composure in the least. I frown at him and he just grins in return. A stupid, gorgeous, bright smile that twists my stomach and sends my heart skittering around my ribcage like a dumb bird that's flown inside and can't find its way out. My heart is a dumb bitch bird.

"I thought you'd be all *brooding businessman*, super un-approachable, or at the very least, less...smiley. I don't know, maybe less talkative and definitely more aloof and secretive. Especially with your background and business. That's how your brothers seem and how you three present yourselves to the public."

I cringe at my awkwardness. It was a valiant effort. My journalism degree and having written countless stories couldn't help the eloquence of that answer if I had a week's deadline to do it justice. Not with him staring at me with that soul-searching look and secret smile like he knows exactly who I am at my core.

There's no way he could even begin to unravel that, but he continues to stare like he's piecing me together and it makes me nervous. I should be the one figuring out who *he* is, chasing down the story of Payton Olsen and what makes *him* tick. I hate feeling like the shoe is on the other foot. *Is this what my subjects feel like when I interview them?*

He laughs. "Hayes and Zander are definitely brooding and far less smiley. You're not wrong on that."

"But you're not," I state, leaning toward him, unable to stop the pull he has on me, wanting to figure him out now. I've always been interested in who people are when no one is looking. What drives them? What makes them tick? If Payton's willing to divulge that to me now, I'm listening, and I'm taking notes.

"All of this is off the record. We're just two new friends getting to know one another over coffee." He gives me a look like he knows exactly what I'm thinking and I chastise myself for potentially broadcasting those thoughts.

I plaster on a poker face and school my features into submission. "Of course."

"I prefer to enjoy life and take things less seriously than either of them. I guess that's why you think I'm smiley." He flashes that grin at me and it flips my stomach again.

I deepen my frown at him. "You smile an annoying amount. Like a total weirdo." I turn away from him and pick up my iced coffee to take a sip, proving that he's incredibly uninteresting and I'd rather do anything other than talk to him. He wants attention and no matter how much I'd like to know who he is, I'd rather not cater to him now that I know it.

I resettle in my seat, returning my attention to my laptop, and refocus on my story, which I should have been doing all along, given I need to turn it in to Reid in a few hours. Sparring with Payton cost me precious time I could have been writing, yet I let him sweep me up in this effortless back-and-forth so easily. Maybe because I felt I owed him for fixing my laptop. Admittedly, I'm intrigued by one of the most powerful men in the city sitting in a silly café and deciding he wanted to smile at *me*.

"Oh, you like me, no matter how much you want to pretend otherwise."

I whip my head back his way, ready to refute his statement, to catch him laughing because he got a rise out of me. "Excuse me. I have work to do and I'm not here to entertain a bored billionaire who has too much time on his hands on a Saturday," I snap.

"You've been thoroughly enjoying yourself this whole time." He looks toward the door as a stunning brunette strides in like it's a catwalk from her past life as a model. He turns back to me with a softer smile. "But it seems like you're in luck because Harlowe's arrived and I'll leave you alone. For now."

I catch his eyes darken minutely and wonder at his meaning behind *for now*. Both relief and disappointment wash over me. I shouldn't be enjoying his attention, so I reach for a barrier to remove the warm fuzzies it's given me.

"Finally. I thought you'd never stop."

"Just know I'll be contacting you about my little favor, and if you're a woman of your word, you'll answer."

I stare at him incredulously, wondering if he's serious. "Don't question my integrity, even over something as dumb as owing you an unspecified favor." I seethe, mostly mad that he cornered me into agreeing to his damn undefined terms in the first place, but this stings, too.

"You're a journalist. How am I supposed to know what you will or won't do?"

I bristle at that but don't get to reply as Harlowe Sorenson, now Olsen, sweeps over in a cloud of confidence and smiles, waving at Payton. He scoots toward me on the banquette, and I lean away from his legs, giving him room. His hand brushes the length of my bare thigh as he moves between our tables, but it's gone before I can pull away. I spend a moment wondering if I'm delusional enough to have imagined that he'd have done it intentionally, or if it was an accident.

I stuff my earbuds back in my ears but keep the music off so I can sit in near silence in this crowded café, with Payton still so close to me, and his sister-in-law, who is a former supermodel, current cookbook author and social media sensation, hugging him tightly. I may also be interested in hearing what could have brought them here, of all places. I return my eyes to my story to give them privacy despite my curiosity, casually typing out a few lines at a time, but without as much force as I normally would.

"Sorry I'm late," Harlowe says, releasing Payton from her hug and looking around the café. "Isn't this place the cutest? I can't wait to bring Hana here when she's old enough for tea parties." She rubs her obvious baby bump through her tight, hot pink dress as a warm smile plays on her face while she takes in the decor.

I tuck away the tidbit of information that the pregnancy she and Zander recently announced on Harlowe's Foulmouthed Foodie Instagram page is far enough along to know the gender—a little girl—and they also have a name picked out for her—Hana.

"We need to talk about your choice of meetup spots. Never again do you get to choose where we meet. Do you know what they put in my Americano? Cinnamon and nutmeg, like it's Thanksgiving in June. And golden foam. What the fuck is that, Harlowe?"

Harlowe laughs, bending forward and slapping Payton on the arm. "Oh my God, you're such a baby! It's just some spice. Live a little." She straightens up quickly. "I have to use the restroom. I drank too much water on the way over and this little girl just kicked my bladder when I bent like that. Let's hope there isn't a crazy line. Order me an iced half-caff magical macchiato, please."

Payton shakes his head as she whirls and makes her way through the café toward the bathroom. I'm surprised when he turns toward me and I'm caught watching him. "Want anything to drink?"

I stop typing and pull an earbud out of one ear guiltily. "No. You don't have to get me anything."

He shakes his head at me with a smile. "I asked if you *wanted* anything to drink, not if I *had* to get you something. Just tell me what you like." He pauses and looks down at my two glasses. "Maybe you don't need any more caffeine. You're already testy enough as is. If I get you another coffee, you might be wound too tightly. Who knows what it'll take to get you to loosen up at that point." His eyes flash an indigo blue, his lips curling up into an entirely different sort of smile from the ones he's given me. This one is pure male arrogance in his sexual abilities to *loosen someone up*. He *is* flirting with me, and his innuendo isn't even veiled this time. I stare him down, not allowing his comment to get the flustered reaction I know he's looking for.

"You *would* be the kind of entitled rich man who isn't used to hearing no. When a woman says no, she means it. I don't want anything from you, even a drink. Now go order whatever it is you're supposed to and leave me alone so I can work." I give him an evil smile as his face falls at the unexpected turn of events. "What, were you hoping I'd ask you to buy me a mocha and let you take me home or something? Men are all the same," I mutter.

Payton laughs and leans back in his chair. "You're a mystery, Ainsley Montgomery, but I'll figure you out."

"Stop saying my full name like that," I insist, knowing I'm just encouraging him to do it more by protesting it, but it's annoying that he can't just use my first name or nothing at all.

He grabs one of my glasses and brings it up to his nose, then—oh God, he isn't—takes a sip from my straw. My stomach plummets as he swallows what's left in the bottom.

"What are you doing? I drank from that and you don't know if I have germs."

"I'm figuring out what you like to drink since you won't tell me," he replies succinctly. "Do you? Have germs, I mean. Other than typical girl cooties, since that's what it sounded like you were alluding to when you protested me drinking from your straw. Iced coffee with...vanilla syrup and heavy cream?"

I lean back and cross my arms over my chest, pissed at how quickly he figured out my drink order from one sip. "Yes, but you just order it as a sweet cream iced coffee."

He sets the glass back on the table and smiles at me wickedly. "Okay, Muffin. Sit tight, I'll get you another sweet cream iced coffee and you can get all hyped to finish your story."

My mouth drops open as he walks away from my table with the confident swagger of someone used to getting their way regardless of the no I told him. *Did he really call me Muffin? What the hell is wrong with this man?*

Four

Payton

Seeing Ainsley's shocked expression was worth drinking her too-sweet coffee straight from her glass. I wanted to get under her skin more than anything, and I knew that would do it. Besides, she taunted me, and I rise to a challenge at the slightest provocation. Ainsley has been a challenge from the moment I offered my help.

I place the order for Harlowe's and Ainsley's drinks and pull out my phone while I wait. I look up the Gazette and find Ainsley's name on a few recent stories to see what she's been writing. She's right, her editor assigns her everything, but her talent is obvious. She can write about even the most mundane neighborhood pothole or elementary school PTA corruption stories with the appropriate fervor, and her prose flows lyrically. She also has a habit of writing in a leading way, drawing the reader along in the story with catchy words and alliterations, feeling punchy when needed, though she can be somber in tone when applicable. Her style feels familiar, which must be her brilliance shining through the stories to evoke that sort of awareness despite not having read anything of hers previously.

Her talent is wasted at a small community paper like the Gazette. She's young, with the skills and work ethic to write for a much better press, and I want to know why she's not. When the drinks are ready, I take them to the table and see Harlowe making her way back from the bathroom.

I slide the appropriately named serendipity sweet cream iced coffee in front of Ainsley with a wide smile. She gives me a murderous look before returning her attention to her laptop. Looks like I won't be getting a thank you from her. She can refuse to drink it, or enjoy the caffeine pick-me-up to fuel her writing. Her choice. She's so fucking cute with her surly attitude and insistence on resisting my charms. I'll win her over. I chuckle and slide onto the banquette next to her, accidentally letting my hand brush along her leg again as I move between our tables. She doesn't shy away from the touch, which I take as a good sign.

Harlowe sits down across from me and immediately grabs her magical macchiato and takes a sip. "Oh, this is heaven. I've been saving up my caffeine today just to enjoy this treat and it's perfect."

"Please explain why you wanted to meet here of all places when I could've met you at your house instead?" I lean back, cross my ankle over my knee, and clasp my hands in my lap. I get a peripheral view of Ainsley from this position, and she's back to speed typing, leaning forward over her laptop like a cute croissant, intent on the screen. She's given up on her blatant eavesdropping from earlier, thankfully, given where I imagine this conversation is going.

"Payton, you're thirty-five. You work too fucking much. When was the last time you went on a date?" Harlowe asks, pointing her drink at me and getting right down to business like Zander said she would. Yeah, I'm glad Ainsley isn't paying attention to this.

"You shouldn't worry about my dating life, Harlowe," I say with a practiced smile. "I'm perfectly content."

"That's just it. I am worried. Both of your brothers are married, with children now. I want that same happiness for you."

"What if I don't want a wife? And who said I wanted kids?" I challenge.

She reaches across the table and lays her hand out for me to take. I sigh, putting my hand on the table, and she grasps it tightly.

"I want you to have someone to share life with, even if you don't want to be married with kids. You need someone to go home to. To destress with. Or at least to fuck the workday out with. You need a damn release. I know what y'all go through at work. Zander comes home wound tight as hell more days than not."

I choke out a laugh at her brazen words and look around, worried about the listening ears that will inevitably share this with a gossip site, but realize no one is paying us any attention. Ainsley is still furiously typing, and the rest of the café is busy photographing their pastries or pastel-tinted cups of coffee to have overheard her. I pull my hand away and run it through my hair.

"You're *so kind* to care about me," I reply sarcastically, giving her an acerbic smile. "But I'm fine." We've had this conversation on repeat the last few weeks, and she's still not getting it.

"That's just it. You're not. I've seen you over the last six months. You work harder than both of your brothers, putting in longer hours and pushing yourself more than you should, and you're not going to make the effort for yourself."

"And that's how I want it to stay. I want to keep working those long hours and pushing myself, which isn't great for a relationship, so it's not worth your time to set me up with anyone," I reason.

"It sucks you're not interested in Jillian or Libby. They're both hot as fuck and the kid thing was a sweet deal, which is your loss. I'm keeping Libby as a friend either way. She's way too sweet to let her get away because your head's too far up your ass. So I invited my friend Kayla for you to meet. She's in a book club with me and has the best taste in spicy romance novels. You'll love her, and she'll be here in"—she looks down at her phone to check the time before glancing up at me again—"ten minutes. What do you want to know about her?"

She bats dark lashes at me and smiles with a look of feline coyness that proves she got one over on me and knows it as she turns her phone around to show me a photo of a stunning, curvy brunette in front of a bookcase, holding a stack of books and smiling invitingly. She's absolutely right. Kayla is gorgeous. A perfect smile, porcelain skin, pretty eyes, and so not someone I want Harlowe to set me up with.

"Seriously, stop. Your friends are absolutely gorgeous, sound amazing, and I'm sure they're all great. I just don't want to date them. I know you mean well, but you don't have to set me up with anyone."

"Kayla has turned me onto the most toe-curling novels I've

read lately. Let me tell you, those books are brain porn for us ladies and we need a release when we're reading them. The girl could use a tall, dark, and handsome real-life book boyfriend of her own to take her frustration out on if you know what I mean." She winks at me like I haven't already told her to quit this whole thing.

I have to put a stop to this or it's just going to get worse. "You're overstepping," I say with forced calm when I want to jump up from the table and flee. When Zander said she was going to ambush me, I didn't realize he meant she was going to have someone meet us here. "I don't want you setting me up with any of your friends, and I mean it. Even more, I don't want you springing a blind date on me."

"You're not getting any younger and you're not doing the work yourself, so someone has to. You can thank me later. Fuck, I have to pee again. I swear that's all I've done lately. Hold on, I'll run to the restroom before Kayla gets here." She points a manicured nail at me with a death glare aimed my way for good measure. "If you try to leave before I get back, I will hunt you down and nail your balls to the wall. You hear me, Olsen?" She gives me a look that tells me she's serious before she pushes away from the table and heads to the bathroom again.

"Fuck," I swear softly, quickly racking my brain for an out that won't embarrass Harlowe's friend, who was unwittingly brought into this scheme with whatever promises Harlowe made her.

Suddenly, Hendricks's comment from a few weeks back about borrowing his girlfriend and it just being pretend surfaces. An idea takes shape that I know I can run with. It's fucking brilliant, actually, and if I can pull it off even half decently, it'll get Harlowe off my back.

I turn toward Ainsley, who's still absorbed by her story. I

pull the earbuds out of her ears, effectively drawing her attention and earning me a scowl. I grip her chin in my hand to stop any protest she could make and force her to look at me.

"I know what I need that favor to be, and I don't have time to explain. You just have to go with it and trust me. I need you to pretend to be my girlfriend so Harlowe will stop trying to set me up with her friends. She has someone on the way here now and I need an out. If you do this, and we can make her believe it, you'll have paid me back for fixing your laptop."

Ainsley's eyes grow wider with each word out of my mouth. "What?" she squeaks, her chin still gripped in my hand. She pulls away and I let go, knowing I have her full attention now. "There's no fucking way I can pretend to be your girlfriend. I don't even know you."

"You know enough. We'll say it's new. We just met. I had you come here so we can hang out after I'm done with this. I didn't want to introduce you to Harlowe just yet, knowing she's been on this kick, but she forced my hand by inviting someone else when I had my girlfriend sitting right next to me. We'll keep the details light. If she starts digging, let me answer for us." I'm quickly spinning the story, giving us a plausible backstory and Ainsley fewer reasons to deny me.

"Payton, no. This isn't like saying I don't want anything to drink and you still buying me a coffee. This is insane." She shakes her head and squeezes her eyes shut like she can remove the crazy idea from her head. She's not even remotely on board, more resistant than I anticipated. Now I have to go for broke.

"Damn, Muffin, I thought you had more integrity than that. You can't even hold up your end of a deal when it's still fresh. I'm glad I didn't wait a few weeks to cash in. Who knows what sort of excuse you'd have given to not own up to it then? I knew you couldn't be trusted. It's the journalist in you that's just looking for a story and not caring about the corners you have to cut to get there."

I'm playing dirty, but I don't care. I need her to buy in right fucking now, and I have a feeling calling her integrity into question will be exactly what does it. Ainsley's cheeks grow pink and her eyes narrow into angry slits. *Bingo.*

"How fucking dare you," she hisses, her finger rising between us and pointing in my face. "I'm fully capable of paying you back for your stupid favor. If you want to use it on me pretending to be your girlfriend so your sister-in-law stops trying to set you up, fine, it's your favor. There's no way she's going to believe it, and you'll have used it up and I'll be rid of you for good."

Her finger jabs me in the chest on her last word and I catch it there, using her forward momentum to pull her into me while looping my other arm around her back. I quickly tip her face up so I can kiss the corner of her surprised mouth, angling my head so it looks like a far more intimate kiss than it is to anyone on the other side of my body shielding Ainsley from the rest of the café. The gasp of surprise she makes is even sweeter when I lick it from her sweet, coffee-scented lips.

Five

Ainsley

W hat in the actual hell is going on? Payton Olsen just kissed me. In public. Is this real? Did he lace my coffee with something and I'm hallucinating?

"Pretend to enjoy yourself. Harlowe's coming and you have to sell this with me. Be a good actress," he whispers, dragging his lips along my jaw and feathering soft kisses to my ear. "Say very little if you want."

His voice is an unexpectedly soft caress to go along with the brush of stubble on his face as it skims against mine. I can't help the shiver it drags out of me no matter how badly I want to shove him away and run right out of here and away from whatever spell he's weaving over me.

I'm vibrating with confusion and lust, it seems because how

do you have a man like Payton, a perfect stranger who is absolutely beautiful, suddenly scoop you into his arms, sort of kiss you, and then *nuzzle* your face and whisper in your ear like he's your lover and feel any other way? Jesus, I need a cold shower and to get the hell away from him.

One of those I can make happen. I straighten my arm, pushing against his chest, and he finally relents, letting me go to reveal Harlowe standing in front of the table with a shocked expression on her face.

"What the fuck?" She places her hands on her hips and narrows her eyes as she looks between us.

I look up, not sure how to handle this incredibly awkward situation, then back at Payton. It's his freaking circus, so he gets to drive the clown car. He smiles wide and wraps an arm around my shoulders, pulling me against his chest. A chest that is hard with muscles and smells of expensive cologne with notes of sea salt and something warm, like amber, which happens to be a heady and delicious combo that invades my nose and sends my head spinning again. He kisses the top of my hat and I'm relieved at the shelter it creates as I duck my head down and escape the appraising look Harlowe is giving me.

"Harlowe, this is my girlfriend, Ainsley Montgomery. Ainsley, this is my sister-in-law, Harlowe Olsen. I wasn't planning on introducing you two just yet, but you're fucking relentless and forced my hand today because you wouldn't listen to me when I told you I didn't need you to set me up with anyone."

He's so casual and sounds perfectly at ease, not at all like he's making this up on the fly. I risk a glance up at him, wondering about his ability to spin any situation. He can't be trusted if this is his default. I turn back to Harlowe with a neutral expression, trying not to give away my feelings of distrust when I'm supposed to be performing.

Harlowe's mouth is open and she abruptly sits in the chair across from us. "No fucking way. I don't believe this." She raises a manicured finger at us. "Why wouldn't you just tell me?"

"You don't know the meaning of privacy. You're all up in my business and live your life in the public eye. I don't. I'm perfectly capable of finding my own partner and just wasn't ready to tell you."

Payton looks down at me and smiles in such a soft way it makes my heart drop into my stomach. This dude is way too charming and good at faking it.

"Things with Ainsley are new. We don't want to rush anything and I didn't want you scaring her away."

He says the words like he means them and I stare into those cerulean eyes, trying not to look too bewildered by the whole situation. I'm supposed to be selling this with him. That's how I'll be able to pay him back and get past this incredibly weird day. Here goes nothing.

"Pumpkin and I are taking things slow," I say, giving him a smile and a stupid nickname of my own. "I'm a bit old-fashioned like that." I smile at Harlowe now. "It's really nice to meet you, despite the circumstances." I reach out my hand toward Harlowe and she eyes me hesitantly before shaking it.

"Sorry we ruined your plans with your friend. You should probably let her know she doesn't have to show up, after all. That'd be embarrassing for everyone."

Harlowe narrows her eyes at Payton. "How convenient to have your *girlfriend* right here when you need an excuse. This seems a little too advantageous if you ask me. When did you meet, exactly, and why was she sitting here like she didn't know you until I told you I had someone coming to meet you?"

Oh, shit. Are we that bad at convincing her? My brain

scrambles as I look for any way to get myself out of this favor to Payton. I think of the story for the Gazette I was just working on. The truth is often stranger than fiction. I twine my arm around Payton's and lace our fingers together as I send him a smile to let him know I've got this one.

"We met at a real estate summit two weeks ago. I was covering the new regulations set in place for downtown development and Payton happened to be there due to the new Olympus International real estate venture. He was so obnoxiously commanding and I couldn't take my eyes off him, even though he was annoying as hell with his perfect smile and easy answers for everything. I'm sure you know what I'm talking about."

I tip my head at Harlowe and her lips twist a bit like she's trying to hide her smile. I look at Payton and he's eyeing me warily, letting me take the lead when he told me to say very little. At least I'm going with a plausible story. We *were* both at that summit, even if he had no idea who I was at the time.

"I bumped into him as I was trying to leave the conference room, and he knocked my coffee out of my hand, then insisted on buying me another. I refused at first because I was mad, but he was very persuasive, and we ended up talking at a coffee shop for hours, arguing over everything, and finding common ground in the most unlikely places. One thing led to another, and now here we are."

Payton's smiling at me like he's proud of the story I've created for us. A shiver runs down my spine and I fight the urge to scowl at him just to cover for the unwanted butterflies he's giving me with this whole situation. He's the worst.

"He is obnoxious and annoying. You're right about that," Harlowe says, smirking at Payton but relaxing back into her chair, and I think she's buying our story. "I wish you had told me." She pouts, grabbing for her phone and typing out a quick message, hopefully calling off the arrival of her friend for Payton's sake. Maybe I can help sell this even more.

"I'm not surprised he's keeping it under wraps even from you. We've been taking things...slow." Payton's relaxing into the banquette now that I'm seemingly doing a convincing job. I look back at Harlowe, knowing I'm talking *way* too much, but it's working. "He's a person of interest and he's so out of my league it's hardly plausible that we'd ever be together. We're staying under the radar for privacy reasons, to get to know one another without being scrutinized in the public eye. I'm sure you know how that goes," I say, appealing to the very real threat of gossip blogs and everyone wanting a piece of the story, which she's had to deal with personally in her own relationship.

Harlowe looks up and rolls her eyes with a knowing smile. "Smart girl."

Payton suddenly tips my chin up with a finger, stealing my attention as his thumb strokes my cheek. "You're everything I could want and more, Muffin. I don't like hearing you say anything about not being in my league. That's bullshit." His voice has taken on a deep, commanding tone, his blue eyes serious, the words jolting me out of the storytelling mode I'd fallen into. I can't look away, feeling something stronger than the lies we're weaving holding us bound together in the moment.

Harlowe makes a sighing noise, snapping the strange thread of tension between us, and we look over. Her eyes are glassy as she fans a hand in front of her face.

"That's seriously so precious it makes me sick and it's everything I've been wanting for you, Payton. I'm so happy."

Payton relaxes next to me, and I hope this means we'll be done with this charade soon and I can go back to finishing my story and making my damn deadline.

"Are you done trying to set me up now?" he asks, leaning back against the banquette, tucking me into his side comfortably. I try not to look too stiff and awkward, willing my body to mold against his side and give in to the appeal of pressing against him again. It's not a bad spot to snuggle up to if I wanted to. Instead, I'm forced to be here and it's wildly overwhelming, making my thoughts spiral and my heart race.

"I don't need to set you up with anyone else now that I've met your cute little Ainsley. I know there'll be someone for you to have at all our summer events and get-togethers." Harlowe turns toward me and I get a sinking feeling in my stomach just as Payton's arm around me stiffens. "I can't wait to get to know you more at everything we have planned."

"What did I say about scaring her away, Harlowe?" Payton chides with a laugh like it's all fun and games, rather than his cunning sister-in-law backing us into a corner. "She's all mine right now and I'm not sharing her with anyone, including you."

I look over at Payton and catch the mask of total confidence quickly replacing the flicker of unease that passes across his stunning profile. He wasn't expecting this from Harlowe, either. So much for a one-and-done favor repayment. Fuck.

Six

The Atlanta Haute List

Our favorite Olsen brothers may have been living quieter lives lately, given two of the three now have growing families, but the unattached middle brother, Payton, was seen at an Atlanta café known more for cutesy cappuccinos and pretty pastries than drawing someone of his caliber. The reason for his visit to the unusual location was revealed later when another member of his family joined him, but our Hauties in the know who initially spotted him were quite surprised. While waiting, the COO of Olympus International looked extra cozy with an unknown blonde patron of the café before his sister-in-law, Harlowe Olsen, met him for coffee, animated conversation, and an introduction to the mystery lady. What we wouldn't have given to have been the object of his attention while he waited! Lucky girl, indeed.

Payton, the mastermind of spin behind Olympus International PR, has always taken a back seat to his brothers when it comes to the stories that are written about his family and business. Cleverly crafted PR planning on his part or simply a squeaky-clean image? We're hoping we'll finally get to know more about the most elusive of the Olsens, who is now the most eligible billionaire bachelor in our illustrious city. As the last to be connected romantically, single ladies in Atlanta, and the South, are salivating for a piece of Olympus, wanting to know him and what he's looking for romantically. Has the mystery woman from the café made a bid for his attention outside of the quick meeting for coffee and cuddles? You know we'll be watching intently, looking for every delicious morsel we can find to share with you Hauties. Remember to hit Like and Subscribe for all the Haute Gossip!

Seven

Ainsley

My phone vibrates as I catch up on my guilty pleasure of trashy TV—tonight it's *The Real Housewives of Atlanta*. I blindly reach for it, wondering if it's Reid with edits for me to go over before he runs my story. Instead, it's a text from an unknown number, and it immediately sets me on edge.

Unknown: What are you up to, Muffin?

I read the text again, knowing who it's from but wanting to make him think I don't. I thought I was in the clear for a while because our performance for Harlowe at the café convinced her she didn't need to set him up, despite her insistence that I join him at the events she's planned.

> **Me:** Wrong number.

> **Unknown:** Definitely the right number. You put it in yourself.

> **Me:** Who is this?

> **Unknown:** I like you playing hard to get.

> **Me:** Tell me before I block you.

> **Unknown:** You get one guess, you overly caffeinated, cranky little spitfire. I told you a third sweet cream iced coffee would get you wound up too tightly.

I groan and drop my phone. He's just as annoying in text as he is in person. I wanted to halt any communication by playing ignorant, hoping he thought I'd given him a fake number. Of course, that's not my luck. I pick it back up and quickly save the number in my contacts. At least now I'll know when he texts or calls and can ignore him properly.

> **Me:** Payton. You obnoxious, persistent prick.

> **Annoying Payton:** You're such a smart girl. Now what are we going to do about you being so wound up? You're just as testy in text as you are in person. At least you're consistent.

> Me: "We" won't be doing anything. Leave me alone.

> Annoying Payton: I can't, you're my girl-friend now. We have to get our story straight.

> Me: *Fake* girlfriend. We created a story already. Now get out of my inbox unless you need me to play along with your id-iotic sham for some reason.

The rapid-fire texting stops. I stare at my phone, wondering if calling him out on his bluff just worked. Maybe he'll leave me alone until he needs a girlfriend for an event. My phone vibrates with an incoming call and Payton's name flashes on the screen. I drop the phone onto the couch and look at it in shock.

"You relentless asshole," I mutter as I stare at the vibrating phone. I pick it back up and swipe at the screen. "Why are you calling me?" I snap.

"It's after eight. Is the caffeine still in your system from this morning, or do you drink coffee all day and let it mess with your circadian rhythm?" he asks by way of greeting.

Why is he like this? He's such a nerd, saying everything he thinks and wanting to crack me open for some reason.

"I stop drinking coffee at noon so it doesn't mess with my sleep," I grumble, not sure why I'm answering him honestly. "Why do you care?"

"I want to know if you're naturally grumpy or if the coffee makes you that way."

"*You* make me that way." I sigh, stretching out on the couch for what is destined to be a long, drawn-out verbal sparring match of our wits. It's almost fun to shut down his every attempt to figure me out.

"I'm sure I do. It must be because I smile too much, right?" he asks, and I can hear the damn smile in his words.

"Absolutely. You're weird for smiling so much."

I can picture it, the way his full lips curl up at the corners, enhancing the little divot in his chin, his stunning blue eyes sparkling in challenge at me. I blink to clear the far too vivid picture from my mind and let the smile fall from my own lips, not sure how it got there, to begin with.

My phone chimes with a FaceTime request from him. I'm in my pajamas, a black crop top that says I heart Gossip, and cotton shorts, my hair piled on top of my head, and no makeup, not that I wear much regularly, but I definitely wasn't planning on anyone seeing me like this other than my roommate, Della, if she happens to get home before I go to bed.

"I don't want to see your stupid face right now," I tell him.

"But I want to see yours. Just accept it, Muffin," he teases.

I sigh and swipe on the FaceTime request, and it connects. His ocean-blue eyes and blindingly white smile greet me. A hint of dark stubble along his strong jaw catches my attention and makes my mouth water because the phone is close enough to show the detail. He's reclining, holding his phone propped in front of him, looking as relaxed as anyone can, and I'm a ball of nerves in contrast. I glower to hide my deep perusal of his features.

"Happy?" I grumble.

"Very," he purrs in great satisfaction. "Thank you, Muffin."

"Why are you calling me that?" I snap, the pet name grating on my nerves nearly as much as the fact that his voice does something to melt the iceberg of my soul that I need very much to stay frozen where he's concerned. He's a threat, and I don't need my life complicated by him stirring up hormones and feelings because he's indecently charming, fucking hot, and has a smile that could drop even panties held up by a chastity belt with a padlock on them.

"You didn't like me using your name at the café, so I came up with something else. You had a muffin on the table with you, so I went with that. Not very original, but it's cute and I bet it drives you crazy because you probably hate anything cute."

Damn. How can he be so spot-on with his analysis of me this quickly? I do hate it because it's cute. "You were using my full name earlier, which is what I didn't like. Just call me Ainsley, like a normal person. You don't have to use my full name or something after a food I was eating."

"What if *I* like muffins? What if they're *my* favorite food and I can't resist them? What if Muffin is the most endearing thing I could've come up with?" he asks, pulling his phone closer to his face, more serious with every word.

My mouth goes dry the closer the phone gets to his deep ocean eyes, those perfect lips of his, and the dimples that come out to play every once in a while. I don't know where to focus, every bit of his face is delicious and worthy of being devoured at close range. I swallow twice before I can unstick my tongue to form words.

"You're lying," I say hoarsely. I clear my throat and continue in a stronger voice. "No one likes muffins that much. They're the cheap, less tasty cousin to cupcakes. You took an easy way out."

He laughs, his Adam's apple bobbing with the movement. "You're right, they're not even my favorite baked good. Peach pie with vanilla ice cream is." He shakes his head, smiling again. "Fuck, you're such a spitfire. What's your favorite dessert?"

I silently stare him down through the phone screen as I lick my dry lips. I don't want to give him that particular answer. I want to be contrary and say something else, but instead, the truth finally comes out. "Peach pie, but with the crumble topping because it's superior to a normal crust," I admit, tearing my eyes away from the screen when his face grows serious, head tilting to the side.

"Really?"

I roll my eyes. "Yes. Are you done now? I was busy before you decided to barge into my night with your incessant questions."

Payton shifts and I realize he's now lying on his stomach, head propped on one arm. "Oh, I'm just getting started. You look pretty comfy. What were you so busy doing before I barged into your evening?" His eyes twinkle with mischief like he knows I'm lying.

I can't tell him I was binge-watching my favorite trashy reality TV show and scrolling gossip online. "Why do you care?" I ask instead.

"Call me curious. How old are you?" he asks.

"Twenty-five," I answer honestly, instead of with the snarky remark of *old enough* that almost slipped out. That could've been construed as combative *and* innuendo, and he doesn't need any encouragement in that area after his flirty banter at the café earlier.

"Why are you working at the Gazette when you're talented enough to be somewhere much better?"

I bristle and narrow my eyes at him. "What's with all the questions? I thought that was my job."

"I read some of your stories today. Your writing is excellent. It's compelling, has heart, and tells the story in a unique way, no matter what you're reporting on. You could work anywhere, but you're at the fucking Gazette, a second-rate paper, assigned shitty stories about strip mall openings when you could be somewhere that would actually challenge you. Why?"

My chest swells with pride at his compliments and my defenses snap up at the same time. "That's really none of your business."

"I thought we were becoming friends, and that's something a friend would ask."

I scoff and sit up so I can direct my ire at him properly. "We're *not* friends. You're an annoying man who won't leave me alone. It was a stroke of bad luck that you sat down next to me today and felt entitled to my time and attention because you managed to fix my crappy work laptop. That doesn't make us friends. It makes me indebted to you. That's different."

Payton sits up, mirroring my movements on his end of the call. I notice for the first time that he's shirtless, his tan skin rolling over his muscled shoulders and chest as his face grows serious. My mouth dries out again. Holy shit, he's built under the suits he's photographed in and was hiding under the casual button-down he was wearing today at the café. I felt those muscles against me, but to see them is something else.

"Why won't you be my friend, Spitfire?"

"Why do you insist on calling me stupid nicknames?" I fire off.

I bang my head back against the couch and close my eyes tightly instead of focusing on his defined pecs and broad shoulders and the way it looks like he's looming over me as I lean back. I'm resolutely ignoring the things that image and the idea of him above me like this does to my dormant libido, which is starting to respond to this antagonistic man when it should stay the hell out of this conversation.

"Because of that, right there, Ainsley."

Oh, shit. He's thinking of fucking me on a couch, too? I lift my head and warily meet his eyes again to keep myself from looking at the smooth expanse of skin below his neck. For once, he's not smiling, he's dead serious, and his intensely blue eyes bore into me through the screen.

"Because of *what*?" I ask hesitantly, keeping a frown on my face to discourage any sexual thoughts on his side of the call.

"You actually show true emotion and let the real you peek through when you're exasperated. The real emotion, good or bad, is better than this prickly persona that you're trying on for size like it'll fit one day. It doesn't suit you."

I bite my lip, my nostrils flaring as I huff out a breath, relieved he wasn't thinking about sex but frustrated he's so damn good at reading me when I'm normally so much better at projecting whatever I want people to see. I can't respond to his comment without giving him exactly what he wants—a heated denial that would serve to prove his point, or me admitting he's right, which would also prove his point. I just shake my head.

"Why did you text me tonight?" I ask instead. I pull my knees up and rest my arms on top.

"I wanted to see what you're up to."

I give him an incredulous look. "You don't have a life, do you? First, you spent your Saturday morning at the Unicorn Café bothering me and meeting your sister-in-law, and now you're spending your Saturday night calling a stranger because you have nothing better to do." A genuine smile lifts my cheeks. "And here I thought fancy billionaire businessmen had more important things to do with their time." I laugh. It feels good to be making fun of him, finally, after he's been laughing at me for the majority of our exchanges today.

"Ah, that's better. Just keep laughing, Spitfire, even if it's at my expense."

My laughter dies. Is he serious? He's still smiling, which is something, and he doesn't look pissed. "It's true, isn't it? You don't have a life," I say, gentler.

"I have my work and my boats on the coast and at the lake. But you're completely right. I haven't given myself much of a life over the last year and a half. Today was the first Saturday I didn't spend working at least part of the day in...damn, I don't know how long it's been. I texted you because it gave me something to do other than turn back to work."

My face softens at his admission, but I don't let him off that easily. "You really have to get a life. How depressing. God, I wouldn't want to end up like you in ten years."

"You were working today, so you're already on your way to becoming me," he says, arching a dark eyebrow.

"That's not the same thing," I protest. "I had a last-minute story to write. I don't work every weekend."

"And what were you up to tonight? Looks like you're home, just like me. Again, your odds aren't looking good. You're definitely going to end up a workaholic without a life at thirty-five just like me." His smile is devilish, popping the slightest hint of dimples into his cheeks that are far too enticing and I hate the way they look. They're lickable, and that's ridiculous on a grown man without a life. Payton is ridiculous.

"I'm not home every Saturday night. I have a life."

"You're just being contrary now. Prove you have a life. Do you have a boyfriend?"

"What? No. I don't date. Why would you even ask me that? I don't have to prove anything to you," I snap, my defenses rising higher as I grow flustered. "You're annoying. Has anyone ever told you that, or does everyone try to kiss your ass because you have more money than God and they want to ride your coattails or get something out of you?"

He laughs. "Fuck, I like you. I'm going to keep you around. Can you say more mean things to me?"

My mouth pops open in shock, not at all expecting that response. Is he serious? Is that why he's been so persistent today? Should I have fawned over him instead, and he wouldn't have paid me a second thought?

"What's wrong with you?" I ask, not sure how to take his comments. He's not normal. There's no way to anticipate his next move or comment, and that freaks me the hell out.

"You're doing a decent job of creating a list of what's wrong with me. I'm weird for smiling so much. I'm annoying. I don't have a life. I have a stupid face. I'm sure given time, the list will grow."

I feel a twinge of remorse for being such a bitch to him. "The list would grow slower if you left me alone like I asked."

"Where's the fun in that? And why? You've engaged with me every time I've talked to you. You secretly like it, even if you want to hate it or hate me, for whatever reason. You would've shut me down and not answered if you didn't want to talk to me."

I blink incredulously at his last words and my cheeks heat with outrage. "You told me if I didn't answer your calls or texts, you'd show up at my house or work." I fume, realizing I had a choice.

I *could* have ignored him, but then I wouldn't have had the chance to get to know more about Olympus and his family. Not that he's been very forthcoming on any details. He's been more intent on asking *me* questions and digging into my history than allowing me any opportunity to get to know what makes him tick or how Olympus runs internally. Goddammit, I've let him distract me so thoroughly, that I'm not even doing my job right!

"Only when I plan on calling in my fake girlfriend favor," he explains patiently, bringing me back to our conversation.

"How am I supposed to know when that'll be?" Exasperation has my brows climbing higher.

"I'll tell you. But we'll need to know each other really well before we appear publicly as a couple to pull this off convincingly. So consider this me starting our friendship. Be my friend, Ainsley."

"Are you so hard up for friends that you have to resort to asking women who don't even like you to be your friends?" I sputter.

"Ah, but I think you *do* like me. You're just telling yourself you don't. Why else would you have stayed on the phone with me for this long? You enjoy sparring with me intellectually. I stimulate you. It's giving you the release you need because you're wound so tight. You like all the verbal back and forth and the mental gymnastics of saying I'm annoying and you hate how smiley I am while you bend over backward to make me smile more. It's cute."

"You're impossible," I spit as I look for a way to refute everything he's said. Am I enjoying this? I mean, maybe, a little bit. But it's not stimulating me or giving me a release. Goddamn, that sounds way too sexual. "This isn't going to work. I can't pretend to date you when I don't even like you."

"Of course you can. That makes it even better. There's no risk of actually falling for me when you don't like me. It's perfect. I just need you to show up in public with me and look like we get along so Harlowe will buy it. You did great this morning. Give me six months of that so she thinks it's serious enough that she'll let her guard down."

"Six months? Hell no, that's way too long. I just met you today. There's no way I'm tying myself to you for that long.

You could be a sociopath." I rub my forehead as I wonder how I got here. I'm arguing with a billionaire about the length of time I'm going to fake date him. This can't be my life.

"I'm not a sociopath. I was tested when I was younger. It turns out I'm just a genius. And you agree, but for less time? Three months. Ninety-day fiancée style."

"What the actual fuck? No. This is insane. No fiancée talk." I shake my head and look back at the screen where Payton appears far too calm and collected. "You were tested to see if you were a sociopath? Were you a weird kid? There are levels here that I need to know about. Did you have trouble connecting, or did you kill small animals? I have so many questions."

He smirks and levels those gorgeous blue eyes at me. "I was too literal and had trouble connecting. I was smarter than my peers and I electrocuted Zander once when we were kids. My mom wanted to make sure I didn't do it on purpose and made it look accidental. To be fair, kids can't be sociopaths, which would actually be a diagnosis of Antisocial Personality Disorder, but they can have Conduct Disorder. You have to meet certain criteria. They asked me a lot of questions and we looked at pictures of facial expressions, checked to see if I understood empathy, and stuff like that. I didn't have that either. Besides, I really like animals. I would never kill them. My favorite animals are dolphins and sea turtles. What are yours?"

"Octopuses and seahorses," I mutter, holding my head. This fucking man.

"We both chose marine animals. I love that for us. So ninety days work?"

My head warps at his persistent back and forth. "What the hell have I gotten myself into?" I whisper, pinching my temples between my fingers.

"I'm glad you agree. I'll work out the details of our fake

relationship and get them drawn up in a contract. This is our little secret. No one else can know it's fake, so we have to sell it well. Now I'll say good night to my amazing fake girlfriend. Sleep tight and talk to you tomorrow, Muffin."

He ends the call before I can get another word in. I'm left holding my phone, my mouth gaping in shock. He's really the genius mastermind I thought, manipulating every situation to his advantage and leaving others three steps behind. My overwhelmed mind spins for hours after, wondering how life could have turned upside down so thoroughly in a matter of hours from one chance encounter with the billionaire I'm now somehow tied to, as a *fake girlfriend for ninety days*.

Eight

Payton

Ainsley dominates my thoughts as I swim laps in the pool on the roof of my loft. It doesn't matter how fast I go or how long between breaths that push my lungs to burning. I can't escape her. Images of her and how I'll use this connection to my advantage chase each stroke that pulls me through the crystal clear water.

My eidetic memory is a blessing and a curse—the vivid recall it provides meaning I have memorized every part of her. Every nuanced motion, carefully guarded look, and grimace she's given me is seared into my brain. I know the way her nostrils flare when she's angry, the way her arched brows pull together when she thinks I'm full of shit, the way the corners of her full lips twitch when I almost get her to smile.

It's the lips that chase me most of all as I think of what they would look like wrapped around my cock, reminding me that I shouldn't be thinking about her like this, especially now that she's my fake girlfriend for the foreseeable future. I shouldn't complicate my life like that.

Ainsley may say she wants nothing to do with me, but I know she's more than a little curious and very interested in a connection despite her prickly exterior. She willingly went along with my charade to fool Harlowe. She played her part admirably, creating a backstory that was more truth than I could've imagined if she was also at the real estate summit like she said. She even melted against me each time I pulled her close and seemed to enjoy at least part of our interaction even if she said otherwise.

No matter how strongly she resists my charms, she's eager to know about me. Perhaps wanting a story on Olympus or on my family motivates it. She could even be drawn to me in the same curious way I am to her. I have no problem dangling the carrot of information and an inside story in front of her. I'll have plenty of opportunity to discover what she wants out of this connection now that we're tied together for the foreseeable future, at least publicly.

The idea occurred to me on a whim as Harlowe backed me into a corner at the café. Having a favor in my pocket and realizing Ainsley would fulfill it regardless of the extremes meant I could ask for it. I don't mind putting myself into a fake relationship if it gets me what I want—my freedom and a reprieve from Harlowe's scheming.

It's the kind of thing I've asked of my brothers when our company was under scrutiny and their relationship statuses could be used. Now it's my turn to take one for the team and use it to my advantage. I just have to work out the details of what this fake relationship will look like and how we'll sell it to ensure Harlowe and the world believe it enough to give me an excuse to be a brokenhearted bachelor again in three months so she'll leave me alone for a nice long time after that. If that means Ainsley and I have to appear to be wildly in love publicly, then that's what it'll take. I'm willing to do anything for Olympus and my freedom, even deceive my family when it's for their benefit.

I pull myself out of the pool and drop onto a lounge chair. My chest heaves from the exertion I've put in before seven a.m., but I don't feel settled. All I have to look forward to today is my continued work of trying to solve a six-month-old cyber breach with cold leads, no closer to putting away Archer Donovan, the assumed culprit of the attack. I can't find any connecting evidence that would mark him as the hacker to turn over to the authorities.

A business associate, Octavius Rex, gave us secondhand information that led us to Archer as the potential hacker for hire with a strong motive against Olympus. We destroyed his father's company, Donner Investments, then sent his father to prison for orchestrating an industrial accident at one of our overseas properties in retaliation. But Archer covered his tracks with his infiltration and never publicly claimed the breach, meaning I can't do shit about it now.

Archer moved through my firewalls and systems with a sophisticated program I've tried reverse engineering to discover how he did it to see if it will lead me back to him. It's been gnawing at me for months that the system I built for Olympus failed at the hands of a twenty-five-year-old punk-ass kid who sold off proprietary information. This let our competitors take our cleaner-burning Pegasus jet engine plans to market before we could. I want to tie Archer to his crimes and turn him over to the authorities—after I've made him pay for his misdeeds in my own way. I want him to feel the same sting of failure and embarrassment I've endured for this colossal fuckup on my part. A petty hacker like him never should have infiltrated my system. I've reinforced the system and made it airtight since, but that doesn't change the past or that I failed in the first place, which is unacceptable.

Shit, Ainsley's right. I don't have a life. I should have gone to the coast this weekend like I wanted. Then at least I'd be working from my yacht with a briny breeze blowing through my hair instead of sweating in Atlanta. *But if I'd gone to the coast, I wouldn't have met the Spitfire who has me in my head today and is now somehow my fake girlfriend.*

She's back in my head with that simple thought. What is it about Ainsley that keeps my mind circling back to her? She's undoubtedly attractive, my physical ideal, with her blonde hair, sun-kissed skin, rosy pink lips, and pretty hazel eyes that narrow in suspicion each time she stares me down, but plenty of gorgeous women have caught my attention over the years. Is it that she says all the mean, unfiltered thoughts that pass through her head, or that she doesn't feel the need to impress me because of my status and power? That has to be it. Ainsley knows exactly who I am and doesn't seem to give a shit. She busts my balls and tells me it means nothing every time she opens her mouth, and I can't get enough.

She's also using it to keep me at arm's length, and I want to know why. Any other woman who's been aware of my family and what our business is has been beyond friendly and willing to fall directly into bed at the first smile from me should I have been remotely interested. It's refreshing to have someone, especially a woman, know my net worth and not trip over herself wanting to get something out of the connection.

Of course The Atlanta Haute List ran a story about me being spotted at The Unicorn Café before the day was even over, linking me to Ainsley as an unknown blonde and setting me up as the newest *most eligible billionaire bachelor* for Atlanta women to salivate over. The story will be a perfect way for me to introduce Ainsley as my new girlfriend to the public and squash that whole narrative.

I'll have to feed a few select details of my own to the gossip site to encourage the connection. I've done this for Olympus over the years, keeping the company name in the news with small tidbits of positive information here and there, so it should work for me, personally, as well. A little PR magic never hurts, and using the Haute List to my advantage would finally be putting the salacious gossip site to good use after all the trouble it's caused my family and business over the last two years.

I slick wet hair off my face as I grab a towel and dry off as I make my way into my bathroom. My phone chimes a few minutes later while I turn on the shower. I pluck it off the counter, thinking it could be one of my brothers, or even Harlowe checking in after reading the Haute List story and giving me a hard time about it, but I'm shocked to see it's not from them at all.

Muffin: Why the hell did you end our conversation like that last night?

I bark out a laugh at the unexpected question, bringing my phone into the shower with me as I type back a response. Thank God for waterproof technology and large shower enclosures where I can keep my phone out of the spray. I don't want to miss the opportunity to spar with her.

Good to know I'm not the only one with a brain stuck on repeat over the person I met yesterday. I put the phone on the ledge next to my shampoo and step into the shower spray, rinsing off until I hear my phone ring, surprised it's the FaceTime sound instead of a text notification. She's the initiator this morning. I smile and it feels wicked. I must've gotten under her skin good last night. I leave the phone on the ledge and accept the call. The camera only shows me from the abs up if I don't step back. It could get indecent if I went far enough, but I can keep the mystery intact unless she requests otherwise. Then all bets are off and she can have whatever she wants. I'm not shy in the least.

"Miss me, Muffin?" I ask, loud enough to be heard over the sound of the shower.

"What the hell, Payton?! Why would you answer a video call *while in the shower?*" she screeches, her pretty eyes popping wide but not averting from my body, dominating her side of the screen.

"You called me. It's only polite to accept." I lift my arms and slick back my hair, giving her a show of my tan, wet, muscled arms and flexing abs with water sluicing down my chest toward other, hidden parts. "Like what you see of your new boyfriend?" I ask as she stays quiet and I catch her lips parting.

Her mouth snaps shut and she glares at me. "Fake boyfriend. It's entirely inappropriate to answer a call like this. You could've declined and texted that you're busy. Why do you have your phone in the shower, anyway?"

I reach out and grab the bottle of shampoo next to the

phone. She moves like she thinks I'm reaching for her. I laugh, water dripping off my face with the movement. "It's efficient. Besides, I don't mind if you watch."

She makes a sputtering noise, her cheeks growing red. "I *don't* want to watch you in the shower! You're all...wet."

I smile at her embarrassment over her blatant interest because she refuses to look away or hang up when that would solve her problem in the simplest way. "Relax, Spitfire. We all get wet when we shower."

She scoffs and rolls her eyes, but they return to me, and I give her a slow, sultry smile as I pour shampoo into my palm and return the bottle to the ledge. She doesn't flinch away this time.

She stays silent, her face set into an uninterested look, but her eyes are burning hot and a rosy glow is creeping up her neck in a way that makes me want to see where else that pretty shade is coloring and how far down I can make it spread. My innuendo and the fact she knows I'm naked in the shower affect her and yet she continues watching.

Voyeur, my brain catalogs about her, while I'm an exhibitionist. Perfect fucking pairing.

"You know getting wet never hurt anyone. I spent the last hour working myself up, getting really wet, so I need this shower."

Now I'm getting into it, playing up the tension, seeing where it'll get me, just because I can. My brothers call me a meddler. They're not wrong. I like to see what kind of reaction I can get from people. Ainsley's easy to provoke. She wears her emotions on her sleeve despite wanting very much to appear unaffected, which is why she relies on her surly attitude and snappy replies more often than not. She started off a bit hard to read, but now she's as clear to me as the newsprint her stories run in. I can read her every nuance, and I'll use that to my advantage at every opportunity. If she were really mine, I'd be testing her boundaries for different reasons.

I lather the shampoo into my hair, really giving her something to watch. I'm not bad to look at. Even if I'm not built as huge as Hayes or as devastatingly handsome as Zander, I hold my own just fine, and I've been told I have eyes that women could drown in. I keep myself fit, maintaining a shredded body to ensure I can keep my brothers from killing each other when their dominant personalities clash in the boardroom—or anywhere, really. Being the middle brother—often the mediator—means I have to step in to soothe ruffled feathers and keep them from coming to physical blows more often than not. I have to stay fit enough to stop the freight train that is Hayes and nimble enough to intercept Zander's willingness to bait him. Not easy with stubborn brothers who are too much alike and too eager to be the authority on everything.

I tip my head back into the spray and rinse the lather from my hair. I may step back a little too far because I hear a gasp over the sound of water hitting the tiles and cascading around my ears. I pull my head out of the spray, stepping forward again. I blink and check the small view of myself in the corner of the screen. She can see the V cut of my low abs but not my cock, so we're good.

"Am I offending you by getting clean, Muffin?" I ask, wiping my eyes and stepping toward the phone.

"You're ridiculous. Why do you insist on staying on the call while you shower?" She huffs cutely.

"We're supposed to be dating. It's only natural that you'd be familiar with my body and I don't mind you watching, but hang up if you want to. I have to condition my hair and wash my body first. Remember, I got worked up earlier. I need to get clean, and you called me, so we can chat while I do it." I reach for the conditioner, shake the bottle a little indecently just for her benefit, and squirt out some product right in front of the camera so she sees the opaque white product hit my hand, to really get her dirty mind going.

"What were you doing this morning?" she asks slowly, her eyes closing tightly like she hates that she even asked. That's my good girl, following the breadcrumbs I'm leaving exactly the way I want her to.

"Swimming laps," I answer honestly as her reward. "I do it most mornings. The pool is salt water filtered, which is nicer than chlorine, but it still needs to be rinsed off fast or it dries out my skin. I'm sensitive."

The look of relief that crosses her face at the innocent answer is hilarious enough to make me laugh as I finger-comb conditioner through my hair. "What did you think I meant? Something dirty, I bet. God, you must be a nasty girl if that's the first place your mind went to. I like it."

She growls in annoyance and narrows her eyes at me. "You're obviously baiting me to think that way. You're an unreliable source. I can't trust anything you say."

"You thought I was doing something naughty. Tell me where your mind went. I want to know just how dirty it got. My hands are slick enough with conditioner, I could do something about what that thought does to me." I want to see if it can get a rise out of her. I'm only semi-hard at the thought, trying not to let my cock take over. Despite how deplorable she thinks I am, I'm actually on my best behavior for her. I'm just messing with her head and seeing where it gets me.

"Payton!" she chastises, dropping her head back against a pillow, and I realize she's still in bed.

"Did you call me from bed, Muffin? Wow, did thoughts of

me not only keep you up last night, but I was the first thing on your mind when you woke up this morning? I like seeing you in bed." I skate my hands from my head, to my chest and start to drag them lower. "Let's play a game. You tell me when my hands should stop moving, and we'll see what I find."

"You're the worst!" she growls. "Don't touch yourself inappropriately while I'm on a call with you. That's gross."

"You're still watching. You don't actually think it's gross, and I'm your boyfriend, so I should think of you when I touch myself, right?" I playfully tilt my head as my hands continue to slide down my torso, nearing the edge of the camera frame. They pass out of view and her lips part, but no sound comes out. Her eyes lower as if following the progress of my hands, the line of my biceps stretching out giving her the only indication of where they could be on my body. I keep my hands moving now because she seems to be playing along, even though I was kidding, initially. "Tell me when," I growl, hitting the V of my abs and feeling my cock jump at the proximity.

"Stop," she says, voice shaking before rolling her lips together. It could be a stop for my hands, or stop this altogether. But I'll take it as the game.

"Good timing," I groan, moving my hands off my lower stomach where my cock is brushing my fingers, but I refrain from wrapping my hand around the hard, thick length. "That could've gotten heated quickly. Who knows what I would've done or said if you let me be gross and touch myself while you're on the call with me," I say, raising my brows and throwing her own words back at her.

She looks away, biting her lip. "You're the worst," she says, lacking conviction while refusing to meet my eyes.

"Oh, Spitfire, you like it. You have my permission to if that's what you're waiting for. Be as depraved as you want to be, no need to let propriety hold you back, or think I'm expecting you to be some squeaky-clean, ethically bound journalist, prickly persona and all. I just want you to be my fake girlfriend. You can enjoy all that entails, fake or not."

"I don't need your permission for anything." She seethes, her lips flattening. "There you go, being a dick and a pompous ass again."

Dick and ass in the same sentence, what a naughty girl, and she doesn't even realize her slip. I bite my lip and lean a forearm on the wall over the ledge where the phone rests, coming closer to the screen, her eyes widening under my gaze.

"Oh, Muffin, you gotta stop now. Those mean words work just as well as knowing that you're thinking dirty thoughts about me. Now let me finish showering without saying any more naughty things that make me want to do bad things while you watch, or let me handle myself and get it over with. What'll it be? My hand's still slick enough to feel good, and I'd like your consent to watch."

"Fucking hell, Payton," she says, breathless and unnerved. "Do whatever you need to get yourself under control. I can't talk to you like this."

"Sounds like you need to take your own advice, Ainsley. *You* should do whatever *you* need to make yourself feel better. Talk soon." I raise my brows at her flushed face and end the call to put her out of her misery. I do take matters into my own hands and finish my shower thinking about her breathy voice, her pretty pink lips, and that blush on her skin that I put there just by saying a few choice words. Ainsley Montgomery with her unrealized words kink is going to be so much fun to play with for the next three months.

Nine

Ainsley

“What crawled up your ass this morning?” Della, my best friend and roommate, asks as I storm into the kitchen.

I’m crankier than usual. I need to fill her in on the developments with Payton and it’s been a few days since we’ve caught up. Our schedules haven’t aligned lately and this is the first morning we’ve crossed paths in weeks.

I think about the FaceTime call Payton answered while in the shower and every glorious bit of him I happened to see. Jesus, that was inappropriate. I should have hung up immediately. Instead, I let his chiseled body, the incredible way he looked wet, the flirty banter, and straight-up sex in his words distract me. I’m a damn professional, not some boy-crazy teen girl lusting after a crush. Fuck me!

I slam a pod into the Keurig, throw a mug under the spout, and press the button to make coffee before I whirl to face Della. "I met Payton Olsen of Olympus International at the café I like to work at on the weekends."

"What?" she croaks, the bagel falling out of her hand and plopping cream cheese side down onto the plate sitting on the table below it. "Why didn't you tell me?"

"That's not the half of it, Dell. He fixed my crappy work laptop that went on the fritz. Did you know he's a tech genius?" I open the fridge and pull out the vanilla creamer as the coffee maker works its magic.

She shakes her head, blue eyes wide as her copper hair whips around her shoulders. "I just thought he's a businessman like his brothers. So you *actually* met him, not just in passing?"

My cheeks heat as I think of him kind of kissing me, the way he held me to his side and touched my face. Yeah, I definitely *met* him. I take my cup of coffee from the machine, pop in a second pod, and make a cup for Della before I pour in an illegal amount of the magical creamer that makes the bitter brew tolerable. I shake my head to dislodge the way his touch felt and what it did to me seeing him through our video calls.

Nope, not going there. I know what handsome, rich, tech-savvy men do to my head and I won't let this one get to me. I've learned my lesson and won't repeat my mistakes. Payton Olsen can stay firmly on the other side of the line I've drawn for whatever this fake dating situation is, no matter how tempting he is.

"He's the most annoyingly chipper, smiley, talkative man I've ever met. He wouldn't leave me alone while he worked on my laptop. Later, he texted, called, and even FaceTimed me in rapid succession, with the same incessant chatter. He's the absolute worst and I hate him."

"Whoa, the same day you met, he called *you*, the meanest woman I know? You had a man not only chat you up but also got your number which he texted, called, and FaceTimed the same day? Were you accidentally nice to him? Did you flirt with him, or maybe smile at him instead of frown and hiss?"

"I assure you, I was myself." I add less creamer to Della's cup and angrily stir our coffees before flinging the spoon into the sink. I fall into a seat across from her. "He gave me not one but two annoying nicknames he's insisting on using because I didn't like him calling me by my full name like a total weirdo." I take a sip of my coffee and push a cup toward her before I continue my tirade now that I'm warmed up. "He said I *liked* sparring with him intellectually, like he could dictate my thoughts. He's such a condescending, arrogant asshole." I bang my mug on the table to punctuate the last word, and coffee sloshes over the edge.

"Girl, he's under your skin." She laughs and shakes her head as she takes her coffee. "What the hell happened? Did you have sexy dreams about the arrogant asshole being nice to you and liking it or something?" She slides her plate with half a bagel across the table to me. "Eat something so you're not hangry in addition to whatever that man did to get you this worked up." She raises her eyebrows at me knowingly.

I take a sip of my coffee, figuring out how much I can tell her. It's embarrassing as hell to explain it all, but maybe it'll help me unravel the complicated feelings Payton has stirred up. I look at Della over the edge of my mug and she meets my gaze with patience. She's always been that way, willing to work through my short temper and cranky reactions with calm indulgence. I don't know how I got so lucky with her.

We met by chance when I moved to Atlanta two years ago

and needed a roommate. I was scared out of my mind, flat broke, didn't know a soul, and was desperate to get away from the worst thing that had ever happened to me. She was a friend of a friend from Charleston, and we met over coffee to see if we vibed, and it worked out. She didn't mind the surly attitude I'd picked up in New York and I could handle her plant lady tendencies. She's a landscape designer who tends to bring her work home with her.

I look around at the fifteen plants crowding our small kitchen waiting to be taken to her next installation as if confirming my decision to give her a shortened version that doesn't include details of our fake dating arrangement. I don't have all the information on that yet, and Payton said it had to be kept a secret.

"He flirted with me incessantly. I wanted to know why he said sparring with him was giving me a *release*, like, in a sexual way, right before he ended the call, which sent me into an anxiety spiral all night, so I texted to ask this morning. Of course his response was some bullshit that I was thinking about him all night, which I had to refute, so I FaceTimed him." My cheeks heat and I take another sip of my coffee before continuing in a muffled voice. "He answered from the shower."

"Holy shit. Did you see him naked?" She sets her bagel down on a napkin and plants her elbows on the table, leaning toward me, fully invested.

"From the abs up, which he has many of, and he's not shy about showing off his insane body." If I thought he was being inappropriate and flirty yesterday, today he was downright indecent. "He's an exhibitionist who likes the sound of his voice and getting a rise out of me, and he knows that's the way to do it. He asked me out, Dell."

I hate not telling her the full story. Still, it's a version of the truth that will be public knowledge soon enough when he launches whatever publicity campaign he thinks will convince the world that we're a couple and he's no longer an eligible bachelor.

"Seriously?" Her voice is incredulous. After a moment, a smile slowly turns up the corners of her lips as she stares at me, reading the embarrassment on my face. "You said yes, didn't you?" She flattens her hands on the table and leans toward me. "You hate him, but you're going out with him! Oh, this is good. A hate fuck is powerful. If you want to get laid by a hot man who likely knows how to make you scream in ecstasy and won't expect anything from you later, this is your chance. He could be a closet freak. I don't know what it is about those cute, smiley ones." She looks off dreamily, and I bet she's imagining the kind of sex she likes best. I've heard about her sex escapades for the entirety of our friendship. I know all the smutty details whether I've wanted to or not.

"No." I cut my hand through the air and bring her attention back to me from whatever sexy place it strayed. "I can't sleep with him. I'm a journalist and I've written about him. It's not ethical to get tangled up with him in any way, and I know he's smarter than that. He's just messing with me because he knows it gets under my skin and he's a world-class manipulator who reads people all too well. He's the mastermind behind all the Olympus PR and marketing, so it's no surprise he would want to fuck with my mind knowing I write the business beat on occasion. I'm not going near that train wreck."

"You sure about that?" she asks, smiling at me and pushing her messy hair behind her ear. "I think he wants to fuck with more than your mind. Tell me about this shower FaceTime. It sounds hot as hell." She shifts in her seat, the conversation getting her hot and bothered. *Same, girl, same.*

I glower at her to hide my reaction. "Didn't you have a date last night? You shouldn't be this hard up for secondhand sexual stimulation if you just got laid." I, however, need time with my vibrator while she hits up the farmer's market later to get myself right. It might take a few rounds before I can exorcize the picture of a water demon with intense blue eyes that can see into my soul from my head. There were...So...Many...Muscles. That won't be erased from my memory anytime soon.

She waves her hand airily at the comment. "It was a quick hookup and he wasn't great. I'd rate him a hard four, at best. I thought from our conversations through the app that he was going to be way more adventurous, but he was vanilla. He didn't even slap my ass or choke me when I asked him to. What is wrong with men these days? They can't even take a direct request when we tell them exactly what we want in bed."

I arch a brow at her. "You asked him to choke you? I thought you wanted the man to take control?"

"Most men think they're so adventurous until they're met with a woman who knows what she wants, then they're faced with the reality that they want the status quo. I like to feel them out and use direct communication to see how they react. If they don't rise to the occasion when given the green light, it won't be a repeat."

"Sorry you dealt with that." I have a feeling Payton is far more adventurous, but I want nothing to do with him in that regard, so it's irrelevant.

"It's fine, but I'm only partially satisfied and have to keep looking for the next hookup who will treat me like a queen in public and leave handprints on my ass in private. Dating these days is so hard." She slumps back in her chair and I burst out laughing until she joins me.

When I rein in my laughter, I raise my mug, feeling less

cranky. "It's a good thing I gave up dating and this Payton thing isn't going anywhere." The honest thought falls from my lips before I can think better of it. *Shit.* That won't help sell our relationship later on. Or maybe it will, given what Della knows about my stance on dating.

Her blue eyes soften with concern as she takes me in. "I wish you'd rethink that. It's been too long, Ains. Not one date since you moved to Atlanta. You're too young to have sworn off men," she says, leaning toward me. "Maybe going out with Payton will be a way to dip your toe in as he weaves sex into your conversations while answering FaceTime calls in the shower." She raises a brow at me and fans her pink face, her scattering of copper freckles standing out on her smooth cheeks.

"It's not good for my journalistic integrity to consider sleeping with one of the subjects of my stories." I look away from her intense stare, feeling uncomfortable even considering this. It's also a bad idea for me to think of fucking a man like Payton for other reasons that have everything to do with my dating mistakes that have kept me on the straight and narrow. Sex complicates everything, especially with a history like mine. I know my limits.

"Oh, please. Like that's stopped anyone in the past, it's not like you write about him, personally, right? You write about his company, their projects, and acquisitions, that kind of stuff. It would be different if you were writing about Payton Olsen, the man, instead of Olympus International, the business. Possible workaround?" She raises a shoulder at me and smiles wickedly.

"Stop trying to make this happen. I don't need anyone telling me what to do." I take a bite of the bagel she pushed over to me.

"I just want you to have every opportunity to enjoy yourself, in whatever way that looks like. You've been so focused on work, and the Gazette has been a shitty alternative to what you could have had before everything went down the way it did in New York. Allow yourself to do something bigger and better, finally. You've more than earned it, and you deserve it. Both professionally and personally, it's time to try again. Maybe going out with Payton will be the push you need to get out of that black time for both."

"Stop," I say, brushing off her well-meaning words. "Payton's an annoyance that's popped up in my life like a bad penny, and it's not so I can ride his dick or use him to get ahead with my career."

"That's not what I'm saying—"

My phone vibrating on the table next to my mug cuts her off. We both look down at it and she chokes out a laugh when she sees the name on the screen with the FaceTime request.

"Well, it looks like your annoying new friend wants another chance to video chat. Maybe he'll start with the lower half of his body this time and you'll see what he's packing and decide if it's worth it to get back into the dating pool for that alone."

"Shut up." My cheeks heat as I snatch the phone and leave the kitchen, heading for my room as she laughs at my retreating back.

"At least let him take you out and show you what his intentions are. Just go with it!" she yells before I slam my door.

I swipe to accept the call. "What?" I snap, mad at what Della said but taking it out on Payton. He deserves it, anyway.

"Still so grumpy? I thought I gave you plenty of time to handle your business and unwind."

I roll my neck, feeling more than the tension he's referring to, trying to get my emotions under control. I'm a professional. I have a solid poker face, and I can usually keep my reactions in check and make it through any interaction without letting them get the better of me, annoying caller be damned. He manages to get under my skin so easily, despite all that.

"This is how I am. If you want to fake date me, get used to it," I snap, running a hand through my hair and pacing around my small room.

"I'm not complaining. I like you just the way you are. I just thought you'd be a little...less on edge if you did what I expected you to. Unless you like being edged. Which I can work with."

"Payton," I warn, my eyes meeting his, humor crinkling the corners. "I don't want this to turn into another conversation full of innuendo and sexual overtures. Stop it right now."

"Anything for you, Muffin," he agrees with a slow smile and darkening of eyes that dry my mouth more effectively than his playful, sexually explicit words managed to. "Are you working today?"

"No. It's Sunday. Even I manage to take a day off. I bet you're working because you don't have a life," I deflect.

"Good. I'm coming to get you. We're going to the lake for the day. I need to get out of the city and we need to work out our relationship details. I'll be there in ten."

"What? No! How do you even know where I live?" Horror jacks up my heart rate as I look around my room and then down at myself, still in pajamas.

"You put your address in your contact yesterday like a very good girl."

I narrow my eyes at him calling me a good girl like a fucking dog despite the quickening of my pulse at the words. "I'm not going anywhere with you."

"Nine minutes, Spitfire. Put on your favorite bikini. It's time we start this fake relationship. I'll text you when I'm outside your apartment. Don't make me wait or I'll come up and get you myself." He ends the call and I'm left staring at the blank screen, my body shaking with adrenaline at the thought of Payton on his way to pick me up to take me out to a lake. What the fuck? I'm overwhelmed and unable to process. I can't do this on my own.

"Della!" I yell, opening the door before turning back and looking at my room without knowing what to do first.

What the hell is wrong with the man, and why am I falling into the web he's weaving around me? I'm smarter than this. Yet...I'm too curious to know who the real Payton Olsen is to give up the opportunity to find out when he's providing it to me on a silver platter. There's a story in there somewhere, and I can unlock it, all his sexual innuendo be damned. And he's right, we have to work out the details of our fake relationship before we start pretending. God, that makes me feel so shitty to even think about it because I'm curious enough to go along with his dumb plan.

"What's wrong?" she says, hurrying into the room and seeing me on the edge of a panic attack. "What did he say this time?" She suppresses a smile as I vibrate in frustration.

"That jackass is on his way to pick me up to take me to the lake. In ten minutes. I did not consent to go anywhere with him. He's such a jerk. What do I wear?"

She bursts into laughter and walks me back to my rumpled bed to sit. "I think asking what you should wear is giving consent, Ains. If you didn't want to go, you wouldn't even be worried about that. You have clean bikinis, right?"

"Of course. Top left drawer. But how dare he make decisions for me when I want nothing to do with him? He's unbelievable."

Della throws a white bikini on the bed along with a few

more items. "Put that on and brush your hair. I'll get sunscreen and a towel. You have flip-flops by the door. You'll be fine. Just have fun, don't think too hard about this, and enjoy your day at the lake, whether or not you want to call it a date."

"Dell, what am I doing?" I ask, panic setting in again. Maybe getting his story isn't worth my sanity. Payton sets me on edge. He gets under my skin, slides through my defenses, and penetrates my guarded walls with ease, and it pisses me off. I don't want him inside with me, seeing what I keep buried, or why it needs to stay locked up.

"You're having something called *fun* that most people partake in on a regular basis. It's good for you. You need it more than most. Please, I beg you, let down your guard enough to enjoy yourself a little bit, for me. Now scoot. You have a few minutes left if your countdown is correct."

I look at my phone and gasp. He'll be here in three minutes. I grab the clothing she picked and race into the bathroom to change. I brush my teeth, splash water on my face, run a brush through my hair, and grab my pink Yankees hat just as my phone vibrates with a new text.

> **Annoying Payton:** I'm outside. Ready for me, or do I need to come get you?

I roll my eyes as my heart slams against my ribs. I type out a hasty reply.

> **Me:** Don't get your panties in a twist, asshole. I'll be down in a minute.

> **Annoying Payton:** I'm not wearing panties, and I sure hope you aren't.

Me: Fuck you.

Annoying Payton: Nice choice of words.
Want to explore that later?

I ignore his text as heat simmers in my veins and throbs low in my body. That man is all sex, all the time, and it's getting me worked up more than I care to admit.

Ten

Payton

Ainsley storms out of her building wearing cut-off white shorts that do wonders for her long, tan legs, and a blue button-down shirt that looks like a perfect match for my eyes. How sweet of her.

Her head whips from side to side, scanning the street. She's wearing the same pink baseball hat from yesterday, but her blonde hair is down, falling below her shoulders, so it blows around her in the warm breeze as she looks for me. She frowns, pulling her phone out of the back pocket of those shorts that highlight her perfect little bubble of an ass that has me biting my lip as I stare.

Muffin: Where the fuck are you, Mr. In-

sists On Dictating My Day But Doesn't Make It Apparent Where He Is?

I give her a minute to stew before I text back.

Me: Blue Maserati MC20. Behind you.

She reads the text and spins around, finally catching sight of me as I wave a hand out the open top of the sports car. She walks down the block to my car and fumbles with the door handle, not sure how to work it. She makes a frustrated noise and glares at me through the top.

"How do I get into this expensive toy, you stupid asshole?"

I laugh, flipping my navy baseball cap backward, leaning over the small space to pull the handle and activate the butterfly door for her. She steps back as it rises at an angle in front of her instead of toward the curb as expected.

"Careful. Remember what I said about your mean words and what they do to me, Spitfire. Now get in here so we can get going. Atlanta is fucking hot and I want to jump into a warm lake with you."

She slides her hazel eyes from studying the door to drinking me in, and for a moment, they don't contain the murderous expression I expect but hold lust, and I smile in welcome to that change. Caught not being prickly, she quickly narrows her gaze and slips into the low car. She's maybe five-foot-three, little enough to fit in my small Italian sports car like a sun-kissed dream. She's fun-sized, and I'm more than ready to have fun with her.

The sunlight glints off her golden legs, drawing my attention to the smooth expanse of skin my hands itch to roam over. I mutter a curse under my breath and look away as she fumbles with the door to close it. I'm once again thankful for the small cockpit of the car, despite being six-two and finding it a bit cramped for my long legs. I still picked it for this drive, knowing it would put us in the closest proximity of all my vehicles.

I lean across her body and she stills. I suck in a greedy breath of her intoxicating coffee and vanilla scent. She smells fucking delicious. I reach up and grab the leather handle right over her hand and pull the door down, shutting it with her. I allow myself to stay close to her the entire time out of necessity but enjoy the feel of her heart hammering against my back anyway. I let go of the door and reach across for the seat belt next, pull it over her body, and buckle it for her as her chest rises and falls quickly under my arm.

"Safety first," I say with a low chuckle. Once she's set, I pat her smooth leg and can't help the caress of my thumb across her outer thigh. Just as I start to pull my hand away, she slaps her hand over mine, keeping it there, and I meet her eyes curiously.

"What's your deal?" she asks, her voice shaking.

"You have to be more specific. I have lots of deals," I answer, wanting her to be very clear about her request.

"I don't date, and you're not even my type, if I did. Why do you want *me* to be your fake girlfriend when I'm sure there are a hundred willing women you could pick from?"

I laugh at her finally getting to the point, but I think she's lying about me not being her type. I see how she looks at me. I'll play along for the sake of answering her question.

"I don't date, either. It's convenient for our fake relationship that you don't like me all that much so you don't fall for me."

She shakes her head vehemently. "I won't, but why are you messing with me like this? Every word out of your mouth is full of sexual overtones for strangers who met yesterday. If you don't expect me to fall for you, why are you flirting with me? Do you expect this to be a friends-with-benefits type of thing?"

I'm shocked she finally got up the nerve to approach my flirting head-on. It does something to me to hear her assertive instead of reactive or reproachful. I want to praise her with a well-placed *good girl*. I bite my cheek to keep the thought internal, despite knowing she'd likely preen under the praise. She's exactly the kind of driven, overachieving, words-of-affirmation woman who'd have a praise kink.

I can't help the involuntary squeeze of my hand on her thigh and she feels it, her eyes dropping to her lap to stare at our hands on her thigh before slowly meeting my eyes again. There's heat in her hazel gaze, shading her eyes more amber than green. Fuck, it turns me on knowing she's feeling the tension, too.

"Do you want it to be a friends-with-benefits type of thing?" I ask her question back to her with significantly more promise in my tone than hers held, unable to be anything but flirty with her. When she stays silent, I change tactics. "You hold all the power, Ainsley." I run my thumb gently along her thigh. She doesn't stop me. "You get to direct what this is in private. I just need a girlfriend convincing enough in public to keep Harlowe off my back. That means we're going to have to touch and put on a compelling enough show for her and others. If we enjoy it along the way, well, good for us, right?"

"That sounds like a cop-out for how much you flirt." Her tone isn't that believable, but she's fighting the good fight to stay prickly.

"I happen to like flirting and you're very fun to flirt with." I turn toward her and she meets my eyes, guarded but receptive. I decide to give her a truth so she'll have some power of her own in our dynamic, given I've already taken so much just by reading her as easily as I do. "I'll say things to get a rise out of you knowing I can. You can give me that satisfaction or not. It's up to you."

I give her thigh one last squeeze and slide my hand out from under hers, enjoying the pressure she keeps on it as if she doesn't want to lose contact. I start the car, pull on a pair of sunglasses, and look over my shoulder for traffic before racing away from her apartment in a roar of Italian horsepower. Ainsley makes a muffled squeal that's too fucking cute as she braces against the door and center console. The wind whips around us through the open top of the MC20, pulling at Ainsley's hat. She quickly presses it down lower on her head and squints against the wind.

"There's a pair of sunglasses in the glove compartment. There's something for you to look over, too," I say, loud enough to be heard over the rush of wind and engine.

She looks at me suspiciously, then reaches to open the glove compartment and sees the gold and pink aviator sunglasses. "Are these the whore glasses?"

I choke out a laugh and manage a quick look at her as I navigate through the early morning traffic in her neighborhood. "Excuse me?"

"Are these the sunglasses that are passed around to the girls who ride in this car with you? The whore glasses."

"I bought those for you this morning before I picked you up. If you don't like them, we can make a stop before we leave the city and get you something you like better. Besides, I don't drive women around, so there's no chance I'd have communal sunglasses."

"Oh," she says quietly.

"I need you to sign the papers under the sunglasses."

Her contrite expression over her misread of the sunglasses

situation sharpens into distrust again. "What are they?"

"Non-disclosure agreement and the contract for our arrangement. Standard forms, nothing untoward or weird, I promise. To protect my privacy and your ethics as a journalist. Feel free to read through the packet before signing. I'm grabbing coffee and the drive to the lake is about an hour. We have time."

"You seriously want me to sign an NDA and a contract to fake date you?"

"Yes." I keep it simple and to the point.

I want to be protected from the start because I'm going to be spending a lot of time with this woman and I won't be cleaning up my own fucking messes down the road like I have with my brothers. I've learned from their mistakes. Well, Zander's, mainly, but Hayes isn't blameless. He married Paige on a whim without a prenup and then fucked up royally when he bought out her hotel legacy without so much as mentioning it. She left him for a few agonizing weeks where we weren't sure if he'd be facing a divorce and subsequent loss of half of his considerable assets. I'll be smart from the start and cut off any potential issues now with a contract that stipulates what can and cannot be said about our arrangement.

I weave around traffic and Ainsley presses her body back into her seat as she pulls the manilla folder and binder-clipped sheaf of papers out of the glove compartment and starts flipping through the document. I pull into a coffee drive-through and order for us while she reads. She doesn't even complain, so I know she's concentrating deeply. I pull forward and pay, take her drink first, and slide the iced coffee between her thighs, making her jump at the contact of the icy cup on her skin.

"Hey!" she says, flattening the papers against her chest and looking down at where her drink is now nestled with my hand on top. I press it closer to the apex of her thighs and she stares daggers at me.

"No cup holders. You're responsible for your own drink, Muffin. If your hands are busy with those papers, your pretty thighs will have to hold it instead." I dry the condensation on my hand along the inside of her thigh, making her squeal in protest.

"Use your own shorts to dry your hands." She swats my arm with the sheaf of papers as she tries to hide her smile, which just makes me laugh.

"Your leg was so convenient, though."

I turn back to the barista and take my drink, catching her slipping a phone away, knowing she likely snapped a photo of us. That happens a lot. People think I'm some kind of celebrity because of my business and status, so they feel entitled to take photos of me or my family whenever we're out. Normally, it'd bug me, but this is convenient, given I want photos of us together to make it online. I tip the barista generously before we get back on the road.

"How'd you like it if I wiped my cold, wet hand on your bare thigh?" Ainsley asks.

"I'd ask you to keep going because I like temperature play and your hands look soft." I give her a coy smile. She smacks me again and I laugh harder.

"You're incorrigible," she huffs, but there's another hint of a smile turning up the corners of her mouth that she's trying desperately to tamp down.

"Oh, I see that smile you're trying to hide. You like it."

"Shut up. I have important documents to decipher and you're distracting me."

I slide my iced coffee between my thighs and move my right hand off the steering wheel over to her bare knee, where I stroke her soft skin and feel goosebumps rise under my touch immediately. "If you want a distraction, I'm good at providing those."

"Payton, focus on the road and quit touching me while I'm trying to read. There's no one to perform for." Ainsley's voice isn't as certain this time, and when I glance her way, her bottom lip is trapped between her teeth and she's staring at my hand on her leg. It looks good, like it belongs there, my fingers lazily making circles over her tan skin as I explore her thigh.

"Practice makes perfect, Muffin. I want us to be comfortable when the time comes to put on the proper show. Shouldn't we know what it feels like and how we'd react in the moment? I'm a hands-on guy. I'll be touching you any chance I get in public. You won't be able to freeze or look uncomfortable with it and you'll have to sell the idea that you enjoy it. So do you?"

"Do I what?" she asks, her voice unmistakably breathy while my fingers roam unchecked up her thigh, still drawing light circles over her skin.

"Enjoy having my hands on you?" I've reached the frayed edge of her shorts and brush along the strands, wishing I could watch her face instead of the road. I let my fingers graze below the edge and slowly slide toward her inner thigh. I feel her tremble before she finally grabs my wrist and moves my hand away.

"You need to drive and I need to read." She evades my question, yet manages to answer it at the same time. She liked it more than she wanted to admit. That's good enough for me.

Satisfied, I keep my hands to myself and stay quiet to let her read through the entire contract while I drive the familiar route to my lakehouse on Lake Lanier. It's about fifty miles northeast of Atlanta and one of the largest lakes in Georgia. It's quicker for me to get there than to the coast by car, and easier than getting the jet ready to fly somewhere farther away.

"I'll sign it, but I want to add my own stipulations."

I look over at Ainsley about fifteen minutes later. She's gorgeous with the sunglasses perched on her face under the pink hat I hoped she'd wear again. I was betting on that when I picked the shades out. The light pink and gold look nice against her tan and the champagne and honey strands of her hair that blow around her face in the breeze.

"I told you nothing weird was tucked in there. It's all very standard, except the whole we're dating for three months thing. So what kind of stipulations do you have in mind?"

"This whole situation inordinately benefits you, even if it's repayment of a favor, which I still think is bullshit." She glowers at me.

"You brought this on yourself by insisting on owing me the favor in the first place." I chuckle at her annoyance at my reminder.

She takes a deep breath and lets it out in a rush before continuing. "I want you to give me a story. I need to get away from the Gazette, and the only way I'm going to do that is with higher-value topics than what our paper covers so I can prove my worth as a journalist. Let me write a profile on you and shop it around. Your name alone carries value to any heavy hitter in the business world, and a human-interest story would appeal to papers that cover soft news."

Ah, there it is. I knew she wanted to learn about Olympus and get her piece of the pie somehow, but this is more than fair. And, frankly, I approve of her wanting to use the story to leave the fucking second-rate paper she's at, so her reasons work for me, even if I'm not sure what she wants to write about exactly.

"There'll be limits on what you can write about. I'm a private person and don't like the idea of letting the world into every aspect of my life. Additionally, there are a lot of sensitive deals that can't be discussed when it comes to Olympus, so I can't be an entirely open book on that, either. I'll need to read a draft of the story before it goes to print to ensure my company and family are shown in the best light. I'll even connect you with contacts of mine at the Wall Street Journal, Forbes, and a few others when it's done. If that's amenable to you, we can include it in the contract."

"Deal," she says quickly. When I glance over, her face is cautiously optimistic, and I like seeing the hesitant smile turning up those pretty lips. Finally, an emotion other than reserved animosity. Fuck yes, it's worth agreeing to a story just to see that smile alone.

"Add the details to the last page before you sign." I pull a pen out of the pocket of my blue checked button-down and hand it to her without looking over. She takes it from me, her fingers brushing over mine delicately, and I wonder if she meant to. Maybe she's trying out the whole touching thing, too. While she's become easier to read the more I get to know her, she still manages to surprise me. Now we'll see if I can surprise her.

Eleven

Ainsley

Payton pulls up to the entrance of a lakefront property, hits a button to activate the gate, and then winds down a driveway that snakes along a hillside until a stunning view of Lake Lanier appears and the house finally comes into sight.

"This is your lakehouse?" I look around in awe as he parks and hops out. He rounds the small sports car to help me with the stupid door and offers a hand to climb out of the low seat. I take it, too caught up in what I'm seeing to refuse. I allow him to keep my hand in his even after the help is no longer needed. I'm getting used to touching him, and honestly, it's not the worst. Payton has big, strong hands with long fingers that looked really good against my leg earlier and feel just as nice laced with mine now. I turn my attention back to the lake house.

It's more of a mansion, which shouldn't surprise me in the least, despite being absolutely insane. The house is a sandy-toned behemoth of modern angles and stone elements seamlessly creating a masculine design that somehow blends into the hillside and keeps it from standing out like a sore thumb against the landscape.

The hillside slopes down to the water. We're at the top, where garages are situated around a courtyard, but I can see the house is four levels in total, each level having an outdoor terrace providing an incredible view of the lake below. One level has a covered patio with a fireplace and an outdoor dining area. Another has a bocce ball court. The lowest level features a stunning sapphire blue infinity edge pool and hot tub perched so it looks like an extension of the lake itself.

Down at the lake, there's a long dock next to an enclosed boathouse with an outdoor slip. A white sailboat is moored in the large cove. It's far more private than I expected. It's a good distance to the wide mouth of the cove, where the lake properly spreads out and watercraft of all shapes and sizes go by.

"Catching flies, Muffin?" Payton asks, his finger stroking under my chin. Apparently, it'd been hanging open as I took in the wealth and decadence of his lakehouse, which is more than most people can hope to have in their hard-earned forever homes. And he's rarely here. It makes me kind of sick, despite how beautiful it is.

"It just seems like...overkill to spend this much money on a place that you visit, what, a few days a year," I say, my mouth turning down with the words.

"Fuck, I love when you tell me how you really feel and insult me in the process," he says, throwing an arm around my shoulders and pulling me into his side.

It's then I realize how much taller he is. My head barely reaches his shoulder, so I'm pressed tightly against his body, my cheek feeling all those beautiful muscles I saw in too graphic detail on our FaceTime call this morning. I push against him for distance because not only does he feel hard and amazing, he smells incredible, too. Sea salt and amber, both invigorating and warm, fresh and sultry. I want to take in greedy breaths of his scent, which makes me take big steps back from him instead.

Self-preservation is my go-to when I'm overwhelmed and wanting what I shouldn't. That means putting distance between me and what I know will hurt me due to my penchant for wanting them. Payton is a walking red flag for everything that could easily ensnare and devastate me. Hot, rich, technologically inclined, interested in the chase, liable to have me eating out of his hand, and using me for his own gain. Yeah, that's a big fat no for me.

I say the first hurtful thing that comes to mind, hoping to push him away. "You're the weirdest man I've ever met. Why do you like being insulted so much? Is it a kink thing? Degradation gets you off?" I cross my arms over my chest, not entirely comfortable talking about kinks with him but wanting to know if that's his so I can avoid it going forward. The less I encourage him sexually, the better.

He raises his eyebrows at me. "I have plenty of kinks, but that's not one of them." He tilts his head, studying me, and I swear he can see into my head with his sharp eyes. Cold fear washes over me and snaps my spine straight. I lower my arms to my sides hesitantly. He smiles at my look of discomfort. It's predatory and pleased.

"Why are you looking at me like that?" I ask cautiously.

He walks up to me slowly, smile not dropping, but his blue eyes heat and I can't look away. His hand reaches out and takes hold of my hip, pulling me forward until I'm flush against his body. His other hand tilts my chin up so I'm looking into his face.

"Is it one of yours, Princess?"

His voice has taken on a deep, commanding tone that sends goosebumps rushing across my skin. The new nickname slips into place far easier than anything he's called me before. I shiver and press closer against him on instinct.

"Do you like being called an eager little cumslut? Get off on being a filthy cocktease who wants to choke on a mouthful of cum, but only if you deserve it? Do you want to be my beautiful little fucktoy? Will you be a bratty whore for my cock? Or is it more of a good girl who takes Daddy's cock so well that you prefer?"

His thumb brushes along my bottom lip, pulling it down slightly and ghosting across the tip of my tongue, making my mouth go dry with need.

"I think you have a praise kink in there, regardless of whatever else you may want to hear." He taps my lips and releases my chin.

His filthy words may have left my mouth dry, but my bikini bottoms are absolutely flooded and my core pulses, squeezing around nothing. I blink at him, not sure how to respond. My jaw works uselessly. Finally, I stutter out a hoarse, "W-what the f-fuck?"

That didn't go as planned and I'm mortified and, oh my God, I'm so wet and...no, I can't be...turned on? This is wrong on so many levels. I've *never* been spoken to like *that* and reacted like *this*. I'd slap anyone for saying those things to me. I refuse to be called names or let a man debase me, but what he said, or maybe it was the way he said it, had an effect on me that I can't even begin to process. He strokes his hand along my hip, his intense eyes drinking me in. I'm frozen as I stare mutely in horror at my reaction. I'm putty in his hands, shaped by the words he spoke to me, molded into whatever he wants to make me.

"I think I hit on something there, Princess," he says quietly. "We'll table that for a later discussion, but know we'll talk about it again." His eyes lower slowly from my lips, down over my hardened nipples peeking through the soft material of my shirt, across my trembling torso, and finally to where my thighs are clenched together. "Unless you want to talk about it now and maybe do something about being this tightly wound up?" His gaze travels back up the same path until he meets my eyes and I still don't have my shit together.

I shake my head, pulling out of the possessive grip he has on me, unable to speak more than a few words. "I need..." I croak, voice breaking as my iced coffee drops to the ground at my feet from my shaking hands while I vibrate in my anxious, now sexually fueled tension.

"I know what you need." He bends and picks up my bag from the car, tosses the strap over his shoulder, then takes my hand in his and drags me toward the house. I fight the lust-filled spell he cast on me with his filthy words and that sexy as fuck voice of his that somehow got deeper and sent me to a place in my head I didn't know existed.

At the door, the lock automatically turns, and we walk into the house that's as modern and gorgeous as you'd expect from the exterior. He leads me through the upper floor which I can't fully appreciate while in my current state. We continue down several flights of stairs to the final level that opens to the pool terrace, where it appears he's taking me. I'm dizzy from the stairs, and still, he continues to pull me along with him.

I'm slowly getting over my shock at his ease with the dirty and commanding words he spoke to me. He said that's not his kink, but he's obviously familiar with dishing out the degradation and had no trouble pulling out easy examples that made me feel some kind of way I've never experienced before.

Do I have a degradation kink? Holy shit, maybe I do. I'm all sorts of fucked up over other things. Maybe I've developed something there, too. I'm not about to explore that with him, though. He doesn't have to know that what he said hit a little too close to home, no matter what my reaction may have told him. I'll have to try harder to have no reaction should he ever make a repeat of his stupid recitation of those types of phrases. They're just words, after all, and I know better than most that words only have the power we give them.

I realize we're on the dock when the ground shifts under my feet. Payton pulls me all the way to the end before finally letting me go and drops my bag at our feet.

"Do you want me to help you with your shirt, or have your hands stopped shaking enough to get those buttons?" he asks, nodding at me while he begins to swiftly unbutton his own.

"I'm not a child," I snap, feeling more like myself now.

"There's my girl," he says, smiling. "Take off your clothes before I throw you in with everything on."

"I'm not your girl." I snarl, feeling stupid as I argue.

I pull my hat and sunglasses off and place them on the dock at my feet where I've kicked off my flip-flops. I unbutton my shirt and let it fall to the dock, then angrily work my shorts down over my hips to step out of them. I straighten up and catch Payton looking me over appreciatively. He smiles when he notices my own gaze rake over his incredible body. His dark blue swim trunks ride low on his hips, showcasing his decadently muscled upper body and the V that points to his muscled lower half, proving it's just as cut.

"Like what you see in person more than through a FaceTime call?" he asks, not at all shy about the attention I'm giving him. He removes the backward baseball hat finally, releasing me from that magical spell. What is it with men and backward hats? It's fucking kryptonite.

"Shut up." I cross my arms over my small chest, self-conscious of my body under his hot blue stare that feels like fiery hands are caressing me.

"Don't hide. You're beautiful, and you look incredible in that white bikini. If you ever want to revisit that friends-with-benefits situation, let me know. But for now, we need to get you even more soaked than you already are."

"What?" I muddle my way through his layered comments that swept through several topics and sent my head spinning.

Before I can get a straight answer out of him, he tosses me over his shoulder and jumps off the dock into the lake. The water is warm but the moment is a surprise and I gasp in a mouthful of water before I kick to get away from him. I break the surface, sputtering and coughing. He comes up beside me, breathing normally. The man must be part fish.

"You're insane!" I accuse, splashing water. He's too close to me. I can't relax.

"You're not thinking about what I said and how it made you feel, though, right? I told you I know what you need. Trust me to take care of you. I can be a very good boyfriend."

"You're not my boyfriend and I definitely don't trust you." I swim away from him. He stays close with ease, not letting me put distance between us. I kick my legs wildly, not nearly as at ease in the water as he seems to be.

"You got into my car willingly enough to come to my lakehouse an hour away from Atlanta. I think that means you trust me a little bit. You signed the NDA and contract, so we're in a relationship for the next three months. For all intents and purposes, I'm your boyfriend."

"I don't think you're a serial killer, but I can't say you're not bad in other ways. And now I've signed your stupid NDA, so I can't say shit to anyone, even if you are." My legs falter their movements at that horrifying thought and my chin dips below the waterline. I suck in a mouthful of water, then sputter it out on a cough.

Payton is there in an instant, pulling me into his arms, turning my back to his front, and wrapping a giant arm around my stomach so I no longer have to swim while he does it for the both of us with ease. I only fight a little against his insistent grip because I was getting tired. Swimming for sport isn't really my thing. I'm more of a *tanning on the side of the pool and hopping in to cool off* kind of swimmer.

"I'm not going to kill you, or do anything without you specifically asking me to," he says next to my ear.

I'm carefully keeping our lower halves apart, letting my legs float out in front of me while he treads water below us, the movement rhythmic and all too easy for him. He did say he swims laps daily, so maybe this is easy.

"Let me go. I'm not going to drown," I snap instead of addressing his comments. I push at his heavy arm around my waist and feel him tighten it more, his chest pressing into my back.

"I don't trust your stamina. It looked like you were getting tired. I can do this for days. You're so little it's nothing."

I scoff. "I know how to swim. I'm a grown woman."

"You sure are," he growls against my wet hair and I shake my head at him for being impossible.

"Don't you dare do anything…" I begin, not sure what I'm threatening.

"Anything what, exactly?" he challenges. "Anything that makes you feel something more than you want to?"

"No," I snap, pushing at his arm again with more force, but it just causes my legs to drop, our bodies aligning, and *I feel him.* His body is hard everywhere—chest against my shoulders, abs against my back, and finally, my ass presses directly into what I was trying to avoid, and oh my God, of course he's hard there, too. And big.

I stop fighting and go rigid, which forces me tight to him. I want the water to swallow me now that I know what he feels like against me. I wish I never let him talk to me in the first place, never let the intrigue of knowing him lure me in at all. I bite my lip to keep the pitiful sound of failure from falling from my throat, sounding an awful lot like a moan. Because I want to feel even more of him now.

"Your heart is beating so fast. Are you excited or scared?" His words are soft against my ear, while his arm is tight where he still holds me against him.

"I'm angry." We both know I'm lying by the breathiness of the words.

He easily turns me in his arms so we're facing each other, and I'm blessedly released from his body. He lets me swim on my own again.

"Why do you want to hate me so much?" It's a rare serious moment where he's not smiling or poking fun at me. He seems to truly want to know.

I look away from the openness that wants to slip under my defenses again, to get in and see *me*. It makes me want to lash out, and my sharp tongue fights the battle for me where my body fails.

"I hate men like you on principle. You're a bored, rich man who's decided I'm some sort of game because it's fun to conquer everything that presents a challenge to you. I'm not a game and I don't want to be conquered."

The words spill out with certainty and venom. It hides the very real sting of having lived through it before and gained the experience. I hope. It might sound bitter and jaded, which is also fine. As long as it doesn't sound needy.

"I don't think of you as a game and I'm not trying to conquer you, Ainsley. I just want to be your boyfriend," he says, sincerity in his eyes when I meet them.

"*Fake boyfriend*. And if only I believed that. Every conversation with you leaves me with whiplash and debating if I should be running for the hills. You don't take no for an answer. You slip sex into every word you say. You touch me like you have a right to. You look at me like you want to fuck me. You act on some misguided instinct that I need you to save me. You have to stop this! You, Payton Olsen, have a God complex, and I'm not having it."

His lips turn up at the corners as he listens to me. "And you, Ainsley Montgomery, are lying to yourself. You deny yourself the truth of what you need because you're afraid to want it. You wear hostility and anger because you feel vulnerable with softer emotions that leave you exposed. You don't want to admit you need connection because somewhere along the line, you were hurt, and that fucker never paid for his mistakes. You don't even want to be playful or explore a friendship with me because it puts you too close to wanting something you refuse yourself. But sure, I'll respect your boundaries if you really want them."

And just like that, Payton Olsen has stripped me bare and knows half my secrets already.

Twelve

Payton

Ainsley's ignoring me.

She swam for the dock and I let her, knowing I'd read her too well and been too honest when she wasn't ready to hear it. It's a fucking curse to see what people try to hide behind; the insecurities, what they don't even understand about themselves. That's where Ainsley's at. She's trying to be something she's not, wearing hard emotions—her control, anger, hostility, hate, and venom—to keep everything good at bay because she knows how easily it can be taken away, or used against her. It's so fucking heartbreaking knowing someone did that to her, made her that way, because no one is hardwired to think like that—they're programmed.

She took her things up to the pool and plopped onto a lounge chair, sunglasses firmly in place, hat back on, not sparing me a glance as she stares at her phone. I followed her sweet little ass calling her name, and now I'm stopped in front of her chair, casting a shadow over her.

"Hungry? Thirsty? Need some sunscreen so you don't burn that pretty skin?"

She doesn't answer me, thumbs flying over her phone screen, messaging someone, probably. She may be telling them she's frustrated or upset at the lake with some guy who's being an unreasonable asshole to her. She'll have to keep details about who it is and what we're doing to a minimum after signing the NDA. I'm confident in her ability to follow the rules, given her profession and how thoroughly she read through the document before signing it. Or maybe she's taking notes for the story I've agreed to and starting off strong with how much of a jerk I am.

Getting no response, I turn and head inside. Maybe some time alone is what she needs. Perhaps I should've waited more than twenty-four hours after meeting her to pull that nugget of information out and throw it in her face. I may have just lost my opportunity at a friendship with Ainsley by pushing her boundaries and my luck.

It's not often my meddling tendencies come back to bite me in the ass, but when they do, it's pretty spectacular, and this feels like it could be one of those instances. I lean against the wall of windows overlooking the pool and watch Ainsley on her phone below. She's beautiful, young, cranky as hell, driven, and lonely. I recognized that part of her so quickly, seeing a reflection of myself in her workaholic tendencies and thinking I'd found a kindred spirit that maybe I could beat back the loneliness with if she'll ever let me close enough.

When I return to the pool, I'm armed with a peace offering. The tray loaded with food and drinks catches Ainsley's attention and she actually looks at me as I walk past to an umbrella-covered double lounger with a table between the cushions perfect for a picnic. I set the tray down and begin to arrange the food without acknowledgment. I can feel her irritation despite being ten feet away.

I pour a chilled sparkling wine into two stemless glasses and set them next to a charcuterie spread full of meats and cheeses, sliced fruit, vegetables, bowls of pasta salad, baguette slices, and a plate of assorted chocolate truffles I hope don't melt in the Georgia heat. Satisfied my picnic is presented to the best of my abilities, I turn to the sapphire pool and dive in smoothly. I swim the length and return to where I started before pulling myself onto the deck, sufficiently cooled off.

Ainsley is sitting up now, looking between the spread and me. I nod at the food as I push wet hair out of my face before collapsing onto one side of the lounger and grabbing a glass of wine.

"Help yourself."

I pick up an olive and pop it into my mouth before creating a sandwich, not waiting for her to make up her mind if she's going to join me. I take a bite and will myself to ignore her as she gets up and makes her way over to me, wearing her button-down shirt over her bikini, the middle open so I can see her perky, palm-sized tits bounce with each step, the ends of the shirt hitting her high on the thighs, not doing much to act as a poolside cover-up and giving me plenty to look at. I blink at the beautiful sight and go back to eating so I don't end up needing to adjust my hardening cock in front of her.

She sits on the other side of the lounger, grabs a water bottle, untwists the cap, and takes a drink. She pops a chocolate truffle in her mouth as she inspects the charcuterie spread and begins to build her own sandwich.

"What, no comment about eating dessert first?" she asks wryly, grabbing another truffle and eating it in between words.

"None at all. I call that a dessert-itizer. You're smart to start with the sweetest bite so you're sure to enjoy it before you get full off the main meal." I resolutely keep my attention on my own food, grabbing a fork and turning to my pasta salad while she quietly stews next to me as I eat. I'm just happy to see her eating what I've prepared, letting me take care of her in this small way.

I keep her guessing the rest of the day. We eat, swim, and take my sailboat around the lake for a few hours. Not once do I touch her. I don't slip sex into the conversation. I don't flirt. She's on edge by the time we're driving back to Atlanta, shoulders slightly sunburnt, and tired from spending the day outside.

"What are you doing?" she snaps when we're nearly back to the city.

"What do you mean?" I ask, keeping my attention on the road, but I can see her arms are crossed and she's staring at my profile. It's cute watching her work out this change.

"You're not flirting. You're acting like a normal human. You haven't touched me since we got out of the lake." She ticks off her accusations on her fingers. "What are you up to?"

I spare her a glance before returning my attention to the road. "I'm respecting your boundaries. You wanted me to stop, so I have."

"Is this another way to mess with my head because you're a master manipulator? You changed it up to keep me guessing?"

"You give me too much credit. Thank you for thinking me devious enough to execute that successfully with you," I say sincerely.

"That's it? You're just going to...stop? It's that easy? Why didn't you stop the other times I asked?"

"You actually meant it this time, and I told you I'd show you I'll respect your boundaries. I'm a man of my word, and even though I really enjoy flirting with you, I'm doing as you asked. Don't you like it better this way? It's what you wanted, after all." I keep my eyes ahead, but I feel her processing this information, warring with her natural distrust.

"So if I flirted with you, or touched you, you wouldn't do anything back?"

"Do you want to flirt with and touch me?"

"Of course not. I was asking about your response. Like, if I put my hand on your thigh right now, or turned the tables and started talking like you've been, you'd respect my boundaries?"

"Oh, little Spitfire, make no mistake. That's not at all what I'm saying," I tell her, glancing over quickly and catching a calculating look on her face, wishing I could see beneath her sunglasses. "If you initiate, I'll follow your signals, but I won't follow for long. I'll take control and then we'll see what you're hiding under that hostility and anger and how fun you can be."

"That doesn't seem fair. Why can't I torture you the same way you've been driving me insane the last twenty-four hours? I should be able to get payback, right? You need to know how annoying you are and how awful it is to have someone not only pick you apart but not listen when you beg them to stop."

I shift uncomfortably in my seat and glance her way again,

debating if I give her what she's asking for or not. Honesty *is* the best policy in the early stages of any relationship, I guess, and strong communication will be the only way we make this work.

"You are torturing me. It's pretty fucking hard not to flirt with you when that's my default. It sucks not touching you when I want because I like how you feel under my hands and despite what you say, your body's reactions tell me you enjoy it when I touch you, too. I read people, so not calling out everything I see that you blatantly ignore is driving me crazy."

I glance her way, seeing her attention riveted on me, her thighs pressed together like she can feel my words on her skin even if my hands aren't. She's definitely a words girl, and mine are doing it for her. I return my attention back to the road, but I lower my voice and slow my cadence, aware it'll get to her even more.

"It's absolutely excruciating knowing I can use a certain tone, say a few dirty words, look at you a certain way, and you'd be rubbing your thighs together for me, looking for something only I can give you, but I have to keep that locked up when I'm certain it would feel so fucking good for both of us to play."

I rub a palm down my face instead of reaching for her thigh like I want to. I drop my hand to my shorts, where my cock is making a valiant effort to strain against the bonds of the fabric in this position, and adjust myself for her to see.

"Is that what you want, Ainsley? For me to suffer as long as you want me to because I'm willing to respect your boundaries?"

"How do you manage to infuse sex into an answer like that?" she asks, her voice husky and tremulous, unable to take her eyes off my cock. My body. Me.

Yes, Princess, look at Daddy and see what you do to me. Want me and everything I can give you. Trust me to take care of you.

"It's a talent of mine," I muse, focusing again on the road.

She clears her throat and shifts in her seat, leaving the conversation there. I swallow and settle myself the fuck down. There's no need to get us worked up over nothing. She has boundaries and I'm perfectly fine staying on my side of them, even if I have no problem telling her how I feel about it. I change the subject, wanting to know more about her if I can't have her the way I really want to.

"Tell me about Charleston and your family. Do they still live there?"

She looks over at me quickly. "Yes," she says warily. "You remembered that?"

"I have a very good memory." That only partially covers it. I remember everything, good and bad. "So tell me about your family. You know about my brothers. Do you have siblings?"

"I have four sisters. I'm right in the middle. Serena and Lana are older. Brooke and Cora are younger."

"So we're both middle children. Funny how that works. Did you have to referee for your sisters like I did for my brothers? Or were you the quintessential middle child who was doing anything for attention since the eldest is usually independent and the parents baby the youngest?"

"Is that why you're so annoying and weird?" she asks, the snarl back on her lips for prying into her personal life again.

"Damn, calm down, Spitfire." I laugh at her quick deflection. "I'm not flirting. I'm just trying to get to know you."

She huffs in annoyance, likely because I'm right. "I guess it was both stifling and lonely in the middle. There was a gap between my older sisters and me, then my younger sisters, so I'm not very close to either set, but they're close to each other. I kept to myself, and I read a lot. Partly it was to get away from my noisy family, but mostly because I loved stories. That love turned into writing my own stories. That's why I decided journalism was the career I wanted to pursue. I wanted to know the story behind everything."

I love how easily she gave up that bit of information without prompting. It makes me greedy, needing more of her history.

"Are you close with your family now?"

Whether they admit it or not, my brothers are my best friends and the closest people in my life despite how often they drive me crazy or do dumb shit I have to clean up for them. My mom is my favorite person, and my dad is my hero. Family means everything to me. Even Harlowe, the evil queen who wants to set me up with every single woman she knows, is part of that.

"Yes, but I don't get to see them much. Lana and Serena live a few states away. Cora is still in Charleston in high school, and Brooke is at the University of South Carolina a few hours away. My parents live in the house I grew up in, so it feels like a time capsule every time I go home to visit. So much changes, yet stays the same."

She's growing more unguarded, less angry, the longer she talks about her family. She's actually pleasant, which is a nice change.

"Did you like growing up in Charleston?"

"It was fine. It's a small town but big enough because of the tourism and local industry, so there's enough to keep busy. We aren't high society and stayed out of the real drama, with just enough to scrape by for a family of seven. My dad's an aeronautical engineer. He teaches at the South Carolina Aeronautical Training Center at Trident Technical College. Sounds fancy, but it's nothing prestigious. My mom is also a teacher but at a local elementary school."

My ears perk at her father's career path. "You know Olympus has a clean burning jet engine project we're working on. We'd have a lot to talk about if we met."

"You'll never meet my dad," Ainsley scoffs with a tone of finality.

"Never say never," I say with just as much conviction, right as I pull up to her apartment building. "Now be a good girl and think about all you've learned about yourself today." She starts to protest and I stop her. "No, really, just give it some thought and explore the ideas a bit to see what you discover. I don't have to factor into it. I'd rather you know the parts of yourself that can bring you satisfaction and pleasure if you let the control go and what that looks like. I'm here if you want to talk, but I'm not pushing you. Thanks for a fun day at the lake."

She looks at me incredulously, shakes her head, and removes the pink and gold sunglasses, tucking them back in the glove compartment. "Yeah, it was something."

When she looks my way again, the fading sunlight catches on her hazel eyes, turning them amber and gold, highlighting a small scattering of light freckles across her cheeks. I find myself smiling at the constellation marking summer on her skin.

"You're really nothing like I imagined, Payton Olsen. Especially not the sex-fiend side of you."

I laugh at that. "You have no idea, Ainsley Montgomery, but if you want to, just say the words. I'm looking forward to being your boyfriend and getting to know you better, so I don't have to imagine anything."

"Fake boyfriend," she huffs, ignoring the rest of my comment before pulling the door open, stepping out, and turning back to me. "Good night."

"Night, Muffin."

She rolls her eyes as she grabs her bag and shuts the door before whirling and heading into her apartment without another word as I chuckle at her haughty retreat.

"You're going to be mine, little Spitfire."

Thirteen

The Atlanta Haute List

Mystery Blonde And Billionaire Spotted Second Day In A Row

Atlanta's newly minted most eligible bachelor may not be single much longer. The mystery blonde he was linked to at The Unicorn Café just yesterday was seen once again with the handsome billionaire businessman, this time as a passenger princess in his six-figure Maserati supercar grabbing coffee to-go Sunday morning. Were the two starting their day together, or ending it? Had they met the day before at the café, or were they previously acquainted? We have questions!

Hauties in the know rushed to provide info on our mystery woman, Ainsley Montgomery, a twenty-five-year-old staff reporter for the Atlanta Gazette, a small community newspaper that barely registers on the radar of news-hungry Atlantans. A search reveals she's not much to speak of, compared to our favorite middle Olsen brother. She has private social media profiles, and her articles from the Gazette don't link to her personal life. She's plain and, well, boring, honestly.

What does Payton see in this Charleston, South Carolina native from a large family with humble roots that are very unlike his own? Maybe he likes slumming with the press, given his role as the head of PR for Olympus International? Her gig at the Gazette doesn't seem like a big enough draw for a power player like Payton. We think there *must* be something more he sees in her because he seems quite smitten from the photos that were sent in where he has his hands all over her while grabbing coffee at a drive-through.

Payton, thirty-five, has kept a low profile during the two years the Haute List has been operating, and as far as we know, hasn't been linked to anyone notable since Olympus was founded ten years ago. He rarely makes our pages outside of business purposes, so it's nice to see him getting out and having a bit of fun now that his brothers have found love and settled down with families of their own. Is that in the cards for Payton as well? We'll be watching! Hit Like and Subscribe for all the Haute Gossip!

Fourteen

Payton

"Tell me about the blonde." Zander accosts me when he enters the boardroom before our weekly briefing.

"Good morning to you too, asshole," I greet with the barest hint of a smile. I've been here for hours, reviewing IT logs and ensuring our servers haven't suffered any breaches or faltered in any way over the weekend while I was away.

"I know Harlowe didn't set you up with her because she was talking mad shit all weekend about how you wouldn't take any of her suggestions and surprised her with some mystery girlfriend out of nowhere. My wife's obsessed with the idea you were hiding a relationship from us like it's the plot of one of her romance novels." He shakes his head with the dopey grin he gets whenever talking about Harlowe. "Hopefully, now that you've found your own hot piece of ass, she can go back to focusing on fucking me instead of fucking with your love life."

I laugh and lean back in my chair, ready to start this charade for my family. "Her name is Ainsley. Didn't you read the Atlanta Haute List yesterday? They gave a pretty good rundown of who she is, despite insinuating she's not good enough for me."

I was pissed when I read that. There's no reason for a gossip site or anyone, for that matter, to think Ainsley isn't a proper match for me, regardless of what they think of her job, family, or social standing. That's all bullshit, anyway. All that matters is who you want to spend time with and who makes you feel good about yourself. Besides, this is all fake, but if it weren't, Ainsley would be a top-tier choice if I ever had one. She's perfect.

"I saw the pictures of you with your hand between her legs in the coffee drive-through, you big perv. I knew you had some kinks but didn't realize you'd play in public, too. If Harlowe let me, I'd have my hands on her pussy any chance I got, too."

"If you want an invite to the club, Zand, just say so. Besides, I was putting a coffee on the seat between her legs because I don't have cup holders, not feeling her up. You know how photos can look. But her thighs are fucking incredible and I love having my hands on them," I finish with a wicked grin, selling the story. He'll inevitably take the news back to Harlowe, and that's who needs to believe this whole thing with Ainsley is legit. I'm planting the seeds and he'll be the one to water them.

"Fuck yes, sign us up for a sex club, and finally, you're getting some. How long has it been?" Zander pumps his fist in front of his gray suit pants while leaning back in his chair just as Hayes comes in, sees what's happening, and rolls his eyes.

"Oh, for fuck's sake. It's Monday morning, Zander. I don't need to see you jacking off in the boardroom. We have deals to close. Grow up and only talk about business." Hayes sighs and settles at the head of the table as our SVPs, directors, and support staff file in to begin the meeting.

"Payton's just filling me in on his new girlfriend. She's hot and almost as young as your Southern belle, Hater," Zander says to Hayes. Hayes glares at Zander, but he shoots me a questioning look as Zander finishes. "Why y'all have to go robbing the cradle to find women willing to fuck you is a question I don't particularly want the answer to." Zander raises his hands to ward off any vitriol from Hayes or myself at that dig.

Luca DaSilva, my SVP, settles to my right with a stack of PR and marketing briefs for me to review. I start flipping through them, trying to ignore my brothers' conversations as Javier Montero does the same with Zander, and Diego Vallarta confers with Hayes. Our admins bustle through with coffee, more documents, and notes.

"Payton, I think it goes without saying that you better watch yourself since everything you do will be publicly scrutinized and tied to the company. We have pending deals that don't need any bad press," Hayes warns. I look up and meet his cold green stare and raise my eyebrows in challenge.

"I know better than anyone, and you should be all too aware of it. How many times have I cleaned up the messes you fuckers created, smoothed over the bad press for Olympus, and made sure we survived every shitstorm that came our way? Oh yeah, every single one. I think I'll be just fine dating an intelligent, hot as hell, driven woman."

"Payton is conveniently leaving out that his mystery woman is a journalist who's written about Olympus and has a new story about our latest real estate project that ran this morning.

She writes for a shitty community newspaper, so it's not like anyone reads it, but their website crashed today when it went live because she's linked to Payton, so obviously their connection is garnering some attention," Luca interjects.

Zander's and Hayes's heads snap my way.

I shoot Luca a look. We're going to have a chat later. He's supposed to have my back, but he lacks a social filter and would throw his own mother under the bus if it appealed to him. If Ainsley thought I was possibly a sociopath, she'd see all the red flags if she met Luca.

"Luca, that would have been the perfect opportunity for you to practice your interpersonal skills to enforce the bonds of our friendship by keeping silent rather than sharing that piece of information," I say, forcing a smile.

It doesn't matter that we've known each other since college and he's one of my closest friends. The man is cold-blooded and refuses to play nice with anyone, even me. But I won't give up on him and keep trying to train the expected niceties and social cues into him.

"A fucking journalist, really, Pay?" Hayes snarls. "Is sleeping with her worth it? Fucking hell. Even Zander in his manwhore days never hooked up with a journalist. They just want to use you."

Zander's nodding next to him. My patience is wearing thin. Fake or not, it's shitty for my brothers to question my choices. I planned for it, of course, and know exactly how I'm going to approach this so it's believable, but damn, couldn't they just be happy for me to have found someone beautiful who challenges me that I want to spend time with, even if she's cranky as hell and wants to put me in my place?

"Let it go. I like her and that's all that matters. I'm going to keep seeing her and you're going to fuck off about it. I'm perfectly capable of handling my personal life and making sure nothing messy comes of it. She signed an NDA, which is more than I can say for either of you fuckers and your relationships." I give them both pointed looks and their alpha posturing noticeably deflates. Yeah, that'll shut them up and give them the impression I'm falling hard and fast for Ainsley. "How about we get back to work and keep my dating life off the table?"

Our support staff are conspicuously silent, keeping their attention on reports as my brothers and I hold our stares across the boardroom table until they both acquiesce and nod. It's not uncommon for our personal lives to be brought up and discussed, given how tightly our family is tied to the company and how often that reflects on the business. We're the Olympus brand. What we do publicly will always end up in the boardroom, which is why they're so worried.

"Let's talk next steps. Now that we've released details about our move into real estate development, we're going to start on our rollout plan. We'll be moving forward on contracts for the lots and land we've been in negotiations for and start pushing construction timelines for the luxury high-rises as well as the arena and entertainment complex."

I start the conversation and allow the proper teams to take over with details of the projects. Real estate development is a new venture for Olympus but one we've gone all in on.

As the meeting drags on, I find my thoughts drifting back to Ainsley, wondering if she's in the office or if she works remotely, and if she's thinking of me or doesn't care. I want to text her, but if I do, I won't be able to stop, and I need to focus on work where I have to manage a million things at once and put out fires left and right without having my head wrapped around her tight little body and that sassy mouth I'm already imagining taking my cock. I shift covertly in my chair to adjust as my dick rubs against the zipper of my pants, ensuring no one else catches me growing hard during a damn Monday meeting because I'm thinking of Ainsley's bratty attitude she gives so well and her plump pink lips wrapped around me. That woman is begging to surrender her control and is desperate for someone to take care of her every need despite how tightly she holds on.

Realizing she'd respond at the lake brought something out of me I hadn't expected when we started. Sure, she's convenient for this arrangement, but there was no expectation I could play with her in a Dom/sub way. Now that I know she's responsive in a way I'm completely comfortable exploring with her—even if she's only just realizing it's something she needs—I can't wait to get my hands on her. Oh, the things I'll do to show her how good giving up control will be. Ainsley will inevitably end up calling me Daddy after how she reacted when I called her my beautiful little fucktoy and cumslut. There was no mistaking how she pressed her hips against me and her eyes glazed over even as her mouth popped open in shock. She wanted all my filthy promises, and I'll more than deliver.

"The Pegasus Project is finally ready, and it's better than the original. How's the marketing plan looking, Payton?"

My head snaps up, meeting Zander's calculating gray eyes across the table as he smirks at me, catching my thoughts drifting and likely knowing the cause is the new woman in my life.

Fucking Zander. "We have a collaborative go-to-market plan ready and the new prototype is significantly better than the original. The extra time after the cyber attack and Nephele Industries beating us to market with the original plans allowed us to get innovative and add new technologies we wouldn't have thought to include previously." I add in the dig about

Nephele to remind Zander it was *his* fuckup not patenting the original plans that allowed our competition to put out our stolen jet engine before us.

I'm able to recover well enough, but this is why I need to stop thinking about Ainsley at work. I have to focus here and she's a distraction. I want her to submit to me too fucking much and I want to reward her by turning her inside out with pleasure for being such a good girl for me. But for now, back to fucking work.

Fifteen

Ainsley

I look at my phone while walking to my car after work and roll my eyes at Payton's presumptuous text. I slide into the hot seat, crank the engine, and blast the air conditioning before I reply.

I can't get him out of my head.

He showed me a side of myself I was entirely unaware of, all because he's some evil genius who can read people so effectively, it's as good as mind reading. The filthy, depraved words he spoke to me and the way it made me feel—confused yet excited, disgusted but needy, wanting to refuse and obey, to balk but give up control, to dig in my heels yet follow his commanding voice and do as he bid—were the antithesis of what I feel about myself as a strong, independent, *controlled* woman.

The antithesis, yes, but I can't deny the allure it created. An attraction I don't quite understand. I'm not the kind of woman who wants to give myself up to a man to debase and degrade. To be put in my place and used for his pleasure. *To be filled with cum and called a whore.* To call a man *Daddy* who isn't my father.

Holy shit, I think I need to change my underwear from the flood of warmth that just hit me as I sift through the destruction that Payton left in my head. He really is a master manipulator of epic proportions who says the shit most people would have the good grace to ignore. He's a dangerous man to be *friends* with.

My phone vibrates on my lap, pulling me out of my spiraling thoughts.

Annoying Payton: You're right. Those fucking lips of yours are always on my mind. I need to see them in person while they say more mean things to me. I'm taking you to dinner at Rare tonight at seven. Prepare your best insults. Wear something sexy. I'm showing off my girlfriend. We'll be front and center for all to see.

My eyes widen at his text and everything it includes. Is he serious? He thinks about my lips and he wants to take me out and show me off? I type back a furious reply.

> Me: You chauvinistic prick, you can't tell me what to wear! I'm not your doll to dress up and show off. You asshole!

> Annoying Payton: *Devil smiling emoji* Keep the insults coming, Spitfire. I like you in pink, but blue is my favorite color. I can't wait to see you again.

He ignored everything I said.

Payton arrives at seven sharp and knocks on my door instead of texting to let me know he's arrived. Della giggles and hops around the apartment like a bunny on crack as I grab a clutch purse and check my blue minidress one last time in our hallway mirror. I didn't wear the color for Payton. It's just the first thing I found that works. I curled my hair and Della forced me to put on makeup, so my eyes are heavy on the sparkly shadow and mascara. I'm even wearing a pink gloss that enhances my full lips to luscious proportions. If he's thinking about my lips, he won't be able to stop now.

"Have so much fun and stay out late. Wait, don't even come home," she says, disappearing down the hallway before I can open the door. I roll my eyes.

"Bye, Dells, I'll see you later," I call back. At least she didn't want to be obnoxious and stand around to meet Payton like a worried parent. Instead, she'd rather make herself scarce so the date starts faster.

I open the door of my apartment and suck in an audible breath when I find the obnoxious billionaire on my threshold, towering above me as he leans against the doorframe, looking incredible in gray slacks and a white button-down, smelling absolutely divine. The knowing smirk on his face drops when he takes me in, and I get a thrill of excitement when his smiley mask slips, his eyes darkening to something so primal and wanting even I can't mistake it for anything other than what it is. *Pure sexual desire.*

"Ainsley Montgomery, you look like the kind of trouble I want to get into." His voice is deep and resonant, sending heat into my core, my thighs clenching as I work to breathe normally.

My cheeks flush at his words. I look away to fight past this flustered feeling. His hand catches my chin and turns my face back up to his as he steps closer, molding our bodies together, his free hand smoothing down my back and keeping me close. His warmth aligns down my front, and though my initial thought is to back up and get out of this, a part of me wants to throw myself into his arms, wrap my limbs around him like a clingy koala, and never let go. That part of me is obviously a horny slut for attention and I work to tune her out as I know better than to give in to her desires, especially with a man like Payton.

Not tonight, demonic koala.

"Good thing we know this is all fake and there's a contract in place to keep us out of trouble," I remind him in a shaky voice, stepping back with more difficulty than expected. Disappointment crosses his face, but an easy smile quickly replaces it as he holds out his hand for me to take and turns us to leave.

Rare is the kind of fancy steakhouse I'd never go to on my own given the cost of a single item on the menu and how hard it is to get a reservation, but of course that's not an issue for a man like Payton. We're led directly to a table when we check in with the hostess. It's set off to the side of the restaurant but still within view of the main dining space, so plenty of eyes are on us as we make our way to our seats. I feel the weight of stares without having to look for them and raise pleading eyes to Payton.

"We want to be seen. That's the whole point," he says quietly, reading my look with stunning accuracy. "You're my beautiful new girlfriend I want to show off proudly." He reaches across the table and takes my hand, then runs his thumb over my knuckles in a way that is both performative for our audience and soothes my anxiety at being watched.

"I'm normally the one watching and taking notes. This is new to me. I don't like it all that much," I tell him. He flips my hand and laces our fingers together on the table, continuing to smooth his thumb along my skin.

Our server stops at our table, keeping me from saying more. He fills our water glasses and takes our order before leaving.

Once we're alone again, Payton returns to the conversation. "This can be a short outing. We'll eat and leave. We don't have to stay long. Now tell me about your week. Has it been busy? Have you given more thought to what we talked about on Sunday?"

I frown. "Which question do you actually want me to answer? The banality of working at a tiny paper, the mundane things that keep me busy, or my research into some uncovered kink and what that could mean?"

"You *were* thinking about it. Do you have any questions?"

Again, he doesn't answer my question. He focuses on what he wants and asks me more. I sigh and look down at our entwined fingers. I have plenty of my own.

"What kind of Dominant are you?" This was something that came up in my research quite a bit. There are variations to the Dominant role that align with different styles of kink or play and meet the needs of different submissives. I don't know if I'm submissive, exactly, but I think I respond to Payton's commanding tone and the words he uses in a way that should be discussed.

He smiles calmly and squeezes my hand. "Good girl, you've been doing your homework."

I blink at the words and a shiver runs through me because he used that deeper, commanding tone when he praised me.

"I fit a few types, but I tend to gravitate toward softer Dom styles. You might've seen it called something like a service Dom or a pleasure Dom, which I think you'd respond to."

"Pleasure Dom," I repeat, rolling the title around my brain. "So you don't do things like spankings or use whips and chains?" I ask quietly. My face heats. I must be bright red at this point, but my researcher brain is fully engaged and I want to know more than I care about my own embarrassment.

Payton's eyes become churning ocean swells at my question, and his smile slides into the sexy one, not the fake one he pulls on for the benefit of others. He leans toward me, his fingers sliding up my arm in a soft caress.

"I'll do anything that brings pleasure to my sub. If the thought of my hand striking your bare ass makes your pussy weep, I'll make your skin blush the most beautiful rosy shade of red, then spend hours worshiping your body so you don't even remember the sting. You'll have the proof of it the next day as a reminder of what I did to your perfect ass."

Oh, sweet Jesus. An intense shiver works its way from my scalp to the tips of my toes. I just experienced a tiny orgasm from his *description* of a spanking. This man is dangerous. He has far too much power, too much of an intense magnetism that my body feels acutely.

"Got it, spankings are still on the table with a pleasure Dom." My voice is husky and has a shake I can't control.

"If you want to test your limits when it comes to impact play of another kind, I have other impact implements and would happily lead you down the path of caning, flogging, or paddling. If you want to experience the heights of pleasure during sensory deprivation, we could try soft silk blindfolds, heavy leather cuffs, and pretty ball gags that would leave your gorgeous mouth so full you couldn't talk back. If you decide that rope bondage is a kink that gets you off as much as degradation does, you better believe I'll be your rigger and turn you into my ultimate rope bunny just as much as my cumslut."

He's slouched back in his chair, relaxed as ever, speaking about the kinkiest shit like we're talking about the weather, whereas I'm leaning over the table toward him, my body wound tight as a spring, practically vibrating with the tension. Our hands are still connected by the barest brush of fingertips and it feels more intimate than it should due to the subject matter.

"It sounds like you're very familiar with this. Have you...had a lot of partners?" I can't bring myself to say subs. Everything about this feels weird. I don't even want to know this much, but it feels necessary. His experience is important.

"I've had many casual play partners for individual sessions when I wanted to release tension, but I've never had a true ongoing Dom/sub dynamic. It's always been too much work to maintain and foster the kind of partnership I'd want with the level of"—he pauses for a moment and levels me with a dark-eyed gaze before continuing—"care...I'd want to provide."

"And your version of care includes spankings and...ball gags?" My voice trembles on the last words, thinking of losing my ability to say something harsh that would keep him out of my head.

"You're really interested in spankings, aren't you?" He looks at me curiously before he continues. "We'd negotiate all that for a play session. Your limits, your comfort level, your curiosity would be discussed, and safe words established. Kink is all about safe, sane, consensual play. Nothing would happen without ensuring your safety, frame of mind, and consent at every step. Submission is given, never taken."

He's drawing small circles along my palm as he speaks, making goosebumps climb my arm. He didn't speak hypothetically. He spoke about *me* like this is an inevitability that's bound to happen.

Our food arrives and stops the kinky conversation but allows me the chance to finally ask about him. I need to put my reporter skills to use and I want to know more about the nerdy side of him he showed me at the café.

"How is it you're head of marketing and PR when you're obviously a tech genius? Shouldn't you be lording it over the nerds in the IT department or hold the CTO or CIO title instead of COO?"

He looks at me over his wine glass before answering. "I do what Olympus needs. We have more pressing marketing and PR concerns than ongoing technology issues. I'm able to oversee both segments of the company through operations, so that's where I'm needed and put the majority of my energy."

"What about situations like the data breach this past winter? Would it have changed anything had you been focused on the technology side of the business, or would that still have occurred?" I press, looking for answers to something no one has been able to pull from the tight-lipped company.

Payton's face darkens, eyes cast down toward his plate with a stormy expression. He leans back in his chair, the movement causing his fingers to finally leave my skin. I close my hand around empty air, immediately regretting that I've caused him to pull away and leave me without his touch after he's been so generous with it.

"There's no way to know for sure. I built the technology and platform our company runs on. I thought it was bullet-proof. I'd run countless penetration tests, gone through every conceivable possibility of attack and still the hacker was able to get in and steal proprietary information. I don't know whether that says more about the flaws of my system or their skills."

"What's Olympus doing with the real estate developments you're working on? You've bought up blocks of downtown Atlanta and are in talks with the city, but you haven't announced what the project is. Can I have the exclusive?" My cheeks heat again but for a completely different reason than before. I'm asking for something that benefits my career and is a bit of a stretch, ethically, due to the complicated nature of our current situation.

Payton smiles and steeples his fingers in front of his face, tapping them softly against his chin. "Look at you, using our relationship to your advantage. I thought you were against mixing business with pleasure." The way he says pleasure is obscene. I know he intended it that way by the sly smile he offers. "Of course you can have it, Princess." He picks up my hand and brings it to his lips. "But you have to shop the story around instead of printing it in the Gazette. That paper's too small for an exclusive like this. At least sell it to a larger Atlanta newspaper with more credibility."

"I can do that, but my editor's going to be pissed."

"Your editor can eat shit. Your paper isn't a hard-hitting news organization known for breaking stories about multi-billion-dollar conglomerates entering into million-dollar deals with the city to build an entertainment complex and bring a professional sports team to the city. That's the kind of story that's better suited to another paper and he can't deny it. If you want to write up a smaller piece that covers the basics that the Gazette would actually run, he should be grateful you're willing to do that."

"You're bringing in a sports team? What kind? Don't we have everything already? And an entertainment complex? We have the Georgia Dome, the ballpark outside the city, and the arena where the basketball team plays. What else could we need?" I'm confused. I know this is huge, but my mind is working to figure the details out. I don't follow any professional sports, so this is beyond my comprehension.

Payton looks around us, ensuring there aren't any listening ears too close before he returns his attention to me, eyes sparkling with mischief. "We're buying an NHL franchise and bringing professional hockey back to Atlanta. The last time we had a team was over a decade ago. Since then, the sport has exploded in popularity. We got into real estate to buy the land and build the complex and entertainment around it. It should be profitable in the long term, but it's a huge initial investment, which is why the city's behind the project because we're willing to take on the financial responsibility."

"That's absolutely crazy. Do you know anything about owning a hockey team, or building a sports complex?" I ask. My mind is spinning through the logistics and what it must take to put together this monster of a project. I'm also filing away everything he says for a story.

"We have a team of experts for every part of this project and we're already interviewing for a general manager and coaches now. We'll be hands-off with the actual hockey part since we don't know anything about it. We've learned how to initiate projects, organize what's necessary, and compile the right teams to run them as needed. It's called delegating." He smirks at me and I scowl.

"You're such a smartass. So hockey and real estate development. I never would've guessed this is the direction Olympus International would be headed in after engines and private jets, hotels, shipping, investments, and mining."

"We diversify our assets and ensure we're always ahead of the curve."

Payton tells me more about the development plans while we eat and I'm already planning out the story I'll write. It has me fully engaged and hanging onto his every word, which keeps him talking. Before I know it, the check's been paid and he's holding his hand out to me, signaling that our dinner date is over. Unexpected disappointment floats through me, despite initially wanting to keep this a short outing.

"This wasn't as bad as I thought it would be," I begrudgingly offer as he opens the door of his Range Rover for me. He waits for me to slide in and hands me my seat belt. He laughs and leans on the doorframe, studying me.

"I'm not as bad as you think, Ainsley. You just want to hate me for all the wrong reasons."

Sixteen

Ainsley

It's been a few weeks of phone calls, texts, and impromptu dates since our trip to Rare, and I no longer have that knee-jerk reaction to piss Payton off every time I hear his voice. In fact, I've started to look forward to his incessant chatter, too smiley face, and the attention he's lavishing on me. I've even changed his name on my phone so he's no longer *Annoying Payton*.

The Atlanta Haute List continues to post stories about the questionable state of our evolving relationship, sharing photos of us that strangers take without our knowledge or permission. It's unsettling to me but good for his end goal of convincing Harlowe and the world that we're really dating. I just have to keep myself from believing it, knowing I'm prone to attachment given the kind of attention he's providing.

That attention has been frequent and fine, but it's not what I've come to anticipate from him. Maybe I expected to experience more of the filthy words that have gotten me so hot and bothered in our conversations, or to experience the form of dominance he explained at dinner. Just thinking about that now sends heat rushing to my core and causes me to squirm in my seat.

I look around the newsroom, my face hot with embarrassment over the errant thoughts that drenched my panties.

Thankfully, no one's paying attention, or even worried about news—or what I'm doing—at a small paper like the Gazette. They're all complacent with fluff pieces and feel-good stories or ad sales for revenue. No one has aspirations of leaving, of climbing higher than this. I'm surrounded by mediocrity, and it stings extra when I remember Payton asking why I'm working here instead of somewhere better. He can't know that I'm here due to an epic fuckup that cost me what I'd worked my ass off for. Now I'm in journalism purgatory, hoping to find absolution for my mistakes.

Will I ever truly overcome my failings and finally earn my shot at a bigger newspaper? Meeting Payton and getting a chance to write a profile on him has given me the opportunity to do more with my work and look for something bigger. At the very least, it's time I get past fucking up royally and embarrassing myself so thoroughly that I was thrown from the path that my hard work at NYU had paved.

Still, it's safer here, tucked away in mediocrity like a bug under a rock, where the spotlight misses me. Here, my mistakes and failures aren't held over my head daily.

Despite all that, I want to start in the direction I was once set on, and the story Payton agreed to will be a huge help. I've begun to outline the story and know it can be good, great even, with the right hook.

I shopped my piece about the Olympus real estate venture into an entertainment complex and new hockey franchise to the Atlanta Free Press, the largest newspaper in Atlanta, and they were thrilled to run the story. It received a great online response, and other news outlets picked it up. They even offered to buy other stories on Olympus I may write, allowing me to publish my work to a larger audience with a reputable press going forward. Reid wasn't all that upset about me publishing with another paper because I wrote a story for the Gazette that was more fitting for our audience and I don't have a non-compete clause in my contract.

My phone vibrates on my desk, breaking me out of my internal musings, and I eagerly snatch it up, thinking it's Payton reaching out. Why I'm so excited is beyond me when I know he's just going to be his annoying self. Disappointment fills me when an unknown number greets me instead of his.

> Unknown: Why are you with Payton Olsen? Are you fucking him? How do you even know him? He's so out of your league.

I've had a few friends reach out to ask me about the Atlanta Haute List stories when photos of Payton and me started to show up more frequently and my name was suddenly thrust into the limelight alongside his. People really will take photos of the man anywhere. I'm trying to get used to that, knowing I'm going to be around him more.

However, this feels more intrusive than usual and I want to know who feels like they can barge into my life demanding answers when I don't even have their number saved. I'm willing to engage instead of immediately block for that reason alone.

> **Me:** Who is this?

> **Unknown:** Are you that desperate to get my attention that you'd pretend not to know? God, you're so pathetic.

No. It can't be him. My stomach drops, realizing who this unknown person could be. I hate that he's reaching out now, just as I was thinking of the reasons I left New York, him being the biggest. I changed my number when I moved to Atlanta to start over. He wasn't supposed to find me here. I thought I'd successfully cut him out of my life. Yet, here he is, somehow messaging me, his hurtful words bringing me right back to the relationship that nearly broke me. My stomach is in knots with panic as I read his messages again, trying to control my breathing, feeling like the twenty-two-year-old girl who was under his oppressive control for far too long.

Archer Donovan knows exactly how to turn me into a weak, insecure mess with his words alone. My shaking fingers type out a halting reply.

> **Me:** How did you get my number?

> **Archer:** You can't hide from me. We were fucking for over a year. The least you could have done was save my number, but you were never a good girlfriend, so I didn't warrant that kind of respect from you, did I?

> **Archer:** My parents were right. You were

> just a desperate redneck scholarship girl who wasn't worth my time. I should have fucked you out of my system and thrown you away like the garbage you are. Your true colors were showing long before you got with this piece of Olsen trash.

A cold sweat beads along my hairline. I swipe at my clammy skin as my past stares me in the face in the form of a text thread, and everything I've tried to put behind me comes rushing back. But I'm a different woman now, with a little more steel in my spine. I can stand up for myself where Archer used to walk all over me. More than that, I can protect my public relationship with Payton, who doesn't deserve Archer's rage just because I'm with him, *even if it's fake*. I push through the fear and let the anger I've allowed to become my personality seep through. I pull it around me like armor and draw a sword of steely words to cut through the bullshit Archer is spewing. I can do this. I'm better than the broken woman he made me.

> Me: Why are you messaging me now if I'm not worth your time?

I swallow a mouthful of bile as I hit send and set my phone down with shaking hands. It vibrates a moment later, and I'm reminded why it's better not to goad Archer. He just gets meaner.

> Archer: Because you were seen with Payton fucking Olsen, one of the assholes who stole my father's company then sent him to fucking prison you brainless cunt, and I want to know why.

Now stop playing dumb bitch and answer me, goddammit!

I cringe at his tone, even through text. I can't believe I thought I was in love with this man at one point. I rub my face and take a deep breath that does little to quell the panic seizing me. I know exactly why Archer hates that I'm with Payton. They have bad blood due to business dealings that went wrong for Archer's father. I'd celebrated the news of the downfall of Donner Investments, knowing Andreas Donovan had gotten what was coming to him, thinking maybe Archer would have learned some humility from watching his father lose everything. That was too much to hope for because I knew Archer better than anyone.

Archer started out nice, like most manipulative narcissists do, but quickly turned into a controlling asshole who put me down every chance he got in insidious ways. It was never this blatant, but I guess the gloves are off now that we've been broken up for years and he wants information on whatever he thinks is going on with Payton. If he's freaking out about my connection with Payton after a few gossip column stories, it's only going to get worse when photos and accounts of my fake relationship with Payton get steamier. Great, just what I need. Archer thinking he should be all up in my business because he has some beef with the Olsens over Olympus business dealings. I type back a quick reply while I have the fortitude to do it.

Me: I don't owe you anything. Get a life.

I quickly block his number with shaking fingers.
"Hey, do you have the Peachtree Plaza story for me yet?"
I jump in my chair as Reid comes up beside my desk, my

face flaming hot in embarrassment. My heart races as I'm caught texting instead of working, feeling like a scolded child. I should've sent my story already. I'm off my game, and it's all Payton's fault. It's not like me to let a man distract me. Well, it's not like me *now*, and I hate that I'm falling into old habits, especially right as my past has come back to remind me of my failings.

"Yeah, I'll email that right over."

"Any fun plans this weekend?" Reid asks, leaning his hip against my desk. Reid's in his early fifties, has been with the Gazette for a decade, and acts like the paper is God's gift to suburban Atlanta. He thinks we need to cover every shopping center's grand opening and pothole petition like they mean just as much as national news. He's a warrior for lost causes, which is endearing in its own way but truly comical when you pick your head up and look at real problems compared to the things he focuses on.

"Reid, we've talked about entering my personal space. Get off my desk," I say with measured calm and a bite to my words that precede a true snap. He stands up without argument, used to my bluntness at this point. It's easier to fall back on that than give in to the panic that's swirling inside of me from Archer's texts and unexpected reentry into my life after two years of silence.

"Oh, sorry. Send me the story and chase down your next. You had some good ideas in our meeting this morning. Run with those and get me something to edit." He starts to walk away before turning with his finger in the air. "And no extra stories this weekend, kiddo. You're too young to waste all that time working. Learn from my mistakes."

He smiles like he's imparting some secret wisdom. In reality, he's the one who assigns me the stories and makes me work on the weekends more often than not. Reid has children my age and tends to treat me like them. I remind him regularly that I'm on his staff, no matter how much he wants the newsroom to be *a family*.

"My personal life is none of your concern. The story's already in your inbox." I close out my email for emphasis. I stopped playing along with social niceties when I moved to Atlanta for a fresh start. I like to blame my time in New York for the curt replies and testy attitude, but it just feels better this way, less likely to get hurt if you keep everyone away.

He waves. "Get out of here, kid."

I look around the office and notice everyone shutting down computers, chatting about evening plans or dinner recipes. I follow their lead, closing my ancient laptop. I'm supposed to meet up with Della for after-work drinks in a bit, which I desperately need following that awful text exchange. My phone vibrates in my purse and I pull it out, wondering if it's her asking where we're meeting up. Instead, it's Payton.

Okay Payton: Miss me yet?

I feel a two-fold sense of relief that Payton's texting me and it's not Archer from some other number harassing me. I wouldn't put it past him to have another way to do just that. I take a relieved breath and smile because the egotistical jerk I enjoy a whole lot more is the one wanting my attention. I type out a quick reply as I head to my car.

Me: Sorry, who is this?

Okay Payton: You want to wound me, but you can't. I missed your insults and crankiness. My life wasn't the same without you.

Damn. I know he's messing with me, but reading that last sentence strikes a chord that feels like a melody I haven't heard in far too long. His attention feels a little too good after the absence and I allow myself a moment to enjoy it before I quickly shut it down, despite wanting more of the reassurance that when I'm not hearing from him, he's missing me.

> Me: I doubt it.

> Okay Payton: Never doubt me, Muffin. Do you like espresso martinis as much as you like iced coffee? There's a bar by Olympus that has the best and I'm heading there now. You're coming with me.

He doesn't even bother to invite me. He sends me the address in a pin with the expectation that I'll join him. It's a bold move that I rather like. I call him out on it.

> Me: You're a smug bastard. I'm meeting a friend for drinks tonight so I'm busy. Can't make it.

> Okay Payton: Not a bastard. Arrogant asshole was a previous insult and it was more fitting. I know you miss my annoying smile. Invite your friend. I have a friend, too. We'll put on a show for them. Get ready for our first double date. See you soon. I can't wait to get my hands on you again. This time, you won't even

have to pretend to enjoy it. I'm fucking
excited.

My heart hammers against my ribs as I let out a sound that's a cross between a sigh and a frustrated snarl as I slide into my car, wincing when I burn my hands on the hot steering wheel that's been baking in the sun all day. I crank the engine of my old Toyota to life and turn the AC all the way up, knowing it won't cool down for several minutes.

Double date? Can't wait to get his hands on me? Holy shit, this is really happening, and I'm kind of into it.

I type out a text to Della, letting her know plans have changed.

Me: Hey, is it okay if we meet up with Payton and a friend of his for drinks tonight instead?

It takes a few minutes for my phone to vibrate back with her reply.

Della: HELL FUCKING YES! Have you seen who he associates with? The men of Olympus are hot as fuck. It's about time you dating him worked in my favor. I'm so glad I finished early and went home to shower.

I shake my head in resignation and send her the address. If she's on board, I guess I can't argue. And now I'm about to play his fake girlfriend in front of my friend and I have to make it convincing. I sigh and let Della know my arrival time so she won't beat me there, and begin the drive.

It takes me half an hour in Atlanta traffic to make it to the bar and another five minutes in the car to talk myself into going inside. Archer texting me out of the blue after years of not hearing from him still has me rattled. Knowing my connection to Payton is what caused him to reach out makes me nervous to be seen with the billionaire because this PDA-filled evening will absolutely make it into the gossip pages again, as planned.

A thought strikes me, and it has me considering the situation from a different angle. Maybe this is exactly what Archer needs to see after all this time, me moving on with someone he hates more than anything. I'll just keep blocking him if he continues contacting me. I don't actually have to interact with him. That's enough motivation to resolve to be as convincing as possible that I'm falling head-over-heels for Payton Olsen.

I slick on my vanilla-scented lip gloss, making sure the rest of my work-appropriate attire and makeup are still in place. I walk toward the bar, knowing I'll be bombarded with Payton's annoying cheerfulness as soon as I find him, and I'll like it more than I care to admit.

Seventeen

Ainsley

T he bar, Dionysus, is close to Olympus International Tower, so I'm not surprised Payton would come here. It's blessedly cool when I walk in. The walls are exposed brick, brass fixtures gleaming against black accents, with sconces casting warm light all around as I take in the room while looking for Payton.

I *feel* his presence and turn, finding him leaning against a booth across from me. His large, powerful body perfectly relaxed, hands in the pockets of his immaculately tailored navy suit pants highlighting his thick thighs, muscled forearms showing below the rolled-up sleeves of his crisp white shirt, setting off his tan skin in stark contrast. My gaze travels up his body, making it to his strong jaw, faint dimples popping in his cheeks from his indulgent smile as he drinks me in and knows he affects me in turn. Finally, I meet his stupid ocean-deep eyes that drown me and I can't look away. I need to be a better swimmer to spend time around Payton Olsen.

His head tips, beckoning me to the booth behind him where a man with cool blond hair and ice-blue eyes lounges, and my feet are moving before I realize I've decided for myself. *Traitors.* I hesitate for a moment when I reach him, not sure what version I'll be getting tonight after several days of not hearing from him. Will he be the constantly joking, can't-stop-smiling fool I met in a silly café, or will he be the Dom I've only heard about? I look up despite wearing heels that usually help give me a bit of height to my short stature.

"Go with it," he whispers in my ear as he bends down to pull me in close and molds our bodies together into a tight hug.

It feels lush and indecent, despite being a fully clothed embrace in public. One of his hands slides down my back, resting just above my ass. The other comes up to my neck and presses me close longer than friendly, ensuring we establish this is more than casual. My arms naturally reach up to his shoulders, fingers threading into the soft hair at the nape of his neck like they're meant to be there, eliciting a quiet groan from him that sends a tremor through me in return. I sigh and relax in his arms, feeling restored just from this small bit of touch that I must have been craving.

I look up at his face in silent question while it's so close to mine. Is he going to kiss me, right here like this? My lips part, and I breathe raggedly against the hold he has on me, my eyes dipping between his eyes and mouth. I don't have to pretend very hard to enjoy this.

"I missed you, Muffin," he says with a gentle brush of his lips against mine in answer before running his nose along my cheek to my ear.

"I'm sure you did." My words come out quick and uncertain, still wanting to put up walls despite how good it feels to fit this well in his arms.

I shiver involuntarily in his hold, my body responding to him dropping kisses along my jaw and pressing closer. He tightens his grip when he feels my reaction and I get a sick thrill that we somehow keep doing this to each other. My eyes widen as he pulls out the pen that's securing the bun at the back of my head, causing my hair to untwist and fall down my back in a heavy cascade.

"That's some fucking hot-for-teacher shit, Ainsley. Don't wear your hair like that around me again unless you want me fantasizing about roleplaying a classroom scene with you, or better yet, setting up that scene for you," he says, voice gravelly and low against my ear. "Especially not in an outfit like that. Fucking hell, woman. Are you trying to kill me?"

He runs a hand over my ass in my tight pencil skirt and looks down as he finally lets me go, but not before I feel the effect I've had on him pressed tightly against me. I'm not the only one reacting to this embrace and he *really* likes my outfit.

This is a perfectly professional blouse that doesn't show any cleavage and a pencil skirt that hits just above my knees. It's business casual and fine for the office. I look back at him as he struggles to compose himself, smiling in triumph to see him lose a bit of the control he always seems to have over every situation.

I reach up and pat his cheek with satisfaction. "You're cracked. There's nothing wrong with what I'm wearing or using a pen to hold up my hair when it's hot as balls out and I don't have a hair tie."

He catches my wrist and lowers it to my side, raising dark

brows at my sassy attitude. "Don't mistake me, Princess. There's nothing wrong with it. I just like it a little too much to stay in a public place if that's how you're going to respond when I mention it. Now sit down before I march you out of here and show you what I really think."

I smirk as I brush past him and slide into the booth, his hand smoothing over my ass before he follows closely behind me. I eye the other man in the booth warily before turning back to Payton for the introduction.

"Ainsley, this is Luca DaSilva, the SVP of operations at Olympus International. Luca, this is Ainsley Montgomery, my gorgeous girlfriend," Payton supplies the introductions for us.

He officially claimed me. My heart races at the thought of people knowing for real now about our fake relationship.

"Nice to meet you," I offer.

Luca nods and looks away without comment.

"Is he always that friendly?" I ask Payton without bothering to lower my voice.

"Don't mind him. He's an asshole on a good day. It's not you," Payton says at the same volume. Clearly, we're not hurting Luca's feelings by talking about him like this.

A flash of red hair catches my eye and I turn toward the door, just as Della takes a few steps into the bar. "My friend just arrived." I wave and catch her attention, thankful for a buffer to this awkwardness.

She sees me and wiggles her fingers before heading to our booth wearing a green silk tank dress. She's dressed more appropriately for this classy bar than me in work clothes, no matter what Payton thinks of my outfit. I need more details about his clothing preferences because this isn't even sexy and if that's a trigger, we're going to have problems.

"Hi," she says, sliding in on the other side of Luca, whose icy demeanor warmed a fraction at her addition. He was giving me a thorough once-over with those cold eyes as if he didn't care much for me. I thought maybe I was invading boys' night or something, but seeing his reception of Della, it appears he wasn't pleased with being the third wheel.

"Hey, Dells, thanks for coming," I say. "Payton, Luca, this is Della Byrnes, my best friend." I provide the introductions this time, but I'm not as loose with the titles as Payton was.

Della raises her eyebrows at me suggestively as if saying we'll talk about all this later, regardless of my lack of titles. I've given her the barest details about our dates, and I mentioned the kinky stuff Payton is into that I learned more about on our date at Rare. She threw herself on the couch in a fit of despair that I found a man who's willing to spank me in private and treat me like a princess in public before she could.

She says hello to Payton with a knowing grin before she turns her attention to Luca.

Luca grasps Della's hand and kisses it, giving her a smile he held back earlier, causing me to snicker. Payton catches on and slips his arm around my hip, pulling me against his side, where I fit perfectly. I try not to appear too awkward since this is supposed to be a two-way thing, and it's not a bad spot to be, tucked into Payton's warm body with his big arm around me. I try out leaning into his chest like I want to be there, and it's not awful, either.

I feel him chuckle against me. I poke his thigh under the table. He squeezes my hip in response, then begins to draw lazy circles that have his long fingers brushing across my thigh and the outer part of my ass. I keep my hand on his thigh for good measure because damn, it's thick and muscular and two can play this game. I flex my fingers against his thigh and he presses his leg closer to mine, giving me more access to anywhere I want to explore, it seems. Goddamn, this man is shameless. I keep my hand safely on top of his thigh and stay away from the monster I know is lurking between his legs.

"Burns? Fitting with your hair," Luca says. He speaks loud enough for us to hear across the large booth.

"Luca, intrusive thoughts stay in your head, please," Payton admonishes with a laugh.

I tilt my head as I look up at Payton's profile from my position tucked into his side. The casual way he said it seems like it's a regular occurrence for them, with Payton having to remind Luca of this fact, so maybe Luca lacks a social filter and they're quite close outside of their working relationship. It wouldn't surprise me that Luca needs a reminder to be nice with how cold his reception was when I arrived. I definitely didn't get the warm fuzzies from him.

"Byrnes with a Y, not a U, but you *are* playing with fire," Della says, leaning into the humor and giving him a wink. Della loves that joke and obviously likes the vibe Luca is giving off if she's willing to be this playful off the bat.

I smile and shake my head, leaving her to it. She's more than capable of handling herself with a new guy she finds attractive, and the way she's looking at Luca, she does. Maybe he'll be the kind of guy she's looking for who'll treat her like a queen in public and spank her in private.

My cheeks heat, thinking about Payton's descriptions of a spanking and how he'd make me forget the sting but I'd have the marks to remember him by. Okay, more than my cheeks are heating and my hand has slid the length of Payton's thigh and back.

I squirm, rubbing my thighs together. Payton's hand stills against my hip, his fingers gripping my thigh tighter like he knows exactly where my thoughts have traveled somehow. He isn't even putting sex into the conversation tonight and that's where my thoughts are straying anyway. Is it me? Am I the problem? Did he break me that easily and now that's what I'll think of anytime I'm with him? He's fucking with my head without even trying. Damn, I need a drink, and fast.

There's an espresso martini already on the table along with a tumbler of amber liquor over ice in front of Payton. I grab the martini. I've never tried one, but I like coffee, and the drink sounds like something I would like in theory. I take a tentative sip and make a face. No, I definitely don't like it. How can both espresso and alcohol fail me like that?

"This is disgusting." I push the glass his way. "Vodka soda with lime." I give him my actual drink order. "Oh my God, I need the taste of that out of my mouth immediately."

He laughs, handing me his glass. "Have my bourbon while you wait."

I take a small sip. The fire of the bourbon burns the espresso martini out of my mouth in phases as Payton signals for a server, who hurries over. He orders my new drink, and Della asks for a gin and tonic. The server leaves and I take another sip of Payton's drink, knowing his lips have been along the same spot.

"You could have given me your actual drink order when I told you where to meet me."

I hand his glass back and he swirls the bourbon around, making the ice tinkle gently. I raise my eyebrows at him incredulously.

"You didn't give me the opportunity. You're quite overbearing and hardly patient enough to allow me the chance to tell you what I actually want when it comes to anything."

"You're usually so vocal and opinionated, I figured you'd tell me either way." He laughs.

He takes a sip of his drink right over the spot my gloss left a lip print, licking the rim of the glass suggestively before he sets the tumbler on the table in front of him. A hint of pink transferred to his lips. I reach up and smooth my thumb along his bottom lip to remove the gloss, and he presses a kiss to the pad of my thumb before I can pull my hand away. I look at him in surprise, not sure if he's just an overly affectionate man, or if this is all for show for our friends. He did say he's very hands-on and that's been true each time I've been around him, so is this just Payton, or is it fake?

"How was your week, Muffin?" he asks with a soft expression as he observes my confusion.

The server returns with our new drinks. I gratefully take the vodka soda and squeeze the lime into the bubbly liquid to avoid thinking too hard about what's real and what's not.

"Fine. And stop calling me that." I look over at him as I bite the straw in my drink contemplatively. I set the glass down. "You haven't messaged me in a few days." I don't want to ask him why; that feels so needy. I want him to willingly tell me why without having to pry it out of him.

"Work is demanding. I've had to focus on that this week." He runs a long finger along the rim of his tumbler, my eyes tracking the movement.

"Ah, the workaholic excuse," I say with less of my usual venom. I shouldn't have expected anything else. I'm trying to play up the fake dating thing, toning down my typical attitude, while not alerting Della to any changes in my behavior. It's harder than I expected.

Della's not even paying any attention. She's deep in conversation with Luca, her body turned toward him, gin and tonic in hand and a smile on her face. Well, fine, I guess I don't have to worry about her. I look back at Payton just as he adds a second finger to the rim of his glass and stretches them off the edge, then pulls them back, almost like he's finger-fucking it, and it makes me shiver. I can't take my eyes off his fingers, the slow, methodical movements hypnotizing.

"I was thinking about you, even if I wasn't talking to you." His words are a quiet rumble, combined with the movement of his fingers, and the sea salt and amber smell of him so close to me sends goosebumps rising along the exposed skin of my arms. I drag my eyes away from his obscene fingers to his face and catch the way he's watching me, taking in everything, seeing my reaction, and using it against me.

"You were thinking of me?" I cringe, realizing I said the words out loud, sounding needy. *Stupid question, Ainsley.* Fuck.

"Of course. You think we'd discover a new side of you that wants to play with me and I'd let you go back to denying yourself? No way."

My eyes snap up, brows drawing together. "What was with you pulling the pen out of my hair and talking about role-playing?" I ask quietly, twisting the ends of my hair where it rests over my shoulder.

"Mmmm, that was giving in to a temptation that was a bit too strong and you nailing one of my favorites a little too well."

"Your *favorites*?" I ask, narrowing my eyes. I look up, which is hard when I'm pressed so close to his side. I scoot away to see his face better. "What do you mean?"

He makes a face as I shift, reaching over to scoop up my legs and drape them over his knees so I'm half in his lap and facing him. He keeps his arm around my back, all but cradling me in this position, seeming pleased. I roll my eyes at him, but I don't move away. I don't think I'd get very far with how he's holding me.

"Let's just say if you'd shown up wearing glasses, we'd have ditched our friends and had some choice words on our way out of here that you likely wouldn't have approved of."

"You have a glasses fetish?" I ask, confused. "How do you make it through the day when so many people wear them?"

He takes a sip of bourbon. "It's more specific than that. Sure you want to hear this?" His voice is low so only I can hear. He sets his tumbler down and places his hand on my bare leg, pressing his fingers under the edge of my skirt above my knee. I'm thankful it's on the longer side, even if it's higher up my thighs now.

"Well, now I do. I need to know what you're talking about, exactly. Call it research so I can avoid an awkward situation in the future, given I do wear glasses on occasion."

"Fuck me," he curses softly. "I didn't need to know that, and now...let's say I have a very vivid imagination and it's running wild." He traces his thumb along the inside of my thigh and damn if it doesn't feel like he's touching me somewhere far more intimate.

"Okay, but that's not explaining the glasses or the favorites comments."

"You're not going to like it. It's all about sex, and your propriety is too easily offended. I don't think you actually want to hear it, so I'll be a good boyfriend on this one." He looks away from me at that, his eyes straying to his glass of bourbon like he wants to finish what's left but doesn't want to remove his hand from my leg to take a sip.

I bristle, hating that he's using this against me. He's baiting me and it's working a little too well. Now I need to know. "Damn you, Payton, that's not fair. I'm perfectly capable of deciding what I can handle," I hiss, sliding my eyes across the booth to Della and Luca, who are leaning toward each other, having their own quiet exchange that's not nearly as contentious as ours. "Explain yourself and stop dodging the subject."

He gives in to his urge to drink his bourbon, takes the last gulp of the amber liquid, sets his tumbler down, and gives me a measured look before he finally shakes his head. "Fine, but I warned you. Drink that." He nods at my vodka soda.

"You're so annoying," I complain, picking up my glass and waving him on.

"You know that for whatever else, I'm a nerd first and foremost. I have a hot teacher and sexy librarian fetish. I love the glasses, bun, tight skirt, white top. Especially with that stern look you do so well." He indicates my outfit with a flick of his hand. "You walked in like you stepped right out of my dreams. The first thing I thought of was you scolding me until I pulled your hair down, wrapped it around my fist, pushed your skirt up, and fucked you over the table."

I choke on my vodka soda, liquid spraying over the table as I cough in surprise. What. The. Fuck. I unwittingly walked into that just like I walked in looking like Payton's wet dreams, one of his *fetishes*, just by wearing business attire and being lazy with my hair. Had I left work later and been driving after dark, I may have been wearing my glasses, and then I'd have completed the look. And he'd have wanted me to *scold him*, which I do regularly with how mean I am to him.

I've been feeding into his fetish without knowing it just by *existing*. I'm in so much trouble with him. I can't even use my normal armor to fight him because he *likes* when I'm mean. I catch Della's eyes across the table as she checks in. I wheeze and sputter as Payton pats my back. I shake my head and roll my eyes, signaling I'm fine, even if I don't look it. She bites her lip to keep from laughing at my look of discomfort.

"I said you wouldn't like it," Payton says, capturing my attention again. I glare at him in rebuke.

"No shit. I didn't think you were going to say you wanted to fuck *me*. I just thought you were going to talk about sex in general. It's different."

"It's a general fetish. You just happened to embody it tonight looking like you do. It's distracting." He looks away and picks up his tumbler, only to see it's empty before setting it back down.

"I would've gone home to change if you hadn't insisted I meet you here. We could've avoided this awkwardness."

"Noted," he says quietly. "But for the record, I really fucking like it on you, Ainsley."

I laugh, and it surprises us both, which has him looking over at me with a perturbed expression that's more suited to me.

"It's funny that you're surly and not smiling for once. Knowing I'm making you uncomfortable just by showing up like this is actually pretty great. Honestly, the more I think about it, the more it makes me laugh. Hold on," I say, giggling and turning away from him, rummaging through my purse while Payton glares.

"You're awfully happy about my discomfort. I'm trying to be noble and keep you comfortable, and you're rubbing it in. I don't have to be nice about this. I can go back to pushing your boundaries."

I find what I'm looking for, turning back and smiling wickedly, enjoying the idea of torturing him a bit more. I'm wearing tortoiseshell glasses that perfectly frame my face and bring out the green and amber in my eyes. His eyes turn into blue fire as his smile disappears.

"I wear glasses when I drive at night, so I keep them in my purse. I think they're cute."

"You're cruel." He reaches out and strokes my hair over my shoulder, clearing a space for his hand to rest against my throat, thumb stroking up to my jaw like he can't stop himself.

"You're not shit and you don't deserve to touch me." My voice is a low purr as I brush his hand off my neck. "You definitely don't get to fuck me and you're lucky I'm sitting here with you, letting you buy me drinks. Now clean up this mess," I say in my meanest tone, indicating the drink I spit all over the table.

His lips part and his eyes burn as they stay locked on my face, and I know I have him under some kind of spell that he gave me the power to wield. I laugh again and pull off my glasses, return them to the case, and throw them back in my purse for safekeeping. When I turn back, Payton's there, a little too close, and I jump in surprise. His hand slips into my hair at the back of my neck and I still instantly, a feisty kitten picked up by the scruff and gone docile, my eyes trained on his fiery blue gaze that sears me to my soul.

Oh, shit.

His voice is a quiet, commanding promise when he speaks just for me to hear. "You think you can be a brat and get away with playing with me and not get it right back, my pretty little fucktoy? If we were anywhere else, I'd bend you over my knee and spank your ass raw before I fucked it and filled my beautiful cumslut up. You can dress any way you want and still be Daddy's little whore, begging for my cock to fill your every hole. Don't think you have the upper hand because I give you insight into one little fetish of mine, Princess. I know what you need, and you're just getting a taste of what that means. Now be a good girl so we can both enjoy our night and not get too wound up or regret anything else."

He squeezes my neck and pulls me closer to him so his lips

brush over mine once and he places a kiss at the corner of my mouth before he pulls back. I moan quietly under the pressure of his fingers, the words he spoke causing wetness between my thighs. I realize my hands are latched onto his shirt, pulling him closer to me as I turn my face up to his. He's looking at me curiously as the sound vibrates from me and my eyelids flutter. He slowly lets me go, his hand brushing down the sweep of my back and over the curve of my hip. I keep holding his shirt until his hand is on the booth between us and I finally let go, my hands flying back to my lap. I can't believe I was holding him so tightly.

"I shouldn't have done that," I say on a shaky exhale.

His smile is seductive and pleased. "Too late for that, Princess. You just showed me you can play exactly how I want you to. You gave me a delicious little taste. Now I'll eat you up."

My stomach drops. I showed far more than I should have, and he's all too capable and willing to use it against me. I condemned myself to whatever sentence Payton plans to dole out. I can't deny that it stokes my attraction and the magnetic pull he has on me.

I want to touch him and have his hands all over me. I'd let him do anything he wants to me, and he can never know.

Eighteen

Ainsley

I snort as I read his text while sipping coffee at my desk. We should both be working, but this insolent fool wants me to tell him I'm thinking about him, just like he has the last few days. This morning he sent me a text that said "Hope thoughts of me didn't get you too worked up last night. I had the best dream of you, though." I'd replied, "Only my nightmares feature you, and thankfully, I've been sleeping soundly."

Looks like I need to take him down a peg. Again. I smile as I type out my response.

> Me: I'm sorry, do you actually believe I give you any time or brain space when you're not driving me crazy with texts or in person? That's hilarious.

He's quick to reply.

> Okay Payton: I feel like pizza tonight. I'll pick you up, and we can get Napoletana to go and come back to my place. I want to see your blissed out on pizza and pleasure face.

What the actual fuck. Is he *Netflix and chilling* me, but with pizza and...orgasms? That has to be what he means by pleasure, right? Jesus, this man is too much. I kind of love it. But I have to shut it down.

> Me: *Rolling eye emoji* We have to fake it in front of people so Harlowe believes this. Going back to your place isn't helping that plan, and no sex.

The Atlanta Haute List ran a Spotted story about our dinner together at Rare and our double date at Dionysus. They shared photos of us looking very cute and cuddly, our hands all over each other. I was completely unaware that I could look at someone with that kind of expression, all rapt and enamored, but apparently, when Payton talks, I lean in and listen like he's the most important thing around. Those are the kinds of outings he needs to convince Harlowe, no matter how disturbing it is for me to see myself like that on a gossip blog.

> Okay Payton: We'll send her a selfie from

my house. She'll love it.

Okay Payton: Besides, we don't need to have sex to see your pleasure face, Princess. You can be my needy little cumslut while still being a cocktease and never getting the brat fucked out of you. But if you're a good girl, I'll make you come before taking you home and you still won't know what my cock feels like in that greedy little cunt.

I drop my phone onto my desk when I read his text, flipping it over for good measure. I look around the quiet newsroom where only a few of my coworkers remain. There's that commanding tone and his degrading words again. Without even hearing his voice, he has the same effect on me, causing a low moan to build in my throat as a part of me wants to take him up on this salacious offer. So badly. I want to see what he can do without fucking me that would have me coming but know I should stay so far away from that temptation and keep my brain and heart from getting my feelings all tangled up in something that is fake, fake, fake. I pick up my phone again and angrily type out a reply.

Me: I have an article to write. I don't have time for pizza and chilling, you presumptuous prick.

Okay Payton: Write the article at my place. I need to read it before you publish it, anyway. See you at six. Hope you

> like pineapple on pizza. I want some-
> thing sweet and you know what they say
> about eating pineapple *Devil smiling
> emoji*

When he knocks on my door at six sharp, I'm in an over-sized, off-the-shoulder T-shirt that says *I Beg Your Parton* with Dolly's face on it over tight, pink shorts. I've scrubbed off my makeup and my hair's messy from work. I went out of my way to ensure he knows I don't consider this a date by any means and haven't put any effort into my appearance for him.

I'm extra annoyed because, with every post about us on the Haute List, I get more vile texts from unknown num-bers—Archer's doing—which has me on edge more than ever. I can't win. Fulfilling my part of the bargain with Payton means lots of public outings with him and inevitably having my photo and name slapped alongside his in gossip blogs, which makes Archer attack me harder. He's even sending copies of the Haute List photos, and more that I haven't seen, with his demeaning messages. His cyberstalking is getting worse and it's making me uneasy that he's escalating. I'm just glad he's in New York and I don't have to worry about running into him here in Atlanta.

I sling my work bag over my shoulder, turning to look at Payton. He, of course, looks incredible in charcoal pinstripe slacks that hug his thighs perfectly, his white button-down so crisp it doesn't look like he spent a full workday in it already. His dark hair is slightly mused like he's been raking his hands through it, but otherwise, he's perfect. It pisses me off.

"Let's go, asshole. I want to finish my story and get back home." I push him out of the way and pull the door closed to lock it.

"That's it, Spitfire, get pushy and mean. I want to play. Get the fuck over here and let me get a taste of my gorgeous little whore." He grabs my hips and pulls me back into his body, my hands still on the keys in the door.

I melt into his body at his commanding words, feeling him all along my backside, his lips at my ear, thumbs massaging my sides. It takes a moment to realize I've arched my back and pressed my ass into him. Apparently, I like having him absurdly close behind me like this. His lips and tongue are traveling along my neck, sending shivers through my body as I roll my head to give him more access. I don't complain when one of his hands splays across my belly, pulling me tighter in a possessive movement that makes me whimper. When my stomach lets out a loud grumble, he finally pulls away with a chuckle.

"Sounds like I need to feed you. But thanks for feeding me, first. You're a fucking delicious snack." He bends and licks along my neck as I bat at his face, belatedly realizing I should discourage him when we're alone.

"Hands to yourself, weirdo. Save it for an audience."

My words are steady, but my heart's racing. I liked feeling him against me and being in his arms far too much. I need to get it together and remember this is temporary. It's for show. All fake and not something I need to confuse with the real thing, no matter how good it feels. Besides, I shouldn't even want this, regardless of what my inner slutty koala seems to think.

"I've missed you, Muffin. I want to eat you up. Now let's

fucking go." He straightens and grabs my hand, pulling me out to his Range Rover.

He drives us to a popular pizza restaurant that The Atlanta Haute List has reported his family frequents. When he parks and rounds the car to my door, I balk at the hand he offers.

"I thought we were just picking up pizza to-go, why am I getting out of the car?" Now my heart's racing for a completely different reason. If I get photographed looking like *this*, I'll be absolutely mortified.

"We are picking up a pizza, but we have to go in and it might take a bit. I ordered it when I got to your apartment. So we'll wait inside where it's cooler. Besides, it's another chance to show you off."

"Payton," I start, venom lacing my tone. "I look like absolute garbage. I don't want to be *shown off* looking like this." I indicate the state of my appearance. I wouldn't have gone to the lengths I did to discourage him had I known we'd be seen together *in public*. This is so fucked up.

"You look incredible. Perfect for a pizza run. Now get your ass out of the car or I'll throw you over my shoulder and walk you into the restaurant in a way that's sure to get more attention than you think you will like this."

"You're impossible," I grumble, stepping out of the SUV, and waving off his offer of help. He grabs my hand and laces our fingers together anyway.

Payton walks right up to the host stand and lets them know we're picking up a pizza. The girl leaves to check on our order, only to let us know we have another ten minutes to wait, just like Payton predicted. I'm miserable.

The restaurant is packed. The tables are full and so is the lobby, couples and families waiting to be seated milling about. Payton leads me to the bar and finds one spot open. He sits and pulls me into his lap as I squirm and protest.

"Don't fight it. This is the only spot and I want you to relax. Either you sit on my lap now like a good girl, or you get your ass spanked raw when I get you back to my place. Your choice, Princess."

I freeze, turning to see if he's joking. He smiles that sinfully sexy smile. He's been in a completely different mood tonight, more commanding, dominant, playful but with an edge that's been missing from his usual lighthearted teasing and innuendo. He's in his Dom persona, I realize belatedly. Fuck me, it's sexy. He told me he wanted to *play.* I just hadn't realized it would be the kinky variety. A shiver runs through me at the thought of exploring some of my *interests* with him. I kind of want to see what those spankings Della loves are all about, but I don't want it as a punishment for this. I work to relax my body, knowing people are watching, seeing the unusual sight of two people occupying a spot meant for one in a classy pizza restaurant. I lean into the protection his body provides.

"I don't like public displays of affection," I mutter. "This is weird for me."

"Good thing we're in public and you know your role," he replies, his voice smooth and low. He kisses my hair and wraps his arms around my middle, holding me close and looking like, for all intents and purposes, we're a happy couple who can't get enough of each other and relish the idea of sharing a chair in a busy restaurant.

The relief I feel when our pizza is brought to us is immeasurable.

Payton's loft is incredible. It's industrial without feeling empty and soulless. The walls are cement and exposed red brick, some areas walled off, but the majority of the space is open and airy. I'm cataloging everything, from the expansive views of downtown Atlanta through the huge windows, to the two-story fireplace. I immediately gravitate to the floor-to-ceiling bookshelves that flank the fireplace, pulling out a book and noticing it's been read. It's a coding book because Payton's a nerd and reads these types of things, of course. The next one I pull out is by a popular mystery writer, and it's also been read, given the tiny tear in the dust jacket. I scan the shelves and see a variety of topics and different states of wear. I turn, finding him watching me, a small smile playing over his lips as he leans against the wall, his arms crossed.

"You've read all these books?"

He pushes off the wall and walks over with an unhurried grace until he's standing in front of me. He places his hands on my shoulders and spins me back around before pulling me into his body, his arms crossing around my shoulders. My hands naturally gravitate to his forearms where they rest across my chest, holding on to the flexing muscles as he rests his chin on top of my head.

It feels comfortable to be held like this. Familiar. It's practiced and easy. I stay silent instead of giving in to the instinct to immediately push him away and say something vile. It might be the first time I accept his touch and physical intimacy without argument or wanting to be prickly. He's getting under my skin. Warping my armor and igniting the part of me that craves this attention and wants nothing more than to be the object of his desire.

Fake, I remind myself as I swallow audibly.

"Most of the books. A few were gifts that didn't really interest me or I haven't gotten around to reading yet. If I'm not working, I'm probably reading."

I tip my head back and look up as he peers down into my face. "I can't even make fun of you for being a voracious reader. If I had a house with all this space, I'd fill countless shelves with books, too." The admission is quiet, honest, and raw. Payton seems to know what it took for me to say it and knows it's a rare compliment freely given. He smiles indulgently.

"If you were mine, I'd build you a library and buy every book you could ever want," he says, kissing my forehead before letting me go and walking back to where he set the pizza. He's nonchalant as fuck like he didn't just say something completely insane and far too real for this fake scenario we've gotten ourselves into. "Make yourself comfortable. We have pizza to eat."

I follow him to the kitchen that's suited to the loft with black cabinets set against the wall and a large island separating the kitchen from the rest of the open dining and living area. Payton puts the pizza box on the island and pulls out a stool for me. I hop up and set my bag next to me, watching as he moves through the kitchen, gathering what he needs. He puts plates and linen napkins on the island, fills two glasses with a red wine that smells full-bodied as he pours, then opens the pizza box and I can't help but laugh.

The pizza is covered in pineapple. Not just a single topping that was sprinkled onto it, but like half a pineapple was chopped up and scattered on top of the crust. It's a wonder I can see cheese and sauce under what has to be the world record for the amount of pineapple on a single pizza.

"Are you kidding me? That's a *lot* of pineapple. Are there any other toppings, or was there no room because of all the pineapple?"

Payton grins like we're sharing a joke. "Pineapple makes cum sweeter. I figured it wouldn't hurt to ask for extra."

I groan. "You're insane. Is everything about sex with you?"

"When it comes to you, maybe." He shrugs, his smile devilish. He turns to the pizza and dishes up slices for each of us. "Now be a good girl. Eat that pizza so you get it nice and sweet for me, Princess."

I roll my lip with my teeth and quickly look away, setting my pizza down and eyeing it dubiously while contemplating his words. They sent a tremor racing through me in anticipation. He's in one of his boundary-pushing moods tonight, ensuring I'm on the edge of discomfort with everything he says to see where I stop him.

I just don't think I want to stop him all that much. In fact, I want to push *him*.

Nineteen

Payton

Ainsley's sitting cross-legged, laptop out, fingers typing away as I lounge next to her. I'm answering emails on my phone and providing details when asked as she works since finishing our *ridiculous pineapple pizza*, as she was sure to point out at every opportunity. She relaxed after realizing I wasn't going to force her into some sex game during dinner, as much as I teased. She hasn't been nearly as prickly as I expected, given the amount I'm pushing her tonight. We're working on establishing her real boundaries, not the ones she uses to keep me out. I need to know what she actually wants, what she's okay with, what scares her, what thrills her. Her clothes won't even be coming off with what I have planned.

"That should do it," she says, her fingers resting on the

keyboard, eyes tracking back and forth across the page. "You can read through it to see if it meets your exacting standards."

I chuckle at the sarcasm in her tone.

"Anything curious happen as you wrote the story?" I can't help but ask as I take the laptop from her with a mischievous grin.

She rolls her eyes. "Your stupid handiwork was evident weeks ago when I was finishing my story on the Olympus real estate news. I had to take this dumb laptop in for service to have that piece of code removed so I wouldn't have to deal with your annoying reminder of the favor I'm still repaying." She glares at me, her eyebrows pinching together. "I can't believe you fixed my code issue just to put another one on there for me to deal with. It was super inconvenient and really mature of you to create a script that scrolled *'Payton is my favorite person in the world'* across my screen every time I typed your name."

I smile wider, loving that she's being feisty with me. "Come on, you loved it."

I reach over and drag my knuckles under her chin, and she grabs my hand, forcing it down between us, not letting it go. Fuck, I love when she does that without even realizing it.

"I didn't want to make your life harder. I would've taken it off for you if you'd asked. No charge and no favors needed."

"Nothing is free, so even that would've had consequences. It's gone now and I'm watching everything you're doing this time." She lets go of my hand and uses two fingers to gesture from her eyes to mine and back as she glares.

I blow her a kiss and return my attention to the screen. I scroll through her story, half tempted to add another quick script to remind her of me this week. I leave her laptop alone in the end because the story she's written is really fucking good, and I'm more interested in reading it than messing with her computer.

"Ainsley, this is incredible. It reads objectively, but your voice is so strongly intertwined in the writing that it feels literary instead of simply journalistic."

I pull my eyes away from the screen to glance her way and notice the bright spots of pink in her cheeks as she stares at me with rapt attention while worrying her lower lip with her teeth. Ah, my girl needs her praise, but she's feeling a bit insecure having me read her work. *We'll fix that right up.*

She pushes stray hair behind her ear and looks away from me, caught in a moment of unguarded vulnerability. "It's okay. But I'll probably need to do a few more passes to tighten the word count. This is the basis of the story I'll shop around for publication, though."

I put her computer on the coffee table in front of us and pull her into my lap. She makes a surprised protest. I want to kiss her fucking stupid for thinking like that so the thought falls right out of her head. I want to grind her hips against me until she comes so many times she forgets her own name, let alone that she's insecure about her writing ability. At the same time, I want to replace those insecurities with the truth by telling her she's incredible, she's so fucking smart, and I love everything she's written. Instead, I turn her face toward mine with my finger and touch my forehead to hers as I give her my most serious look.

"It's perfect, just like you. Do whatever you need for the word count but know you've already written something that is exactly what it needs to be. I can say the same about you." I pull back and give her a slow appraisal so she knows I'm appreciating her beauty. "Now that you're done with the article, let's get you out of your head." I stand from the couch, keeping her in my arms and relishing the quick way she grabs onto me in shock.

"Put me down or I'll kick you in the balls," she threatens, her feet already swinging, looking for parts of me she can make contact with. I keep her cradled in my arms and all parts of me safely out of her reach.

"Relax, Spitfire, I have longer legs, so it's faster this way. Think of it as your princess treatment."

I wanted an excuse to scoop her up and have her in my arms like this, protests and all. I walk into my bedroom, but I don't throw her on the bed like I'm sure she imagined I would. Instead, I place her gently on a padded stool I put here while she was busy writing. A candle is burning on the nightstand, the room filled with the scent of peach from the Broken Wax Co. candle burning on the nightstand. "Play With Me" by Rendezvous At Two is currently playing from the Bluetooth speaker connected to a playlist I made especially for her. Perfect timing for that song as I'm about to show her how I like to play.

I've noticed Ainsley gets in her head and refuses to process what's happening in the moment, spiraling and freaking out over the smallest details instead. I can connect her to her body, have her feeling more and thinking less, remove that feeling of overwhelm, and help her process by controlling what she's experiencing physically. She's spiraled tighter lately, as the stories about us have become more frequent, and I feel shitty that I've caused that. I want to make her feel good, get her out of that busy brain with something easy, and show her she can trust me. I roll my sleeves up as she fidgets on the seat. This will be how I initiate a scene with her going forward.

"Stay there," I command, dropping my voice into Dom mode. Her eyes grow wide at the change. She stops moving, her hands gripping the edges of the stool at her hips.

I walk into my closet to grab a few things and when I come back out, she's still where I put her. Task one is complete. I approach her, winding a silk scarf around my hands, letting it slip through one palm as she watches until I'm directly behind her. I drag the ends of the scarf up each of her arms in turn, noting the changes as she shivers and goosebumps rise in the wake of the cool black silk against her golden skin.

"What are you doing?" she asks shakily.

"You wanted to know what kind of Dom I am. I'm going to show you a little of what I like to do and the kind of pleasure you can get from it." She has no reply to that bit of information, but the way I like to play, I can't take her silence as an indication of her acceptance. "Do you want to play, my perfect little cocktease?"

She looks up at me, biting her lip and radiating tension, but there's a flare of need that lights in her amber eyes, and she nods. "Yes," she says quietly.

Unfettered joy and desire burst in my chest that she wants this, too. "That's my girl."

I walk around the stool again, letting her track my movement with tense anticipation. I nudge her knees apart with my thigh so her legs bracket mine and she has to look up at me. I trail the scarf over her exposed legs while she's distracted, making her jump.

"We're playing with sensations. What do you smell, hear, see, feel? Next, we'll take away one of your senses so you can experience how everything else is heightened." I drag the scarf up her shoulders to circle her neck. I'd love to run the ends between her gorgeous tits, along the soft skin of her stomach, down her back, but she's in a big T-shirt and I'm not getting her out of anything tonight, so this will have to do. I slip out from between her thighs and move to her back.

"I'm going to blindfold you. Do you want to know what it feels like to have my hands on you when you don't know where I'm going to touch next, Princess?" I whisper in her ear.

She shivers again and leans into me. "Maybe."

"Maybe won't cut it when we play. Yes or no, like my perfect cocktease."

"Yes," she exhales, a hesitant expression still on her gorgeous face despite her affirmation.

"Good girl. When I check in, I need you to let me know how you're doing. Red means stop immediately. Yellow means change what you're doing now or we'll have to stop. Green means you're enjoying yourself. Do you understand?"

She nods, blinking quickly as she takes it all in while willingly letting me guide her like this. Fuck yes. I've only dreamed she'd let me do this. To have it happening makes me ecstatic.

"What are you going to do?"

I hold the black scarf in front of her. "You're not supposed to know in this game, but you'll enjoy it. Close your eyes and tell me if this is too tight." I bring the scarf to her face and wait for a nod to allow me to cover her eyes. I run my fingers along the edges, checking the tension, satisfied it shouldn't hurt her, but significantly reduces her ability to see what's happening. "How are you doing, Princess?" I ask, checking on her comfort as well as her ability to follow directions.

"Green," she says after some hesitation.

"That's right, you're already so good at this," I tell her, running my fingers lightly along her neck with my praise.

She relaxes by a degree, her head following the path my hand takes as I drag it along her arm. She's curious as I expected but not able to relinquish her control, still wanting to anticipate the next move. She's wound so tight and just needs to let go, to surrender to the sensations and let me ground her here, show her she's safe, that she can shut her brain off and nothing bad will come of it, that she can actually relax and enjoy herself. I pull my fingers away and watch as she straightens in anticipation, unsure where the next touch will come from. I open a box on the dresser next to us.

"Open your mouth," I command, popping in her reward when she does.

"Did you just give me candy?"

"Taste is another sensation we're playing with. You earned it by following directions like a good girl."

"What was that? It's good."

I smile, watching as her pretty mouth sucks on the treat. I knew she'd like it because we both love peach pie, and this is one of my favorite sweets. "Peach Sour Patch candy." I also have a box of chocolates to reward her with to change things up.

I play with her like this, alternating using my hands, a feather, and a spiky metal Wartenberg wheel until a thin sheen of sweat coats her forehead, knowing I have her endorphins flowing with the anticipation of what sensation to expect next. The music, the scented candle, and the chocolate and candy I feed her keep her other senses overwhelmed in the best way. I reach into my pocket for my next toy, slipping it onto my fingers before I run it lightly along her thigh. She jumps at the feel of the thin metal claws, so different from the soft pads of my fingers or the feather, and different from the rolling motion of the wheel.

"What's that?" Her hands are already reaching to feel where the claws were before her question is even finished. She can't stop reaching out for the tools, her hands searching and looking for me, trying to figure out what I'm doing throughout the session, and she won't fully let go because of it. It's time to try something new.

I capture her wrists with my hands and lean into her ear, my voice taking on a disappointed tone. "Are you going to be a good girl and let me play, or do I need to bind your hands so you keep them to yourself?"

"I'll be good," she says, pulling against my grip like I'll let her go that easily. I chuckle at the words.

"Bullshit, Princess, it's cute you think you could. Be honest. You're my feisty little cockwhore with a sassy fucking mouth. Be that all you want, baby. I'll work with whatever you give me, and I can't wait to see you tied up for bratting too hard and tempting the consequences."

Her lips tip down like she's considering the pros and cons of that end. Her shoulders straighten and she turns toward my voice. "Tie me up, then, you arrogant asshole. I won't be able to stop reaching for you otherwise."

Jesus. Fuck. My cock swells and I swallow down the building desire with that perfect retort from her smart fucking mouth I want to fill so badly. She's so goddamn adorable, ready to tease and provoke during a game she doesn't even know all the rules to. My adrenaline surges, my heart racing with excitement at her willingness to play with me. This is better than I could've imagined. She's already everything I want.

"Take off my belt," I command, bringing her hands to my hips so she can feel her way to the task I've given her.

Her hands glide along the leather, fingers trailing against my stomach, making my abs contract. Fuck, her touching me feels good, even like this. She finds the buckle and pulls, fumbling as I work to stay still. She frees the belt with some tugging and holds it out. I take it, cupping her face and running my thumb along her cheek just under the blindfold before I return to my task.

"Put your wrists out in front of you."

She puts her arms out like she's made for this.

I slide the end of the belt through the buckle to create a loop and slip it onto her wrist before creating a second loop for her other hand. I double the tail around and pull it through the buckle. Her wrists are bound but not in a way that will cut off circulation or keep her from moving, but the idea that she's restrained is enough to have her chest rising and falling faster. It's perfect for switching her brain off and letting me take over.

I take a step back and stare at her, looking like my fun-sized bondage dream. She's blindfolded, my belt wrapped around her wrists, willingly waiting for me to touch her. I hold back the groan of pleasure working through me and return my attention to pleasing her.

The next time I drag the claws over her skin, it's along her inner thigh. She jumps and lets out a breathy moan that surprises her. She's shaking her head when I look up. I smile, not at all convinced she's not enjoying the shit out of this, too.

"How're you doing, Princess?" I need her answer when she's in this heightened state of anticipation and arousal. If she's uncomfortable, we'll stop now. I continue running the claws along her legs while I wait for her response and she shivers.

"Very green," she says quickly, her knees moving apart as she shifts her bare feet on the stool rungs.

Fuck. Yes.

"Does my cumslut like being blindfolded, tied up, and scratched all over her beautiful skin?" I ask in a teasing tone, taking stock of the thin red lines crossing her exposed skin. They're superficial, only from pressure, but I love seeing her marked anyway. She looks like...mine. That's a little more real than I expected to be thinking right now. I fucking like it.

"Something like that," she says, her tone breathy but still

holding a note of sass that tells me she's not sufficiently in line with me and still fighting to remain in control. I smile and want to kiss her smart mouth.

"There's my little brat. Do I need to spank it out of you so you can enjoy the rest of this session?" I tease.

The visible shiver that runs through her is beautiful. Her chin lifts and she turns her face toward my voice. "Yes."

I drop to my knees in front of her and rest my face on her thighs, my arms circling her hips and holding her to me as I shut my eyes in ecstasy at that one word spoken so confident-ly. Her bound wrists tentatively settle over my head, fingers threading into my hair and pulling gently. I groan into her legs at the contact, needing more. Needing everything she could possibly give me. Yet she's already given me so much in this one session that I never expected from her.

Her trust is so fucking sexy. She barely has enough for me outside of this situation to have a normal conversation where she isn't using her prickly words and put-downs to keep me away. Yet here she is, far more vulnerable, giving up control in a way that allows me to take care of her every need, whether or not she realizes it. My heart pounds as I drop kisses down to her knee reverently.

I rise to my feet, take her hands, and walk her to the bed. I sit on the edge and direct her over my lap, stretching out her bound wrists onto the mattress in front of her for balance. I rub my palm along her back and she arches into the touch, pressing her hips up as I get lower. She's already primed for this. This is her first spanking. I want something with an in-timate connection to monitor how she's doing easily. I'll feel everything she does with her body on mine like this.

"Is this okay?" I ask once she's positioned, her ass temptingly in the air, waiting for what she asked for in such a cavalier manner.

"Yes," she says, wiggling her ass, teasing me with the way her hips move over my lap.

"You remember what to say if you want me to change what I'm doing or stop?"

"Of fucking course I do," she says with more attitude, turning her face to rest on her arms.

I laugh, the sound dark and ready to tame the bratty attitude right out of her. "How long will it take to have you begging me to stop? Will you promise to be a good girl after one, or will you be stubborn and hold out through more?" I rest a hand in the middle of her back to keep her on my lap once we start.

She opens her mouth like she's going to answer, but I bring my open palm down on her ass and she lets out a cry of surprise, jolting up onto her elbows, her whole body going rigid before she settles under the hand I have holding her in place.

"Fuck you, asshole," she grits out between clenched teeth.

This earns her another slap on the opposite cheek, quickly followed by a third right in the middle. She squirms across my lap with each one.

"You'll be nicer to me before this is finished, won't you, Princess?"

"Not a chance, motherfucker." She seethes, her face red from the exertion of holding herself together through the bursts of pain.

"Do you feel what your mean words do to me, Princess?" I growl as she writhes over my rock-hard cock. I'm loving every minute of this. So is she. My eyes are focused on the apex of her thighs. She's soaking her panties *and* her tight pink shorts.

"You're the fucking worst."

I bring my hand down twice more, biting my lip as her wiggles turn into thrusts, seeking friction against me, her noises of pain sounding more like pleasure. I'm pulling my strength, letting this be more of a lesson than a punishment, inflicting the least amount of pain I can while still letting her feel the sting of my palm as I continue to alternate sides.

At ten, I pause and watch as she writhes, my chest heaving with the exertion of holding back and keeping her still. "Have you had enough yet? Ready to stop? You can tell me you'll be a good girl or call out red anytime you want, Princess." I can barely keep from groaning with her every time she grinds her hips into me. It's exquisite torture.

"Don't you fucking stop now," she pants, and I smile in triumph. My girl wants this as badly as I do. I'm going to make her feel so fucking good.

She's rocking against my lap with each swat, grinding down against my cock instead of flinching away, and I know she's getting close to release by the way her hands curl into the mattress and her knees push off the bed for more pressure. She's so far gone, she just needs a little push, and I'm right there with her, feeling every movement.

"Come for me, you gorgeous little slut. I want to hear my filthy cockwhore scream," I growl, slapping her ass harder this time, watching as she tips over the brink.

"Oh, fuck, yes," she moans, her blindfolded face thrashing. She's enthralling and I'm lost to her. She owns me now. She silences her cries by biting her arm, thighs quivering where they rest over my leg. She's a sight to behold, flushed and sweaty, writhing against me in pleasure, fully free of the strict control she normally holds over herself. She's more beautiful than ever.

I soothe her ass with soft circles as she comes down from her release, her back rising quickly with each breath, syncing with mine. It's euphoric to be this in tune, to have felt everything right along with her, and to have released at the same time she did, even if it means I finished in my pants like a fucking inexperienced kid. It's worth it to have this moment with her.

I pick her up and hold her to my chest where she curls into my arms as naturally as if this is what we do all the time. I free her wrists before moving to sit against the headboard, running my hands gently along her arms and legs. She's even resting her head against my chest, her hands on my neck, holding me back, while fully relaxed in my arms. I take my fill of this trust until she's breathing evenly. I don't want to change her trusting mood, but I have to take the blindfold off and bring her down from the floaty place she went to on the back of the endorphins she's riding coupled with the fun orgasm she had.

When I uncover her eyes, she blinks at me blearily, a look on her face I've yet to see. She's calm, and, damn, I think she's completely unguarded. I brush hair off her face and smooth my hand to the back of her neck, kneading her muscles to keep her that way.

"Did you enjoy that, Princess?"

She stares dreamily. "Mmmhmm. I didn't expect to like it, but..." She pauses, her flushed cheeks darkening.

"You came really fucking hard from being spanked and you liked it despite the initial pain," I supply for her. "It's not bad to enjoy something like that. If it brings you pleasure, makes you happy, or gives you any measure of joy, don't feel even an ounce of shame."

I reach over to the side of the bed and grab a piece of chocolate, then hold it up to her mouth until she lets me feed her from my fingers like I've been doing, but now she can see me doing it, which makes her uneasy. My unguarded Ainsley of minutes ago has gone back to her citadel of solitude and slammed the gate shut on me again. At least she's still in my lap, letting me provide her with the necessary aftercare to deal with her first impact session. The sensation play I wasn't worried about, but spanking her until I'm sure her ass is cherry-red and may be bruised tomorrow is another.

Good thing I'm patient and focused on making sure she gets everything she needs.

"Come with me to the coast this weekend."

Her eyes focus sharply. "Why would I go anywhere with you for a weekend?"

She's probably terrified to spend that much time alone with me. She wouldn't be able to fight whatever reaction she has if she's around me for days on end, which is exactly the point.

"I spend a lot of weekends on the coast, so it's only natural my *girlfriend* would come with me," I clarify, my smile wicked, seeing her unease, knowing where it stems from. "I have a boat. It has lots of space. I need the ocean air, and you need to be with me."

She gives me a withering look. "*I need to?*"

"We need to feed the rumors and see how far we want to take this. I also need to get you comfortable with what we can do together." I need more of her just like this, pliant and relaxed in my arms.

A shiver of anticipation runs through her and I smile, knowing I've won.

Twenty

The Atlanta Haute List

Blonde and Billionaire Fanning Relationship Flames

Billionaire businessman, Payton Olsen, and his new romantic interest, humble journalist, Ainsley Montgomery, are making a bid for most PDA-filled outings. The new couple who have yet to confirm their relationship status have been spotted out and about around Atlanta and can't seem to keep their hands to themselves. Payton has been pulling out the stops for his new paramour, letting actions speak louder than words when it comes to their status. Fancy steakhouses, the best pizza in the city, candlelit picnics in Piedmont Park, a trip to the suburbs to catch a baseball game at the ballpark, and plenty of small one-on-one trips around town have set tongues wagging.

We can't deny the attraction they seem to have for one another, given the photo evidence our Hauties in the know have submitted of them. While this behavior seems unusual for Payton—who, as we've previously reported, hasn't been romantically connected previously—it's great to see that he's capable of such romantic gestures now that he's found someone he's deemed worthy of his time and energy. Yes, we heard the collective sound of Southern women weeping over this conclusion, also.

Ainsley, however, is still a mystery to us at the Haute List. What does Payton see in her, and how did she snag the last eligible Olsen brother? We certainly know what she's getting out of the relationship, going by the recent article published in an Atlanta newspaper breaking news about the latest Olympus venture into a professional hockey team. Could she be taking advantage of the man who appears so besotted with her, or is this a mutually beneficial relationship, and, if so, what's Payton getting out of the coupling?

We'll be keeping an eye on this unusual pairing. Remember to hit Like and Subscribe for all the Haute Gossip!

Twenty-one

Payton

"That's yours? It's huge."

"Thank you, Muffin, just what every man wants to hear."

I laugh at her expression of disdain when I turn to her and see her looking between me and the yacht as it comes into view. I chuckle and pull her by the hand along the dock in the private marina off the Georgia coast where the yacht is moored. She's letting me touch her far more tonight, even when it's not for show and I'm taking every opportunity she'll allow me to do it.

"I told you it has lots of space."

"You said you had a boat. This is basically a cruise ship. The two are not the same. I was expecting something else entirely," she mumbles as we board the yacht.

"I'll let you berate me about the differences all you want later, but first, you have to meet the small crew who'll be on board with us." I wave at the people waiting in the main cabin. "Ainsley, this is Captain Roycroft. Evans is our chef. Grant, Eamonn, and Brockway are our deckhands. Everyone, this is my girlfriend, Ainsley Montgomery. She'll be staying with me and should be afforded the same treatment and respect you'd use for me," I direct to the crew, whom I've already messaged this information to but figured Ainsley would benefit from hearing it as well.

She squeezes my hand in warning, and when I look down at her, she gives me a murderous look that's not well-hidden before she schools her face and returns her eyes to the crew. "Nice to meet you."

"We'll have our food in my cabin whenever it's ready, Evans," I instruct.

"Yes, sir. Your requests were received and I delivered your meals myself a moment before you arrived," Evans responds with a nod.

"Perfect timing. Thank you," I say before turning us away and leading Ainsley toward a hallway into the heart of the yacht.

"*I'm staying with you?*" Ainsley whispers in indignation as she follows along, her hand tugging to be released from my grip. I hold on tighter. "I thought *this boat had space* was code for I would have my own room and spending the weekend with you meant I'd see you in common areas only, not that I'd be staying in the same room as you." Now she sounds pissed.

"Of course you're staying with me. My staff is discreet, but even they can't know about this arrangement. Outside of us, everyone has to believe this is real." I push into my room, wishing it could be real for us, too. The huge bed looks more than inviting after a week that took more from me than I care to admit.

"There's only one bed," she says, sounding positively mortified.

"Yes, and it's nice and big, but if you want to cuddle, I won't mind." I smile as she rounds on me, her hazel eyes flashing angrily at my humor.

"This isn't a good idea. In fact, it's terrible. We shouldn't be in the same room, let alone the same bed. This is all wrong."

I drop her bag on the floor and walk her over to the bed she's so worried about until her knees hit the edge and she's forced to sit, then lie back. I keep moving until I'm hovering over her body, feeling her chest heave under mine as I hold myself on my forearms above her.

"What are you so worried about, Muffin? Think you won't be able to keep your hands off me if you have to sleep next to me? Or maybe you're worried about having a naughty dream and I'll hear you moaning my name and grinding against me looking for a release?" I roll my hips against hers for the briefest moment and feel her unconsciously rise to meet me before I've lifted again. "Or maybe I'll see you unguarded and raw, and that scares you more than anything else." I trace the soft curve of her cheek with my finger as she stays silent below me, her face pink and her eyes simmering pools of golden-flecked amber in the low light.

Her small hands find my chest, but instead of pushing me away as expected, she leaves them there, tentatively curling into my shirt as if she's fighting the urge to pull me against her. I decide for her and move away, her hands dropping as I do. I walk into the closet, hanging my jacket before returning and finding her holding her face on the edge of the bed where I left her.

"You're a real mind fucker." She scowls up at me.

"When was the last time you ate?" I nod at the small table and chairs where the dinner service is set up. "Maybe you'll be a little nicer after we get some food in you."

"I don't do nice with arrogant assholes who aren't used to hearing no."

Her face is set in that perpetual pout that's way too cute.

"I'm fine with hearing no, Spitfire. I just think you need someone else to take control and give you a chance to relax for a change. You're so rigid and stuck in this angry, prickly thing you have going that you're missing out on a whole lot of the fun life offers. We're going to work on that together. Starting right now."

Ainsley visibly bristles as she rises to her feet, still considerably shorter than me even in heels, and stomps toward me.

"The audacity you have is unmatched. I have no interest in working on anything with you."

"Wrong. You've agreed to be my girlfriend, you've joined me here, and you've come at my hand turning your ass red. You fucking loved giving up control and submitting to me because you trusted me to give you what you needed. You're going to work on a shit ton with me, and it starts right the fuck now, Princess. Now sit on my lap so I can take your shoes off and feed you some fucking dinner."

I sit at the table and pull her down onto my lap, settling her on my thighs as she squeals in protest. She's in the sweetest silky pink skirt that floats around her thighs and lets me feel the heat of her on my legs. I toe off her heels under the table and kick them away so her feet dangle above the ground. God, I love that she's fun-sized and fits perfectly right here against my chest, her head lower than mine so I can see over her, and my body wider than hers so it's easy enough to move around her.

"Payton," she warns once she realizes I'm not joking. "I'm not a fucking child who needs to be fed." She vibrates in frustration against me, not sure what to do with herself and me as I push her need for control and independence that wars with her need to be taken care of.

I've already boxed her in with my arms to uncover the trays of perfectly cooked chicken, mashed potatoes, and vegetables on the table. "Relax and let me take care of you, Ainsley."

She turns her head and looks at my profile, and I pause from cutting the food on the plate to meet her stare.

"Why the hell do you want to take care of me? You've said that a few times when we've been together. What delusional world do you live in where that's the default for a perfect stranger who has never asked you for anything?"

She looks truly curious and a little put out. I abandon the silverware and wrap my arms around her waist to hold her against me, her eyes growing wide, but I don't miss the amber warming right along with the heat from her body against mine. I confuse her further by kissing her nose, getting a huff of surprise. She's so fucking cute when she's indignant.

"How long have you been taking care of yourself?" I ask instead of answering her question.

Her eyebrows bunch as she considers. "That's a weird question."

"Did you have to grow up quickly because you were a middle child in a large family, slightly overlooked, a bit shy, reclusive, and left to your own devices more often than not? As a child, were you packing your own lunches, organizing your own school things, and in high school were you babysitting for extra spending money so you weren't a burden on your parents?"

She stays silent, her eyes growing wide, so I know I've nailed the conclusions I've drawn from the little she's told me about her family and upbringing.

"I bet you worked through college, too. Where'd you go?"

"NYU," she answers sulkily, guarding her answers as usual, but she relaxes against me a bit, and I take that as a win.

"New York would suit you with that attitude. No wonder," I tell her, nuzzling her cheek as I chuckle. She ducks her head but doesn't pull away, and she crosses her arms over mine where they rest around her middle. I open my fingers and lace ours together. Surprisingly, she lets me. "What did you do for work in New York?" I ask quietly, bringing my face next to hers as she relaxes further into my body.

"I did a bunch of things," she replies, sounding introspective.

She curls her legs up into my lap and I tuck an arm under them to support her. She's so little and adorable, I just want to keep her here forever.

"I wrote for the school paper, took food service jobs, interned at *The New York Times*. I even worked at an investment firm as an admin for a summer."

"See, I knew you were a hustler and likely haven't had anyone take care of you for a long time. Let me. Allowing someone else to take care of you and remove that burden from your shoulders, even for a little while, doesn't undermine your independence or say anything bad about your ability to do it yourself."

"Is that another one of your *things*?" she asks quietly, turning her head, which is now fully resting against my shoulder.

I can't fight the urge and place a lingering kiss against her forehead because it's *right there*. She doesn't pull away from my kiss, and her eyes are soft when she opens them and meets mine.

"Yes, baby. I want to take care of you. Make you feel good. Find what works for you. Explore anything you like and do that for you. I hate seeing you deny yourself the things you want. It drives me fucking crazy knowing I could give you everything so easily. Let me be what you need."

"You don't have to do that. There's no one here to put on a show for. Isn't the point of all this to prove to Harlowe that you don't need her to set you up with her friends? It's not about what I need or want. I'm here filling a role as a favor, which is fine."

I can feel the tension in Ainsley's body despite her relaxed posture.

I consider my words before replying. "That might've been what got us here in the first place, but why shouldn't we get something out of the charade that's beneficial? I want to take care of you, and you have needs that should be explored. I can be a safe way for you to do that. Completely outside of our arrangement, of course. This has no bearing on what we've agreed to do in public for my image as a perpetual bachelor. Though it could lend credibility to the story of me being in a committed relationship if we look sexually satisfied."

She stiffens in my arms. "You're saying we could have sex and it wouldn't be real or mean anything, but it wouldn't be for our fake relationship? Why even do it, then? Why not just keep it off the table completely and not complicate the situation any more than it needs to be?"

"I didn't say it wouldn't be real." *Fuck, how I want it to be real.* She'd go running if she knew that, though. I try a different tactic. "How wet do you get when I call you my pretty little cumslut?" I ask, voice low and commanding.

I feel the change in her posture immediately. She goes soft and attentive, her face turning toward mine, eyes wide, lips parted, back arching as her ass grinds into my lap unconsciously.

"W-wet," she says haltingly, her cheeks growing pink either from embarrassment or desire.

"I bet if I slipped my fingers up your skirt, I'd find my sweet cockwhore's panties soaked for Daddy, wouldn't I?"

She subtly parts her legs in invitation, and I take it, sliding a palm between her knees and up to the apex of her thighs, where I feel her hot and wet for me, just as expected. I groan as I stroke the tips of my fingers under the edge of her lace panties and she lets out a breathy sigh.

"Oh, God," she says quietly, turning her face into my neck, her whole body shaking from that one light touch. Fuck, she's more responsive than I could have imagined. I haven't even brushed her clit or sunk a finger inside of her and she's already trembling. I reluctantly remove my hand from her thighs.

"Tonight, it's Daddy. Now eyes on me."

I taste her on my fingertips while I wait for her to turn hazy eyes to mine. She's sweet, as expected, and it makes my cock harden, digging into her ass where she's still curled on my lap. I want to bury my face between her thighs and feast on her while she eats her dinner.

"You could get off just from my voice and the filthy words I say because I want you to. Isn't that right, Princess? Now taste yourself and suck."

I move my hand to her mouth and push two fingers with her arousal coating them across her parted lips and she sucks them in, swirling her tongue around. She keeps her eyes on mine as I press them farther into her mouth and test her reflex. She may be confused about her reactions to what she wants, but she has no problem acting on them in the moment, and she can deepthroat my fingers just fine. I push until she gags, eyes watering, before I pull my fingers out.

"The next time I tell you to suck, you'll be on your knees, begging for my cock and I'll be watching your pretty pink lips suck me off." I brush my thumb along her cheek and smile at her. "You took it well. You're so fucking perfect, Princess. Such a good little slut. And that's why we're going to explore this together."

She blinks, clearing the sex haze from her eyes when I let my voice return to a normal tone before she unfolds out of my arms.

"How are you doing that? What sort of mind games are you playing with me?" she asks, eyes narrowing as she stands on shaky legs and moves to her own chair without me stopping her. I would prefer she stay curled up right here in my lap, but she needs her distance to think clearly, and I'm happy to give her that.

"I'm not playing mind games. I just tapped into something you need and respond to that I'm capable of providing. If you want to play games, that's something I'm quite good at and we can come up with all sorts of scenarios that would be lots of fun." I grin at her as she shoots me a glare that could freeze the fiery pits of hell. I push the plate of food toward her. "Now please eat. I know you're hungry."

I pour us each a glass of wine before I take my own plate while she eyes me suspiciously. Finally, she takes a bite of the food I cut for her and lets out the most erotic-sounding moan of pleasure that instantly makes my cock hard again. My head snaps up at that noise and a small smile tugs on my lips when I see her eyes are closed and she's finally making a happy, blissed-out face. Okay, so she likes tasty food. If that's one way to get her to relax and stop being so prickly, I can work with that. If I can get her to make more of those hot little noises and her face to look like that when she's experiencing pleasure without food involved, I'll call this a successful weekend.

"This is incredible. Your chef is amazing."

She takes another bite and tips her head back and forth like she's doing a happy food dance to some internal music only she can hear while she hums her pleasure. It's the most innocent and sweet she's been around me. All over food.

Fuck, this is a side of Ainsley I want to see more of. Her prickly personality and wanting to figure her out up until now has intrigued me, but this authentic joy is something I could easily want to make mine. I've just doubled down on my resolve to loosen Ainsley Montgomery up and see who she is under her layers of anger and control because she could be exactly what I need and I already have her right where I want her.

"So are those noises you're making. They're making me as hard as when you were in my lap. You do realize we're sharing a bed tonight. I've felt how wet your pussy is for me, figured out how far you can deep throat, know I can probably make you come with words alone, and see you're pacified with good food. You're giving me all the power here, baby, and as much as I fucking love it and will use it to my advantage, I want you to be the one to direct where this goes."

Her eyes grow wide as she swallows her mouthful of food and sets her fork down. "Am I that easy to read?"

I reach out and stroke my thumb over her cheek, not able to resist touching her. "I'm sure to most people you're a locked down vault. To me, you were a puzzle I wanted to solve as soon as I met you, and I'm really good at reading people."

"Why do I…respond…to all this kink stuff? To what you said. I don't like it. That's not me at all." Her tone is accusatory like I've forced the response out of her rather than evoked it from somewhere she's repressed.

I nod in understanding as I take a sip of wine. "You don't think you *should* like it, is what you mean. You think because you're an independent, empowered woman who takes no shit from men, those words are belittling and not at all aligned with the image you've created of yourself."

She nods. "I don't like it. I shouldn't. It's all wrong." She sounds less sure with each statement.

"You fucking loved it when I had you blindfolded and tied up, begging me to keep spanking that perfect ass of yours."

She blushes and frowns in annoyance. "I asked you a serious question and you immediately turned it into something that would make me uncomfortable. Don't be a dick. Just help me understand."

I take her hand in mine and run my thumb over her knuckles in a soft motion, reassuring her that I'm taking her seriously.

"Degradation can be healing in a way. It may help you overcome past trauma by reclaiming the words that were used to hurt you, by turning them into something that makes you feel sexy and powerful instead. The moment that changes for you, this stops. My words are for your pleasure, not punishment or disrespect." I give her an understanding smile. "It's okay to like it. There's nothing at all wrong with the things that bring you pleasure, even if they differ from what you think you should want."

She blinks at me, but she doesn't stop me, so I continue.

"There are a lot of reasons to want to submit and freely give up control—to take you to the edge of your boundaries, to test your limits with pain, or to discover what brings you pleasure that's outside of your comfort zone." I stand and walk behind her, letting my hand trail along her arm. "Maybe you want to relinquish the control that you hold onto so tightly in every other aspect of your life. Maybe you need someone to finally take care of you. Or maybe you want to let go of the image you have of yourself as the morally righteous, squeaky-clean, does all the right things woman so you can be the filthiest version of yourself possible. The desperate slut who wants to be dripping with cum and have every hole filled by a Daddy who'll tell you what a good girl you are for giving yourself up for his pleasure."

She visibly shivers and closes her eyes as if that'll stop her reaction. I pull her up into my arms and walk her to the bed where I sit and place her in my lap. I wrap her legs around my hips to hold her to me, even if it pushes her skirt up toward her hips. She's so damn little, yet she fits around me so perfectly.

"Hey!" she protests, weakly fighting me to let her go.

"Just hold on to me. Look, I'm not even touching you."

To prove my point, I lean back on the bed and let her see my arms are behind me, not on her body. She tentatively puts her arms around my shoulders and leans away from me, so we're not flush together the way I'd initially positioned us, which is fine. Whatever she's comfortable with as long as she stays here with me. I've had a taste of what it's like to have Ainsley trust me, letting me touch her as I please, and now I can't get enough. I want her in my lap, my hands on her, any chance I get. Fake or not, I'm interested, and that's more than I can say about any woman who's crossed my path in years.

"Will you stop saying all that shit about sluts and daddies and stuff tonight? I can't handle it," she says, her face angry, likely at having to ask for the concession at all.

"There's a part of you that wants it very badly, judging by your reactions," I tell her quietly, all the humor gone from my tone. Her legs tighten around my hips a fraction as if in confirmation.

"Well, the rest of me isn't comfortable with it, and that's enough to want you to stop." Her face is set in determination, yet there's a war going on that's evident in her struggle to meet my eyes.

"Okay."

Her eyes snap to mine, mistrust in the hazel depths. "Okay? That's it? From you?"

I smile at her again. "I'm fully capable of respecting your requests when you mean them. Just remember, I can read you better than anyone and I'm going off that more often than what your words say."

"You're so arrogant!" she snaps, her eyes flashing.

"I sure am, but you know I'm right. I'll stop like you asked." She visibly relaxes as I speak.

"But you have to be honest with me about your requests, and yourself."

"I'm being honest," she says forcefully, and it's cute to watch her grow prickly again as she's wrapped around me, vibrating with indignation.

I chuckle darkly. "You want me to call that bluff and lay you bare? I can and you're not going to like it, even though I sure will."

"I don't know what you're talking about," she says, maintaining the denial, and I know it's going to suck when she realizes I know her this well. She needs to come to terms with her own body, needs, and desires.

"I warned you," I tell her as I bring a hand to her back and she stills. "You're so tightly wound and into the slutty submissive side we've discovered that you've been subtly grinding your sweet little cunt against my abs since I put you here, and I have a much better spot for that if you want to get off quicker, no touching on my part needed unless you want me to spank you again. I can just lie back while you straddle me and rock all you want."

Her face blanches in horror at her body's betrayal and she unhooks her ankles from behind my back, but I keep her pressed to me.

"Let me go," she protests, eyes wide as she pushes against my chest.

"You sure about that, or are you just embarrassed that I noticed how your body was reacting and read you so easily? Get used to it. I see you, Ainsley, and I like everything, whether or not you do."

She lets her head tip forward in defeat, relaxing in my arms and burying her face in the spot between my neck and shoulder. I hold her gently so she knows I'm not keeping her against her will. She lets out a groan before she picks up her head again, and I see her mortification, cheeks flaming red, eyes a raging fire of anger at us both.

"You're the most infuriating man I've ever met. I need to shower and get ready for bed. Can I do that now, or do I have to ask for your permission, *Daddy*?" she asks sarcastically.

I smile brightly at her use of the honorific for the first time, loving hearing her say it, even with that tone. "Say that and mean it next time, Princess."

Twenty-two

Ainsley

Payton can read me like a book. Absolutely nothing gets past him. On top of that, my own damn body is betraying me where he's concerned, humping him like a horny puppy and letting him feel me up because he has the sexiest voice known to womankind and I have an inner slutty clingy koala who spreads her legs when he asks if I'm wet for him and wants to be in his arms every possible moment.

Of course I'm wet. I'm a woman who sees his appeal and what he said was sexy as hell to a twisted part of me. I know what he's capable of, what he can do to me with his hands, a silk scarf, and some choice words. For whatever reason, I like when he calls me a cumslut, a cockwhore, or Daddy's little whatever.

Fuck. I turn the shower to cold and blast myself with an icy spray to cool the inferno of lust that simply thinking the words stokes in me.

While I won't tell *him*, I loved everything about the sensory session he put me through. I've been waiting for him to initiate another, but since that one instance, every interaction we've had has all been for show in public. It's a good reminder that this thing between us isn't real and I shouldn't expect anything from him outside of the fake roles we're playing, even if he says we can introduce sex. Yeah, because that wouldn't complicate things even more.

He may tease me mercilessly with his never-ending innuendo, but we haven't talked about how I asked him to tie me up *and* spank me, which got me off. I submitted to him willingly and gave up control in a way I never thought I'd be able to. It was *easy* to trust him when I wasn't able to see and didn't have the use of my hands. I was dependent on him in a way I otherwise wouldn't have been. I couldn't have my walls up in that situation. I needed what he could give me, and he needed me to be honest and let him in. I told him what I wanted. He gave me that and more I didn't realize I needed.

I crave it. To be at his mercy and just a little out of control of the situation, letting him do what he wants to me because he's capable of making me feel good no matter what he does. The way I came while grinding on his lap as he spanked me and called me his whore was unexpected and hot as fuck. When he took off the blindfold and we locked eyes, it clicked that we had a level of mutual trust that doesn't come easily to either of us. Later, I realized he'd come, too. Despite his immense amounts of control, he'd been so turned on by bringing *me* pleasure, he couldn't help himself. I'd broken that part of him while he broke down my walls. It was a revelation that made me feel so powerful. I blast myself with more icy water.

My next dilemma is clothing. The pajamas I packed—a tank top and boy shorts—are for the privacy of my own room, not sharing one with Payton. I sigh. He's seen me in a bikini, so I guess it's fine.

I open the door and find him reclining in bed, phone in hand. My mouth drops open when I look at him, shirtless, only wearing a pair of loose shorts, dark hair wet from his own shower. He looks up with a smile, but it slips and his blue eyes quickly darken when he gives me a slow once-over that feels heavy as I put my bag away and walk toward the bed, trying not to feel too awkward under his perusal. I snatch up my own phone and crawl into what I assume is my side of the bed, ignoring Payton. I cross my arms to try to hide that my nipples are straining through the thin material of my tank top.

"What?" I snap, unable to take it any longer.

"Want to talk?"

I shake my head.

"Want to cuddle?"

I roll toward him and prop my head on my hand. "Why would I want to cuddle with you when I know exactly where that would lead?"

He rolls to mirror my position so we're only a foot apart. His naturally intoxicating scent is mixed with a clean soapiness that is divine.

"I can cuddle without having sex. Why? Do you only cuddle when sex is involved? That's so sad. Cuddling's nice. It releases feel-good hormones. It's been a while since I've had another person in my bed to cuddle with. I figured the same for you since you said you don't date."

My phone vibrates on the bed between us, the screen lighting up with an unknown number texting me. We both look down at the same time and I quickly put my hand over it, hoping he didn't see the screen. I swipe away the notification as my heart hammers a rapid staccato beat. It vibrates again and I silence it.

"Who's texting you from an unknown number, Ainsley?" Payton asks evenly as he gives me an inscrutable look.

"Probably spam," I evade. "I need to block it. Happens a lot." My face heats as I evade his probing eyes.

"Why would a spam number mention my name and call you a fucking whore?" Payton's voice is deadly quiet and I've never seen him look so serious. There's no trace of his usual smile or effervescent energy. He doesn't even get the same reaction using the word whore now, in a different context. I guess it's good to know I don't have to worry about always reacting to the word, only to the way he uses it in certain situations.

I sit up and bring my knees to my chest, wrapping my arms around them to keep from shaking. "It's nothing. Just some ex drama I'm dealing with."

Payton sits up against the headboard and pulls me between his legs until I'm leaning into his chest. He wraps his arms around me, holding me together, too.

"What about you being with me makes your ex want to call you names?" he asks quietly as he runs his fingers through the ends of my hair, sending goosebumps dancing along my skin.

God, why does him holding me feel good? I shouldn't like the way he's comforting me, and there's no reason for him to even care, yet for some reason, I know he does. The way his whole demeanor changed told me everything. And now I want to tell him everything. I sigh and shift deeper into his hold, his arms closing tighter.

"This is personal to him. Olympus led a hostile takeover of his father's company a few years ago, but it was after we broke up, so I wasn't around to know the details. It's no surprise that created bad blood he's not over. We've been broken up for years, but he contacted me a few weeks ago out of the blue after he saw us on the Atlanta Haute List. He's been pretty nasty in his messages, which was standard for the end of our relationship. I changed my number when I left New York after our breakup, but he's kind of a tech genius, like you, and has always had a way of finding information, so I guess he tracked me down. I've blocked every number he's used, but he hasn't stopped."

"Who's your ex, Ainsley?" Payton asks quietly next to my ear, his fingers stilling the delicious movement in my hair.

"His name is Archer Donovan. Do you remember taking over Donner Investments? That was his father's company." I partially turn to look at Payton's face. "His dad was part of the group that went to prison last year for orchestrating all that stuff with the mine collapse y'all were framed for. It's no surprise Archer's pissed at me." I let my head fall back against his shoulder in frustration before leaning forward again.

Payton swears under his breath. "No, Princess. You're not to blame for anything and Archer shouldn't be taking his frustration out on you, even through texts. His issue is with Olympus and what we did. He's cyberstalking you." He brushes my hair away from my neck, kneading at the tension that's jacking my shoulders toward my ears.

"He has easier access to me to take that frustration out on, so I'll be fielding his aggressive texts, not Olympus. Mmm, that feels good."

Payton has magic hands, strong enough to work out the knots that have settled in my overly tense muscles but gentle enough to send shivers racing down my arms and to lower places.

"Tell me how you met Archer." His voice is quiet as he works at stubborn knots in my shoulders and neck. This could be a very effective interrogation tactic because I'm willing to tell him anything as he touches me like this. I even want to grind my ass against him a little. I don't care if that's his motive. It feels too damn good.

"I worked at Donner Investments as a summer job before I started my grad program at NYU." My words are quiet as I sink back into the sludge of memories that are hard to dredge up, knowing where the story ends. "My scholarships wouldn't cover as much of my tuition so I needed more money than my internships or odd jobs were getting me. The admin position a friend hooked me up with paid better than anything else I'd had before. Mmm, right there. Good God, your hands are amazing."

He chuckles. "I'll leave that comment alone for now, but know it's taking everything not to crack an inappropriate joke." He ghosts his lips over the shell of my ear and I shiver. "Keep going with your story, Princess." His voice carries that note of command that stirs something low in my body as his hands work up my neck, effectively turning me into putty in his grip. It takes me a moment to collect my thoughts through his effect on me.

"Archer came into the office occasionally. He liked to lord it over us plebeians who had to work for our paychecks and found it funny that his father was always stressed over the market and deals. He hated everything his father did."

"He sounds like a real winner," Payton deadpans.

I laugh quietly and drop my head down, remembering seeing Archer around the office and being attracted to his tall, blond, lean build and cocky attitude, but knowing he was off-limits because of who he was. It made him that much more appealing.

"I was taking notes on a deal, and Archer saw me when I left the meeting. He followed me back to my floor and asked me out. I turned him down. I knew about him and didn't want to get myself into trouble or lose the one job that was actually paying decently. Archer's a narcissist, but I didn't know that at the time, so he took it hard that I wasn't instantly his and I became a challenge. He pursued me all summer, and I agreed to give him a chance when my internship was up, thinking it was finally a safe time."

"It sounds like things turned ugly for you if you realized he was a narcissist and was nasty to you."

Payton sweeps his thumbs up the sides of my spine and I moan at the incredible way it feels. Not seeing his face while I reveal this makes it easier to divulge the details. At least it's been the simple stuff so far. Now he's asking for the hard. The lump already rises in my throat as I dig for the strength to open this box, share the ugly truths, and reveal my weaknesses to a man who's far too similar to Archer, at least on the surface.

"He was great at first. Attentive, doting, made me feel so special, and like the only woman in the world who mattered. I was so dumb. I realized later that's exactly what a narcissist does. A few months in, he asked me to move in with him. He wanted me to focus more on school and not worry about paying rent. It was too good to be true and I was head over heels for him, so I was thrilled. But he quickly changed. He became possessive and controlling. He didn't want me to hang out with my friends and demanded all my time be spent with him. He said he cared and didn't like when we were apart, but he was jealous if I wasn't focused on him. He even interfered with school and work. I kept my newspaper internship but quit my waitressing job because he didn't like me out late, so

I became financially dependent on him, as well as dependent on him for my housing. He was super manipulative. Every argument became my fault when I knew he was the cause. It was so messed up. He had the upper hand at that point and I didn't know what would happen if we broke up over something stupid, so I'd apologize to end the fights. I was walking on eggshells, trying not to upset him, worried that I'd suddenly be left without anywhere to go or a way to get by. It was scary to realize later just how much he'd manipulated my situation so I needed him for everything and couldn't leave even when I wanted to."

I shrink with this admission, becoming smaller as I round over my knees away from Payton's hands. I hate this part of the story. I was so weak and stupid. To not realize that was gaslighting...God, listen to me, I'm still making it my fault. I don't want to admit the rest because it only gets worse from here and it's already bad enough.

"He sounds like a fucking nightmare. You didn't deserve to be treated that way." Payton pulls me back against him, threads his long fingers into my hair, and massages my scalp, eliciting a little moan from me as my body relaxes against his minutely. "Tell me the rest of what he did to you. I know that's not the worst of it. I want to know everything."

I sigh and squeeze my eyes shut. "He tracked my phone, I think, because he'd call or text and ask who I was with and why I was at a certain place if I hadn't told him I was going to be there. It was all super weird. I knew it wasn't healthy, but I was in so deep by then I couldn't end things. Where could I even go and how could I pay for it? I'd alienated all my friends and I didn't have a way to afford a Manhattan apartment on my own. It was such a change after he'd been so good to me, at first."

I sniff and force the tears that blur my vision not to fall. I won't let Archer make me cry again. I clear my throat and shake my head. He's had enough of my tears. Enough of my anxiety, my fear, my pain. But not tonight.

"His parents hated me. They made sure to mention that I was a scholarship student from the South every time I had to see them as if that somehow made me less. They insisted he'd never marry someone like me and made it known they thought I was dating him for his money. I guess it looked that way. I was living with him and he was paying for everything. Looking back, that's probably what he wanted them to think. How sick is that?"

I shake my head, shame settling over me as I unburden myself of the shadows of my past to a man who is too much like Archer in his wealth and status that he could think the same things. Payton could be a carbon copy of Archer if he wanted to be, given a malicious streak. I should worry what he'll think of me after hearing how naive and dumb I was to fall for someone like Archer and his manipulations. I'm supposed to be smarter than this.

Payton's hands still against my neck and he pulls me back against his chest. "Archer's a predator. You didn't do anything wrong. You know that, right?"

I stay silent.

He grips my knees and spins me around to face him. He wraps his arms around my back, holding me close. It's incredibly intimate being face-to-face with him like this.

"He's the one who fucked you over and that's why you don't date, right?"

"It's a pretty good reason not to. He's horrible and I was so stupid."

He tilts his head like he's seeing something I'm not saying, and I look away, not wanting him to pry into what I'm keeping from him, but in true Payton fashion, he catches on too easily.

"It was you who ended things, right? How did you finally break up with him?"

I nod, still not meeting his intense ocean-blue eyes. "It's a long story and it's already late. I'm sure you don't want to hear it, especially since it's not relevant to our fake relationship." I wave at him to deflect, looking for an edge of anger to add to my voice, but I can only muster embarrassment.

Payton captures my hand in his and pulls it up to his lips, kissing each of my fingertips in turn. "It's relevant because it happened to you. Besides, it's going to be too hard for me to sleep with you next to me if you won't let me cuddle, so I have all night to listen to your story, and I want to hear it. Please tell me, Ainsley, even if you're embarrassed or it hurts. I won't judge you."

I look at Payton, seeing the truth of his words and the openness on his face. I hate sharing this part of my history with anyone. It took me a year to tell Della, and my parents still don't know the full story. But for some reason, I want him to know. I blink and look at the stubble on his jaw before I can work up the nerve to tell him. I take a deep breath of his glorious scent to fortify myself before I can begin. When I blow it out, I see him shiver a bit from my breath on his neck.

"He asked me to do something for him, to write a story using information that he said was from a source at the company. I agreed, and the story was really good, one of the best I've ever written, but it ended up costing me my integrity in the end. My editor was able to substantiate the claim, but I shouldn't have accepted the information. It's a story that earned me a really great scholarship that would have paid for the rest of my grad program. It opened doors for me after my time at NYU—it landed me an internship at *The New York Times*, which led to a promised spot on their staff once I graduated."

I laugh bitterly, remembering how great my life was going for about six months before it all came crashing down on my head. I risk a glance up at Payton. He's looking at me sincerely, with no judgment in his stare, just patience.

He cups my cheeks in his big hands and forces me to maintain eye contact.

"I'm listening. I know this is hard. I won't judge you for anything you say."

I swallow the lump in my throat, hating the next part and the way it reflects on my character, and possibly how he'll feel about me, despite what he says.

"Everything was going so well after that story. My confidence was at an all-time high, so my writing was better than ever. I won an award for it. Everything was great. Until I found out it was all a lie. Archer's father, Andreas, had provided the insider information I was given. Donner Investments had fabricated the whole thing. Archer used me, knowing I was desperate to prove my worth as a journalist. I didn't care when I wrote it that the story would have the kind of life-altering consequences it did. When I heard Archer and his dad talking about how they'd used me, I was devastated."

I hug my arms around myself as my stomach twists even now, years later, thinking of walking up to their table to meet them for dinner without them seeing me and hearing them discussing how easy I was to manipulate. I'd stayed long enough to hear all the incriminating evidence because they were planning to do it again now that they'd been successful. The repercussions of my actions and how Archer manipulated me using false information for the financial gain of a company that already had more money than they knew what to do with still affect me.

I swallow the lump in my throat and glance up at Payton, feeling guilty even admitting it now. He cups my jaw and brushes his thumb over my cheek before he leans forward and kisses my forehead tenderly, lingering long enough for me to relax into the intimate gesture. I blink a few times to hold back the tears pricking my eyes.

"What did you do when you found out?"

"I tried to have the story retracted. I begged my editor to pull it even though it had been out for over six months by then. I said I'd own the fuckup. But he had substantiated the story and it was true at the time, so there was nothing we could do. The company I wrote the exposé about had quickly collapsed after it ran and Donner Investments bought them out at bottom dollar, which was the whole point in Archer giving me the information to begin with. I cost a lot of good people their livelihoods because my ambition blinded me. Everything happened so fast after that. I outed myself to NYU for using falsified information in a story, which cost me my scholarship. I had to drop out of my grad program without a way to pay for my classes. I needed to break up with Archer, but I had nowhere to go and felt so alone, and honestly, I was afraid of what he'd do. I begged an old friend to let me stay with her for a while just so I could leave him. Archer didn't take it well when I told him my reasons. It was nasty. He punched holes in the walls next to my face as I packed my stuff up, pushed me onto the bed when I tried to move past him, broke glasses as I was trying to leave, so I had to walk through the shards, and he probably would have done worse because he had his hands on me, shaking me when my friend arrived to help me leave and buzzed the intercom. That finally made him stop. The last thing he wanted was for anyone to see him as less than perfectly in control and the greatest."

I stop and take a quick, trembling breath as I sink through the deepest, darkest memories of my adult life. I feel like a wreck, the same mess of a woman I was when Archer was raging at me as I tried to leave. I hear his taunts, his screams, feel the terror, not knowing if I'd make it out alive. All because I'd made the wrong choices.

"Was that the end of things, or is there more?"

Payton is rubbing comforting circles on my back, his voice soft as his caress, but I know he's angry. I can tell by the set of his shoulders and the way his jaw ticks while I talk. He's being so calm, for me, knowing I need this more than him raging against the treatment I received. It softens my heart even more toward this stupid man who just wants to comfort me and make me smile for some reason. He's been so good to me when he's had absolutely no reason to, and now he's proving once again that he knows exactly what I need without me even asking. It gives me the strength to continue the story.

"He was pissed at me and embarrassed that he'd ever be the one dumped, especially by a nobody like me. He hacked into the NYU newspaper server and ran a story that was supposedly by me about the false information incident that wasn't very flattering. Of course my editor retracted it the next day when he realized what had happened, but once something's on the internet, you can't pull it back completely and Archer ensured there are still sites where it lives on, so it's haunted me ever since. I can't exactly get a job at a big-name paper with an unfinished master's degree and unflattering stories that pop up when you do a deep dive while researching my name. Archer made sure of it."

I roll my lip between my teeth and the sting of tears pricks the backs of my eyes and chokes me again. I had everything

I wanted right in front of me. It was so close. Then it was snatched away because I made the wrong choice. I blink and a tear tracks down my cheek.

Payton swipes it away with his thumb and tilts my face up, making me meet his eyes. "You're right about one thing. Archer and his father used you. They manipulated you. You wrote the story you did on the information provided. You did your duty vetting the information. It was substantiated, so you ran with it. There's nothing you could have done differently at the time."

I shake my head at him, having gone down this route so many times in the last two and a half years. "I could've refused to take the information from my boyfriend at the time because he was a bad source. I could've stood on the principle that I was too close to the story, knowing the company was one Donner Investments had an interest in had I only looked a little deeper. Instead, I saw an easy story handed to me and I ran with it. Not only that, I fucking thrived under the attention and success it brought me after. I was so stupid to think I could have a win like that and not have to sell my soul for it. Now I know life doesn't work like that. There are no such things as handouts, favors, or free rides. Life will always expect its fair share for every scrap of luck I receive, and I know I'll have to pay for every bit of good that comes my way."

Twenty-three

Payton

Waking up with Ainsley wrapped around me wasn't how I imagined starting my Saturday after she refused to cuddle before bed. We threw the covers off at some point because it's warm in here with her covering me, even in the scraps of clothing she calls pajamas. Barely there boy shorts and a tiny tank top that leaves little to the imagination made her a walking temptation, yet I somehow managed to refrain from fucking her into the mattress, which is a credit to my restraint.

I blink slowly as the early morning light filters in and glints off her tan leg where it's thrown over my thigh, her small foot tucked under my calf like she couldn't get close enough. Her pussy is snuggly pressed into my hip and her upper body is draped over my torso. Her cheek rests on my bare chest, her hands tucked under my shoulders. I became a life-sized body pillow for her at some point in the night. She's snoring softly and may have drooled a bit, but it's fucking cute that she felt comfortable enough to sleep that deeply. It's nice. I was serious when I told her I like cuddling, even if she scoffed at the idea.

After Ainsley told me her story about the ordeal she went through in New York, I just wanted to hold her longer, but I let her leave my arms and go to sleep. I can't believe she's connected to the fucking asshole I've been dying to get my hands on for the last six months. Learning Archer hurt and manipulated Ainsley, discredited and forced her out of her graduate program, sent her running away from everything she'd wanted for herself, and is now intimidating and harassing her because she's with me made my blood boil even more than him costing my company millions of dollars. He fucking put his hands on her.

More than ever, I want to hurt the punk-ass kid, embarrass him, make him feel small, and show him what it feels like to be scared and powerless the way he's made Ainsley feel. It was business before, but now it's personal. All because of a chance meeting with the blonde spitfire wrapped around my body, who's afraid to embrace her desires and represses her needs because he taught her to fear intimacy and gave her trust issues.

He's fucking up my life even more than he knows. Not only will I make his life a living hell, I'm going to pick up the pieces of the woman he crushed and make sure she knows she's treasured, important, amazing, and so fucking strong. She'll walk away from our arrangement better than I found her. If I can let her go at all.

I tighten my arms around Ainsley's back, holding her to me as I make that vow to myself, grateful for the chance to even hold her and maybe have a shot at helping her come into her own and take down her shitty ex in the process. But at this very moment, I've got a cock that likes her soft body lined up with mine a little too much, and if she wakes up and sees us like this, she's not going to like it, no matter how far we've progressed.

Her hips move against my thigh and she lets out a quiet moan. I stifle a groan of pleasure so I don't wake her. This is exactly what I teased her about last night, and fuck if it's not the hottest thing ever to know she's having a sex dream while I'm holding her. I trace my fingers down her back gently to see if that slowly wakes her up so she's not grinding that hot little pussy against me and ends up embarrassed. I keep rubbing her back, but her hips are moving in erratic attempts to provide her needed friction, and I'm half tempted to wake her up and offer to help.

"Payton," she murmurs into my chest. I look down to see if she's awake now. Her eyes are closed, and she seems to be asleep, so she's dreaming about me as she grinds against my thigh.

"Fuck, Ainsley," I mutter as I let my head fall back on my pillow, not wanting to be a good guy. Instead, I want to pull her on top of me, nestle my cock between her thighs, and let her ride out her dream over my hard length. I don't have to be inside of her to make her feel good, and fuck would that be nice for us both. Instead, I keep my cock out of it and press my palm against the top of her ass and move her hips in a steadier rhythm than her dream motion was able to establish and feel her arousal seeping through my shorts to my thigh. Jesus. Fuck, I want to bury myself in her sweet pussy and feel that for myself. My fingers, my tongue, my cock. All of the above. I groan as the feel of her, hot and wet even through layers of clothing, teases me. Fucking hell.

Ainsley gasps and shudders against me, and I slow the

rhythm of my hand at her back until she's still again. I'm sweating from the effort of restraining myself from turning her onto her back and taking over, but that's not what this is about. She's dreaming, not asking me to fuck her. She can grind against me anytime she wants, but I won't take that as an invitation unless she explicitly offers it. I'm a hedonist in my pursuit of pleasure, but I know she wouldn't be happy if I didn't have her conscious consent.

Ainsley wakes, her eyelashes fluttering against my chest, her body stiffening as she realizes how entwined we've become. She rolls away, untwisting her leg from mine and leaving me cold without the heat of her against me. She sits up, looking confused.

"Good morning, Muffin." I stretch as I look at her surprised face. Her hair is tangled and wild, a crease down the cheek that was pressed to my chest, and her nipples are hard enough to cut glass as she stares at me like I've just appeared out of a horror movie wielding a chainsaw. I don't look that bad in the morning, and my morning breath can't be any worse than hers at the moment.

"What was that?"

"It looks like you're a cuddler after all. I woke up with you draped over me. I told you it was fine, so I guess you took advantage of the opportunity at some point and came over to my side to snuggle."

She shakes her head. "Did I—" she cuts herself off and closes her eyes.

"Snore? Not very loudly. Just cute little sounds that were totally fine."

Her eyes fly open. "I don't snore! And that's not what I was going to say. I was...dreaming." She looks down at her hands twisting in her lap.

"Oh yeah, what were you dreaming about?" I ask as I sit up against the headboard and pull a pillow over my lap to hide the evidence of what having her draped over me and watching her dream did to me.

"Stop it and put me out of my misery. Did I make any noises? Like talk in my sleep or anything...weird?" She's so uncomfortable, I just want to kiss it out of her. She shouldn't be worried about what her subconscious plays out in her sleep.

"Nothing weird. Just some sexy noises that still have me hard." I pull the pillow off my lap to show her, hopefully easing her tension and putting the focus on me instead. I don't want her uncomfortable with her body or her sexuality around me at all.

She covers her face with her hands. "Oh my God, I can't believe I had that kind of dream while I was sprawled on top of you."

"If it makes you feel better, you can tell me all about it in graphic detail," I say hopefully.

She drops her hands and glares at me. "You'd like that, wouldn't you?" she says sarcastically.

"You have no idea." I drop a hand onto my shorts, stroking my cock that's painfully hard, and lean my head back against the headboard. "I'm ready when you are, Muffin. This is better than breakfast in bed."

I'm surprised when the bed dips and I open my eyes to find Ainsley crawling into my lap. She's playful in the morning. I smile as she removes my hand from my cock and picks up the other, lacing our fingers together. She lifts onto her knees so she can press my hands back against the headboard by my shoulders and leans into me until her breasts rub against my bare chest as she slowly settles her ass into my lap right over my cock that jumps at the feel of her hot pussy just a few pieces of clothing away.

Fuck, what is this little minx doing to me now? Does she want to start something I'm more than happy to finish, or is she teasing me? I've warned her that I won't let her tease me for long and I'll take control back if she wants to play games. She had better be ready for a taste of her own medicine if this is how she starts her day.

"I wasn't even dreaming about you, but if I was, it would have been a nightmare where you wouldn't stop smiling and annoying me."

I smile at that and lean forward until our noses are touching. "Liar," I say playfully. "You moaned my name and came against my thigh." I was ready to keep that little fact to myself. If she's going to tease me like this now, she's going to get it right back. "Your pussy felt *so good* rubbing against me, and those noises you make are pure heaven."

Her eyes go wide, busted in her bravado, but I don't give her a moment to get embarrassed. I flip her onto her back below me, getting a surprised sound from her as I settle into the cradle of her hips like I wanted to earlier. Her thighs spread and she wraps her legs around me in reflex, holding me tightly.

"That's my good fucking girl," I growl out at her reaction that could've been to knee me in the balls.

"Oh, wow," she says, realizing how lined up we are.

"You're allowed to dream, even the sexy kind. You don't have control over those things. It's what you do when you're awake that counts, and I want to eat you up after all the teasing you've done this morning." I drop my mouth to where her neck meets her shoulder and nuzzle, breathing in her intoxicating vanilla scent. I lick and suck gently along her neck and she writhes under me.

She sighs and wraps her arms around my shoulders. I try

not to show my surprise since I expected an entirely different reaction. Maybe sharing her story with me last night also changed something for her. She's certainly more receptive to my playfulness and touch today.

"Why do you feel so good even when I don't want you anywhere near me?" she asks quietly, her fingers raking down my bare back. I groan into her neck, making her shiver, and buck her hips up into mine. I press her harder into the mattress for the friction she's looking for and she digs her heels into my ass as she dry humps me with the same ferocity.

"Your body wants me near you, even if you don't. We've discussed this." I trace my thumb along her ribs as I kiss up the column of her neck. I swipe along the side of her breast and she arches against me with a moan.

"Why does it feel all too real when it's supposed to be fake?"

I hum against her neck. "It's only as real or fake as we make it," I answer. I take her earlobe in my teeth and suck before I let it out with a pop as she shivers. "How real do you want this to be?" *Please want me.*

"I don't know," she says, her voice breathy. "This is supposed to be fake."

My heart sinks. I place a kiss on her flushed cheek and reluctantly pull myself off her despite her hands trying to pull me back down. "Until you know for sure, I'll hold the boundaries for you. Now get up and get dressed. We have a full day to look forward to."

The disappointment on her face is worth the case of blue balls I just gave myself. It means she's seriously considering exploring something with me that could feel so fucking good despite this all starting out as a ruse to throw Harlowe off her mission. Now that I've had her submitting to me and woken up with her in my arms, I want her begging to be mine for real.

I stare out over the South Georgia water on the starboard side of the top deck. Up here, I can enjoy the Atlantic breeze that cools some of the oppressive summer heat, reminding me why I like to escape here from Atlanta as much as I do. My phone vibrating pulls me back to the moment as I wait for Ainsley. I pull it out and stifle the groan that automatically rises.

> Harlowe: You've been keeping Ainsley away from us long enough. Bring her to a family function so she gets to know us better. Otherwise, this isn't as serious as you say and you're just fucking around. In which case, I have friends I want you to meet. What'll it be, lover boy?

I tap back a quick response, hoping to cut off this line of inquiry.

> Me: We're taking it slow, remember? I don't want her to get scared away by how insane the rest of you are. I'm keeping her to myself as long as I can.

She's just as fast with her insistent reply.

> Harlowe: Time's up, and you've overused that sorry excuse. We'll see her at the Fourth of July and you should bring her to the wrap party for my show next week. It's at this awesome spot my

production company found and everyone will be there, even Paige, who just
had a baby, so no excuses.

I sigh, wanting to chuck my phone overboard. I don't hate the idea of having Ainsley around my family. In fact, I really want to show them what an incredible woman I've found and impress them with how intelligent, capable, and funny she is. I'm more worried about her reaction to them. Will she freak out seeing how over-the-top in love both of my brothers are with their wives and how insanely protective they are of their families? Will that push her away from me, wanting to avoid that possible fate for herself when she realizes that maybe this isn't as fake for me as it may have started out? Because it's becoming more real for me by the day, and I want to make her mine more than ever. That is, if she'll let me. I'm already fully hers. That was made obvious to me with my knee-jerk reaction, wanting to protect her, and my murderous thoughts toward Archer for his treatment.

"Where are we going?" Ainsley asks, pulling me out of my churning thoughts.

I turn, catching my breath as I take her in. She's in cutoff jean shorts and a cropped white tank top, looking like a summer dream, the briny ocean breeze ruffling her golden hair that shines in the sun.

I hand her an iced coffee and wrap an arm around her waist, leaning back against the railing. She leans into my chest and takes a sip of the light drink I made for her. She makes a happy sound and I know I made it how she likes.

"We're headed out to one of the barrier islands. I thought you might be interested in helping with a project of mine tonight. I have a foundation that contributes to the Georgia

Department of Natural Resources sea turtle recovery efforts. During nesting season, we can help with their efforts to track Loggerhead turtle nesting sites." She twists in my arms and looks up at me, her hazel eyes crinkling in mirth.

"You keep surprising me. I thought you were just a friend-less, boring, workaholic businessman with too much money. Now I know you're a sex-crazed tech nerd who likes sea turtles and spankings."

I tip my head back and laugh. "Wow, you think highly of me, don't you?"

She tips her head back and forth. "I'll admit, you may be growing on me. Like a fungus."

"So complimentary in the mornings, aren't you, Muffin?"

"Well, you did bring me coffee."

She laughs as I spin her around so she's facing me. "And I helped you have an orgasm on my leg. That has to count for something."

She smacks my chest with her free hand. "Oh my God, you really don't stop, do you? You can't take credit for what happens in my dreams."

I drop my hands to her ass and roll her against my thigh much like I did this morning. "I can take credit for moving your hips in a better rhythm and letting you grind on the most unfulfilling parts of me. You pick spots I never would have chosen for your pleasure, but if that's what you want, I won't stop you." I tilt my head toward her and raise my eyebrows suggestively. "Though I'll remind you that I have a very nice cock, magic fingers, and a filthy mouth all happy to be taken off the bench."

Ainsley's mouth opens, eyes blinking as she processes my rapid-fire statements. "You what? Good grief, Payton." She laughs and shakes her head. She steps between my legs, leaning into my body. I clasp my hands above her ass. "I may be amenable to taking your favorite playthings off the bench," she says, looking down at where my hips are pressed into her stomach before bringing her eyes up to mine and giving me a cheeky smile that I really fucking like the looks of.

"Oh, really? I knew I'd convince you." I roll my hips against her and she laughs before giving me a stern look that isn't nearly as powerful as most of her surly expressions.

"For research purposes. To ensure we sell this arrangement in public, and maybe because I'm curious about what else you can do," she says with a roll of her eyes as a flush creeps into her cheeks.

I nod in understanding. "You want to keep playing with me, but you still don't think this can be serious." I don't even touch the topic of real or fake with her now. She's barely on board with this much.

"Should it be serious? I barely know you and you immediately asked me to fake date you to throw your sister-in-law off her mission to set you up. You've been hell-bent on making me uncomfortable with your Daddy vibes and slut talk even though I have no idea how in the hell you figured that shit out when I had no clue it was something I'd want."

I cup her cheeks and push my fingers into her hair, tipping her chin up so she meets my eyes. "If I have Daddy vibes, you have your own vibes I was drawn to and wanted you to be aware of. When you responded the way you did, even that first time, I knew you were absolutely perfect for me, and if you wanted, I'd give you everything you need to fulfill those repressed desires."

I smooth my thumb across her cheek and down to her pretty pink lips that are parted as she listens to me speak. I trace the Cupid's bow of her top lip before I drag the pad of my thumb down to her bottom lip gently. I keep my eyes trained on her lips where my thumb rests as my tone changes to one of patient dominance.

"Do you want me, Princess?"

"Yes, Daddy," she says sweetly, eyes on me as her lips part, sucking my thumb into her mouth that can be so vicious when it wants to be, yet just passively told me I can take care of her and be in control, at least in the bedroom. A shudder rolls through me at her acceptance and first serious use of the honorific.

She's going to be mine.

Twenty-four

Ainsley

Telling Payton I want him and I'm willing to explore this Daddy-Princess thing didn't result in him taking me back to the bedroom to fuck me while calling me his filthy little cumslut like I thought it would. Instead, he smiled and kissed my forehead before taking my hand and leading me to the dining room where a breakfast spread was set out for us. He pulled out a chair for me at the dining table and asked what I wanted to eat, then made us both plates of food while I tried to figure him out.

I feel emotionally hungover after unloading on him last night. He took every sordid memory I unleashed and validated my experience in the most calming, comforting way imaginable. He didn't swear to kill Archer or to make up for what I'd experienced. He just sat with me and listened, hearing my pain and loving me through it. Wait, nope. That's a clingy koala thought. *Slow down, you slutty demonic koala.* Just because you've decided to fuck him does not mean you need to show up claiming to be in love. Back the fuck up.

I frown at him. "I'm perfectly capable of getting my own food and you're a billionaire with staff to do this. Why are you insisting on serving me like this?" I ask as he sets a plate piled with waffles, fruit, bacon, and scrambled eggs on the table before taking a seat next to me.

"I want to. More iced coffee?" He motions at my empty glass. It was perfectly made, just the right amount of vanilla creamer, and the ice hadn't melted, so he must have allowed the coffee to cool before he made it. It's really thoughtful and attentive because the stupid man pays attention to everything and I wish I could fault him for it.

I snort a laugh. "No, one coffee is fine. You think I'm wound up and cranky with multiple caffeinated beverages."

He leans over and traces his nose along my jaw to my ear, where he whispers playfully, "I like you bratty and unfiltered, Spitfire. Remember that the mean things you say do it for me just as much as the rest of your...very...impressive...package," he says, nipping at my neck with his teeth between each word, causing my head to roll to the side for him as he traces kisses along my skin.

Good Lord, he knows exactly what to say and do to make me crave more. My nipples are painfully hard and goosebumps rise over my skin when he finally pulls his lips away.

"Should I put on my glasses and scold you so you'll do that again? Or what was it you said? Push my skirt up and fuck me on the table?" I taunt, but it's a little breathy and less sarcastic than intended.

Payton's eyes grow dark with desire as they dart between me and the table, and I know he's thinking of doing just that.

"Mmm," he growls, and it vibrates deep in his chest as he catches his bottom lip with his teeth, staring down at me. Fuck, that's so sexy. "I like you being a little cocktease. You want me to fuck you so badly now, but you have to wait. We have plans and they don't include a marathon sex session right now, as amazing as that sounds. Be a good girl for me until I get you all to myself later. I want you wet and squirming thinking of what I'll do to that needy cunt. You'll be begging for my cock before the day is over. Just know I'll have you coming on my fingers and mouth before I ever give it to you. You'll be a dirty little whore for me today, right Princess?"

I nod, pressing my thighs together as my core throbs with each filthy word he utters in that commanding tone of his that sucks me in. "Yes."

He takes my chin in his hand and gives me a look that says he likes me in this obedient state. "Yes what, my perfect cumslut?"

I know what he's looking for, and I'm willing to give it to him despite how foreign it feels to the independent, controlled woman I am in my everyday life. There's a part of me that thrills to use the term with him, to give up control and place my trust in his hands in a safe space, knowing it'll precede something my body and mind needs for whatever reason. "Yes, Daddy." I tremble as I say the words and he smiles.

"That's my good girl."

He releases my chin and caresses his hands down my bare arms, smoothing over the goosebumps his deep voice and dirty talk cause. He brings my hands to his lips to kiss my knuckles.

"Please eat your breakfast before I feed you by hand."

I laugh as he drops my hands and turn back to my food, feeling lighter, though now I'm wet and squirming in my seat, just the way he wants me.

We take a tender boat into Jekyll Island and Payton treats me to a day of touristy activities. He takes photos of us every time we stop somewhere he deems picturesque, or he likes the background for a selfie. He's posting them regularly to his personal social media pages, knowing his family and the thousands of people who follow him will see them, for the purpose of spreading our couple status. He's really convincing at playing a besotted boyfriend, and it's pretty hard to distinguish the lines between real or fake with him when he keeps pulling me back into his arms, kissing my head, and tucking me against his side, even when no one's around to see us.

My text notifications are going off like crazy, mostly from Della wanting to know how things with Payton are going, and what we're up to, so I give her regular updates. She's thrilled, obviously, and wants details, but I don't have much I can say. She hearts my photos when I send her a few I've taken of us, including one where Payton is standing behind me, his arms wrapped around my shoulders, kissing my head while I scrunch my face up in a mix of a smile and grimace. Her response is in all caps and curse words, so I think she's both shocked and happy.

I'm also getting regular nasty messages that I know are from Archer, and I keep blocking those unknown numbers. Payton notices each time I tense up or sigh in frustration but doesn't say anything. He pulls me closer and runs his fingers through my hair or smooths his hand down my back until I relax again.

He doesn't seem to mind that I pull my phone out often while I'm with him. He just gives me an indulgent look and smiles when I catch his eye as I finish up whatever I'm typing. I take plenty of photos of him looking incredible against the coastal backdrop and historic scenery for research purposes. And maybe for my own use. The man is drop-dead gorgeous, after all.

We visit the Mosaic Museum where Payton patiently allows me to pull him along as I learn the history of the island and the stories of the people who shaped it during the Gilded Age.

"I could fuck you properly in the back seat of a car like that," he whispers in my ear as we pass a classic Studebaker on display in the middle of the museum. "Should we try it before more kids crowd inside?"

I raise my eyebrows at him. "Are you trying to get arrested today?" I hiss as I drag him away from the car when he looks a little too serious about his suggestion. "That's certainly one way to make headlines."

He laughs. "Harlowe's asking how serious we are and if I need her help finding a girlfriend I can be serious with, even after all the stories in the Haute List about us. I need to up my grand gesture game and make sure something a bit more outrageous runs so she knows the rumors are true and I'm completely crazy about you."

My face heats when he says that, even though I know he means it all for show. I shake my head at him in warning. "We should be out in Atlanta if you want the Haute List to be running stories about us. We shouldn't be spending so much time alone. No one is going to recognize us here in South Georgia on a barrier island doing tourist stuff."

He turns, wearing a sardonic smile, and taps me on the nose. "That's where you're wrong, Muffin. We've had at least five people take photos of us since we stepped onto the island this morning." His smile drops as he pulls me into his side when we exit the museum and he grows uncharacteristically serious.

"I didn't even notice." I'm shocked to hear this. I look around, expecting to see paparazzi stalking us now, or at least some tourists with cell phones pointing our way that I'll be able to see for myself, but I don't see anything out of the ordinary.

"I'm used to it since I see it more than you're used to, even though you've had a taste of that sort of *fame* now that you're with me. People think they have a right to take pictures of me and my family and write shit about us and our personal lives. We never asked for that. We run a business that happens to do well; we're not celebrities. Well, Harlowe's a celebrity, and she knows how to handle that, but the rest of us are far more private and never asked for that life."

I feel a prick of guilt, being lumped in with the journalists and people who've written about his family.

"You're all public figures. It comes with the territory," I say, sounding defensive. "You're incredibly fascinating. Not many people find the kind of success and wealth your family has. It makes a compelling story, and that's good journalism to write what will sell papers. Your business deals and the things that happen at your level make waves that affect the world and markets at large. Of course it's going to make the news, and so will you."

"If it stopped at our deals and what happens during business, sure, but what about all the after-hours stuff? Gossip sites have hounded my brothers and their wives from the beginning of their relationships. Pictures of their kids are splashed across the internet all the time. Pregnancies were announced and baby names were shared online before our extended family or friends were even told about them. They can't even go out to dinner without the outing becoming a story. That's not business, that's invasive."

"I'm sure the gossip sites just see it as y'all being people of interest." My heart pounds as a wave of fear passes through me. This feels like a black mark against my profession, something he holds against me as a journalist. I'm in damage control mode. "You can't really blame them for seeing your family and wanting to write about everything that happens to you because you're Southern gods. All of you are insanely good-looking, ridiculously wealthy, and blessed beyond belief when it comes to every business deal that comes your way, with lives that seem like fairy tales or far more interesting than average. Even the bad stuff is worthy of reporting on because of who you are. You make for epic entertainment, fair or not."

He pulls me off the path toward a secluded stand of ancient oaks ringed by fat-headed, pink hydrangea bushes and pushes my back against a huge oak tree dripping with Spanish moss. He leans an arm on the trunk over my head as he looks down at me with a troubled expression. "Now I'm using the same gossip machine against my own family for personal gain, and I've forced you to be a part of it. It's fucked up."

I reach up with one hand to smooth the tension from his forehead and he leans into my touch, closing his eyes. I slide my hands behind his neck and pull his head toward me as I press up on my toes, molding our bodies together, which brings our lips a breath apart, hoping to provide what little comfort I'm able to, given my job is part of the problem causing his distress.

"You're doing what you have to."

I hate seeing him troubled, and it's a peek inside the head of a mastermind. I know he carefully crafts every move and calculates his plans, but this is the first time he's shown that he feels the weight of each one far more than he lets on.

"I'm always doing what I have to, not what I want to. I put Olympus, my family, and everyone else, first. It's the only way to keep what we've built intact and moving forward."

"You're a good man, but you shouldn't have to sacrifice everything you want to make all that happen."

He seems vulnerable for the first time and it makes me want to cut my skin open and pull him inside with me so we can be raw together while I keep us safe with my prickly exterior. It increases my growing feelings of attachment. Sirens for the warning system I put in place after Archer devastated me are wailing now. Still, I can't help my natural inclination to want to be close to someone who opens up and shares themself with me, who turns the spotlight of their attention on me, who holds me and shows me affection and gets the good feelings flowing that turn me into a red-flag-waving, clingy koala bear that won't let go even when I know it's no good for me. I pull my face away the slightest, hoping to give myself space to remember why I don't do attachments now, but can't bring myself to fully disengage, wanting this closeness even more than self-preservation. *He's not Archer. This isn't the same.*

"My life is about sacrifice. That's my role. It's not about what I want." His eyes finally meet mine. He keeps his face close like he needs the contact to be this open.

"What do you want?" I ask, threading my fingers into his hair and looking for some way to comfort him now that he seems to be opening up and dropping the enthusiastic and overly smiley thing he's had going since I met him. Maybe that's his own armor, like I use my attitude and prickly persona. It wouldn't surprise me. It must be exhausting to be that *on* all the time. He's genuinely nice and happy, but he's allowed to feel something other than enthusiasm and excitement. He can experience the full range of human emotions, rather than simply the good ones that people expect of him.

"I want you to let go of your control with me, give in to what you actually need, and let me show you what unguarded pleasure looks like as I take care of you completely. I want you."

My breath stutters as I process his request and my warring thoughts. Fuck it. *I want him.* It's more than just wanting his dominant side that spanks me, or wanting to introduce sex into our fake relationship. He's shown me this other side, one that's not masked by his easy smiles and carefree attitude. He's given me so much with this admission and openness that I want to do the same. I let my thoughts and intentions spill into my face, finally letting down my guard, not wearing my anger and hostility to keep him away. I need him close and I want him to know. I brush my nose against his gently as I lick my lips, wondering if I'm going to have to initiate this first kiss, or if he will. I nod my acceptance slowly.

"I want that, too."

"That's it, Princess," he breathes as his hands circle my waist, pulling me up his body.

I hold on to his shoulders and wrap my legs around his hips while he closes that tiny distance, crashing his mouth down on mine. The soft petals of the hydrangeas tickle the skin of my legs. A quiet moan escapes when his tongue teases my lips apart and I let him in, eager to taste and feel more of him. His hand tangles in my hair, pulling tight and angling my head as I gasp into his mouth. He rumbles a pleased groan as he kisses the hell out of me, but he does it slowly and thoroughly. The scent of green foliage, damp earth, the sea salt and amber smell of him surround me, and I'm lost in the feeling of Payton against me.

I bury my fingers in his soft, dark hair, keeping him just as close. My tongue tangles with his, tasting mint and man, realizing he's my new obsession. He kisses me slowly like he's learning every bit of my mouth without hurry, teasing out a desire that has my body burning with need. I grind my hips against him and he rolls his slowly in answer, matching the cadence of this kiss, staying slow, hungry, deep, like he's fucking my mouth and my pussy against the tree.

I whimper as so many sensations wash over me all at once. The bark of the oak against my back. The petals of the hydrangeas. The feel of Payton's cock rubbing my clit through our clothes. His hair in my fingers. Hot breath and low groans mixing. I'm in a frenzy of lust and he's so unhurried, and—oh God, we're right off a public path and someone could see us. My eyes fly open as I pull away from the kiss and grip his shirt to make him stop.

"We shouldn't be doing this here," I whisper, my voice coming out husky with need because I don't want to stop but know we definitely should. I try to look around his shoulder to see how far off the path we are and just how much of our PDA someone can see.

Payton hasn't stopped moving his hips in that slow, hypnotic rhythm, his thick, hard cock rubbing against my clit continuously, and holy shit does it feel good and it's just dry humping. What's this man capable of without his clothes on? A giddy feeling rushes through me, knowing I'll find out. I tip my head against the tree, panting from holding myself back while wanting him.

"We're not stopping until you get off, Princess. You're coming like this with your clothes on or I'll get on my knees, rip your shorts off, and bury my face in that sweet cunt and eat you right here for anyone to see. Tell me what you want, baby girl."

A flood of warmth greets his words and my core clenches,

tipping me over the edge of my release. He slams his mouth over mine, catching my moans, and lets me ride out my release while he kisses me senselessly. He slows our kiss even more, stilling his hips against mine, and peppers my face with soft kisses as I breathe hard through my come down.

"You were right," I say, the words coming out breathy and low as I keep my eyes closed, head tipped back against the tree trunk.

He chuckles as he kisses down my neck. "About what, exactly?"

"You can make me come with words alone. But friction helps."

He lets out a deep laugh and buries his face into the hollow of my neck and shoulder. "Yeah, it really does. And you actually used my cock to get off this time. Such a good girl," he purrs, and it sends a shiver through my body. He straightens up and gently sets me on my feet, fixes my clothes, and smoothes my hair. "You look freshly fucked and those perfect, puffy lips can't be helped. Just the way I like it. I want everyone to know my little fucktoy was just used and is freshly satisfied."

I blink at him and bring a hand up to my mouth. My lips are a bit puffy from our kiss, and I'm sure I look like a hot mess, but damn, if that's what he likes...I laugh. I brush hydrangea blossoms and bark off my legs as he adjusts himself discreetly, and I realize that he got me off, but he didn't come.

"I can take care of you." I reach for his shorts and he gently grabs my wrist, stopping me from dropping to my knees.

"You're my priority, and I'm satisfied. You'll be dripping with my cum later if that's what you want."

I shiver at his dirty words and the promise in them.

"I have an IUD, and I haven't been with anyone in years. I want to feel you inside of me when you fill me with cum."

I look up at him shyly, not sure if I should be asking this or if that's what he's saying. Payton's eyes widen in shock and quickly transform into a look of intense pleasure.

"Fuck, baby, you can't say shit like that to me."

"Never mind." My heart hammers hard as I realize what I've asked for.

He backs me into the tree again so I feel him, hard and ready, pressed against my stomach. He grips my chin and makes me look up at him. "You want me to fuck you bare and come inside your pretty pussy, Princess?"

I try to pull away in embarrassment. "Just forget I said anything."

"I can't forget it. I don't take that lightly. I've never fucked a woman bare, but goddamn do I want to bend you over right now and have my way with you. I won't be able to stop thinking about it, and that means I'm going to do it. Jesus, Ainsley. It's one thing planning to have you choking on my cum and decorating your beautiful body with it, and another thing to fill your tight pussy with it. Fuck, I want to see you dripping now." He scrubs his palm down his face as he looks at me and my face burns red hot, but I can't stop my lips from twisting into an embarrassed smile.

"How was I supposed to know you were all talk? I saw it so vividly in my head; my mouth, pussy, and ass full of your cum. That's all I've been able to think of around you." I give him an innocent look and his eyes go nearly feral with desire. I like knowing I can get him to lose control like this.

"Stop talking or we'll get arrested for indecent exposure for sure. I'm half tempted to put you on your hands and knees on the grass right here and fuck you stupid, but I want you somewhere more comfortable the first time I get you naked and fuck you the way you need to be. Let's get out of here. Our day isn't done."

I take the hand he offers me as we leave our secluded spot, which I'm happy to see was well hidden from anyone who could've wandered by.

Twenty-five

Payton

Ainsley has a needy cunt face.

After her resistance and pushing me away with her prickly anger for so long, it's a welcome change. She's trying to play it cool, but she keeps studying me when she thinks I'm not looking, and whenever I catch her, she's biting her bottom lip, hazel eyes hungry, and I know she's thinking about when I'll fuck her. My perfect little cockwhore is so ready for me.

I take her to lunch. I touch her constantly. I buy her ice cream and tease her mercilessly outside of the shop while I lick her fingers clean. Finally, she groans and bangs her head against my shoulder.

"I give up. You win. You're better at this game than I am.

Just take me back to the boat and fuck me already, please."

I tip my head back and laugh before bending down and kissing her sweet lips, getting her eager moans. I pull away and look down at her. "I never thought you'd admit defeat, my beautiful little warrior woman."

"It's not defeat. It's getting on the same page. There's a difference," she corrects, slipping her hands under my shirt to caress the skin of my back. It feels damn good, and I like the idea of her initiating the contact.

"I like you on the same page with me. It's definitely time to go back to the boat."

The bright smile on her face falters as her vibrating phone distracts her. She pulls it out of her pocket and swears softly as I catch another unknown number text with vile words harassing her. I grab the phone out of her hand before she can block the number like she's done with the rest.

"Hey," she protests, reaching for her phone as I read the full message, keeping it out of her reach.

> Unknown: A pathetic whore like you would get on your knees for any rich man who showed you the slightest interest and promised you a story. What's he offered to make it worth it? Answer me, you filthy piece of trash. That Olsen fucker is a shit stain on the world and you need to stay the hell away from him.

The more I read, the hotter my temper grows, and it takes everything to keep from hurling the phone on the ground. I'm the calm, collected one of my brothers. I don't usually have a temper, and I certainly don't rise to insults or let anyone get under my skin these days. This isn't even directed at me. It was sent to Ainsley, and I want to beat the shit out of Archer for thinking he has any right to send even one word of the text to her. How the fuck dare he? If he has a problem with me, he should man up and come to me with it, not continue to send her nasty texts, trying to get her to stay away from me.

I turn her phone on silent and pocket it so she doesn't have to deal with the asshole any longer. I don't want him to take her peace away or put a damper on our time together. I turn and see her worried look as she searches my face.

"Let me take care of those texts. I hate that you're reading even a single word of that nasty fucker's vitriol, and if you let me, I'll install a program that will route any unknown numbers directly to my phone so I can track and deal with him in my own way."

Her face falls, suspicion darkening her golden features. "You have a program that would route things from my phone to yours? Sounds like something I've been through before."

Of course she'd be hesitant to let me do anything with her phone after Archer showed her the worst a partner could do to her with his jealousy and manipulation, tracking her phone and controlling her. I take her hand and start toward the marina again. It's time I shared just how connected our paths are.

"You remember the Olympus cyber breach last winter?" I ask.

"Of course," she answers, sounding puzzled.

"I have good reason to believe Archer Donovan was the hacker behind the attack. I've been looking for a way to tie him to the breach. I reverse-engineered the program he used to get into the Olympus servers, but it hasn't helped. He's good, and I hate to admit that because it means he got through the system I designed without leaving a trace other than a signature in his code that alluded to a bow and arrow, for Archer, I guess, because he's an arrogant fucker," I mutter. "This aligned with information we received a week after the attack. I've hated the slimy weasel for what he did to my company—getting into our systems, stealing proprietary information and plans for the Pegasus project, selling them on the dark web, and allowing our competitors to take the jet engine to market before we could, which cost us millions—but now that he's harassing you, I want to fucking kill him."

I run a hand through my hair, flustered by the uncharacter-istic anger and emotions to protect what's mine. I feel more like my brothers than I ever have before, and I finally get it. I have something in my life that I would go to war for, and it's a fucking fake girlfriend who smells like vanilla and coffee and fits in my arms like she was made for me. Ainsley is more than a plaything or a means to an end to avoid Harlowe's matchmaking. She's someone I want to take care of, to protect from assholes like Archer, and to repair the damage he's done to her heart. She's someone I want to...love.

Ainsley's eyes are huge, her lips parted in shock as she processes all I've told her as we approach the marina where the tender boat is docked. "Archer was the hacker," she says, shaking her head as her brows draw together. "And you need proof that the code was his."

"Yes. Apparently, he's a hacker for hire and does this shit all the time but hasn't been caught, so his signature is known, but he doesn't take credit for it, and it can't be linked to him di-rectly. It's fucking infuriating to have the information offhand but not be able to link it concretely. I can't take hearsay to the authorities, and it wouldn't stand in court either way."

She looks away, staring out over the choppy water of the marina as I help her into the boat. She takes a seat next to mine while I unhook ropes and push the boat away from the dock, before starting the engine and navigating us out of the marina.

"I'm sorry. I know what it's like to be on the receiving end of Archer's wrath and destruction," she says, finally meeting my eyes. I swear there's guilt clouding her hazel depths, but I can't pinpoint why she'd feel guilty about Archer now. Maybe she feels bad that he's texting because of the Haute List stories about us. "You can put the program on my phone if that will help you."

"Who knows if it will get me any closer to connecting him to the cyber attack, but it'll make me feel better that he's not harassing you anymore. I'll monitor how often he's messaging you and what he's saying, and I'll fuck with him a bit to see if he likes a taste of his own medicine."

He might not like the hateful messages when he's on the receiving end of things, and I can be just as persistent as he seems to be. He'll be getting some very special messages from me just as soon as I fix Ainsley's phone.

We stow the tender boat on the yacht with help from Eamon and Brockway, and I follow Ainsley into our cabin, feeling her subdued mood. Archer Donovan is more than a nuisance. He's also a cockblocker, and I'm adding that to the list of reasons I hate him. I'm going to fix this texting issue first.

I grab my laptop from my work bag, pull out a cable, and connect her phone directly to it as I settle at the table in our room and get to work. Ainsley takes a seat next to me and watches over my shoulder, probably to ensure I don't fuck with her phone any more than I've said I will. She doesn't even have to put in her passcode for this to work, so I pull up a program I created called Delphi and see every unknown number that has texted her recently.

Archer's been a busy boy, and he's been heinous with his treatment. Every one of his messages has been disgusting. How has she managed to go on with her day like nothing's happening, smiling, enjoying the tourist crap we've done, entertaining my whims, and playing up this fake dating shit, when all along she was getting these nasty messages? She's a stronger woman than I knew. I'm so fucking impressed by her.

I grab my phone and see all the numbers now in my inbox. I pull up another program I've created called Theseus that can work for this purpose and initiate a spam system, adding all those numbers to the registry. I quickly type in a handful of horrible messages of my own that should give him a sample of what I want to start him out with and then get creative with even more. I want him to need a shower because his soul feels dirty after he reads these. I let the program AI learn from my messages and set it to produce more messages and additional sending numbers as needed when he inevitably blocks the first before I close out my side of the program so it can run without my assistance. I disconnect the phone and hand it back to her.

"It's done, and you shouldn't get anything more from him. I'll take care of this."

"You're really an evil genius, aren't you?" she says warily, having just witnessed a side of me most don't get to see.

I gave up my hacker days in college, and haven't been this vindictive for about as long. I learned that carrying a chip on my shoulder or always one-upping others didn't make me feel any better, for the most part. Carrying that weight around just made me feel heavier, whereas I could let it go and allow people to sort themselves out in their own time without my interference and it would serve just as well.

However, in some cases, I'm willing to turn to my old ways and take the situation into my own hands to make sure it's dealt with efficiently without waiting for karma or fate to get around to it. This is justified vigilantism.

"You could say that. He more than deserves it." I sigh when I see she hasn't softened at my explanation and probably still thinks I'm just as bad as her manipulative ex. "Believe it or not, I was bullied a lot growing up. I wasn't always six-two and full of lean muscle. I was your height and nerdy as hell until I was fifteen. Hayes was always huge, Zander was always hot, and I was always too smart for my own good. Kids are cruel, and when my brothers weren't around, I got shoved into lockers, beaten up, called names, and picked on. I hated it. So I got back at people the only way I knew how. I outsmarted them every chance I could and I had to get creative. I hacked into the school servers to change test grades that caused my bullies to fail classes, made school-wide automated announcements calling John Williams a micro dick panty sniffer, and even revoked college admissions from a few of the worst offenders. That one nearly cost me my spot at MIT, but I somehow got through it on school probation. I was a mean little shithead and angry at the world, but I fucking hate bullies. I'll do anything to make sure a bully is put in their place, and that's what I'm doing with Archer Donovan."

"Wow, you're also a vindictive tech genius." The wary expression finally leaves her pretty face. "I'm sorry I ruined our afternoon with my ex drama. I hate that he's still controlling what happens in my life years later. He shouldn't be able to do that. It makes me sick."

I gather her up into my arms and walk her over to the bed, placing her sideways on my lap so I can take her shoes and socks off.

"Consider Archer Donovan handled and you won't have to hear from him ever again." I kiss her temple. "And he can't ruin anything for us. There are no expectations for this, Muffin. If you want to take a nap, watch a movie, swim, or spend time alone, that's what you get to do. It doesn't matter what we talked about before. You have the power for what happens now, got it?"

She turns and straddles my lap, putting her arms around my neck. "I was so ready, and then he had to go and cockblock us and it's frustrating. It feels like there's a malevolent presence in the room and my thoughts are racing now instead of enjoying what I was looking forward to."

"Sounds like I need to get you out of your head and make you forget about any other man but me."

"Please, I need you to fuck me," she begs, her eyes beseeching as she pulls me closer to her.

Twenty-six

Payton

Ainsley begging me to fuck her is beautiful.

I take that as all the invitation I need. I grip her perfect ass in my hands and pull her flush against me as I crash my mouth down on her soft pink lips, teasing them and making her work for the deep kiss I keep just out of reach. I bite her bottom lip playfully and she moans, her tongue swiping out, looking for mine. I finally meet it, tasting her and feeling all the want and need surge again. It takes so little for me to lose myself in this woman. One taste and I'm gone for her.

I want to see her naked, spread out under me, to trace every line of her body, to feel each dip and curve of her. My fingers tangle in the hair at her nape and pull gently. She groans, her tight body rocking down on my cock, which gets harder with each touch and kiss. Her fingers fist in the neck of my shirt and she pulls, gathering the material and yanking it off until we have to separate. I toss the shirt on the floor and return my mouth to her neck as her fingers trace over my skin, sending shivers of longing racing through me. I love it when she touches me.

I trace kisses along her collarbone and down the neck of her tank top to the swell of her breasts as I inhale the sweet vanilla scent of her that gets me fucking high. I groan with my face between her tits, my tongue swiping out and licking along her skin, tasting what I've only imagined, and it's as sweet as I hoped. Her fingers are in my hair, holding me right where I want to be. I slide my hands up her ribs, lifting her tank top and pulling it over her head, my hands returning to her waist as she shivers and I trace the sides of her breasts. I hook my thumb in the material of one cup and pull it down, letting her tit pop out into my waiting mouth to swirl my tongue around her dusky pink nipple that's so tight. She's a perfect handful, just enough for me to suck and bite and make her feel so fucking good, given the way she's rocking in my lap and the sounds coming from her mouth. I unclasp her bra and pull it away, her arms untangling eagerly.

I pull back to take her in, savoring the moment I get to see her bare tits with her pink nipples straining for attention, her blonde hair falling over her shoulders and shining around her in the golden afternoon light that slants in through the windows. She's a fucking dream.

"Why'd you stop?" she pants, her lips red and puffy from kisses, her eyes heavy-lidded and needy, but there's hesitation on her face. I need to replace that right the fuck now and ensure she knows she's safe, treasured, wanted.

"I'm deciding what I like most about your gorgeous body, my perfect little fucktoy. These perky tits with the most delicious nipples I've ever tasted that I want to see covered in cum, or the cunt I haven't even explored yet but know I'm going to worship with my mouth as soon as I get these shorts off."

Her eyes close and her whole body rocks with a tremor as she moves in my lap. I smile at the visceral reaction my words have on her. She really is so perfect, and God does she like dirty talk. She scoots off my lap and stands, her hands coming to her shorts to pop the button and unzip them slowly. I lean back on my hands and watch with a smile as she shimmies the shorts over her hips and stands in her blue cotton panties in between my spread knees.

"My shorts are off. Now what, Daddy?" she asks, a taunt in her tone. Ah, my bratty baby girl is here to play.

"Show me how wet you are, Princess. Slip your fingers in your panties and touch your needy pussy."

She slowly slips her hand down the front of her panties and cups herself. Seeing the outline of her fingers and knowing she's feeling her arousal that I'm dying to taste has me aching for her. She withdraws her hand just as slowly, her middle finger glistening, and I groan at the sight of it.

"You're soaked, baby," I growl.

She nods and holds her hand out for me. I take it, slip her finger into my mouth, and suck it clean, groaning at the taste of her. That's all it takes. One taste of her pussy off her fucking finger and I'm dying to have her. I lean forward to pull her panties down her legs until she steps out of them and take her hips in my hands so I can shift her onto the bed.

"Um, this hasn't worked before, but you're welcome to try," she says breathily from the pillows as I kiss down her stomach toward the most alluring pussy I've come across. I've thought about this exact moment with my hand wrapped around my cock so many times over the past month, and none have done it justice. Her pussy is pink and gorgeous, groomed and glistening with need, ready for me.

"Are you saying you've never had an orgasm from being eaten out properly, or that no one took the time to do it right?" I kiss along her hip bones and into the crease of her leg, bite her inner thigh, and suck until she gasps.

"It's always been an uncomfortable experience."

She sucks in a breath as I lick her from slit to clit with a groan before moving to her other leg and kissing her hip.

"What was uncomfortable?"

"I couldn't get there, no matter how hard they tried. It was too soft, just not enough."

"The boys you were with before were amateurs. I'm going to show you how a man pleases his Princess. You'll forget every other before me. This pussy is mine. Say it for me, my perfect little cumslut," I command, moving up to where a little blonde landing strip points me exactly where I want to spend the rest of my days. I eat pussy like it's a sport, but for Ainsley's sweet snatch, it'll be the fucking Olympics and I'm going for gold.

"This pussy is yours, Daddy." Her voice is a breathy plea as she writhes against me.

Fuck, that sounds good. I trace my fingers up her legs and grip her hips. I kiss back down her pussy and bury my tongue inside her, tasting her sweetness and groaning in pleasure. I point my tongue to lap at her entrance greedily while she writhes, but she's not letting go completely. She's probably in her head, worried about something that shouldn't be an issue. I want her to lose herself in the moment with me, to feel every ounce of pleasure I can wring from her body.

"Fuck, you taste so good. Ainsley, baby, I've never wanted

anything more than I want your pussy in my mouth. You're so goddamn perfect. This is the prettiest pussy I've ever seen. Every part of you is incredible." I'm delirious with desire, caught up in what craving her does to me. I drop my mouth back to her center and feast, feeling her relax at my praise.

She squirms and I press her body into the bed with my forearm and reach for a nipple, stroking and mounding her breast in my hand before rolling the tight bud in my fingers. I suck her clit and slip a finger inside her. She gasps and her pussy tightens around me as I caress her. God, she feels so good and it's only one fucking finger. What's she going to feel like on my cock? I slip a second finger in and stroke her rhythmically, pressing into her spot and feeling it swell with each pass while I continue to suck and flick at her clit, pinch and roll her nipple. I'm dexterous and used to multitasking. This is nothing.

I find a pace she seems to like, feeling how her body responds. I listen to the noises she makes, paying attention to the way her nipples tighten and her skin flushes, what makes her eyes close, and the way her back arches and toes dig into my sides, and I do more of that. This moment is seared into my brain, the memory one for the ages as the best fucking pussy I've ever eaten and the woman writhing under me the best fucking thing to come from a chance encounter.

"Oh, I'm close." Ainsley gasps, her hips rolling into my face, and I let her ride it out as she holds her breath just before she gets there. She's still struggling to maintain control, not wanting to relinquish it, desperate to keep her walls in place despite all we've accomplished to get here.

"Let go, baby," I command, dropping my mouth back to suck her clit, pressing into her G-spot with my fingers hard enough to nearly lift her off the bed, and she finally breaks, releasing the death grip she has on her control and going wild in my arms.

"Payton!"

Hearing her cry out my name is the most amazing thing. Her fingers pull at my hair and grip my arm where it rests against her stomach. Her pussy clamps down on my fingers over and over as the orgasm crests, and I coax her through it, drawing out each contraction of her body and eliciting moans of pleasure long after her initial release. Her limbs release me, falling to the bed as she finally settles, her body going limp and relaxed under me. I cover her pussy lips with kisses as I gently pull my fingers out of her gold medal pussy and suck them clean, relishing the taste of her.

Holy shit. If that's what it feels like when she comes on my fingers, squeezing the life out of them, I'm going to lose my fucking mind when I bury my cock in her tight cunt and she comes apart around me. Fuck, I get to feel *that* bare. I push up on my elbows and lean over her, seeing her looking sated, with a sleepy smile on her face.

"You're so fucking beautiful when you let go, Princess. I think you'll look even better with my cock buried inside that tight pussy. Do you think you've earned it yet?"

Twenty-seven

Ainsley

I'm ready for Payton to deliver on all his filthy promises. That was the first time a man has made me come from going down on me, already a huge win in my book. What he did with his mouth and fingers should be illegal because I'd do literally anything to feel that again. If what he just did were a drug, I'd be addicted after that one hit.

I've never come so hard, by myself or with a partner, and it was with his mouth on my clit and his fingers in my pussy. I normally get too up in my head about having someone down there, wondering if they actually like it or if they're just going through the motions. Archer once said my pussy lips look weird and compared them to lunch meat, and I wonder if I taste funny because he didn't like it, so it didn't happen often.

Every time we tried it, I was thinking about anything but getting off, so it just never happened and we both ended up frustrated until I'd fake it or we moved on. But Payton pushed every thought out of my head with his enthusiastic praise and how he devoured me. All I could do was *feel* him and what he did to my body until he told me to let go and I was free-falling. He's right. He'll replace every other partner because he's that much better than anyone I've had.

"I think you'll look even better with my cock buried inside that tight pussy. Do you think you've earned it yet?"

I tip my head back and my whole body shudders in need.

"Yes, oh God, I want you."

I lift my head and meet his eyes, my hands reaching for his face and pulling him toward me. He's still half-dressed and covers me with a barrier between us when I want him naked. I make a frustrated noise as I look down at his shorts.

"My cockwhore doesn't like being denied." He chuckles, thoroughly amused. He brushes hair out of my face as he holds himself above me on one forearm and traces my lips with his thumb. "I want to hear how pretty you beg for my cock, Princess. Put this smart mouth to work." He nips at my lips.

What the actual hell? I already told him I need him. He knows I want him to fuck me. We're on the same page. Why does he need me to beg? But his damn deep voice is commanding and the way he's looking at me makes me want to do exactly what he asks, which overpowers the part of me that wants to rebel out of spite and tenacity.

I blink, my lip pouting and his eyes track the movement. I wrap a leg around his hips and pull him flush against me, shorts and all. I trace my finger across his lips and roll my body against his.

"I want your cock so bad, Daddy. I've been dying to see it,

to taste it, to feel it, to have you buried inside me since the day I met you."

My voice is needy, husky with the heaviness of my desire for him. I reach for his face and pull him down until I can rub my cheek against his and luxuriate in the feel of his afternoon stubble rasping against my skin. I pull back enough to meet his stunning blue eyes, seeing the heat and need that mirrors mine.

"I've dreamed about your cock and the dirty things you'd do to me, and now I want you to make my dreams a reality. Please fuck me. Pretty please, Payton." I make sure he knows I want *him*, all of him, whether it's a Dom, a Daddy, or the man who makes my coffee just right. I know they're the same person, anyway.

"Such a good girl." His voice breaks as he captures my mouth with his and kisses me deeply. He pulls away, still staring at my face with that pleased expression as I pout again. He backs away, standing to remove his shorts with a grin like he knows I can't take my eyes off him.

I push up on my elbows to watch, eager to finally see what this man has been teasing me with. He pushes his shorts over his hips, his boxer briefs straining to contain the hard length of him. When he pulls the waistband of his underwear away and his cock springs out, I make an audible whimper because good God, he's huge and hard as he grips the base and strokes up his shaft to the crown while I watch. And holy shit. He's...pierced. A column of silver barbells runs the length of the underside of his shaft, probably six in all. *He's ribbed for my pleasure.* It's so fucking unexpected from the billionaire businessman who wears suits and is a total tech nerd. But he does have a dark side and is familiar with the pleasure of pain, so it shouldn't surprise me that much. I want him even more now. I moan in longing, needing to feel the metal-studded cock for myself.

"My needy girl wants this cock. Crawl for me, Princess, and I'll let you have a taste."

I'm on my knees and crawling to him, my eyes riveted on his hand and the way he strokes himself over the metal. Dicks don't usually garner titles like beautiful or make my mouth water, but Payton has a work of art between his legs, complete with jewelry. I want to touch it, taste it, and learn every ridge and vein. It's calling me like a damn siren and I'd crawl over glass for it.

"My greedy little cockwhore. Show me how good you can take me. Open your beautiful mouth. I want to see you choke on my fat cock." He taps my cheek with the head of his dick and I smile from my knees, thrilled at that filthy promise like the twisted woman I am. "Get it wet and messy, Princess. I want to see you drooling around me like the fucking animal you are."

I moan and let Payton guide me as I settle in front of him. My hand replaces his and his fingers thread into my hair, gripping hard to control my movements. I smooth the moisture at his tip over the broad head with my thumb on my next stroke while licking my lips and he makes a feral sound of pleasure. I look up at him as I slide his cock slowly past my lips, realizing how impossible it'll be to take much of him given his length, but I can do what he wants. I'll make a mess of us both.

His eyes are blue fire as he watches me work his cock in and out of my mouth, drool pooling and leaking from my lips as I swirl my tongue around his length and feel the unfamiliar bumps of his piercings stroke across my tongue. His hips buck as his fingers clench against my scalp on each harsh thrust and I relish the pricks of pain that radiate into a warmth of pleasure that skates down my spine. I grip his thigh and hollow my cheeks, breathing through my nose to take him deeper as he pistons into my face. He groans as I stroke and twist my hand up from his base to meet my lips, slipping on the drool that's coating my hand now. He takes his fill of my mouth while I take my fill of him, loving the salty taste of his precum as I lick and work him deeper down my throat on every stroke until I feel the sting of tears in my eyes. He pulls back on my hair sharply just as I reach my limits, gagging and choking on him just like he said I would.

"Your mouth is too good, Princess. You only get a taste. You can have a mouthful of my cum another time. I want to be fucking your pussy the first time I come in you." His voice is strained, the words harsh as he fights the urge to keep fucking my mouth instead.

I let his cock pop out of my mouth, a string of drool connecting us, and lick the tip, making it jump. I wipe my mouth delicately, wanting more, though he keeps me just out of reach with his hand fisted in my hair. "Promises, promises," I tease.

He laughs and bends down, lifting me into his arms and falling onto the bed with me as he peppers my face with kisses. "I want to fuck this tight little pussy. You want this cock?" he asks, teasing my entrance with the head as he thrusts against me, hitting my clit and sending shivers dancing across my skin as those magical piercings provide extra stimulation.

"Yes." I gasp, moving with him.

I lift my leg over his hip and angle my body to catch his next thrust. He fists his cock and drags it to my opening, pushing in slowly. The exquisite fullness has my head dropping back, a moan leaving me. I can feel every delicious inch of him as he works his cock in, my body is so ready for him but I still need him pulling out and thrusting back in to take him all the way.

"Fuck, you feel so good," he grits out as he pauses once our hips finally meet. He dips his head to my chest, his tongue drawing my nipple into his mouth and sucking as I wrap my arms around his shoulders, loving the feel of him everywhere around me. He fills me so perfectly. His big body covers me entirely.

"Show me what it's like to be your fucktoy. Make me your cumslut," I rasp into his ear, wanting to know what all his talk has been about.

The smile he wears when he raises his face from my breast is pleased, and it sends my heart pounding against my ribs hard enough he has to feel it.

"I knew you were a brat, but I should have expected you to try to top from the bottom also." He laughs. "So my little cumslut needs to be used hard until she knows what a fucktoy feels like. Hold on, Princess, I'm going to fucking wreck you and you won't be able to walk straight tomorrow."

"All talk until you prove it," I say, rolling my hips under him and making him groan. I'm growing more confident the longer he stays still, wanting to see how far I can push him to fulfill every dirty taunt he's made since we met.

"Nothing about me is all talk, Princess."

I gasp as he smoothly sweeps his arms under my knees and pins them up by my shoulders, spreading me wide and folding me in half as he pulls out and slams back into me. He does some *Magic-Mike*-type shit with his hips, thrusting into my pussy with a force that leaves me breathless and hits exactly right but also rubs over my clit with a precision focus that has me seeing stars by thrust three. I'm chanting his name now, and on the next wave-like thrust of his cock, the breath leaves my body. I'm having a religious experience, proving that the god above me pounding his perfect cock into my pussy is deserving of a freaking cult following.

"Oh, God, Payton, fuck, I'm..." The orgasm that detonates is quick to break and unexpectedly strong, sending my head back and my hands clawing at the bed as I moan his name, but he doesn't stop. He rides me hard through the waves, leaving me gasping and shaking, unable to move from the folded-up position he put me in.

"Take it, you filthy fucking slut. Look at you coming apart around my cock, squeezing me like you want my cum. You like being used like this, don't you?" He pushes my legs together against one shoulder, making me infinitely tighter around him as he fucks me relentlessly.

I moan and clench around him harder as I grip the pillows where my hands are fisted next to my face as his words set off another flutter of pulses. Fuck, he's going to do me in with his words and the way he moves in me. I can't get away from the assault of pleasure with how he's turned me into a pretzel. I don't want it any other way. This is the best sex I've ever had, and it's the first time Payton has fucked me.

Once my pussy semi-recovers from the earth-shattering second orgasm of the night, he pulls out and I think I'll get a breather. Instead, he rolls me over, yanks my hips up, and widens my knees by shoving his thigh between mine, pushes back inside my pussy, and shows me how amazing he feels from behind.

"Oh my God." I gasp into the bed, the side of my face pressed down flat as he fucks me, and I feel him deeper as he bends over me. He wraps a hand around my neck to hold me in place while the other finds my clit, circling as he continues to thrust into me.

"Your pussy feels so fucking good, Princess. Your whole body was made for me. Look how well you fit tucked into me like this as I fuck you like a whore. My perfect little fuckdoll, taking my cock so well as I stretch this tight cunt that I'm going to fill. You're going to take it and you're going to love it, aren't you, my beautiful cumslut?"

"Yes," I whine, completely lost to the sensations. Another orgasm builds at his filthy words and at the way his cocks hits me on each thrust as his fingers circle my clit. He knows just how to touch me, where to angle his hips, and what to say to have my body respond. The pressure is building low in my belly and I'm gripping the bed in anticipation, my body tensing. "It's so good. Keep doing that." I gasp, feeling unintelligible. He's fucking me stupid.

"Stop resisting."

"I'm not." I push up onto my elbows to argue, but he squeezes my neck where his hand rests and forces me back down.

"Let go and come for me, Princess. I want you strangling my cock with this tight pussy. Squeeze the cum out of me, baby. Take every. Last. Fucking. Drop," he growls, his hips slamming against my ass in a punishing rhythm before he slaps my ass, hard.

My mouth pops open in surprise for a moment, but his grip subdues me and I feel more of him while thinking less. Once I release the tension, the orgasm hits me, my knees giving out as the waves roll through me and I moan my pleasure into the mattress.

"Fuck, Ainsley," Payton growls as I pulse around him, my pussy holding him tight. His thrusts become more erratic until his hips press hard against my ass and I feel him swell and release with a feral groan as he falls apart right along with me, whispering incoherent praise and curses.

It takes me a moment to gather my wits and realize the gravity of our situation. What the hell was that? That wasn't sex. That was something a million times better that only he could deliver.

He lets go of my neck and smooths my hair away from my face as he pulls me up onto my knees to lean back against him, his cock still pulsing inside me. I'm limp, barely able to raise my arms to wrap around his neck as he holds me to his chest. His heart beats wildly against my back, matching the frantic hammering of my own as I try to steady my erratic breathing. He runs his hands across my breasts, tracing long fingers down my stomach to where we're joined as he lifts me off his cock with one thick arm wrapped around my waist. He places his chin on my shoulder and watches the path his hand takes. He cups his fingers in my pussy and I look down to see him rub his cum along my inner thighs like paint.

"My own personal cum canvas. You wear it so well, Princess. I won't be able to get enough of you. Fuck, I love that you're full of it right now." He presses his fingers back against my pussy, pushing his cum inside of me and sweeping his thumb across my sensitive clit. "You're fucking mine now."

I shiver against him and he holds me tighter, his hand splayed against my stomach. His mouth finds my neck, biting the skin and sucking, marking me possessively. I whimper and let my head fall back on his shoulder, surrendering to the feel of his mouth on my body, needing more of this from him. I want to wear him with me everywhere, have his marks on me, to be his. I've let down my walls and given in completely. I'm fucked.

There's a reason I don't date and won't do casual sex. I can't. I get *attached*. I'm a fucking clingy koala. The way I'm feeling right now, in Payton's arms, lets me know I didn't grow out of that particular habit with a few years of celibacy and staying out of the dating scene, or by gaining my prickly attitude and wrapping myself in anger after leaving my last bad relationship. I'm not sure if I can handle the kind of obsessive, all-consuming desire I'm feeling after fucking him just once. I want him in every way. I want to belong to him, to have all of his attention. To be his sole desire. It's a sickness I thought I could cure myself of with time and an attitude change. Instead, it seems I've found someone even more addictive and overwhelming. The inner slutty demonic koala has won.

I'm in way over my head with Payton, and I may have just sealed my fate by giving him my body and letting him fuck me bare. I have no control over my growing obsession, and if he's feeling even a portion of that, too, there's no hope for me. He's looking at me like he won't be letting me go when our fake dating arrangement is over. I can't decipher whatever's in his deep blue gaze and what that means for my independence. It reminds me far too much of the look Archer got when he realized I'd be a challenge and he wanted me. I quiver, and it's only partially from post-orgasm aftershocks.

I know through the way he holds me, the way he wants to mark and possess me, that he felt the same thing I did. We may have just fucked for the first time, but there was something very different about the way we connected, the way our bodies responded to one another. The way *we* respond to one another. I don't know what he thinks, but it doesn't matter if this is real or fake to me. My brain has flipped the switch and decided I'm done for either way.

I'm terrified of the power Payton Olsen holds over me. I'm far too willing to do anything he asks of me and would give him anything he wants, including every piece of my soul. I just need to keep him from realizing he has this ability when he's been too good at picking up on my every tell so far.

Twenty-eight

The Atlanta Haute List

Billionaire and Blonde Escape Atlanta For Weekend Rendezvous

The Haute List has readers throughout the great state of Georgia keeping tabs on our favorite new couple, Payton Olsen and Ainsley Montgomery. The pretty pair were spotted on a South Georgia barrier island looking cozy and cute and setting tongues wagging about their relationship. It's pretty clear from the photos and accounts that were sent in by our Hauties in the know that these two lovebirds are getting hot and heavy and are making their fling into a thing. We were fanning ourselves when we saw the photos of their quick tryst outside of an ice cream shop and how pleased they both looked about Payton licking ice cream off Ainsley's fingers. Where do we sign up to hang out at cute ice cream shops with dripping cones waiting for our own billionaire to swoop in to clean us up?

While we still can't explain the draw of a lowly journalist for a billionaire businessman, we're happy to see the last eligible Olsen brother finding love and settling down after watching his brothers experience familial bliss of their own. It's still early on for the pair, but with the way the Olsen men work, it may not be long now before he's locking her down. We'll be watching and reporting. Remember to hit Like and Subscribe for all the Haute gossip!

Twenty-nine

Ainsley

I can't wait for my day to end. I have plans with Payton. Big plans. Now that I know what his dick feels like, piercings and all, I'm taking every opportunity to enjoy it. I just have to get through another fifteen minutes of work and he'll pick me up for a trip to his lake house for the Fourth of July celebration he's famous for throwing. I have a bag packed and I'm anxious to leave, not getting much done the day before a holiday. I can tell the whole newsroom feels the same, with casual conversations and a lackadaisical approach to work permeating the air.

The front door to the office opens and I look up. Hope rises that it's Payton arriving early. My stomach sinks when I see who it is instead.

Archer Donovan. Cold sweat prickles along my hairline, my

stomach knotting as he casually looks around, examining the humble space I've ended up in. When he spots me, I shrink as if that will keep him away. He gives me a cold smile of triumph and starts toward me.

I want to run, throw up, scream for someone to make him leave, but I do nothing. I'm rooted in place, my tongue stuck in my dry mouth as bile rises in my throat. This is a living nightmare. His texts were bad enough, but seeing him in person brings back every horrible feeling and emotion of the year we spent together. It reminds me of my failures and fuckups and how easily he manipulated me, then discredited me when I wanted to get away from him.

"Ainsley, look at you," he croons when he gets to my desk. "You've really taken a turn for the worse, haven't you"? He stands over me with his hands in his pressed trouser pockets, a cruel smile playing on his lips. His blond hair is longer, but his sky-blue eyes are just as sharp and cunning.

"What are you doing here, Archer?" I ask when I find my voice. It comes out shaky and low, my eyes darting around to my coworkers, who are watching our exchange curiously. I never have visitors who aren't here for a story, so they think he's either here for interview purposes, or it's personal. It's way too personal, and I don't want him exposing everything that happened between us in front of everyone.

"Can't I visit an old girlfriend to *catch up*?" he answers. He's here for more than a catch-up session, and this can't be good.

I stand quickly, feeling unsteady in my heels, and attempt to push past Archer toward the door, expecting him to follow. His hand snakes out and grabs my upper arm, just hard enough to let me know he's serious but looking to anyone else like he's helping to steady me when I wobble a little. My skin crawls where he touches me and I want him to let go, but I don't make a scene, letting him half drag me out of the office into the shade of the building facade. Maybe out here we can have whatever conversation he came all the way from New York to have. I hate that I'm still afraid of him, that he can have power over me like this without repercussions. He's a menace and I want him out of my life for good. I'm tired of hiding from him, worrying about what he'll do to me if he's unhappy, and being scared of him.

"Cut the shit. You don't have any business in Atlanta and you don't care about me enough to want to catch up. Why are you here?" I ask again, my anger bubbling through my fear.

"Payton Olsen isn't who you think he is. Whatever lies he's feeding you to get you to fuck him are just that. He's a sick sonofabitch who destroys businesses and breaks up families. You saw what they did to my dad's company and now my father's in prison because of them. You can't trust him."

"That's rich, coming from you!" I seethe, unable to stop myself. "You and your dad are just as bad. Andreas took advantage of companies in the same way and didn't have any scruples about saving family businesses. He took what he wanted however he could and used anyone to do it. You're no better, you fucking nepo baby with a giant fucking chip on your shoulder. You're so insecure, you have to make yourself feel bigger by hurting others." The words rush out of me in a torrent fueled by years of hurt. *Holy shit, did I just say all that?*

Archer's eyes narrow and I see the moment he snaps. His grip on my arm tightens and he shakes me until my teeth clack. My head spins and my heart races, realizing he's dangerous and could hurt me, for real. I look around for help, but the parking lot is empty and no one's around to flag down easily. I could try to go back inside, but he'd be able to stop me before I made it three steps. Oh, fuck, this is so bad, and I've made him even angrier. I can only hope there are security cameras somewhere capturing this, or someone will drive by and take pity on me.

"You dumb clingy bitch. You can't see what's right in front of your face. He's using you for media coverage and doesn't care about you. Why would he want someone as broke, ugly, and stupid as you, when he can have anyone he wants with his money and connections? You're a means to an end for someone like him. I'd know. I used you for the same thing, remember?"

My heart clenches and my stomach feels like I've swallowed hot rocks that are burning me from the inside out. He hits on every insecurity I have, flaying me alive and staking me where I can be picked apart the easiest. He knows just how to fuck with me, every button to push. I have to get away from him. He's not the kind of person to see reason and come to a compromise with. He escalates and gets worse unless you appease him. I'm not about to stroke his ego and fall back into those old habits of our relationship.

I pull against his grip as I push his chest with my other hand. I have to get away from him. "Fuck you."

His other hand grips my neck and squeezes, cutting off my words and forcing me to look at him as I fight for breath. My hands latch onto his arm, trying to pull away, but he's relentless, a cruel gleam in his eyes.

"You would want to fuck me again, you sloppy, degenerate whore. But I don't do repeats with the same trashy, bad lays," he says cruelly. "I don't want you, but you sure as hell aren't fucking Payton Olsen. I see you with him again and you're going to regret it." He squeezes my neck and shakes me again, forcing a cry out of my clenched teeth when it goes beyond what I can tolerate.

"Let me go," I beg hoarsely, holding back tears and grasping onto anger so he doesn't see just how badly he's hurting me. I wrench my arm hard and pull free of his grasp, using both hands to pry him off my throat. It hurts like hell and I flinch, which thrills him.

"Touch her again and I'll put you through that wall, motherfucker."

We both spin around at the growled threat. Payton's stalking toward us through the parking lot, his eyes deep blue flames, face set into a menacing scowl, anger radiating off him in palpable waves. He's scarier than I ever imagined he could be, but to me, he's a beacon of hope and safety, my harbor in this shitstorm, and the one I want to tread water for me when I feel like I'm drowning.

He doesn't stop, grabbing Archer by the shirt and around his neck, and lifts him off the ground before slamming him into the wall of the building. Archer looks shocked, his face gone bloodless, eyes wide. He's never been handled like this in his life, not knowing what it's like to be on the receiving end of treatment that scares the shit out of him.

"Do you know who I am? You're going to jail for touching me!" he squeaks out, finding his outrage at this treatment, sounding unbelieving that anyone would look at him as anything less than a god worthy of worship.

Payton growls, pulling Archer off the wall, only to slam him back into it, forcing out a breath and rattling his head against the brick with a sickening thud that makes me cringe. Oh fuck. Payton's not exhibiting the tight control he usually does. I might not be able to stop him now that he has Archer in his grasp after everything Archer's done.

"I know exactly who you are—a blight on this world. Listen closely. I won't be repeating myself. Harass her and I'll make your life a living nightmare. Look at her and I'll carve out your eyes. Put your motherfucking hands on her again and I'll cut them off and feed them to you digit by digit. Come for my girl and I'll end your miserable life. Got it?" His voice is deep, serious, vibrating with wrath and menace, unlike anything I've heard from him.

I hear a splattering sound and see Archer's pissed himself. I gasp in shock, Archer whimpering in embarrassment. I take a step toward them and place my hand on Payton's back, trying to soothe him.

"He's not worth it. Let's go."

Payton doesn't look at me, a muscle ticking in his jaw as he keeps his eyes locked on Archer's terrified face. "Bullies get the treatment they dish out. Remember that. You put your hands on my girl, payback is tenfold." He squeezes Archer's throat until he gurgles painfully and shakes him. "If I see you again, you're not walking away." He glances over at me. "Did he touch you anywhere else?" he asks, sounding murderous.

"No, just my arm and neck. Put him down. Seriously, he's not worth it. He's nothing."

His jaw clenches, his stare returning to Archer, who visibly shrinks under the scary look. "You're lucky I don't end you now and do this world the favor it deserves." He snarls, tossing Archer to the side so he stumbles to his knees.

Archer stands and collects himself as much as he can with wet pants, a disheveled shirt, and his hair a mess from being shoved against a wall and shaken like a ragdoll.

"You're going to pay for this, Olsen." He points a shaking finger at us as he walks backward toward his car. "You just signed away everything you've ever loved or wanted. You're going to regret putting your hands on me." He turns and walks quickly to an unfamiliar black BMW, slams the door, and peels out of the parking lot while we watch.

Once the car's out of sight, Payton turns to me and gently cups my face in his hands, his expression now one of concern, though his features are harder than usual. "Are you okay? Where did he hurt you?" He doesn't wait for me to answer, his hands softly running down my neck and shoulders to my arms and pushing up my sleeves to where Archer was gripping my arm. He hisses out a breath and scowls. "I should have knocked his teeth out for marking you."

I look down and see the red mark from Archer's tight grip on my arm already starting to bruise. "I don't care about that now that he's gone. Let me get my bag from inside and we can leave. We'll put this behind us. I don't want Archer to ruin another thing for me."

"He put his fucking hands on you, Ainsley. He hurt you." His voice breaks and he shakes his head, jaw clenching again. "He came here to intimidate you, right? To say more horrible things and get under your skin because of me. What did he say?"

"It doesn't matter what he said. Archer sucks and he's gone now. You scared him so bad he pissed himself and that means he's going to come back swinging the only way he knows how, which is at me. Just let it go. You've done enough and I don't want to think about this."

"*I've done enough*?" he repeats, his voice rising. "I'm trying to protect you and put that punk-ass kid in his place. I want him to know it's not okay to touch what's mine, and he has no business harassing you."

I'm mad, confused, and scared, and this isn't helping anything. I don't want to fight with him after dealing with Archer's bullshit. Payton has no right to claim me like that when all we're doing is faking it in public and opening ourselves to sex because it's fun, not because he thinks it's real.

He's acting out of possessiveness, not because he's in love with me, and he doesn't like seeing another man's hands on me because he thinks of me as his property.

"Stop pretending I mean anything to you. I'm playing a role for a stupid favor and you're getting something extra out of it now that I've let you have my body. That's all I am, a fake plaything to enjoy for a short time to meet an end goal. You couldn't possibly want me for real because I'm not your type. I'm so beneath you it's stupid to even pretend that you'd want me, so it's better if we don't bring sex into the mix anymore. It'll just hurt me more in the end," I say, balling my fists and pressing my nails into my palms to anchor myself when my mind is spinning down dark paths Archer opened up.

"Don't you fucking dare," Payton says, the words coming out in a low whisper laced with the rage I heard earlier directed at Archer.

I shrink inward and close my eyes, putting up the walls he so recently dismantled. I shouldn't have let him in. This is it. This is when I see the other side of the happy-go-lucky guy he's presented this whole time. This is when he shows me his true colors and I'll know what I'm dealing with. I take a step back, letting his hands fall from my arms. My heart beats erratically in my chest and adrenaline surges through me, prepping me for fight, flight, or freeze. I have to leave before my instinct to freeze kicks in so I won't be stuck with another abusive asshole. I'll put myself first this time.

"Don't put yourself down or say you're not my type. You're perfect for me and I want you. I'm not fucking you as a fake plaything. It's because we have a connection and you're someone I want to give my body to. I sure as fuck hope you feel the same because we're good together. I'm drawn to you." He snarls an exasperated sound and pauses, running a hand through his hair in agitation as he looks up at the sky. "Fuck it. You need to hear everything I feel, no matter how crazy it sounds." He levels me with that churning sea stare and I freeze. "This isn't casual and it's not a game. You're the fucking moon controlling my tides. You mean...everything to me, Ainsley." His words are hurried and passionate but not angry. He's desperate for me to understand him, I realize.

I blink and look away from the unguarded emotion he's showing me. This isn't good for the attachment and obsession I'm already feeling. His words draw me in and make me hope for more when I know I shouldn't. It doesn't matter what nice things he says now. We have a three-month contract. When it's over, there's no reason for him to want to keep me around, connection or not. I have to remind my heart that, as good as it feels to be wanted by him, to have something special, and to hear his words now, there's no guarantee I get to keep him at the end of this. I sigh in defeat.

"Fine. Let's go to the lake."

"Fine? That's how you end a conversation after an encounter like that and me fucking pouring my heart out to you? You want to suppress your feelings and not deal with the emotions of seeing Archer again, let him get into your head, and pick a fight with me because I want to make sure you're okay? We're not doing this your way, Princess. We're doing it mine." He bends and tosses me over his shoulder, his arms banding around my thighs as I shout a protest. He ignores it and marches me inside the building. "Which one is your desk?"

My face is hot with embarrassment from being carried over the shoulder of my fake boyfriend in front of my coworkers, who are staring openly, some laughing. I point at my desk. He walks to it, picks up my overnight bag and purse, slings the straps over his other shoulder, and turns around to leave. At the door, he pauses for a moment.

"Happy Independence Day. I'm taking my workaholic girlfriend to the lake a little early and this is the only way I can pry her away from work." He turns back around after his explanation and exits as I wave sheepishly and see Reid smiling at me.

At his Range Rover, he places me in the passenger seat and hands me the seat belt before stowing my bags.

"You're a caveman," I accuse once he's settled and we're pulling out of the parking lot.

"You bring out my more primal side, Princess. Now take off your panties and spread your legs for me."

There's no question. It's a command and I'm compelled to obey without further argument. I huff in annoyance but a thrill goes through me as I shimmy out of my panties and hold them up for him. He takes them from me and runs them under his nose with a groan before they disappear into his pocket. Fuck, he's sexy with his unabashed desires and willingness to act on every one.

"Put your right foot up on the dash. Good girl," he praises when I follow his direction. His hand moves under my skirt to the apex of my thighs, fingers sliding through the slickness at my entrance from the anticipation of whatever he's going to do to me. He drags the wetness to my clit and rubs it in circles, causing my hips to roll into his hand. He pinches my clit and I jump. "Now tell me why you think you're not good enough for me while I make you come. We'll see who gets their point across first."

It's a game he is unequivocally skilled in and gives him an advantage that has me coming faster than I can try to explain how my brain works and why I think he couldn't possibly want me. He makes me come four times on the drive to the lake and I forget that I'm supposed to be arguing my point with him. He has me seeing fireworks brighter than those that pop and burst over the lake the next night as we spend the evening around the pool at his beautiful lakehouse with his family and close friends. Through it all, Payton makes sure I know I'm wanted with every action and word, reassuring me at every turn that I'm enough for him. It feels good to be wanted, and it sinks me deeper into my obsession with him which will be even harder to climb out of should he decide to be done with me at the end of our contract.

Thirty

The Atlanta Haute List

Billionaire Brawls Over Blonde In Broad Daylight

Who could bring the mild-mannered middle Olsen brother to violence over his pretty paramour? That would be Archer Donovan, son of incarcerated business rival, Andreas Donovan. Sounds juicy, right? The details become even more sordid the more we dug. Archer was previously connected to Payton's lady love, Ainsley Montgomery, while she attended New York University. We even received unconfirmed accounts saying Archer has anger issues and their relationship ended badly.

We did some snooping and found dirt on Ainsley from her time at NYU with copies of her last story that was quickly retracted from the Washington Square News, the NYU student newspaper, that painted her out to be quite the lethal opportunist. However, a letter from the editor that followed refuted the story. It alleged that *an unnamed bitter individual* had hacked into the NYU journalism department's server to post the unflattering story about Ainsley. It hinted strongly at the person being a disgruntled former lover. Ainsley was quickly forced out of her master's program and sent fleeing to Atlanta shortly after all this went down in New York. We'll go ahead and name him if that editor wouldn't. We're disgusted by that allegation and wish all the worst to Archer for his part in that situation.

Archer in Atlanta now makes us believe he's not too pleased seeing his former flame moving on. The bad blood between the Donovans and the Olsens probably doesn't help, making Archer look more desperate and pathetic. Archer, honey, bless your heart. It's time to return to New York, where you belong, leaving our billionaires and their relationships alone. We're pro-Olsen on this blog and won't tolerate New York interlopers stirring up trouble in our city. As always, hit Like and Subscribe for all the Haute gossip.

Thirty-one

Payton

My phone vibrates on the boardroom table, drawing my attention from the meeting with the city planners for the arena project. Heads all around the table look my way and I smile disarmingly as I make a carry-on motion. Fuck. This is not a meeting I want to be interrupted by an errant notification about a new Atlanta Haute List story or something else I'm keeping tabs on. Hayes sends me a venomous look, letting me know the faux pas has not gone unnoticed, no matter how quickly I silenced my phone and slid it off the table. I look down to put the offending device on silent, only to see Ainsley calling.

My heart lurches. She never calls me during the day. She's made a habit of rarely reaching out at all. I hate having to send her to voicemail, but this meeting is incredibly important, and I have another hour until I can call her back. I return my attention to the meeting, tapping a finger against my tablet in agitation. This could be an email, but we have to smooth over every little wrinkle with the city to stay on their good side so we can force through our building plans faster than they'd typically approve construction plans. Everything hinges on keeping them happy.

My phone buzzes in my lap and I look down, seeing a text from Ainsley.

> Princess: I'm sorry to call. I know you're working. I just got off the phone with my apartment manager. A water main broke and our whole floor is flooded. I don't know what to do. You're the first person I thought to call.

Fuck. She's coming to me for help. She's vulnerable and telling me she *wants me* when she needs help the most. And here I am, a fucking asshole, not picking up her call. I run a hand through my hair and look around at the city officials and my brothers in the boardroom. They're more than capable of handling this meeting without me, no matter the importance of the deal.

Ainsley needs me. She knows I can take care of her when she needs me the most, and I'm not about to disappoint her when she finally gives in and realizes it. I stand and collect my things.

"Going somewhere, Pay?" Zander asks with dangerous calm from across the table.

"Sorry to run out. I have an emergency. I hope you understand." I direct my brightest smile at the city planners. "You're in good hands with our team. I apologize for leaving like this."

"Payton." Hayes's voice carries a note of warning, like he's about to grab me by the collar and yank me back into a seat. "I'm sure whatever it is can wait."

I turn a lethal gaze on Hayes, letting him know there's no arguing with me right now. I'm leaving, even if I have to bull-doze my way through both of my brothers.

"My girlfriend needs me." I look at the faces around the table with calm resoluteness. "Here at Olympus, we put our family and loved ones before business. I hope you understand," I direct the last bit to our guests, who nod in confusion, looking between me and my brothers.

Hayes and Zander are brooding and unhappy but not about to stop me now that I've pulled out the family card. Both of them have established that their families come before work, and if I'm using that rationale with them, they know this is serious. I get a nod of acknowledgment from Hayes and a hand wave from Zander, who turns back to the table and moves on to the next topic of discussion as if my interruption hadn't occurred.

I pull my phone out as soon as I leave the boardroom, texting Ainsley on my way to the elevator.

> Me: Where are you? I'll be there as soon as I can.

She texts back almost immediately as if she's been holding her phone, waiting for my reply. It breaks my heart that she had to wait even this long.

> Princess: I'm headed to the apartment to see if I can salvage any of my things. Della says it's bad. There's a foot of standing water and it's coming in from the ceiling.

Most of our stuff is ruined.

Me: I'll meet you there. Don't worry about anything. I'll replace whatever you need and we'll pick up any necessities before we go home tonight. I'll take care of you, baby.

Princess: I hate this so much *crying face emoji* I don't want your help.

Me: I know, Princess. Good thing you're mine to take care of.

When I pull up to Ainsley's apartment, restoration vans are parked outside, and crews of workers move in and out of the apartments, creating piles of soaked drywall and collecting rolls of sodden carpet on the sidewalk. I scan the area, looking for Ainsley before I head up to her floor and find her wearing a pair of pink rain boots, standing in a foot of water that's collected in the hallway outside of her apartment. She looks lost, holding a duffle bag at her side as she stares inside.

"Ainsley," I call as I close in.

My feet slosh through the water, ruining my Prada leather Oxfords in the process. It's worth it when she turns and hope lights up her despondent face. I open my arms and she buries her face into my chest as I wrap her in a tight hug that I hope can hold her together when everything feels like it's falling apart.

"Thank you for coming," she says, finally pulling away from my chest but not letting me go. It seems she needs a lifeline in this flood, and I'm good at treading water for us both. "I'm sorry to pull you away from work in the middle of the day."

"Shh," I say, kissing her forehead and stopping her apologies. "You needed me, so I'm here. What can I do? Anything inside that I need to grab?"

She shakes her head and tears well in her eyes. "I got what I could. My personal documents and my laptop from my desk that stayed out of the water, some clothes that didn't get wet, and my toiletries. Everything else is destroyed. It's bad." Her voice breaks. "Who knew an apartment could flood that quickly? It's insane the damage water can do."

Just then, Della, Ainsley's roommate, sloshes out of the apartment wearing yellow rain boots, looking just as sullen as Ainsley.

"We can probably come back for our dishes and things that can be cleaned. Our furniture is toast. Hey, Payton," she says, seeing me holding Ainsley in the hallway. She can't muster a smile, stress evident on her face as well.

Luca will likely be taking care of Della after work. I learned he spent the weekend with her after they met at the bar when Ainsley and I went to the coast. Now he's mentioning her frequently and seeming a bit attached himself, unusual for the cold almost-sociopath. He's not even divulging the details of their sex life the way he normally would, which leads me to think he's gone over her.

I can relate.

Fucking Ainsley is a religious experience. She's a drug I became addicted to with one hit. There's no other way to explain it. Coming inside her changed my brain chemistry. I was a different man after that first time, and now everything I am is rewritten to her code. I wanted to keep her in my bed, learning her body and giving her all the pleasure possible, but the point of heading to the coast together was to show her the work my foundation, the Trident Trust, does for sea turtles. We almost didn't make it out of bed that night to track the nesting sites. It took all I had not to pull her into the dunes and have my way with her again in the dark.

Once I had her back in bed, I kept her there, coming on my face, my hands, and my cock until she was begging me to stop. But we both knew the only words she could use to make me stop would be to call out red, and she never did, so she finally passed out from pleasure. I got to clean her up, put her in one of my old MIT shirts, feed her, and read aloud from the smutty romance book she brought while she lay in my lap and I played with her hair until she was sufficiently recovered to be fucked again. We repeated the whole thing until we had to fly back to Atlanta.

She was even a total trooper at my Fourth of July party, handling my family admirably. She slipped into host mode alongside me, complementing everything I normally do so beautifully. The best part is watching the change in her from a reluctant partner in my schemes, not wanting to be touched and rebuffing every attempt to get to know her, to thriving under my attention and care. She's warming to having someone she can depend on.

Ainsley shifts in my arms and I'm jostled out of the rosy memory of when everything changed for us and brought back to the dreary reality in front of me.

"I guess there's nothing else we can do. The building manager said it could take a few weeks for everything to dry out and the work to be completed. We have rooms at the extended stay hotel they've arranged for displaced tenants. It's not fancy, but I don't need much. I'll head over there now and see what I need to replace immediately."

"Like fuck you are," I growl, an unfamiliar feeling rising in me. It's protectiveness morphing into possessiveness. "That's not safe enough for you. You can both stay with me. I have plenty of room at my loft."

"That's nice and all, big man, but I'd rather not be a part of your sex-fest, as hot as it sounds, so I'll respectfully pass and let you two play kinky house," Della says, a mischievous smile curving her lips.

"Della!" Ainsley hisses, her cheeks growing pink as she steps out of my arms in embarrassment. "I'll never tell you anything ever again."

"What? I liked hearing you were having your back blown out by your billionaire boyfriend on the regular and he was kinky as fuck. Sir, carry on with that shit. She needs to have a safe space to not be so uptight and rigidly in control of herself. It's good for her."

I laugh darkly and shake my head slowly. I hadn't expected Ainsley to divulge that much, but I also hadn't expected her to stay completely silent about what we're getting up to.

"Sounds like my little brat's been running her mouth and needs to learn what's acceptable to talk about and what isn't when it comes to our playtime. What do you think, Della? Should I cuff her to the bed and strap a vibrator to her clit, only to turn it off just before she comes and edge her for hours? Or should I put nipple clamps on her and attach them to a chain so I can lead her around on her hands and knees like my good little pet until she learns her lesson?"

Della and Ainsley stare at me with wide, surprised eyes. Della clears her throat and seems to recover quicker. "Edge her until she's begging. Make her squirm." She turns to Ainsley and pats her on the shoulder. "You lucky fucking bitch. I'm so glad I love you and you introduced me to my own kinky king, so I'm not at all jealous. Speaking of, I have my own safe place. Luca's letting me stay with him, but thank you." She directs the last bit at me, confirming my suspicion. He normally wouldn't even think to offer his home to anyone in need, so he must be completely into her.

"I'm glad you do. Now let's get you ladies something to eat. What would make today better?"

Ainsley and Della look at each other, sharing a conspiratorial smile before saying in unison, "Mama P's."

They introduced me to their favorite hole-in-the-wall, family-owned restaurant in the neighborhood near our planned sports arena and entertainment district that they claim has the best Southern comfort food. It turns out, a flooded apartment and losing nearly all your worldly belongings is made somewhat better by Southern soul food. Atlanta staples like chicken and waffles, mac and cheese, shrimp and grits, and biscuits with honey, along with lots of sweet tea for Della and icy Coke for Ainsley seemed to do the trick. I can't complain after trying it for myself.

Thirty-two

Ainsley

Walking into Payton's home knowing I'll be staying here for an extended period feels like the edge of a slippery slope into a situation that's far too familiar and scary. Archer conveniently created a reason for me to live with him and I was stuck, completely dependent. When the world fell out from under me, I didn't have anywhere to go and no one to ask for help.

I follow Payton into his room and watch as he puts my bag into his closet. "Wait, I'm staying in here with you?" I ask, a note of accusation in my tone I can't help, given where my thoughts have strayed.

He turns around slowly and gives me a dark look that promises punishment for my insolence. He's in Daddy mode, and my knees weaken as butterflies gather in my stomach just from that look. He walks toward me slowly, unbuckling his belt as my breath catches in my chest with anticipation. Hell fucking yes. I need him to put me in my place and wipe every thought right out of my head with his particular brand of dominance.

"If you think you're going to be in my house and I'll be okay with you anywhere but in my bed, I think we're going to have to discipline that idea out of you right fucking now. Once you get it through your head this is where you belong, I'll put you on your knees and show you what you'd be missing if you chose to sleep elsewhere."

A spark of rebellion lights in me, knowing it's safe to push him because his punishment for doing so would be even better. I set my feet and cross my arms, fully ready to be a brat, as he likes to call me.

"How dare you assume I want to share a bed with you? I need my own space. I need my autonomy and not to be stuck with you all the fucking time. Needing a place to stay doesn't mean it needs to be in here, you presumptive prick. I have half a mi—"

He grips my chin and kisses me, stopping my tirade that's getting us both worked up. It's bruising and allows no argument as his tongue demands entry to my mouth, and I welcome him in. His taste is pure heaven, making me moan with need as I kiss him back. I want to devour him and show him I'm just as capable of putting him on his knees as he is at making mine weak.

I twine my arms around his back, dragging my nails down his skin as he gathers me to his body. He groans and nips at my lips as he pulls away, peppering my skin with soft kisses he trails along my jaw. He licks along my neck and bites at the sensitive spot where it meets my shoulder, sucking until my knees give out and he's holding me up. I'll have a mark from that, and the thought thrills me for some stupid reason. He's claiming me, telling anyone who sees it that I'm his. Not just to kiss and fuck, but to take care of, which seems to be of even more importance to him.

"Take off my belt, you naughty little slut. I need to remind you how good it feels to let go and be with me."

I eagerly drop my hands to his hips and work his belt free, holding it out for him and presenting my wrists with a smirk when he takes it. He's finally going to turn my brain off again, let me come undone under his hand, and feel safe to fall apart, knowing he's guiding me through every floaty moment of un-thinking bliss. It's a welcome relief after a day of stress, making me jittery with excitement for the scene that will take my mind away from my stupid situation. This is addiction in its purest form, my attachment. I need a hit of what Payton can provide.

He takes the belt and stands back, observing me impatiently rocking from one foot to the other. "Strip."

His one-word command sends bolts of desire streaking through me. I'm already barefoot, having kicked off my pink rain boots at the front door. I unfasten my skirt and push it down my legs, letting it pool on the floor around my feet before I start working on the buttons of my blouse. My damn fingers shake with anticipation, the simple task taking twice as long. I finally work the buttons free and let it fall at my feet, leaving me standing in my bra and panties, which don't match, but Payton doesn't seem to mind as he takes me in. I reach behind my back and unfasten my hot pink lace bra, the straps sliding down my arms, nipples peaking in the cool air that caresses my skin. I hook my fingers in the straps of the simple black thong and slowly work it down my thighs, his chest rising and falling faster with each piece of discarded clothing.

I step out of my pile of clothing. I want so badly to step out of my life the way I did my clothing. To discard the stress of losing everything I own and my living situation in a matter of hours like I tossed my rain boots at the door. I need Payton to show me what he's been saying all along—that he can take care of me when I need him to, without taking advantage of me. "I'm ready for you, Daddy." My voice quivers with need and vulnerability.

Payton walks around me, sliding the end of his leather belt against my skin and making goosebumps rise in the wake he creates. "Bend over and put your forearms on the dresser," he commands.

I turn to his long dresser with the large mirror hanging above it. Taking a tentative step toward it, I bend and place my arms on the top. It forces me to look directly at the mirror, and I watch as he comes up behind me, still holding the belt. He stands so close I can feel every ridge and hard muscle mold to my body as he leans over me. He inhales deeply, blowing out a breath as he moves along my spine. I'm nearly jumping with need, held in place by his weight. He drags the belt up my side, letting the tail touch my heated skin. I expect him to put it around my wrists like cuffs again, but he loops it around my neck and tightens it so the excess runs down my back to his hand. He stands back and groans when he looks at the image of us reflected in the mirror.

"You look fucking amazing with my belt around your throat. I can see you wearing a collar for me all the time, show-ing the world you're mine in every way. My cockwhore. My bratty baby girl. My princess. My everything." His cock presses into my ass insistently. He really likes this idea. It thrills me in a way I never expected when I first met this annoying man in a café and ended up owing him a stupid favor by accident.

"Collar me if you want that so badly," I taunt, knowing full well the implications of what I'm saying. I did the research for my degradation kink.

Being collared means commitment. It symbolizes a relationship between a dominant and a submissive. It's far more than the fake relationship we've engaged in. It goes beyond the play or the sex. It's a physical representation of the very obsessive, very real attachment I've developed due to being with someone as compelling and charismatic as Payton, reinforced by the care, attention, and devotion he's given me. He's made me feel safe in a way I never expected.

Payton's eyes dart to mine in the mirror and he pulls back on the belt, forcing me up until my back's against his chest. I gasp as the belt constricts and he lets it loosen. His arms come around my body, banding me nearly as tightly.

"You want to be mine?" he asks, voice low and serious, our eyes locked in the mirror.

I swallow against the leather around my throat, but it's dry for another reason altogether, my heart hammering in my chest with the vulnerable thought I need to say. "Only if you're all mine."

He drops his face into my hair, his shuddering exhale ruffling the strands of gold that float around my shoulders. He's expelling a tension I wasn't aware he was under and surrendering a weight I didn't know he was carrying. When he looks up, a new man faces me, unmasked and even more stunning than the one I'm already obsessed with.

"I've been yours since the moment I stopped you from throwing your laptop on the ground. I needed to know you, to have you in my life in whatever capacity you'd have me. I wanted to get past your walls and attitude to see who was behind the vicious words. I knew you were exactly what I wanted—*needed*—and nothing else would do. Knowing you want this, too, is the best fucking thing to ever happen to me."

Butterflies burst into flight, warmth spreading within me at his words. "It's not all fake?" My voice is quiet, tentative, worried there's still a part of this he wants to stay for show, only to prove to Harlowe that he's fine alone, despite his pretty words.

"It's never been fake to me, baby. I've always wanted you. Having an excuse to get to know you was convenient and thank fuck for that. I don't know if I could've gotten past those walls without the extra time and reasons for you to give me a chance."

Tears prick at my eyes, knowing how persistent he's been, how much time he's spent trying to make me smile and gently pry away my defenses to get to know me inside this prickly shell. He's seen the worst and still wanted me. He knows my darkest secrets, endured my most horrible treatment, and was never deterred. Instead, he was patient, understanding, kind, calm, caring, and resilient. He's everything I needed, whether I knew it or not. He even managed to show me a new side of myself, allowing me to feel safe in my vulnerability and give up control to explore it.

"It's not fake to me anymore," I admit. He smiles gently, like he already knew that and was just waiting for me to catch up. "But there's something you should know about me before you commit to this." I swallow a lump in my throat that feels like it's stuck on the belt that's still wrapped around my neck.

"You're not going to scare me away, Princess, no matter what you say," he assures me, tugging gently on the end of the belt. "You can tell me anything you want or need. I'll be able to handle it."

I close my eyes tightly and find the courage to lay myself bare to him. He's already seen so much. If this is the thing that breaks us and sends him running, I need to know.

"I struggle with attachment issues. I'm the worst sort of clingy and obsessive and catch feelings when I shouldn't, to an unhealthy degree. Everything's a million times worse once sex is introduced to the equation. I need you to know now because that's already happening and I'm sorry if that's not what you're looking for, despite what you're saying. I can't help it, and I know it's a lot, especially so soon, to know that the person you've been fake dating is falling in love with you like a psycho," I ramble, my hands gripping the edge of the dresser and my eyes dropping to where his fingers are splayed across my stomach.

"Eyes on me, Princess," he says, yanking on the belt sharply, halting my tumble of words and self-loathing over my *issues*. "You better fucking be falling in love with me because I need you on the same page. I can't be the only one stupidly in love here. When I fuck you like a dirty whore, I want to be able to tell you I love you and know you love me back. When I collar you, I want you to know it's out of love and respect and my own submission to you that I do it. When I smile and annoy the shit out of you, I want you wildly in love with me even when you say you hate it."

"I love all of that," I admit quietly, my eyes finally leaving his in the mirror as I turn in his arms. "And I love you. I'll let you do all that and even take care of me. You've loved me consistently, despite everything I did to make you hate me. You've shown me you're unfailing and true to your word when others were all talk. I trust you."

He scoops me up and plants me on the dresser, his mouth landing on mine in a bruising kiss that's filled with longing and passion. He kisses me savagely, imprinting his taste on my mouth, stealing my breath, and making me wild for him. I wrap my legs around his waist and pull him close, hating that he's still clothed while I've been naked and vulnerable this whole exchange. When he finally pulls his mouth from mine, his pupils are blown wide, turning his blue eyes nearly black, wearing a feral expression I know will only lead to very good things for me.

"I love you, Ainsley Montgomery, but right now you're my perfect little cumslut that needs to be treated like my fucktoy. Turn around, bend over, and let me spank that insane ass before I fuck it."

I hop down from the dresser and turn, bending over again as commanded. I'm already vibrating in anticipation and need, dripping wet, the slickness coating my thighs. I look over when he opens a drawer and pulls out a black leather paddle from a collection of toys. Another toy with soft leather strips hanging off a handle catches my eye. I point at it before he closes the drawer.

"What's that one?"

Payton pulls the toy out by the handle and shows me the long leather pieces hanging off of it. "This is a flogger. It's best used on backs, or at least it's better on your ass when you're lying down instead of standing because the falls"—he drags the leather pieces along my skin before he continues—"can wrap around your thighs or hips and hurt too much rather than feel good. Paddles and crops are better for this position." He tosses the flogger back in the drawer and closes it.

Satisfied with his explanation, I resume my position and wait for whatever comes next. "Is this going to hurt?" I ask hesitantly because I don't want him to stop if he thinks I'm not down for this. I just want to know what to expect.

"There'll be some pain. If it's too much, you know what to say to make it stop. Use your words like a good girl and you'll be fine," he tells me, his voice low and sexy as he drags the paddle up the backs of my bare legs. "But remember, Princess. You're getting your ass marked because you wanted to sleep in a bed that wasn't mine. This *is* a punishment. I'm reminding you that you're mine and I won't have you spending another night without me."

He pulls the paddle off my legs and I feel the swish of air before it connects with my ass, making me jump and hiss out a pained breath.

"That fucking stings!"

"Tell me whose bed you're sleeping in from now on."

I'm mad as hell, my ass cheeks still burning, and my nerve endings are on fire. He's not in control of what I do. "I'll sleep wherever the hell I want," I sass. "You have other—" Before I can finish the sentence, the paddle connects with my ass again and I jump, letting out a breath so I don't cry out. Fuck, that's way worse than his hand. I rise up on my toes and shake, fighting the lingering pain.

"I want you to tell me where you're sleeping," he repeats, and without waiting for my answer, he paddles me again. I let out a pained cry and wiggle, trying to get away from the hold he has on the belt that keeps me in place.

"Your bed," I breathe, voice thick with tears I'm desperately trying to hold back.

"And why are you sleeping in my bed?" he asks patiently like he's not holding a leather paddle ready to swing against my burning ass.

"Because you're a possessive asshole who wants me there," I spit out, already knowing I'm going to regret it. The swish of the paddle swinging through the air and the smack of it connecting with my skin are familiar enough that I tense and muffle the initial yelp and moan I make when the sting sets in. Tears track down my face and drop onto my arms. I can't look at myself in the mirror. I can't look at him. I regret my sass and know I'm bringing this on myself. I can't help it.

"Use your words, Princess," he says quietly, smoothing his palm over my ass. "You know what to say that'll make this stop."

"Yellow," I say quietly, dropping my face onto my arms and feeling my shoulders shake with sobs that have nothing to do with the sting of the paddle that has already faded. "Red," I cry out, ready for this all to stop, overwhelmed by so many feelings and emotions I'm instantly overstimulated.

Payton drops the paddle at our feet and removes the belt from my neck before he picks me up and carries me to the bed. He gently lays me down on my stomach and opens a drawer on the nightstand. I continue to sob as he smooths a salve on my raw ass. He removes his shirt and pants, crawls onto the bed, and pulls me on top of him in only his boxer briefs. He runs his hands up and down my back soothingly, kissing my hair and murmuring for me to let it out.

"I'm proud of you for using your safe words, Princess. I know it's hard to ask for help or end a scene because of something hard. You're brave and strong, and I'm so fucking impressed with you. You're such a good girl."

I bury my face in his neck and my sobs start to abate. I love hearing his praise, especially when he calls me a good girl. But his words are tinged with double meaning. He's not just talking about this scene like my tears aren't just about the pain from the paddling.

"I'm sorry I'm a mess," I say, wiping at my face. I've gotten snot and tears all over his neck and chest. I'm so pathetic.

"No apologizing for a natural reaction. You experienced a traumatic event today. Instead of stuffing it down and repressing everything, you need to process your emotions and grieve what you've lost. Feeling physical pain can ground your emotions in reality and help you deal with what you may not fully understand yet. Let the tears out and know that using your safe words stopped the imminent pain and allowed you to have control of the scene when you didn't have control of the situation you experienced earlier. Processing what happened to you today through a scene is healthy."

"I didn't realize it would come out like that. I was looking forward to a spanking, thinking it would be like last time and I'd get off on your lap. I just wanted to have an orgasm and turn off my brain," I admit, a bit of a whine to my tone.

Payton's chest rumbles under my ear as he chuckles. "Don't worry, Princess. You're going to come plenty of times once we make sure you get what you need right now."

Thirty-three

Payton

Ainsley looks up at me, and even with wet lashes and a red face, she's still the most gorgeous thing I've seen. "We're not done?"

I smile and kiss her nose. She has to know I'd give her anything she wants. All she has to do is ask, or just look at me with the hint of desire in her eyes, and I'll drop everything to make sure she's satisfied.

"Of course we're not done. We've only managed the impact session. You still need to come until you're a puddle of drool, completely incoherent with pleasure. I have plans for my pretty whore."

Her eyes brighten and she wiggles over me, her lithe body feeling incredible against my bare skin, letting me know she's working through her emotions and processed enough to want sex now. It would have been fine if she just needed to be held all night and never wanted sex. As long as her emotional state is taken care of first, I'm good.

She sits up, straddling my hips, and looks down at me. "What if I have plans for you?"

Oh, fuck, yes, she wants to play. I grip her thighs and roll my hips up against her, watching as her eyelashes flutter. "If your plans have you coming so often you're seeing stars, I think I can get behind that."

"I like your plans better," she admits, rocking over my cock that's notched snugly against the apex of her thighs. "You seem to have a handle on my pleasure."

"That's right baby, anything to make you feel good."

I gently roll her over, put a pillow under her raw ass to keep it elevated, and slide down the bed between her legs. Fuck, this pussy is my favorite. She smells good, tastes phenomenal, and has gorgeous, plump pussy lips, with the inner pair slightly longer and perfect for me to suck on. I lick up the taste of her arousal from her inner thighs, relishing the tease before I get to dive in. Ainsley's watching me, lips parted, breaths coming in short pants, eyes heavy-lidded and hazy with lust already. I keep eye contact as I lower my mouth to her entrance. I slowly lick up her slit and groan in satisfaction at the taste of a fucking good pussy now exploding on my taste buds, her thighs quivering on either side of my head.

Her eyes flutter closed, her head dropping back onto the pillow, hands at her sides, clutching the duvet like it'll keep her anchored when I plan to send her to outer space with my tongue. I worship her beautiful cunt, licking and sucking as she bucks her hips before moving to her clit and really start my fun. I spread her open with my fingers and suck her clit like she's my favorite peach milkshake until she nearly flies off the bed, her hands grappling at my head, trying to push me away.

"Fuck, oh my God, that's too intense. It's too much." She gasps and writhes under me.

She's not using her safe words, so I keep going, sliding two fingers into her pussy and pumping her in time with my tongue and lips sucking at her clit. Her hands stop pushing me away and begin to grip and hold me in place, letting me know I have her exactly where I need her to be. Her hips are rolling against my face, grinding down on my hand as I slip in a third finger so she's full, letting her fuck my hand at her own pace while biting and sucking her. She's close, her rhythm speeding up and her moans growing louder as she chases the orgasm I'm leading her to. She pushes her hips against me hard, holding my head in place as she screams her release. Her legs go rigid next to me, her pussy spasming around my fingers and gushing down my hand as I work her through the intense moment. Her head thrashes from side to side, her pretty blonde hair sticking to her wet face as she moans loudly, chest heaving until she finally stills and her pussy lets my fingers go.

I give her another lick, savoring her taste as I push up onto my forearms and look down at my gorgeous girl, looking rosy and sated, blinking sleepily at me as she smiles. "You're so fucking hot when you come apart on my face like that, baby. I love making you come almost as much as I love you."

She beams and reaches for me, stroking her fingers along my jaw and hairline gently. "I love you, too, but I think you can make me come harder if you fuck me with your insane pierced cock. I still can't believe you have all that metal tucked away every day in your business suits."

I laugh, pulling back to remove my boxer briefs and drop down to kiss her until she's sighing against me. I roll my hips, and she meets me, looking for my cock to slide home. Entering her feels like falling in love all over again. It sets off every nerve ending in my body. I'm fully attuned to her as soon as my cock is seated to the hilt, and I want to live right here, just like this. I keep kissing her as I move slowly, my movements languid and deep, our bodies flush and friction building as I hit her clit with every rock of my hips.

She's gathered in my arms like the precious treasure she is, her hands still on my face, softly stroking through my hair or across my cheek as she kisses me back at the same unhurried pace. I move again and hitch her legs around my hips, her ankles crossing, which pulls me deeper and makes me groan into her lips. Her pussy was made for me. It hugs my cock and she fits against my body exactly the way I need her to as I keep making love to the woman I'm desperately in love with. The woman who somehow loves me back. I feel her tensing, building toward another orgasm. I angle my hips just a bit and press into her harder with each slow pass, swallowing her moans of pleasure.

Her sharp inhale precedes her stilling and exploding around me, her pussy pulsing, face contorting beautifully as she breaks away from my mouth to scream her pleasure.

"Yes, baby, let go and feel good."

I keep moving through her release until she falls limp, her legs dropping from my hips and hands coming up to push the hair off her sweaty face as she breathes heavily.

"You're so good at that. I love how you make me fall apart."

I pull out, her sensitive cunt jerking at the sensation. I move one of her legs up toward her chest where I hold it and make sure she's still comfortable before I straddle her straight leg, dropping the other across her body. I slowly slide back in with her in this new pretzel position that will let her relax while

I continue to do the work that will get her off. It makes me insanely happy to see her that blissed out, and I think a third orgasm will do it. I move faster now, my fingers playing with her clit and finding the pattern that works best for her. I know I've found it when she gasps and her back bows off the bed, a gush of warmth hitting my balls as they slap her ass. I keep circling at that speed and intensity, listening to her moans and whimpers and feeling her clench around me as she approaches her release.

"Right there, don't stop, I'm so close," she begs, her hands coming to her beautiful tits because mine are busy. Fuck, she looks so good, head thrown back in abandon, fingers tweaking her nipples, a rosy blush spreading across her skin as I fuck her harder. I made love to her before, but now I'm using her like my whore and she's loving every second of it.

"Come for me, my little slut. I want to see you fall apart on my cock," I taunt, slamming into her and pressing down viciously on her clit.

She tips over the edge with a moan and comes so hard I think she stops breathing for several seconds. The squeeze her pussy has on my cock is insane, her pulses constricting and sending me right along with her. My cock pulses as I empty inside her while she continues to throb around me. Goddamn. Fucking her bare and feeling her take my cum has ruined me. I pull out of her slickness and look down at our mess.

"Push it out and show me what I did to my fucktoy," I command, eagerly watching as she whimpers and contracts her abs, pushing my cum out in the prettiest cream pie she could've made. "Fuck, you're beautiful. Seeing my cum on you does something to me. You rewired my brain and now all I want is this." I slide my fingers through our cum, smearing it along her thighs so she'll smell like me, be marked as mine, and push it back inside her pussy gently where I want her to keep it.

"Do you have a breeding kink?" Ainsley asks quietly, and I look up at her face, searching for fear or rebuke of something she doesn't like. All I find is hesitant curiosity.

I shake my head. "It's cum play. I don't want to breed you or get you pregnant, and I don't need you to have my babies. I just like seeing my cum on you and fucking love the idea of you wearing it. It's more primal, like an instinct to mark you as mine. The most feral part of my brain wants you covered in my cum. Does that bother you?"

"No," she says quickly, reaching down and placing her hand over mine where I still have my fingers pressed to her pussy. She slides her fingers through the mess and between mine, meeting me in this obscure fascination with her pussy and my cum without judgment. "It's just..." She looks down at our entwined fingers before she can meet my eyes and continue. "I don't know if I want babies. Is that a deal breaker for you?"

I squeeze her fingers and give her a reassuring smile. "You're the only baby I want to take care of. Anything else is up to you, in whatever time frame you want. If you decide you never want kids, that doesn't bother me. If you end up wanting four, I'll fuck you until you have everything your gorgeous heart desires and show them how much I love their momma. It's you, Ainsley. You're all I want."

She visibly melts, relief softening her features as she stares at me in what I can only call adoration and wonder. Fuck, I want her to look at me like that every day. I've just decided it's my new challenge and I gladly accept.

"Right now I want to eat you out while my cum's still inside you so I can taste us together." I voice the insistent need screaming in my head, hoping she won't freak out.

She gasps, slightly shocked by the absurdity of the request. I'm ready to pull back to where she's comfortable when she moves her hand to my head and pushes me down, urging me to do as I said. I unlace our fingers and move them away from her glistening pussy to lick her clean, feeling her writhe under me as she gets into it, too. I push two fingers into her, coating my fingers in us, and bring it to her mouth. She eagerly sucks them in, tasting us, and I growl against her with the desire that stokes in me. This is going to be a long night with how badly I already want to fuck her again.

She bites down on my fingers as an orgasm rolls through her. I take the pain to ground myself while I fuck her with my tongue and get high off her exquisite taste that's mingled with my own. I can get used to this. I want her riding my face, my fingers, my cock, with my cum dripping out of her any chance I can get.

Thirty-four

Ainsley

I slam my laptop shut in frustration and stifle the scream that wants to come out. I have work to do and my shit isn't working. I stand and pace the living room, silently raging at the unexpected inconvenience and what this means. I've never had my credentials fail before, and I can't reset them now. Fuck!

"What's wrong?"

I spin on my heel, my heart hammering against my ribs as Payton leans in the doorway, running a towel over his chest on his way down from the rooftop pool after his morning swim. He looks incredible, water droplets still clinging to his tan skin tantalizingly.

"Nothing. It's just a work issue." I rack my brain for a better explanation but can't come up with anything. I don't want to tell him because he'll insist on fixing it.

"Work issue? I bet I can help with over half of your work issues. Tell me what it is and I'll fix it."

I hold back a groan. I don't want him anywhere near this. "Seriously, Payton, I don't want your help. I'm just frustrated. Stop trying to fix everything."

He walks toward me, eyes serious. "You're mine to take care of. It's better if you remember that, Princess. Your problems are mine to solve, and your frustrations are mine to ease."

He pulls me in and I can't resist the appeal of being held by him. I drop my forehead to his chest, breathe in his wet scent—pool water mixed with his cologne—and want to live here where nothing else matters.

"I know you mean well, but this is one of the few things you can't fix, and it's not a reflection of your skills but the nature of the issue. It's okay. I just need to freak out a bit right now. I'm sure it'll be fine."

I have to convince myself of that more than him at this point because my brain is fifty steps ahead on the anxiety spiral I've taken and everything looks bad.

Payton lets me go and walks over to the bookshelf flanking the giant fireplace in the living room. He pulls a book off a shelf and walks back to me, holding it out. It's *Pride and Prejudice* by Jane Austen, one of my favorite books, something I told him early on. His favorite book is *The Great Gatsby*.

I take it and look up at him, trying to hold back a huffy response that now isn't the time for a reading break, but I realize the pages are interrupted toward the back of the novel and flip to that location. The book opens to reveal a dainty rose gold chain. I hold it up to the light and notice the chain lengths lead to a small ring in the center. I look over at Payton, catching his smile. It's insanely sexy and mischievous at once.

It's his Daddy smile.

"Is this…"

"A discreet day collar. You can wear it daily without anyone being the wiser of its meaning, all while we know it symbolizes our commitment," he finishes. He takes the necklace from my hand and puts it around my neck, fastening it so it sits at the base of my neck, nearly in the hollow of my collarbones.

I read the pages where the necklace was tucked, realizing he chose the scene in which Darcy proposes to Elizabeth the second time. I love this part. When I look up, Payton is staring at me, his fingers brushing along the skin of my neck under the necklace. Bringing my fingers to his, he guides them over the chain and ring.

"Does it look nice?"

His eyes meet mine, full of fire and hunger. "It looks beautiful, just like you. It makes you look like mine."

I can't stop the stupid smile that tugs at my lips at that, rising on my tiptoes to kiss him. He hauls me up his body, my legs wrapping around his waist as he kisses me deeper, and I realize his swim shorts are getting me wet. I pull away from his mouth, laughing.

"Thank you. I love it. But you have to put me down so I can get ready for work or I'll be late."

"Just remember, that collar means I take care of you and if I want to fix something, you're going to let me," he says, growing serious as he sets me down.

I bite my lip, knowing this is one problem I can't ask him to fix, no matter what he says. "I'll remember."

My day is getting marginally better. At least my human interest story about Payton and Olympus is coming along great. This feels like one of my best pieces of writing, and I'm excited to see what I can do with it. He's read what I have so far and likes it. I just have to tie up some pieces and edit before I begin querying it to potential papers. The door to the office opening barely registers until I feel a presence looming over my desk. I scowl, ready to snap at Reid because he's the only one brave enough to interrupt my writing flow after I've scared off all my coworkers. I raise my face, lips set in a snarl already.

My throat goes dry and fear streaks through me when I see Archer leaning against my desk.

"You shouldn't be here," I tell him, quickly standing so there's less of a height disparity.

"Oh, this is worth it and will be the end of my Olsen issue. I told you both you'd regret fucking with me."

This motherfucker doesn't know what's good for him. If Payton finds out he's here...but before I can finish my thought, he irrevocably turns my world upside down.

"I know your dirty little secret."

Thirty-five

Payton

Ainsley seems off and I know something isn't right. She was frustrated this morning, but it's ten times worse when she gets home from work and she brushes off my attempts to figure out what the issue is. I keep reminding her that I can handle anything and to let me do this for her, but she says it's nothing and she's fine. She's not fucking fine and if we had time, I'd paddle the information out of her. Instead, we have to attend the wrap party for Harlowe's new cooking show at some pretentious restaurant downtown, which forces us to change and leave soon after arriving home.

"Baby, let me help you with whatever is causing this."

She looks up at me, her face a mask of emotions I can't begin to unravel before her cheeks turn pink and she looks away.

"You can't help with this. No one can. It'd make you hate me if you knew," she says quietly, anxiously smoothing her hands down her dress.

When she looks up again, her hazel eyes are tortured, and I want to pull her into my lap and kiss away the tears that are pooling at the corners, telling her whatever it is can't possibly be as bad as she thinks it is. Nothing could make me hate her. Her bratty attitude, her mean words, nothing she can do has pushed me away, and nothing will.

She's quiet and fidgety on the way to the restaurant, not letting me play with her or make her happy. She's barely listening to me when I tell her about my day. Fuck, what's wrong, and why is she icing me out after all we've worked through to get to a place of open communication and understanding? I just want to take care of her, but she's closed herself back inside her citadel, throwing up walls and hiding from me. This won't fucking stand. Not anymore.

I look over and brush the gold ring shining prettily at her throat while stopped at a light. It's a silent reminder to her that our relationship has taken on a deeper meaning now, and she's supposed to be on the same page. She glances over and smiles, but it doesn't meet her eyes and she quickly looks out the window again. Too soon, we're at the restaurant and forced to perform and pretend there isn't something hanging over us that I need to make right.

"Fashionably late, but at least you brought Ainsley," Harlowe says, greeting us when we walk into the restaurant. "I loved that berry flag cake you made for the Fourth of July. It was delicious. Hana did, too. Now I have mad cravings for it. I need you to send me the recipe so I can make it this week," she says to Ainsley.

"Of course. I can email it over, but it's just Ina Garten's flag cake recipe. I'm not really a baker, so I keep things simple." Ainsley shifts on her tall, strappy black heels that make her legs look insane. She's wearing a hot pink minidress that's structured through the bodice to look like bondage with black straps that crisscross around her chest exactly how I'd tie her up if I were showing her the ropes of Shibari. It gives me ideas of what I'll do when we get home to make her talk.

"Perfect, I love Ina. Her recipes are so approachable," Harlowe says, guiding us into the party and waving over a server with a tray of cocktails. "These are the Harlowe, which is a spicy mocktail kind of like a jalapeño margarita, and that's the F-Bomb, which is a French 75 variation with a rose cordial and rosé champagne," she says, gesturing at the two drinks on the tray. They're both perfectly fitting for her. Ainsley takes the pink bubbly drink and I grab the green mocktail with a red rim.

"Congratulations on your show," I tell her, tapping my glass first against Harlowe's and then Ainsley's.

"Thanks! But you're on your own now. I have to mingle. Zander and Hayes are somewhere over there." She gestures toward a corner as she gives us one of her supermodel smiles and wiggles her fingers before turning toward another group of people.

I face Ainsley, intent on finding out what her deal is now that I have her to myself. "You're going to talk to me. I don't care what I have to call you or what it takes. You'll let me in and give me this burden to carry. You know I can handle it. I hate seeing you like this. Don't fucking say you're fine again. I know you're not," I say, cutting off the retort she's about to interject.

She shakes her head, looking ill, and now I'm getting worried. What the fuck happened? She was irritated this morning, but something is wrong now.

"There are some things I can't let you have," she whispers, her voice strained and face warped in a way I've never seen. "I wish I were a better person, someone who didn't have regrets and mistakes and irreparable things in my life that would absolutely destroy us."

Destroy us? What the fuck is she talking about. She's not going to slip away from me that easily. I can get past anything. "Baby, we can work through whatever it is. If there was someone else, or you did something you think is wrong, I can get past it. I just want you and what we've built together."

My phone vibrates in my pocket at the same time I hear text tones go off all around the room. It buzzes again and I look around as people pull their phones out. Faces turn our way, people talking behind their hands like that'll disguise that Ainsley and I are the focus of their conversation. I spot Hayes and Zander making their way toward us, their faces set in scowls that make people move out of their way without complaint. Paige is behind Hayes, her hand in his and a worried look on her face as she bites her crimson lip and looks from me to Ainsley. Harlowe gets to us before they do, holding her phone in front of her.

"Is this fucking true?"

I look over Ainsley's head at the screen and my blood runs cold. At the top, in crisp, bold font, I see exactly why Ainsley was worried I'd hate her earlier. The headline is spelled out clear as day, and I know exactly who has been writing about my family for the last two years.

The Atlanta Haute List
Gossip Girl Uncovered: Ainsley Montgomery the
Whore Behind The Haute List

That's right. The traitorous bitch now reporting on herself and her new *relationship* with a fucking Olsen brother has been behind this gossip site for over two years. Want proof? I have receipts. I built this site for her three years ago to use. The dumb skank didn't know how to cover her tracks well enough to keep me out when I discovered she's still using the same platform. Of course I gave myself a backdoor to get in whenever I wanted, and the code was exactly the same. She just changed the domain and the design, the ignorant twat.

And Ainsley, your VPN wasn't enough to hide from me, you cunty bitch. You shouldn't have spread your legs for the first rich man willing to give you a story and a place to stay when you once again fucked up your life. You're so pathetic you couldn't even get out of the hole you dug for yourself. And it had to be a fucking Olsen. I might've left you to your own devices knowing you'd blow it up on your own, but you picked him? That can't stand.

But that's not the worst, is it, you twisted fucks? You're not even fucking together. This whole relationship has been for show. The brainless cunt had the fucking relationship contract saved to the site with notes on how to be your girlfriend.

Damn, you're both pathetic.

Payton, you slow-witted prick, the girl is a fucking fraud. She's using you and the blog post drafts on this site are proof. She's planning to run a story about your Fourth of July party tomor-

row and another about some investments you've been making into local real estate and how that affects the city. Looks like even your business deals aren't sacred when it comes to the snooping slut. She'll use anything against you, even if your contract says she should keep her dick-sucking lips shut. I'd say watch your back, but I hope you go down in flames, you entitled piece of shit. You deserve to have your life fucked up by someone as messy and devoid of feelings as Ainsley. She'll fuck you over and fuck herself in the end, every time.
Deuces, dickbags and anyone who reads this stupid shit.
Bow and Arrow

I scan the article, every word committed to memory without any desire to remember it, feeling myself growing angrier and more detached with each line. When I finish, I look down at Ainsley, who's shaking, her face ashen and eyes glassy with unshed tears.

"My ex-boyfriend is trying to ruin me," she whispers to Harlowe. "He's mad I'm with Payton because of some business dealings between his father's company and Olympus. He's cruel and manipulative and everything he says is hurtful and meant to break me down."

"But it's true," Harlowe presses, popping her fist on her hip as Zander puts his arm around her waist. Hayes and Paige flank our other side, effectively shielding us from the rest of the party, but creating a hostile huddle that has Ainsley looking around like she's trapped. She's about to bolt. Do I want to let her go, or keep her here? The choice is harder than I thought it'd be.

Her next words slam a knife into my heart and rip it to shreds.

"I did start the Haute List, but what Archer said is meant to—"

"We don't care about Archer. We'll deal with him. We care about the countless stories you've written about our family. About my wife and child. Everything you've posted has harmed us in some way, and I don't suffer anyone who fucks with my family," Hayes says, his presence more menacing than ever as he towers over Ainsley and gives her a green-eyed death glare that makes grown men shit their pants.

Ainsley shrinks into herself even more, the smallest person in this huddle by several inches from the next woman, and a foot shorter than Zander and Hayes each. I want to defend her, to stop my brothers from intimidating her, but they aren't wrong, and she admitted to being behind the Haute List. Her words and stories have played a devastating role in our lives as long as she's had the blog. She's been critical, judgmental, shared sensitive personal and business information, and made choices that are now coming back to bite her in the ass.

She couldn't have expected to remain anonymous forever. She had to know there would come a time when she'd have to own up to the fact that she was behind the page.

"Ainsley," I say with quiet authority, and everyone looks at me.

Paige's gaze is full of sorrow and pity. Harlowe is pissed. Zander and Hayes are waiting for me to cast my judgment with hard expressions. Ainsley slowly brings her eyes up, like a weight is attached to her neck, making it the hardest thing she's had to do. They're red-rimmed and full of tears that begin to spill over her lashes when she meets my eyes.

"Is this what's been weighing on you today that you wouldn't tell me? You didn't trust me enough to help when Archer was blackmailing you and had you locked out of your site that I could've gotten into if I'd known?"

"I couldn't," she says, her voice thick with tears, eyes pleading.

"I'd do anything for you. I just need you to trust me. To accept my help. You couldn't fucking do that when it mattered the most."

Ainsley drops her head and covers her mouth as silent sobs rack her small body. She looks so tiny, more so than usual. Her normally sassy attitude gives her a larger-than-life quality, and missing it, she's a shell. I could've gotten past this had she come to me with it immediately. If she'd been honest about Archer and the Haute List today, we could've worked through this together. Instead, she let Archer win because she pushed me away and I don't want to bridge that gap now.

"I'm sorry," she says, pushing through the circle of my family and heading for the door with her head down. She stumbles as people veer into her path, and my heart pangs to go after her, to make sure she's okay, but I can't right now.

"What the fuck did you do?" Hayes asks. "You put our business in jeopardy. Not only are you dating a journalist, which was bad enough, but you found the worst imaginable who's had it out for our family for years."

"Fuck you." I'm only willing to take so much criticism. "I didn't know she was behind the Haute List, and she's only written stories about Olympus through her legit job that were good for our image. There was nothing to warn me that this would happen."

"I had so many amazing friends ready and they weren't good enough for you. None of them would have done you dirty like this, or have reported on your every dalliance in a gossip blog. Damn, Payton, you really know how to pick them."

I meet Harlowe's dark gaze head-on.

"This is your fault," I say, raising a finger and pointing at her.

I feel like kicking this hornet's nest and rattling everyone up because I'm hurt and pissed and want to go back to yesterday with my girl in my bed, trusting me to take care of her every need. I'm being the meddling middle brother at my worst.

"I wouldn't have been looking for a fake girlfriend if you weren't pushing for me to date in the first place. I needed an escape from your matchmaking attempts and Ainsley came along at the perfect time. We didn't expect it to become real. At least I didn't think I'd find someone so seemingly perfect for me, no matter how badly she stabbed me in the heart. So if you want to blame someone, blame yourself."

"I think the fuck not." Zander steps up so we're chest to chest. "You made your own choices. It's not Lowe's fault you picked the worst woman in Atlanta who fucked you over even though it's all fake. That's on you, and if you get in her face, you're going to feel my fist in yours."

"Stand down, Zand. I'm not going to fight Harlowe over this." I smile antagonistically. I want to feel something other than betrayal. Maybe him punching me is just what I need. "But you have to admit she overstepped. Even you warned me she was ambushing me with blind dates, telling me to run from your wife. What's your home life like if that's your advice to your brother?"

Zander shoves me and I rock back with the force, relishing a pain in my chest that's not my heart caving in from Ainsley's deception and duplicity.

Hayes grabs Zander by the jacket and hauls him back just as he cocks a fist to punch me. I was ready for it, willing to take the hit, to bleed for my mistakes, and take a punishment fitting my failure. Instead, I face the disappointment of my family.

"You should go after her."

Surprised by the words full of empathy and concern amidst the anger and frustration, I look over. Paige's worried face peeks out from Hayes's side.

"If she wanted me, she wouldn't have kept this from me or left when it came out," I say simply.

I look away at the party. People are still focused on our huddle, some with their phones trained on us, taking photos or videos, waiting for this to get ugly. Great, more gossip fodder. The only silver lining to this is there's no Haute List to share gossip while Archer holds it hostage. There are plenty of papers that would print the photos and stories on their society pages, though.

"Don't be an idiot like your brother." We all snap our heads Paige's way now, then look at Hayes, who wears a sheepish look as he pulls her into his arms. "Go after her if she's what you want. If Ainsley's special to you, and you see a future with her, even after all of this and how it started, don't let her get away. I don't think she's the kind of woman to come back if you figure this out too late. She's a runner and she's so guarded. You'll never get through her walls again once they're up. I liked her at the Fourth of July party. You were good together."

Harlowe makes a sound of annoyance and waves her hand. "Fine, she's not the worst. I liked her, too, and that's saying something. She's either a great actress or you have something real now. This gossip blog bullshit is a real fucking downer, but the way she looked at you when you were together was pretty adorable. I'll never forgive her for printing my unborn baby's name, though. And didn't she dox you when you bought the Savannah house?" she directs to Paige.

Paige shakes her head. "She printed what was sent to her. Our realtor sent the information. She was careful not to give too many identifying details about the house, but there are only so many houses facing Forsythe Park, so it's not her fault people found the house and camp across the street when we're in town."

My heart swells with admiration for my sweet sister-in-law. She can see the good in everything, and she's carefully defending Ainsley despite what happened tonight. I straighten my sleeves and turn away from the group.

"Where are you going, fucker?" Hayes calls.

I turn, taking in my brothers with their wives again. I once thought they looked good this happy, and I loved that for them but never wanted it for me. Turns out, I just needed to find the right woman to realize I was desperate for that kind of connection and companionship for myself. Yet I just let that woman walk out of my life, likely to run as far and as fast as she can to get away from me.

"Paige is right. I need to go after her and see if it's worth salvaging what I've found with Ainsley."

"Go get your girl," Paige calls, jumping up and down at Hayes's side with a bright smile. She pauses and shakes Hayes's arm. "Encourage him so he doesn't do something dumb like you did and let her run away for good."

Hayes looks down at Paige with a scowl that slowly morphs into an indulgent smile he gives only to her before it drops and he faces me. "You know what to do. Be a fucking Olsen."

I leave my family, going after the girl who just broke the shit out of my heart.

Thirty-six

Ainsley

Humiliated. Furious. Condemned. Miserable. Regretful. Hating myself.

My brain vacillates through so many emotions, my head spinning as I take a rideshare back to Payton's loft, knowing this will be the last time I come here. The look on his face when he read Archer's post is seared onto my brain and flashes every time I close my eyes. I hunch forward, holding my stomach as pain lances through me from the knowledge that I caused it. I made him—the man who makes my coffee perfectly, who just wanted to take care of me, who took the time to slowly peel back my layers and take down my walls, the man I've fallen in love with—look like I sucker punched him and destroyed his favorite electronics while telling him he was nothing but the dirt under my shoes. But it was actually so much worse than that.

Through The Atlanta Haute List, I've written and shared some of his family's most intimate, embarrassing, and silliest information for the world to read. I've posted photos of him, his brothers, and their families for all to see. I removed their privacy and encouraged readers to view them as entertainment.

I knew the Atlanta Haute List had an expiration date, that no matter how careful I was, or how much I masked my identity by writing in a plural voice, or kept my personal feelings out of the reporting, there would come a time when I'd either have to shut the site down or own up to it. I foolishly believed that I'd shut it down before someone ever caught wind of the anonymous writer behind the blog, but I should have known life wouldn't be that fair to me.

The Haute List was my way to hold the Haves of the world—the billionaires, celebrities, businessmen, nepo babies, and the like—accountable for their actions knowing someone was watching them and reporting on their misdeeds. It was done under the guise of gossip to keep a light tone, but the heart of the site was about accountability, and I saw it in action. Once a spotlight was shown on the behavior of some nefarious person or business, they'd magically straighten up, at least publicly, wanting to maintain a good image. There's a thread of good to the Haute List, despite all of the harm it caused. I can see that so vividly now.

The car pulls up at Payton's and I hop out, moving as fast as I can in these tall heels through the dark front yard and up the path. I step on gravel, my foot sliding, turning my ankle in my haste and pain explodes up my leg.

"Shit!" I swear, coming to a stop and reaching for my foot.

I think I just sprained my ankle on top of the rest of the crap that's happened tonight. Hot tears fill my eyes, this time from pain and embarrassment instead of heartache and regret. I unstrap my heels with shaking hands and hobble barefoot into the loft. I've only been staying here for a few weeks and it's already started to feel like home, but tonight, it's a reminder that I fuck up everything good that comes into my life.

I don't have much to pack. Payton bought me a new wardrobe, but I won't take everything with me. I stuff my duffle bag with clothes for work and my necessities and find my work bag with my two laptops—the hand-me-down Gazette-issued dinosaur, and the sleek black laptop with extra encryption and a robust VPN that I use for the Haute list, not that I'll need it with Archer locking me out. I change out of the pretty pink dress Payton brought me into shorts and my cropped I Heart Gossip t-shirt, which feels so fucking stupid now. I catch sight of myself in the big mirror over the dresser in our room and notice the hint of gold at my neck. My hands come up to the collar and I want to cry. I need to take it off and leave it after only having it for hours. I don't deserve the reminder of his commitment and care. Of his willingness to do anything for me while I was lying to him and living a double life that hurt him, even when I never intended to. A sob escapes as my shaking fingers unclasp the chain and I set the dainty necklace that means so much to me on the dresser. I turn and head for the door, ready to leave Payton's life for good so he never has to deal with my duplicity and damage again.

The door flies open as I hit the first floor, and I skid to a stop. Payton stands in the doorway, his chest heaving like he's been running for blocks, his face a tangle of emotions that are so different from the relaxed smile and air of control he normally wears.

"Where the fuck do you think you're going?" he asks, slamming the door behind him and taking slow steps toward me, scaring the shit out of me. He has a wildness about him, feeling unhinged and dangerous. *Feral.* He's a savage man, wind-ravaged and storm-tossed, a vessel lost at sea without direction. It breaks my heart to know I did that to him.

"I'm leaving. I've done enough damage, there's no reason for me to stay." I palm my phone to order a car from a rideshare app because my car decided today was the time to die and wouldn't start. Payton stalks toward me and rips it out of my hand when he sees what I'm doing. "Hey!" I grab for the phone but he pockets it before I can wrestle it back from him.

"You're right, you've done enough damage. I'm still not letting you leave until I say you can."

I look at him, angry and confused. "I don't want to hurt you any more than I have. I need to go and I need my phone for a ride. I'm so sorry." My voice breaks on my apology, tears pooling in my eyes as my skin crawls with the urgency to be out of his condemning presence.

"You need to make this better. What are you doing to do to fix us?" he asks, arms crossed.

I look up into his stony face, anxiety racing through me thinking of anything I can do to make him let me go. Wait...I may have what he needs. "I can't change what I've done, but I might be able to help you take down Archer. If I can't win against him, you deserve to."

Payton takes my hands as I fight to pull away, not worthy of his touch now. It's too intimate when I deserve to be blocked from everything good that he's given me.

"What do you mean, take him down?"

Thirty-seven

Payton

Ainsley's eyes are brimming with tears when they meet mine again. "You need proof that Archer was the hacker that attacked Olympus. I may be able to help..." She looks down and shakes her head sadly, pulling her hand away from mine.

"How can you help?" I ask, hating her warring emotions and pain and knowing she's struggling because she wants to help me. I love this woman and I don't want to see her hurting in any way, despite everything I've learned tonight.

She sets her duffle bag down on the coffee table and pulls out a sleek black laptop that clearly isn't her work-issued equipment, and must be her personal computer. She sits on the couch and I follow, staying close to her as she opens the computer and powers it on. The home screen is simple, and the operating system is Linux, which is unusual for anyone not in the tech world. She looks over at me, but won't meet my eyes.

"I need my phone, please," she says quietly, shoulders slumped and her whole countenance defeated.

I pull her phone out of my pocket and hand it over to her. She activates a hot spot, connects her computer, then clicks on an icon on her laptop screen and pulls up a VPN, clearly comfortable with this process and knowing her way around her own tech and how to hide her movements online. She pulls up a web browser and types in an IP address.

She's surprising me left and right. This is a vastly different woman from the one I met at the Unicorn Café who lost her shit over a temperamental laptop with a screen of code on it. Between this and learning about her secret identity behind the Atlanta Haute List, I don't even know her, it seems. The address loads a white password-protected screen and she quickly types in her credentials, which are both hidden. It opens a storage site that she navigates through with ease, pulling up a folder and opening a backup copy of a website with a resource library on the left, a navigation screen across the top, and a blog feature in the middle where the meat of the website obviously lives. It's a copy of The Atlanta Haute List.

My knee-jerk reaction is to delete it and remove the code so it'll never be created again, but I refrain and let her show me what she wants to. In the end, it's something that could change everything.

Thirty-eight

Ainsley

Payton stares at the backup of my website and I shake silently, blinking back tears as I wait for him to throw my laptop at the wall. It was one thing to see a post that Archer had clearly written calling me names and outing me as the woman behind the site, and another for me to admit it and show him proof. I expect him to turn on me in his rage. I know he's capable of violence after his encounter with Archer. He can be cold and brutal when he wants to be.

He runs a hand over his face and nods for me to continue. I swallow the lump in my throat at his restraint. I don't deserve his patience and grace. It's too much to ask for.

With trembling fingers, I scroll down to the code section of the backup, which isn't as current as the site Archer is holding hostage, but it's exactly what I need to help Payton now. I click the toggle that converts the site to code and turn the laptop toward Payton. I point at a section I think will be useful for him.

"Archer built this for me when we were together. I wanted something professional looking for my articles when I started interviewing. He coded the whole thing and showed me where he put his signature."

My voice is high and shaky, but I'm doing this to help him, even if he'll never speak to me again after what I've done. I've already lost absolutely everything, the least I can do is offer this crumb of help.

"The narcissist made sure I knew exactly how he did everything and how special it was that my site would have his name in multiple places. He wanted to own anything he did for me. I've always hated that, but I didn't know how to get rid of it without crashing the site, so I pretended it didn't exist. When we broke up, I got a new domain and used a VPN to access the site for the Haute List. Archer never gave me credit to consider doing it this way, until now, so I think that's why he hadn't put it together before that the site he built is the skeleton of the Haute List. I think the last few Haute List stories I wrote pissed him off because I painted an unflattering picture of him and he went snooping to see what he'd find. It was a mistake doing that, and now I'm paying for it in the worst way."

Payton scrolls through and highlights a section of code. "This is the same signature he used in the code for the program that got into the Olympus servers." He scrolls up and highlights another section where it says *Archer Donovan has the biggest dick and fucks like a beast*. "Shit like this is pretty incriminating if you're able to corroborate the timeframe and can pinpoint when he built this site, somehow. Anyone can build a website and write code to say whatever you want it to. It doesn't matter that he admitted to building your site in the post he made today. He didn't put his name on it, only the bow and arrow reference like his signature."

"I have a video of him coding, typing that exact phrase," I say, hurriedly tapping the screen he just highlighted. "I took it while he was feeling particularly pleased with himself and was gloating. I kept it after we broke up because it was proof that he was a narcissist and I could show it to people if I ever had to defend myself against him with those allegations."

I open my phone, tapping on my photo library to pull up the very first video I transferred when I got my new phone here in Atlanta. It shows a twenty-three-year-old Archer sitting at a desk typing into a laptop and voicing what he's coding out loud as he laughs. I ask him about the site he's creating for me, and he answers in a condescending tone that it'll be the best thing I'll ever have because he's building the whole thing for me. I have the camera trained on the computer screen, with Archer in the frame, and it's more than incriminating.

"It should more than corroborate anything you need." I pull my knees up to my chest and wrap my arms around my legs. I'm still waiting for Payton to lose his shit on me. I press my face into my knees, feeling too much shame to look at him.

"Why, Ainsley?" Payton's voice is guttural, full of hurt and anger. I hate that I've made him feel that.

I pull my face up enough to look at the table. "Why what?"

"Why would you give me this information now?"

I sit up a little straighter and bring my gaze to his chest but still can't meet his eyes. "You need the information to connect Archer to his crimes. This is the only way. I'd rather you hate me while I lose everything than keep it from you and let him get away with fucking over more people without repercussions. He deserves everything that's coming to him. And so do I."

"What do you think you deserve?" His voice is so different. Hard, not at all the humorous jokester who's constantly pushing my buttons and trying to rile me up with innuendo. I miss him and he's sitting right next to me. It breaks my heart more that I'm the one who put this distance between us.

"Whatever terrible things you think are fitting for the last two years of stories I've posted about your family and business. Never speaking to me again." A tear slips down my cheek at the last words and I turn my face away to swipe at it. I can't even muster up the anger to put up my normal guard when I need it most.

Payton shifts, and I wish it was to reach out to hold me. He only crosses his arms over his chest and it creates more of a boundary between us that makes me ache for him.

"Tell me why you started the Haute List." His voice is so cold and distant. I hate the change.

I swallow the lump in my throat, feeling all of the emotions, especially guilt at having kept this from him as we've grown closer, even fallen in love. I nod, knowing I owe him this much because no matter how hard this will be for me, I've put him through worse.

"Archer fucked with my head before I left New York," I say, trying to make him understand the place I was in when I came to Atlanta. "He was rich, entitled, didn't care who he hurt when he wanted something, and was willing to use others for his gain. I watched too many people just like him do the same thing in New York. Celebrities, businessmen, socialites, politicians, nepo babies, tech bros, you name it. I was so sick of the class divide and unstoppable arrogance, the unchecked and rampant misdeeds of the wealthiest people who should be giving back and doing the most for others. When Archer and his father used me like they did, I'd had it. I realized I was just another tool for people like them to get what they wanted—in their case, more money when they had more than they knew what to do with." I shift in my seat, wishing I could curl up. I'm so exposed.

"What happened when you'd had enough?" he asks, his voice rumbling and deep, but not in the way that tells me I'm his Princess. This tone is all rebuke, and I feel small and selfish when I hear it.

"I'd had too much wine one night after I'd moved to town. *The Real Housewives of Atlanta* was playing and more celebrities were acting out while I was reading the financial news on my computer as I gathered information for an article. I saw the story of Olympus International buying out Donner Investments. I felt like things would never change, just one billion-dollar business buying another, perpetuating the cycle of wealth and arrogance. I wanted a way for normal people to see what billionaires and celebrities were like in their private lives. If there was an anonymous site we could share tips and post photos, or stories could be published that called them out on their bullshit on occasion, it might make them realize they were being watched and held accountable. I didn't expect it to change anyone on an intrinsic level, and I knew it would be a gossip site at heart, so it had to be fun and light. I'm still able to add my love of research and journalism to the stories on occasion, digging into celebrities, or businessmen, sometimes finding real dirt, and exposing things I'm sure no one wants to ever see the light of day. The Haute List has been my way of feeling accomplished when the Gazette has been such a letdown compared to what I could have had before Archer ruined me. It's my way of getting back at people just like him,"

I finish weakly.

Shame fills my cheeks with heat, my hands fisting in my lap, wishing I could hold onto Payton, knowing he's one of those people. I targeted the Olsens because they reminded me of Archer and Andreas Donovan. From the outside, Olympus International looked just like Donner Investments had, and they'd bought out Donner Investments, so in my mind, they were worse. Why shouldn't I have vilified the Olsens and made them the main characters of my gossip blog?

"Were you ever planning to stop?" Payton asks.

"No," I answer honestly. "Not before I met you." I swallow past the desert in my throat. "The Haute List basically runs itself now, with tips and leads coming in around the clock. Any time I open it, I have something to write about, and it gets incredible traffic. If I monetized the site, it would be an insane source of income, but I've never wanted to profit off of gossip because that would make me just as bad as the people I report on. This has always been a way to even the playing field and bring you down to our level. But, now that I've gotten to know you as a person, and know your family, I'm finding it really hard to write about you."

"As it fucking should. We're just people, Ainsley. We never asked to be made into entertainment for anyone to speculate on."

He drags a hand through his hair, staring at me, his face holding something close to disgust on it. I look away quickly, my stomach flipping, heart racing. I wipe my hands against my shorts to try to get rid of the sweat that's making them clammy, but nothing seems to be working for me right now.

"You've had so many opportunities to tell me about the Haute List and you never fucking said a word. You've just gone along with this fake relationship, even when it became real, writing about yourself and looking like a backwater nobody for fuck's sake. Why did you put yourself down and disparage your accomplishments as part of your coverage? You couldn't even fucking tell me this when I told you about Archer being the hacker. You kept the code on the website to yourself and told me you were sorry he did that to us, and let me go on thinking I'd never have a way to connect him to his crimes. Why the hell would you tell me at all if you wouldn't tell me then, before I fucked you, gave myself to you, fell in love with you?"

I feel my anger seeping back into my body. I grasp the tendrils and yank it back into place where it feels good. I've missed this armor. "Why would I tell you about the Haute List? It's anonymous for a reason. No one is supposed to know who's behind the site, especially the people I write about the most. I was terrified of you finding out, and this is exactly why. I couldn't exactly talk myself up or give myself a glowing review when I'm nothing compared to you. I was being a realist when I wrote about Ainsley Montgomery dating Payton Olsen on the site. I have nothing to show for myself when you think of it. I write for a tiny paper that prides itself on picking up every strip mall opening and follows PTA drama like it's the Supreme Court. I dropped out of a master's program and have a few controversial stories that pop up if you dig back far enough, so I keep a low profile to ensure I don't make big enough waves to uncover them. When paired with you, I look like an uneducated, lowlife journalist eager to get a story out of you that you're pity fucking so your family will stop trying to set you up. I'm a means to an end, and I think my usefulness has come to an end."

"Like hell it has." Payton stands and paces across the room. "I'm not fucking done with you, but I'm mad as hell right now.

I want to punish you for everything you've kept from me, not for what you did. That I can get past. It's the secrets and not trusting me that fucking broke me, Ainsley. You should have come to me as soon as you knew there was a problem with Archer. You submitted to me, told me you trusted me to take care of you, then wouldn't let me when you needed it the most. I'm going to remind you of that commitment. Now get your ass into the bedroom and put your shit back where it belongs."

My jaw drops at his assertions, unsure how he could say that. There's no way he means it. This is unforgivable and will always hang over my head. I don't want to be in a relationship with another man who holds an unfair advantage over me. He'll use this against me, eventually.

"I don't belong here, Payton!" I explode to my feet and pace on my side of the coffee table, away from him. "I've done something unforgivable and need to leave. You can't keep me here against my will."

"You don't have anywhere to go," he says, his voice serious and quiet. "Your apartment isn't ready yet, and that fucking hotel isn't safe for you. You're staying here, even if I have to chain you to my bed, which sounds like more fun than punishment if you ask me."

"Why the hell do you want me to stay?" I huff in exasperation, stopping in front of him and slapping my hands against my thighs. "I fucked up and don't deserve to be here or for you to offer me a place to stay out of pity. I'll be fine on my own wherever I go."

"Always such a spitfire, spouting off instead of just fucking listening to me." He shakes his head, skirting the coffee table and rounding on me. I take a step back, but he's faster, catching me around the hips and tossing me over his shoulder.

"This is ridiculous!" I pound on his back with my fists and

kick my legs until he traps them with his arm.

"You're staying with me and we'll work through this. You don't get to run away and hide behind your walls this time. You don't get to shut me out or use your anger as a shield. You're going to let me in and we'll fuck it out if that's what it takes, but we're doing this together."

I stop pounding on him as we enter our room—no, this is his room, not mine—and he throws me on the bed. I scramble up to my knees growling in anger, watching him warily as he unbuttons his cuffs and begins to roll up his sleeves, which is his way of initiating Dom mode. He's so calm and collected, his expression almost serene in his determination. It pisses me off. I'd be more comfortable with him throwing me out on my ass and telling me to never show my face around him again for what I did.

"Why do you still want me?" I scream, tears threateningly close to overflowing. I swipe at my eyes, angry that I can't control my emotions.

Nothing good has ever come to me without strings attached and ready to take a chunk out of me in exchange. There's no reason to expect anything different now when I've seen this happen over and over. I just have to get it through his thick head that he should be done with me and let me go so I can lick my wounds in peace and figure out my next steps.

"I'm the worst thing that's happened to you. I've attacked your family time and again, shared your secrets, called out your business practices, and made you a spectacle. You should hate me more than anyone. Why are you insisting I stay when we both know it's better if I go?" The tears fall and the weight of my inadequacies and failures forces my head down, unable to meet his eyes. I stare at my hands and hate the words they've typed and the hurt they've caused.

His fingers press into the bed, meeting mine in the gentlest reminder of our connection. His voice is the deep, commanding rumble I love when he speaks, sending a shiver through me that speaks to my bruised soul.

"My love isn't fickle. It won't be easily swayed by one bad day, or a thousand. I gave you my heart and it'll always be yours. You can stab it as many times as you want, shred it to pieces, or throw it away—it'll still belong to you."

The words I'd use to push him away dry up and blow away like husks of the insecurities he's worked so hard to overcome to get me to trust him. My claws retract and anything prickly I could pull around me is missing from my arsenal after not needing them with a man as patient and understanding as him. He brushes his fingertips against mine and I flex involuntarily. I want so badly to reach for him. Tears drip off my face and drop onto the back of my hands. There's safety in his touch, even when I don't deserve it.

"I fight for what I've earned, and fucking hell, Ainsley, I earned your trust *and* your heart, you can't deny that."

My soul's undergoing a seismic shift that rattles my foundations, toppling everything I could hide behind. Mortar crumbles and bricks clatter from the walls I've erected around myself. His fingers inch up, covering mine, taking my tears as I cry harder with each word he patiently utters.

"You're mine to take care of, and I want to, now more than ever. Your past and what you've hidden won't change that, and nothing will. We can get through this."

The last of my walls fall, clouds of dust rising within me as everything I've used to keep him out is demolished by his steadfast patience and dedication to what we've built together, slowly, despite everything I've done to avoid him. I raise my burning eyes to meet his and find determination, dominance, acceptance, and understanding staring back.

"Why are you doing this? No one's ever fought for me before. I'm not worth the effort."

"Every moment with you is worth the effort. But I don't need a reason, and you don't have to earn my love. This is the bare minimum, not the exception. You are deserving of good things even when you fuck up, and I won't use my love as currency. I give it freely because my soul feels its match in you and I'm not letting that go for any reason now that I've found it. I love you, Ainsley."

"I don't understand how you can be this forgiving and still love me after you found out what I did. I'm always going to expect this to bite me in the ass down the road, or for you to hold it over my head as leverage of some kind," I admit, voicing my worst fears.

"The only thing biting you in the ass will be my teeth."

Thirty-nine

Payton

I think I've finally gotten through to her. She's fucking stubborn and intent on driving me away because of what she's done rather than let me show her we can move past it, but I've never lied to her. I'm all in on this and I want her, every flawed, broken, secret-keeping, slow-to-trust part of her.

"Forgiveness is free, but you're going to clean up the mess you've made. There are repercussions that don't look good for us, my family, or Olympus. First, we have to get your site back from that sniveling asshole with a big fucking mouth I'm going to punch the next time I see him."

I turn and leave the room, hearing her gasp from where I've left her on the bed. I return a moment later with both of our laptops and settle next to her, handing her the black one, indicating the screen.

"How do you usually access your site, not the backup?"

She opens another browser and quickly types in an IP address that I repeat on my own computer. It loads a white screen with fields for a username and password.

"My usual username and password aren't working, but the username is G0ss1pH0und, capitalize the G and H, the Os are zeros and the I is a one."

I look at her in amusement. "That's original."

She glares at me, but I ignore it as I open a program called Orion that hunts through code looking for backdoors and weaknesses to break into websites. I run it now as I pull up another program called Cyclopes that will virtually smash security protocols to remove any trace of my cyber breaking and entry from watchful eyes. A third program, Antaeus, wrestles control away from whoever is holding a site and kicks them out, allowing me to take over. These are a few of my tech babies I've created and they're doing my work as Ainsley stares over my shoulder while I set everything into motion.

"I shouldn't be surprised by your tech skills, yet here I am," she muses softly, shaking her head.

"You're going to be thanking me for my tech skills shortly." I lean over and kiss her forehead, reassuring her we'll be okay. We'll get through this. I'll make sure of it.

Orion breaches suddenly, quickly followed by Cyclopes shutting down any encryption and security measures Archer may have put in place, and Antaeus gains control of the site, all in rapid succession. I dig around the source code, looking for anything he may have planted while in control of the site, removing a few unnecessary bugs and code he's fucked with. Now it's time to write better security protocols that'll keep him out for good. I spend a few minutes intent on my task, beefing up her site in a way Archer only wishes he could. I install my own program for defense called Trident that uses a three-pronged staged set of advances that fuck with anyone attempting to breach a site and turn every hack and maneuver back on them, allowing me access into their space if I want it. I have this as part of the Olympus security system on our servers, too, so she's getting every protection I can provide. Once all is in place, I reset her username and password.

"Try Buttercup01 for the username and AsUW1sh!," I say, instructing her on where to add capitals and numbers.

"Princess Bride references, really?"

"You're my Princess. Might as well make it one who's a feisty Domme."

"What do you mean, Domme?"

Oh, this will be fun. "I have a theory from the lens of my particular interests. Princess Buttercup is absolutely a Dominant and Wesley is her service submissive. Everything he does is to please Buttercup in some way. His catchphrase is *as you wish*. How much more submissive can you get? Even when Wesley goes off to sea and becomes the Dread Pirate Roberts, his whole goal is to come back with enough money to set them up so he can be with her, ideally, to serve her. Saving her from Humperdink is his greatest act of service, and even when he's tortured, he says he was doing it for *true love*. That man was a sub who had it bad. Buttercup was in control of their relationship, and he submitted to her freely, because that made him happiest."

She shakes her head at me and types in the username and password I gave her. "It worked! I didn't think I'd ever get this back." Her voice is a mix of awe and regret, and I know it's because of the hurt the site has caused.

"Take that brutal fucking post of his down now. I never

want to see what he wrote again. The things I'll do that son of a bitch are certifiable."

"He's not worth anything you could consider doing. He's a pathetic, little man who puts others down so he can feel better about himself. Besides, your dick is way bigger and he never made me come."

I look over quickly and see her looking down at her hands where they rest on her keyboard. "I'll make it up to you. For every orgasm you missed out on when you were with him, I'll give you three."

"I actually believe you will. You've been really good at fulfilling all of your filthy promises this far." She navigates through her site and deletes the nasty post Archer created, a disgusted look on her face as she reads over the vile words again. I'll have to scrub it from the internet because it's probably been shared or reposted in a number of places.

Fuck, I'll kill the punk ass kid for the things he said about her. About us. The way he degraded her is far beyond anything we'd use in our own play, despite many of the words being the same. His use of words like whore and slut were to tear her down, hurt her, and make her feel small. My use is to build her up and make her feel powerful in her sexuality. We take back the words and give them new meaning that's all about our trust and me seeing her as a goddess when I call her my cumslut, my cockwhore, my fucktoy. She preens under the words that are anything but insults when we use them in the bedroom. For Archer to undermine the trust we've built and to use my playful endearments as slurs is unforgivable. His sins are piling up and I'll be the one to cast judgment and issue punishment when I get my hands on him.

While she spends time cleaning up her site, I capture the site backup, prepared to send it to the FBI contact we worked with throughout the cyber attack and another contact who helped put Archer's father behind bars for his own, more violent, attack on Olympus. I include information on how it was obtained, and how we can leverage this. But I don't hit send. I want a little time with the scumbag who put his hands on my girl and then thought it wise to publicly humiliate her first.

It doesn't take long for the fallout of the Haute List post to reach mainstream news. I wake up to notifications about Olympus, my family, and mostly, me. Our relationship starting as fake is being speculated on and articles are questioning if my personal choices reflect our business practices. My phone vibrates again and I slip out of bed to not wake Ainsley, leaving her curled up with the dawn light making her golden hair shine across my pillows. I look at my phone and see the group chat with my brothers already going off.

> Zander: Your girl fucked us. You knew better than to get in with a shitty journalist who happened to be behind the worst gossip site known to man.

I type back quickly, not about to let him start in on her.

> Me: Talk shit about Ainsley again and I'll release the photos of you with acne and a bowl cut and lock Harlowe out of her social media accounts.

> Zander: Fuck, I forgot about that un-

fortunate haircut. I thought I got rid of everything.

Me: I can find anything on the internet and always have shit to hold over you and Hayes. Why are you texting so early when you should be curled up with your wife?

Zander: The city is getting cold feet for our arena plans. There were emails from zoning and planning saying they needed to "reevaluate the speed at which our project is being pushed." They don't trust us after that bad press Ainsley caused. Turn this shit around now before we lose out on billions.

Me: This is your last warning, Ainsley isn't your scapegoat and I'll punch your fucking face when I see you if you continue with this. Besides, Ainsley didn't write that post about herself or put us in any sort of situation we wouldn't have gotten in ourselves.

Zander: It's still her fault for the Haute List and making us look like fools because you got into a fake fucking relationship with her.

Me: Blame Archer Donovan. He's the cause of yet another issue for us. Thankfully, Ainsley, my beautiful goddess, love of my life, is saving our asses and he's about to learn the hard way why you don't mess with Olympus.

Hayes: What the fuck could she do to help? He annihilated her in that post. Her credibility is ruined and she'll never be taken seriously again. Good thing you're still willing to take care of her through this fake-ass thing or she'd be running for the hills.

I bristle as I move into the kitchen to get the coffee started so I can let it cool for Ainsley's iced coffee. So both of them are up and after my girl now. They're going to feel my wrath if this is how they want to start the day. Ainsley isn't ruined, she's just getting started, and I'm going to make sure she has every opportunity to rise to the occasion now.

Me: I'm going to ignore both of you idiots, but know I won't stand for either of you talking shit about her, got it? That's my fucking girl. What we have is real, no matter how it started or what's happened since.

I take a deep breath, pushing through the anger and irritation they bring out in me. Normally I can handle so much more from them, and would be pushing one or both of my brothers instead of the other way around to see what kind of reaction I'd get. Instead, I'm in this protective headspace ready to fight them over their words about the woman in my bed who needs to be treated gently after everything she's gone through. I put one of Ainsley's pink to-go mugs of coffee in the refrigerator to cool. It's these little, normal things that help ground me and bring me back to rationality before I reply.

> Me: She gave me the proof we need to tie Archer to the Olympus cyber attack. We can finally put him away. You're going to be biting your tongues and wishing you'd never said anything bad about her. Or I'll make you do it. She's mine and she'll be sticking around. Get used to it real quick or I'll change your attitudes for you.

> Zander: Oh, Pay's finally found someone who brings out the caveman in him. Look at that, Hayes, he's threatening us with violence instead of stopping us from fighting this time.

> Hayes: How does it feel to be wrapped around a woman's finger, ready to rip the world apart if it so much as dirties her shoe?

I lean back against the counter looking around at the pops of pink showing Ainsley's presence. Her emotional support water bottle, as she calls it, that goes everywhere with her is on the island. A pink fuzzy blanket is draped over the back of a chair by the fireplace, her worn copy of Pride and Prejudice still on the seat where she set it after I gave her the day collar necklace. A pair of pink sneakers remain by the door where she slipped out of them after her run the other day. I like seeing her in my space. The little reminders of her femininity and trust are a balm to my frayed nerves as I calculate how best to approach this PR nightmare we've found ourselves in. I pick my phone back up and reply.

Me: It's the best fucking feeling in the world.

Forty

Ainsley

Fired.

I was fired from the fucking Gazette by a chino-wearing, mid-level editor who thinks the new median beautification project should be the focus of our front page instead of real news. I've sunk to a new low.

Reid even said, "You've done good work here. Great even. I had high hopes for our paper with you on staff. But your work on the Atlanta Haute List, while attracting quite the fervor, doesn't align with the values of The Gazette. We've had hundreds of calls, emails, and inquiries for comment since you were revealed. This isn't the way we want The Gazette to be represented."

He was certainly happy enough when my involvement with Payton doubled his subscribers and crashed our website because so many people wanted to check out the paper. Firing me because The Gazette is receiving more views, interest, and people actually caring about the paper is so fucking hypocritical. I didn't have a non-compete clause in my contract, and it was never expressly stated that I couldn't have a hobby that happened to be a public blog I'm not even profiting from. I handed in my decrepit laptop and told him to pony up for a new one the next time a reporter is hired because it sucks, turned on my heel and left while holding back angry tears.

Now I'm hiding in Payton's loft, eating Payton's stash of peach Sour Patch candy by the handful and mindlessly doom-scrolling news sites as I wait for Della to arrive so she can commiserate with me. Ugh, this is so depressing. Story after story assaults me as I read through the headlines about the Olsens and myself.

Olympus Businessman Hoodwinked by Gossip Queen.

Payton Olsen's Dating Habits Shed Light On Olympus Business Practices.

Billionaire Businessman's Fake Relationship Casts Doubt On Olympus Credibility.

City Officials Pause Arena Construction Plans Amidst Ongoing Speculation Brought On By Olsen's Fake Relationship.

Olsen's Use of Gossip Site For Company Gain Revealed Along With Fake Relationship.

Unethical Journalism And Business Practices Bring Scrutiny To Olympus International Real Estate Development Plans.

Archer achieved exactly what he set out to do—shatter my credibility while fucking with the Olsens' business. It doesn't matter that the story was only up for a few hours. It has lasting effects that are haunting me. Was this my last day as a journalist? Certainly no one else will want me after *another* very public screwup. I need to fix this. Not only for me but for Payton and his company. They don't deserve to go down with my sinking ship, no matter what Payton says. I gave him the only thing I could to take down Archer, but maybe I can do more on my own.

I reach for my laptop and jump through Payton's new security hoops to access The Atlanta Haute List site. I feel sick opening it and seeing the hundreds of posts I've made staring back at me, the majority about the Olsens in some capacity. It feels especially cruel to consider writing another story about them now, but I'm desperate to clear the air and make things right.

I open a new post and stare at the white screen with the blinking cursor accusing me of my misdeeds and the hurt I've caused through this site by writing about others.

It's now or fucking never and about time I took back my power, admitted where I went wrong, and hope to do better.

The Atlanta Haute List
A Reckoning For A Reticent Reporter
Hi, it's me, Ainsley Montgomery, the voice behind The Haute List and your partner in entertainment for the past two years. The previous post on my site was written by an angry ex-boyfriend who gets off on belittling and controlling others. That was made extremely clear by his raging rant. Instead of naming him now, I'm going to do something I should have years ago—rise above it and find the good I can do instead.
This will be the last post of The Atlanta Haute

List.

The Haute List was started with good intentions, despite all the bad it has done. I wanted to provide a public arena to call celebrities, socialites, nepo babies, and yes, even businessmen, out for their bad behavior. The intention was to be an all-seeing eye in the sky to let them know someone was always watching, hoping it would make them behave better. However, intentions aren't always obvious, and they certainly can change as the situation does. What began as a place to keep people on their best conduct soon became entertainment based. I unfairly targeted the Olsen family and Olympus International, setting them as the villains of my blog in some posts and fodder for amusement as I painted them into spectacles for your enjoyment. My own biases were showing in my reporting as soon as the family made it into my writing. I couldn't be objective when I'd been manipulated and controlled by people so similar while I was dating the author of the previous post. You can probably tell how well that relationship ended by his tirade revealing my identity, trashing my credibility, intent on destroying a business, and calling my relationship with Payton Olsen fake.

What hurts the most is that it's partly true. Payton and I initially began our relationship as a way to serve a need that doesn't need to be discussed in public (see, I *can* do better). However, the more time I spent with Payton, the more he became a real person to me, instead of this vilified caricature I'd created in my head. He's sweet, caring, patient, helped me see my own worth when I'd lost it, defended me, and is so respectful. I somehow managed to fall in love with the man, not the mystique, while pretending to be together. This wasn't the plan for either of us.

I hated him at first, but he was determined to earn my trust and show me where the bar for the bare minimum should be set in a relationship by treating me better than anyone has before. The way he treats me shouldn't be the exception but the rule for all of us. Dear reader, don't settle for anything less than someone who sees all your vices, flaws, and failures, yet builds you up and shows you unconditional love despite it all.

I managed to find the love of my life, my soul's complement, the man who knows me better than I know myself, while trying to keep him out and only pretending to date him. Now this site has jeopardized not only the love we've grown together, but both Payton and his business have been unfairly lumped in with my actions and words.

Olympus International and the Olsen family operate with the highest integrity, making calculated business decisions that may sometimes appear unfairly weighted in their favor. That's how I always saw it, at least, but I'm learning to put my biases aside and evaluate the situation from a neutral standing as I always should have. Through that, I've discovered that I judged them unfairly for what can only be called shrewd business practices. They haven't done anything any other business wouldn't do, yet I set them apart due to my own history with a similar company. I created the problems they're now facing, and I plan to help make it right.

I'm deeply humbled, at my lowest, and realizing where I went wrong. It's with the sincerest heart that I apologize for what I and the Haute List have caused. Not only that, but I apologize to each person I've made into entertainment by reporting on their personal, as well as their public, lives. The words *I'm sorry* will never be enough to express my extreme mortification at what I've created and brought to others who never deserved to be thrust into the spotlight the way I allowed. While realizing the errors of my ways is just the first step in righting the wrongs I've made, there's a lot more ahead that I must do to seek forgiveness and begin to redeem myself.

My hope is that you'll learn from my mistakes and treat each person you encounter as a human, not a story or for your personal entertainment. We're all just doing our best and trying to get by. If my failings and how I'm seeking to fix them can provide context and guidance, then they weren't made in vain, despite how painful it is to acknowledge that I was in the wrong and was misguided in my vigilante reporting.

I'll be leaving this last post up and removing every other in my final act as The Atlanta Haute List. It's appropriate that my public apology be the only post to grace this site going forward, given

how loud it must be to even be heard by those
who deserve it the most.
No need to click Like or Subscribe now. The
Haute gossip is finished for this reticent reporter.

Next, I open my email and start querying my feature on Payton and his work at Olympus to the biggest-name newspapers I've collected that may be interested in this story. It's time I shared who he really is and how his influence has shaped the business world quietly. Hopefully, this will work toward clearing his name and raising Olympus International back to the venerable business it should be seen as. I've done enough with my writing to bring them down. They deserve to have my words finally build them up.

Forty-one

Payton

I straighten the cuffs of my hand-cut suit as I enter Ambrosia and Nectar in Manhattan. My purposeful strides take me past the host, who nods at me in greeting, and toward a private room I've reserved for the evening. A special guest is waiting for me, thanks to a few calls to connected associates here in New York. I pull the door closed behind me and know we won't be interrupted. There's no beverage service needed at this high-class cocktail lounge tonight.

"About time you arrived," Octavius Rex, Hayes's former best friend and our begrudging business partner, greets me from his spot leaning against the arm of a cognac-colored club chair.

"I had to make a few arrangements. Forgive my tardiness,

Rex." I look over his shoulder at the man gagged and tied to the chair. "Seems you managed to secure our guest without issue."

Rex is just as huge as Hayes and equally scary. They went to college together before Olympus bought out Rex's family business and drove a wedge between them. Now Rex is our inside man to a group of businessmen who've had it out for Olympus, thanks to a fortuitous partnership in which he helped save our company from ruin and asked for our help getting away from the group of shitty humans in return.

"This idiot narcissist actually believed he was invited here to celebrate his *technological accomplishments*. He strutted in preening like a fucking peacock and wasn't prepared for an uppercut to the stomach and to be choked out in record time. I'm actually kind of mad he didn't put up a better fight. I was itching for something physically demanding to take my mind off a few things. Now I'll have to hit the ring when I leave."

I walk over to Archer Donovan while he tracks me with narrowed eyes. He's scared out of his mind but pissed all the same. I squat in front of his chair and he squirms like a worm under the brutal sun. I pull the gag down from his mouth, chuckling as strings of drool drop down his chin and he takes a ragged breath.

"Hello, you piece of human garbage. Miss me?"

"Your fucking life is over, Olsen. You can't get away with kidnapping and holding me like this. My lawyer—"

I forcefully stuff the gag back in his mouth and punch him for good measure. Try talking shit around a gag with a swollen lip, motherfucker. I promised to punch him in the mouth the next time I saw him for what he wrote about Ainsley, anyway. I'm not normally the one doling out beatdowns—that falls within Hayes's realm of expertise—but this called for a personal touch, given the trouble Archer has caused both my company and my woman.

"Shut the fuck up, you Brooks-Brothers-looking microdick motherfucker. I'm not here to listen to you run your mouth. You've had plenty of time to do that. You're here to listen to me now. Nod if you understand."

Archer glares at me, blood dripping from his nose and soaking into the gag. He refuses to comply. I sigh as I stand, pull my leg up, and kick one of his hands hard enough I feel a sickening crunch under my leather brogues. Finger bones are quite fragile. I probably broke a few. He won't be writing code or hacking into websites anytime soon. He screams behind his gag and makes a pathetic whimpering as his eyes fill with tears. This is quite cathartic, actually. Maybe if I'd fought some of my bullies in high school, I wouldn't have needed to hack into their digital lives to fuck with them that way.

Nah, who am I kidding? I'm a lover, not a fighter, but I'm willing to defend my love when necessary, and he's put his hands on Ainsley more than once while fucking with her life.

"I told you not to come near Ainsley again," I say, my voice low and threatening. "Coming for her virtually was included, you delinquent coward. Remember what I said I'd do to you if you targeted her again?"

Archer blubbers, bloody snot bubbling from his nose as he breathes heavily, fear in his eyes.

"Looks like you do, but apparently, you didn't think I was serious. Let's refresh your memory." I take one of the fingers of his non-broken hand that is tied to the chair and pull it up as he fights against my grip. "I told you if you harassed my girl, I'd make your life a living nightmare." I crank his finger back quickly, dislocating it, and he wails. I take another finger. "If you came for her, I'd end it." I yank this finger in a different direction until it pops. "You're not so smart. Not only have you harassed her, you've come for her livelihood, her integrity, and her dignity." Archer screams behind his gag as I bring my fist down on the dislocated fingers. I'm not worried about anyone hearing him. The music in the cocktail lounge outside is loud enough to cover anything in here.

"He's a dumb motherfucker," Rex says from where he's leaning against the wall, observing my lethal calm and the punishment I'm dishing out. "But I have to know just how far you're taking this, so if we need a cleaner, I can get them on the phone and here when we need them." This is why I brought Rex in. He's connected to all the right people and wouldn't bat an eye at what I had planned.

I nod and look back at Archer, his eyes bloodshot and wide as he takes me in, his chest pumping as he hyperventilates. I've seen adrenaline spikes brought on by pain and fear plenty of times in my play with subs, and this pathetic little boy is experiencing the rougher side instead of the fun of it. He won't be getting any pleasure from this torment. While I'm not a sadist, I'm enjoying this a bit too much after the hell he's put Ainsley through.

"I think one more finger will do it. He won't be able to code or break into websites for a very long time after this. He should learn his lesson about not messing with my woman, my family, my business, or me. Right, asswipe?" I ask, turning back to him and taking his thumb. It trembles in my grip.

He nods violently and whines, the sound so unbecoming and sad, I almost stop. But then I remember his hand around Ainsley's neck, shaking her outside the Gazette office, and red masks my vision. I don't even remember breaking that finger, but his cries tell me it was successful.

"See how good you feel about yourself when you need someone else to wipe your ass for the next few months," I tell him, ruffling his sweaty, limp blond hair. I pull the gag out of his mouth and he breathes in gulping breaths while I fish my phone out of my pocket. "Now I've fucked with your livelihood by breaking your hands and fingers, so we're even when it comes to you messing with Ainsley's work. You're not going to say shit about how it happened or this little chat we're having because I have you cornered."

I turn my phone around so he can see the video of him shaking Ainsley that I pulled from a stoplight camera. I swipe through to another video that has his eyes widening even more. The Trident security program I installed on The Atlanta Haute List site allows me to access the computer of anyone who tries to break into the site. Archer made several attempts to get the site back, failing at each. It allowed me a chance to look around his computer, take screen recordings, and use his own camera to find out what he's been up to. He's been busy. Blackmail photos and videos, financial extortion, emails from the who's who of the criminal underworld securing his hacking services and brokering deals for the work he'd do to get them what they wanted. Even an accounting of his monetary exchanges made through the dark web. Nothing's too difficult for me to find when I set my mind to it, and damn if Archer didn't give me plenty of motivation.

"How'd you get that?" Archer asks, his voice thick with pain and the swelling in his nose. "There's no way you should have any of that."

"There's no way?" I scoff. "You dumb fuck. I'm better than you in every way possible. A better businessman, better with technology, a better hacker, and better at pleasing my girl than you ever were. She comes for me every time I touch her and sometimes just from my words alone. But you wouldn't know about that, being a selfish prick who only cared about yourself.

Nice guys finish last is a saying you should really take to heart in the bedroom."

Rex chuckles, and I look over.

"Save some for me. He can stand in for his father in some of the aggression I need to take out." He cracks his knuckles slowly, his eyes focused on Archer.

I look back down at Archer, who's crying again.

I grab the sniveling man's chin roughly. "It's not so fun when the shit you do online behind a keyboard that fucks with others is brought into the real world and you have to pay for your actions. Now do we have an understanding? You're going to keep your stupid mouth shut about this or I'll release the information I have on you and let your *business associates* know you've revealed their activities." I pause and run a hand over my cheek in mock contemplation. "You know, maybe I should just release it and let trash take itself out."

"This isn't fair. I'm sorry about Ainsley. Don't release that. They'll kill me!" Archer is wide-eyed and pleading now, but I don't think he fully understands just how serious I am.

"You don't get fair anymore. I'll fucking kill you myself if you so much as think about Ainsley or fuck with us again. Remember that."

"N-no, I won't. I swear! We're cool. I won't say anything," Archer stammers.

I step back and turn to Rex as he takes my place in front of Archer. "I think I got my point across, but you should enforce it."

Rex bends down and looks into Archer's terrified face. Rex is a much scarier motherfucker than I can ever hope to be.

"We're going to have a little chat of our own," Rex says, grabbing Archer by the hair and slapping him hard across the face.

"Have fun," I tell Rex, who smiles brightly and waves, shaking Archer's head by the handful of hair gripped in his fist.

I wipe my hands on a handkerchief as I turn and leave the room. I have a plane to catch so I can get home to my princess and show her just how well Daddy can take care of her.

My phone vibrates in my pocket just as I board the jet, ready to be back in Atlanta. It was a quick trip to New York but it was worth it.

I pull it out and see a notification for the Atlanta Haute List that pauses my steps toward my seat. Is Ainsley really posting again, even after everything that happened? I click the link and see the post she's written, acknowledging her faults and apologizing for the Haute List. She owned the culpability for the site and the last post that caused so much trouble. Despite it being my idea to begin a relationship that would all be for show that came back to bite me in the ass, she took responsibility for that, too. Knowing Ainsley and going on what she wrote about our business practices being blameless, she's trying to absolve Olympus of any wrongdoing brought on us by the bad publicity.

Fuck, I love this woman. I need to get home to her and show her just how much.

My phone rings as I exit the airport in Atlanta. I answer it over the car speakers.

"I didn't expect to hear from you today," I say after greeting my caller.

"Turns out business needed to be conducted after hours

today," John Buckman, the editor-in-chief of the Atlanta Free Press, says. "I received an interesting email today. Did you know your"—he pauses, clearly looking for the right word—"girlfriend, wrote a story about you and Olympus? She sent over the synopsis today. I've already told her I'd buy any story she wrote about your company, but she says the focus is *you*."

I smile. "She's been working on this piece for a while. What she's written is powerful, and I'm glad she sent the story proposal to the Free Press. Are you going to pick it up?" My curiosity is piqued. Ainsley could use a win today if he says yes.

"I think Ainsley's an excellent writer, and her reporting is top-notch. But there's the whole issue of her journalistic integrity after this Haute List scandal. You have to understand something like that follows a person. It doesn't look great that she's written so many inflammatory posts about public figures, you included, many of whom can make or break the paper's subscriber base if they call for a boycott of a paper that runs her stories now that her identity is linked to the site."

My jaw ticks as I clench my teeth. I won't let this *scandal*, as John called it, ruin Ainsley's chances of getting the job she's been working so hard for. Everyone deserves to be judged on more than one mistake, even as far-reaching as this one.

"John, you know I can send a message to my contacts at the Wall Street Journal, Forbes, or the Washington Post tonight and get that story picked up, leaving you high and dry. It's up to you how you want to manage your paper and the stories you publish. But if Ainsley came to you first, she's demonstrating her integrity by honoring your previous partnership and offering the story to you before other papers."

"As much as it pains me to say this, we may have to pass on the story, though I know she'll have written something that'll do it justice. Her last post on the Haute List showed she's intent on fixing the problems she's brought to your doorstep, and you're right, she has plenty of integrity to come to the Free Press with the story first. I can keep her in mind for freelance stories that don't center around her romantic partner in the future."

"It's your loss, John," I say, my voice rumbling with the effort to keep my anger at bay. "Ainsley will come out on top after all this blows over, just you wait, and you'll be kicking yourself for not picking her up while you had the chance."

I end the call and put my foot down on the gas, more anxious than before to get home to Ainsley. I need to ensure she's holding it together. She's had more than her fair share of bad news and blows recently. If I know her at all, she's suppressing her feelings and not acknowledging what she's been through. It's time she processes her emotions, and I know just how to get her out of her head and feeling everything.

Forty-two

Ainsley

Della makes a killer peach margarita, and we've enjoyed plenty at this point. I'm blissfully numb, my brain fuzzy and no longer endlessly spiraling through every bad thing that's happened to me and is bound to come. She berated me and asked how I could've been behind the Atlanta Haute List for two years and not told her before she let me have my first margarita, but she showed up when I needed her, and that's what counts. She's hurt I didn't tell her about my covert machinations and the site I ran, but that was the point of staying anonymous. I needed to keep the site to myself or risk exposure. I know she's trustworthy and would have kept my secret, but I didn't tell *anyone*. The guilt has magnified with each margarita, and I'm feeling particularly contrite now.

Della flips through a streaming app on Payton's giant TV, finding my favorite comfort movie, the 2005 Keira Knightley version of *Pride and Prejudice*. "Here you go, doll, I found your movie. Now you can feel all cozy and enjoy watching Mr. Darcy reform himself because he realizes the errors of his ways, just like you have."

"Have I told you how pretty you are and how nice you are to be my friend?" I say, rolling my heavy head along the back of the couch to look at her sprawled out next to me. "No one else puts up with me like you. It's good to have a friend." I hiccup and let out a small, sad laugh.

Della snorts and looks over at me. "Wow, I'm getting mushy Ainsley? You must really feel bad. I've already forgiven you for keeping this huge secret from me, so don't let it eat you alive. I just want to know some of the crazy things people sent in that you *didn't* post."

"My lips are sealed. My gossip-mongering days are over." I mime zipping my lips and throwing away the key.

She hits play and chucks a pillow at me that I fail to catch. It hits me square in the face. I sputter and pull it down to hug against my chest as she tosses my fuzzy pink blanket over our legs. We cranked the air conditioning up so we could turn the fireplace on and get comfy on the couch. It doesn't matter if it's almost August in Georgia. Here, we're experiencing a chilly British day that requires *ambiance* to watch my favorite movie.

My phone vibrates in my lap as Lizzy walks through a field toward her house. I pull it out and blearily read the screen. I tap on the notification for a new email and see the sender is from one of the newspapers here in town, The Southern Sounder. They tend to sensationalize news stories and always have a lean to their reporting that I'm not a fan of.

From: Carlton Daley <cdaley@southernsounder.com>

To: Ainsley Montgomery <ainsmontgomery@memail.com>

Subject: We have an offer for you

Dear Ms. Montgomery,

Allow me to introduce myself. My name is Carlton Daley and I'm the editor of the Lifestyle and Entertainment section of the Southern Sounder. The editorial staff has long followed the reporting of the Atlanta Haute List, and we're impressed not only by your latest post taking ownership of the Haute List, for better or worse, but by the years of stirring posts you've authored following the who's who of Atlanta. We've enjoyed the tone of the posts, as well as the thought that went into each one, despite being a gossip site with the ability to exaggerate the melodrama or only report the most basic of details.

We would like to offer you a position on our Lifestyle and Entertainment team as our new page six gossip columnist. This would be a role that aligns with your considerable talents and continues the work of the Atlanta Haute List in a legitimate space. We like your writing style, the voice you've created, and would love to have you join the Southern Sounder.

We look forward to your reply and hope to discuss your addition to the team!

Regards,

Carlton Daley

I groan, letting my phone drop into my lap as tears well in my eyes.

Della pauses the movie just as Lizzy is learning that Mr. Bingley has let Netherfield Hall. "What happened now? Why are you in tears?" she asks, scooting across the couch to wipe my cheeks with her thumbs.

I hand her my phone while I drain the last of my margarita,

looking for the buzz I lost when I read the email. She quickly scans through it and looks back at me in confusion.

"This is great news! They offered you a job and they're one of the bigger papers here in town. Why are you sad?"

"They didn't offer me a legitimate job. They based this offer on my notoriety and want me to continue the work of the Haute List, reporting gossip." I pull the pillow tighter against my chest. "I'm done with that, Della. I've been busting my ass for over two years at the Gazette so I can move up to a better paper writing about serious issues. They don't want me for that. They just want me to resurrect the Haute List for their paper. I can't do it. I've committed to doing better, and this is the same thing that got me to this miserable place where I'm humiliated and I've jeopardized my credibility as a journalist, *again*."

I can't believe I'm disappointed about a job offer with a large paper when I should be thrilled that someone wants me after how badly I've fucked up. It's what I've longed for since prematurely leaving NYU and hiding away at the Gazette. But this isn't how I wanted to make a name for myself. I have to set my standards higher and look for something that wants my writing for real news, not the gossip I'm now known for.

"What if you look at it like a foot in the door for the paper?" Della muses, sitting back against the couch and looking at me as seriously as she can through a peach margarita haze. "Maybe you start out writing the gossip column and move to other entertainment stories, then to hard news? It might be a good option for you now that you're *fun*employed."

She's so good at looking for the positives in every situation, and she's not wrong. I could look at it that way. My heart sinks, realizing that's not going to be enough for me.

"I don't want to settle for this when I could do better with my career. I don't want to only be known as a Gossip Girl, a real-life Lady Whistledown. I need to hold out and pursue something that'll actually fulfill my need to report on hard news and restore my credibility. I'm hoping to hear back about my story on Payton. I sent a proposal to about ten different papers and business magazines. Maybe seeing it published will help my job search and make me more desirable for the kinds of offers I'm looking for.

"You'll find something and anyone who passes on you will be kicking themselves when you're given a Pulitzer Prize for one of your stories. I can see it now. We'll manifest that shit and within five years, you're going to look back on this moment and realize it wasn't the darkest night of your soul but the moment everything started looking up. You're like a phoenix rising from the ashes already."

Tears spill over my lashes and I wipe them away. "Your faith in my ability to rise out of this and make it better is very sweet. I just don't see it yet."

"Trust me, it'll all work out."

Forty-three

Payton

I park the Rover in my garage next to Ainsley's bro-ken-down Toyota.

I scowl at the beat-to-shit Corolla. She insists it just needs a new battery, but I hate that thing. It's old, dangerous, and she needs a better vehicle. I've already called the Aston Martin dealership and ordered her the new DBX SUV. I need my peace of mind preserved when she's out on the treacherous streets of Atlanta or driving I-85. That's even where Zander and Harlowe reconnected, proving any manner of shit can happen on that interstate. Besides, she likes British things and deserves something nice after everything she's been through lately. Getting her a decent, safe, reliable car is the least I could do.

I hear the strains of music playing when I enter the loft and instantly recognize it as the ending credits of *Pride and Prejudice*, Ainsley's favorite. She told me Della was coming over to hang out and make her feel better, which included copious amounts of alcohol and her comfort movie. I've already texted Luca and he should be here soon to collect Della.

I have plans for my Princess that don't include an audience.

Ainsley looks up from the couch, where her head's in Della's lap, her hair being stroked comfortingly, when I enter the living room.

"You're back early. How was your trip?"

I didn't give her reasons for my quick trip to New York, only that I'd be back by the evening. "I accomplished exactly what I hoped to."

The doorbell rings and Della narrows her eyes at me after studying her phone. "Did you call in the cavalry to get me out of here? Luca says he's outside. I'm here to comfort my best friend. You can't kick me out like this. We're not even drunk anymore. We ran out of margaritas two hours ago before Kitty created a scandal with Wickham." She puts an arm around Ainsley, who's sitting up now.

"I'm fine, Dell. I don't want to take up your whole evening. Go see your hot boyfriend and enjoy your night."

I feel the slightest twinge of something hearing her call another man hot, but it quickly fades. She's not interested in Luca, and I'll be more than enough to keep her attention, especially with what I have planned. I walk to the door and let Luca in.

"Della's insisting she doesn't have to leave. Want to clear that up?"

He gives me an appraising look with his ice-blue eyes. The man can be so cold, even after fifteen years of friendship. He looks over at Della, thawing a little at her giddy smile, his own turning up his lips.

"Miss," he says, holding out his hand. "It's time to go. We can get tacos on the way home where I'm going to have you for dessert while you try to read that latest Haute List post without stopping as I make you come."

"Yes, Sir," she says, popping off the couch like she's been shot from a cannon. "Sorry, Ains, I'm not passing this up. You understand." She hugs Ainsley before making her way over to Luca, who still holds his palm out for her to take.

"Go, be annoyingly cute and get everything he's offering. I'll be fine here, and I'm sure Payton will be plenty entertaining to keep my mind off the shittiest day I've had in years."

Once Luca and Della have left, I turn to Ainsley.

"Turn off the movie and get in our room. Strip and lean over the bed, hands on the mattress," I command, my voice low. Now it's her turn to hop off the couch like it's burning her ass.

"Yes, Daddy," she says, and I feel myself melting for her even more. She hurries down the hallway and I give her a few minutes to comply before I make my way in after her. I take my jacket off and unbutton my shirt, removing it so I stand in just my pants, barefoot.

She dropped her clothes in a pile on the floor and is posed exactly as I asked her to. I slap her bare ass, making her jump and moan. My handprint blooms red on her skin, marking her as mine to use. My cock stiffens as I move around her so she can see me. I take one of her hands and wrap her fingers around my length through my pants.

"Look what you do to me, my gorgeous little cockwhore. I've never been as hard as I am around you. You fucking do it for me, you filthy little slut. Just knowing you want me to spank you and fill you up with cum has me planning out every unspeakably sexy thing I can do to you."

I drop her hand to the bed and move to her back. Goose-bumps rise across her skin as I trace my tongue up her spine until I'm bent over her, my lips at her ear.

"Please," she begs, her voice husky with desire and already delirious before I've even touched her how I intend to. "Do whatever you want to me. I'm yours."

I wrap my arms around her, burying my face in her neck and breathing deeply. Fuck, how is she so perfect?

"That's right, baby, you're mine, and I'm yours even more. No one else gets to touch this flawless body that wants to be painted with my cum, and you're the only woman I see. Everything about you is perfect." I wrap her golden tresses around my fist. "This silky hair. Your goddamn perfect face that stays with me night and day. Your sassy as fuck mouth that turns me on faster than anything has before. Your tight little body that fits me so perfectly." I run my other hand up her stomach to her tits and roll her nipples between my fingers until she arches into me. "And this cunt that was made for my cock." I drop my hand to her pussy and grind my palm against her clit until she cries out.

"Fuck me, please, Daddy. I need more. I need you inside of me." She rocks against my hand shamelessly and I grin.

"Show me how bad you want me. Get on your knees and open that bratty mouth of yours I'm going to fill. I want to see that pretty pink tongue that loves telling me off."

She turns, my fist still in her hair, and drops to her knees in front of me, her eyes looking up at me with beautiful trust. I take my time unbuckling my belt and pulling down my pants enough to free my cock. She licks her lips as her eyes flick between my face and what she's about to suck. She opens her mouth slowly and sticks out her tongue exactly the way I like best, soft and ready.

I fist my cock and pump before tapping her tongue with the head a few times. She moans and lets me rub the crown across her lips.

"That's my good fucking girl. Spit on it."

Ainsley looks up at me, confused. "Spit?"

"Get it wet for me so I can use you like my favorite fucktoy. Make a mess for us, baby."

She looks at my cock with determination now that she's been given an order. Her mouth works until she leans forward and opens, letting her spit fall onto my cock, getting me nice and wet. I'm so hard and ready for her to take me into that hot mouth. She parts her plush lips and lets me feed my cock between them, her tongue licking along each barbell of my piercings.

I groan when she closes her lips around me, her cheeks hollowing, sucking the best she can. I'm too big for her to take all the way into her mouth, but it feels fucking amazing all the same. I take her hair in my fist again and she steadies herself against my thighs. I use her hair to pull her off me and push her back down.

"That's my good girl. I love seeing you on your knees. You're taking me so well like the perfect cumslut you are," I praise. She hums and sucks me harder. "You like when I use your holes, don't you, Princess? You want to be my fucktoy and choke on my cum." Her fingers tighten against my thighs as she moans, her eyes going unfocused in delirious pleasure.

This Ainsley is so different from the standoffish woman I met in a café a few months ago. Instead of doing everything in her power to keep me out, she's allowed me in and willingly partnered with me in this. She's compliant, letting me fuck her face slowly as she keeps her eyes trained on me, but I know that look. She needs to come. She's squirming, looking for friction against her heels to ease her need.

"Touch yourself, my pretty girl. Make yourself feel good while I use my favorite toy."

She drops one of her hands from my thighs to her pussy, her fingers sliding through her arousal and back to circle her clit. The lewd, wet noises coming from her cunt and mouth as I fuck it make me feral. I pump harder, holding her head steady, reaching her limits in how much she can take with each thrust. Her eyes water and drool drips down her chin, dropping onto her tits with each rock of my hips, but she doesn't pull away or complain. Fuck, seeing her dripping like this turns me primal. I fuck her face faster and she moans around me, her eyes closing in pleasure, hips rocking into her hand as she continues to work herself.

"That's it, baby, come with me and don't swallow," I growl, my release building at the base of my spine, my balls tightening and ready to explode into her perfect mouth with the slightest push.

She blinks, a hazy look in her eyes as she hums, mixing with the wet sounds of my cock in her mouth becoming more beautiful than ever. She cries out around me, the sound muffled as I thrust harder, pulling out enough to watch as hot ropes of cum shoot onto her tongue and chin while she rides her fingers through her own release. Like the good girl she is, she doesn't swallow, just moans around her mouthful of cum.

"Show me," I command when her orgasm fades. She looks up at me and opens her mouth, displaying how beautiful she looks holding my cum.

I drop to my knees and kiss her, tasting myself on her tongue, loving that she's mine in this way. She swallows as I lick the cum off her chin before thrusting my tongue back into her mouth so she can suck it off. I want her to have every bit of me. To smell like me, taste like me, and be full of me.

"Holy shit," she pants, looking at me. "You really just did that."

"We're not done yet. That was just the appetizer. You need to get out of your head and process your feelings from today."

"I was processing. That's what peach margaritas and *Pride and Prejudice* are for," she sasses. "I've felt enough today."

I pull her up off her knees and move her to the bed before walking into the closet to my toy drawer. I find what I'm looking for and return. Her eyes grow wide and she opens her mouth.

"That's right, my personal Fleshlight, I'm going to put this plug in your tight little ass while you take your spanking."

"It has a...pink jewel on the end. What am I, a treasure troll?"

I smile. "I have all sorts of butt plugs, but this one is pretty like my favorite fucktoy and will prep you to take me in that gorgeous ass I have to fill with cum. You're my favorite set of holes and I need to use them all tonight."

She shivers and looks up at me with hazy eyes, her brain buffering from the new degrading endearment.

"On your hands and knees, Princess," I command.

She turns over, presenting me with her stunning ass. I approach and run my palm over the tempting curves. She arches under my touch.

"Have you worn a plug before?"

She shakes her head.

"Have you had anal?"

She tentatively nods, but her face is less enthusiastic.

"Not your favorite experience, I take it? Tell me why."

She glances over her shoulder at me as I continue to caress her cheeks.

"It didn't feel great. It was kind of a surprise and it hurt."

"A surprise? Someone fucked your ass without asking or doing any prep? Let me guess, it was that fuckwad, Archer."

She averts her gaze and nods. Red washes over my vision and I wish I'd shoved my foot up Archer's ass along with breaking his fingers. He should know what it feels like to uncomfortably take something when you're not ready and how that fucks with your brain. I'm close to leaving the room to call Rex to put in one last request, but Ainsley's comfort is more important than righting this wrong. Archer will get what he deserves soon enough.

I tug her back into my lap, pulling her tight against my chest. I bury my face in her hair and breathe deeply to center myself in her sweet vanilla scent. It calms me when I want to fly into an uncharacteristic rage. Having her to take care of, as mine, has unlocked a part of me I wasn't aware of. It turns out I'm possessive, protective, a little jealous, and will go to any lengths to ensure she's safe, wants for nothing, and all her enemies are dealt with at my hand. Right now, she needs reassurance, not me flying off into a crazy rage.

"We don't have to do this. We'll only do things you're comfortable with. Your limits will always lead our play, Princess."

She half turns and looks up at me. "But I want this. I trust you."

I sigh out my appreciation for those three words that mean the world to me and kiss her forehead, hugging her tighter. "I fucking love hearing that from you, but I don't want you to say it because you feel pressured in the moment. Your consent and desires are far sexier than anything we could do together." She brings her hand to my cheek and brushes her fingers into my hair. I turn into her touch and kiss her palm.

"I'm serious. I know you'll make it better than what I've

experienced before. Everything with you has been amazing. I know that won't be an exception. Besides, I've been anticipating this since the moment you said you'd fill every hole with cum. You shouldn't leave one out and make a liar of yourself," she teases.

I chuckle in surprise. "Fuck. How do you go and get more perfect every day?" I shake my head as I decide to trust her back. "Remember to use your words if you're uncomfortable or need to stop. You're in control of everything we do, got it?"

She pulls back and gives me a look that sets me on fire with the brattiness of it and has my palm itching to show her what that will earn her.

"Enough talk. Spank me and fuck my ass already, Daddy."

"Oh, girl. You're going to get it now."

I lean in and bite her shoulder. She yelps and swats at me as she scrambles off my lap, laughing.

"Turn around, Princess, we have to tame that bratty attitude."

Forty-four

Payton

Ainsley naked on her hands and knees in front of me is a sight to behold. Her lithe curves and heart-shaped ass are tormenting. I bite the swell of one cheek and she yelps.

"You're a freaking alligator today! I'm going to have teeth marks all over me."

"Good. It should be apparent to anyone who sees you that you belong to me. You can bite me back anywhere you want and I'll wear your teeth prints with pride to show that you own me."

I drop down and lick along her ass crack and she lets out a startled sound that quickly turns to a moan as I tease her puckered entrance. Fuck yes, she's okay with ass play. I get her nice and wet while heightening her anticipation. She's even pushing back against my face for more as I show her what proper prep should feel like. Fuck, every part of Ainsley is amazing and tantalizingly good. I pull her cheeks apart, stretching her and massaging what I'm going to play with.

I give her one last lick and pull away, popping the cap on a bottle of lube, and pouring a trickle down to her tight ring. I swirl it around with my finger, coating her properly and dragging it down to ensure her pussy and clit are coated, too. She's arching, rocking back into my fingers, and looking back at me with heavy-lidded eyes. My girl wants this. I coat the metal plug with lube and hold it up for her to see.

"You're going to take this just like you're going to take my cock, because you're my good little slut who wants me to fill every hole."

Her lashes flutter and she lets out a delicious moan. I take the opportunity and press the plug against her ass, pushing it into the tight ring of muscle with steady force while massaging her clit. She cries out and pushes back against me, taking the plug easily and grinding against my hand. I let her rock against me while pulling on the jeweled base. In seconds, she's coming apart, her face dropping to the mattress, her pussy pulsing in a quick rhythm that has me growing hard and ready to plunge inside of her.

I growl in pleasure as she moans into the bed, half tempted to keep her in this position, but I want her closer for what comes next. I need intimacy and closeness with her when I'm inflicting pain and punishment, even if she likes it. I need the connection as much as she does.

I sit at the end of the bed and pull her to straddle my thigh, facing me, before bending her forward under my arm toward the bed. She's languid, letting me position her without a fight until I have her secure with my arm around her waist and ass up, her legs dangling on either side of my thigh so her toes brush the ground. She'll be able to push off the ground for leverage and grind on my thigh in this position, but won't be able to get away from me.

"How do you feel about losing your job at the Gazette?" I ask her.

She sighs and props her head on her folded arms, "I'm fine. They're a second-rate paper and I can do better."

"You truly can, but how do you *feel*, little Spitfire?" I drop my voice low, taking on a commanding tone.

She squirms on my thigh, her pussy rubbing against my pants, the movements making the jeweled plug in her ass wink at me, and she huffs. "I'm fucking fine, just drop it already."

I swing my arm and spank her ass, hard. She flinches and cries out, the sound beautiful but not close to her breaking point. She's clenching around the plug, which is going to make her release even better when she gets there.

"You're not fine. You weren't prepared to lose your job on top of losing your gossip outlet because you were exposed by a spiteful ex. How...Do...You...Feel?" I ask, bringing my hand down on her ass with stinging efficiency between each word.

She whimpers, her toes pushing against the floor as she writhes against my thigh. She's holding out from losing her shit, but close to getting off from the pain of the spanking and the friction of my thigh, which is the point of this position. I swing my palm again and connect with a stinging slap over the reddened cheek I've focused on. I haven't pulled my strength this time, knowing she can take it, or use her words if not.

I turn to watch as she rocks forward, her head thrown back as she screams and bucks her hips against me, her thighs quivering with her release.

"That's it, you're doing so well," I growl as she continues to rock against my thigh.

Her face quickly transforms from ecstasy to agony as she drops her head down onto her arms and bursts into tears.

"I fucked up *again* and no one will want me now. I'll never make it as a real journalist," she sobs, her voice muffled and thick with tears, her back heaving under my arm.

I rub soft circles against her skin as she cries. "Let it out, sweetheart," I coax.

"I can't do anything right and I'm a failure."

"You're doing so good. Keep going, baby."

She needs this emotional release, and it turns out the physical pain from our play is a good way for her to connect and process her feelings. I've learned she'd rather keep everything bottled up inside, building walls and keeping me out, but I'm not going to allow that from now on. She's going to deal with shit as it comes, and we're going to do it together so I can hold her up and give her my strength when she doesn't have enough of her own.

"I can't even make it at a second-rate paper. I don't deserve anything better." She presses her face into her arms and bawls.

Okay. That's enough of that self-defeating nonsense she's used to tear herself apart. I scoop her into my arms and hold her to my chest, letting her cry into my shoulder as I soothe her. It's time for me to build her back up.

"You're one of the most talented writers I've ever read. Not only because of your work on the Haute List, which has always been entertaining and evocative, but for your real news stories that have managed to make even the most mundane subjects interesting. You have a brilliance for storytelling that goes beyond reporting facts or gossip. Millions of people read the Haute List because of your writing, not just your subjects."

I kiss her temple and smooth hair away from her face. Her

sobs have stopped and her tears slowed, but she still carries an aura of despondency that I need to eradicate with praise and a plan.

"You're not a failure. You'll figure out what comes next in due time. You've been given an opportunity to pursue any avenue you want now that you're not tied to the fucking Gazette where they wanted to keep you mired in mediocrity. Your time to shine is here, and big things are coming for you, my love."

She looks up at me through red-rimmed eyes, her dark lashes wet and spiky. "The Southern Sounder offered me a job as a page six gossip columnist today."

I smile brightly and place another kiss on her forehead. "See, it's already looking up!" I'd connected with that paper earlier with an inquiry about a position for Ainsley on staff. She could easily write circles around everyone that's currently part of that paper. I'm glad they reached out to her after all. It wasn't guaranteed, but they do owe me some favors for a few stories I've given them first access to.

"I'm not going to take it. I don't want to write gossip and resurrect the Haute List in newspaper form, and I don't want to work for a paper that's only interested in me because of my notoriety. I want to grow, not stay complacent in my mistakes."

My heart swells at her integrity and dedication to doing what's right. She has an opportunity to take a job that would be so easy, a natural next step, and a solid income, yet she's not content to stay within the gossip sphere where she was unintentionally hurting people with her words. I'm so fucking proud of her for making this choice, as difficult as I know it must be when she's so uncertain of her future. It doesn't bother me at all that the little bit of coaxing and string-pulling I did was for nothing. I'd rather Ainsley make this decision herself and feel good about it than take a job she hates and feel like she's contributing to the problem.

"The right opportunity will come along and feel like the perfect fit. You have something special that others will recognize. Wait and see. In the meantime, I need to fuck this perfect ass of yours and fill my favorite fuckdoll up with cum."

Ainsley stares into my face with a confused expression. "You still want me after I've had a total breakdown?"

I lick her cheek, tasting salt and sadness.

"I like it when you cry," I growl. "It turns me on when you experience true emotion and release those pent-up feelings instead of boxing them away and not dealing with the shit that comes at you. I especially like it when you come apart and the tears come with it. So, yes, Princess, I still fucking want you after your breakdown. Now, take off my pants like my good slut and show me you want me to fuck you like a whore."

Ainsley slides off my lap and obediently works my pants free. I lift my hips for her and watch as her eyes grow hooded with desire when she sees my cock swollen and leaking precum for her again. She runs her finger down the line of barbells, making my cock twitch and I groan. She crawls back on the bed and points her backend my way, pressing her face down into the mattress, stretching her arms out in front of her so her ass is in the air and showing off the jeweled plug. One of her cheeks is cherry red and has an impression of my palm standing out in stark relief. This woman is so fucking hot. So mine.

"I'm ready for you, Daddy, come use my holes."

My control was barely holding on by a frayed tether before her taunt. Now I'm at her back, fisting my cock and sliding into her wet cunt before she can finish her amused laughter. She groans at the fullness, grabbing the duvet cover and shaking with the unique feeling of being so full. She has no idea what she's in for.

"Not so funny now, is it, Princess?" I growl.

I roughly fuck her, bottoming out in her dripping pussy and she gasps with the fullness. I slide out to the tip, gripping her hips to slam her back down on my cock. She makes an unintelligible sound and claws at the bed, drool dripping from her plush bottom lip as her mouth hangs open. Good. I managed to shut off her brain and she's out of her head with desire and simply feeling in a primal sense now.

I haul her up on her knees and against my chest, wrapping my hand around her throat so I can keep her close and kiss her while I play with her clit. Her hands come up to my forearm and behind my head, holding me tightly and keeping me as close as I can be as she kisses me back fiercely. Don't worry baby, I'm not going anywhere.

I pull away from her mouth, dragging my lips to her ear. "You're my perfect cock sleeve, here for my pleasure, and you're not going to come until I tell you you can."

I continue my brutal rhythm, her sounds growing more erratic and urgent as I slowly circle my fingers at her clenching pussy and squeeze her throat tighter. She's desperate, her body closing in on the release I keep just out of reach. It feels so good to hold her here, edging the elusive orgasm she wants so badly, not able to take a full breath. I move my fingers faster.

"Be a good girl and come for me, Princess."

Her breath stutters, cunt clamping down on my cock as she races to her climax, no sound releasing through the hold I have on her. I ease up my grip, needing to hear her beautiful sounds. She gulps in a breath and instantly whimpers her pleasure, an aphrodisiac to my ears.

"Just like that sweetheart. You sound so pretty coming for me." My voice is guttural. I fucking love the way she feels around me and how hard she makes me with her noises. I could get lost in a moment like this, give her anything she asks for, and more. She's my queen. My goddess. The fucking sun I orbit.

"Payton," she gasps, pulling me back to the moment with her nails raking down my arm as waves continue to roll over her.

Hearing my name from her lips is the most satisfying sound. Her sweet voice full of pleasure brings me to the edge. I groan into her hair, spilling my load as she flutters around me. Her pussy sucks my release from me, spilling down my shaft when she's too full to hold anymore.

I slide my hand down to where we're joined. "Look at the mess you made. Clean it up and don't waste a drop, my greedy girl." I swipe my fingers through our cum and bring it back to her mouth. She sucks my fingers clean, her tongue darting out and catching every bit, sending a thrill through me. My growl of pleasure rumbles through my chest as I praise her. "Good girl."

Forty-five

Ainsley

Payton kisses me hard, his hands roaming my body and painting me with our release. I smile, close my eyes, and tip my head back against his shoulder, enjoying the feel of his fingers coasting over my skin. He really loves this part of sex, marking me as his in such a primal way. It makes me feel closer to him. Wanted, cherished, needed. His.

"Don't you fucking fall asleep on me, Princess. This ass is mine to take. We're still warming up." He pumps his hips and I can feel his dick hardening again inside me.

My eyes snap open. Seriously? *This man.*

"You've come twice already. How are you going to go a third round so soon? Don't you need a nap? Some water? You're a decade older than me, after all," I tease, trying to hide the smile that wants to take over my face.

"I've fucked your face, spanked your ass, and choked you to orgasm and you're still a brat," he muses in my ear, his Daddy voice sending shivers racing down my arms. "What's it going to take to tame you?"

"You'll never tame me," I taunt, wanting to push him to see what else he'll introduce in his quest to see me tamed.

He bites my neck right where it meets my shoulder and sucks, the sensation lighting me up and turning me liquid in his arms. I mewl and shudder in his hold.

"I love your wild spirit, Spitfire. I want you bratty and mean and yourself," he says quietly in my ear, soothing the spot he bit with a gentle finger. "I also want you vulnerable and raw and open with me so I can take care of your every need. Don't keep me out with the bratty attitude when you need me the most."

An unexpected prick of tears hits me and I blink quickly. I push off of him and turn so we can be eye-to-eye. He sits back on his heels, watching me carefully, probably thinking I'm about to freak out. I take his hands and lace our fingers to reassure him I'm not.

"I'm yours, Payton Olsen. Every part of me, every need, everything I could hope for, is yours. It's not easy to open up and be as vulnerable as you want me to be, but I'm trying, and you seem to have a way of getting me there." I stop and swallow hard, about to give him a deep truth I'm not sure I should expose because it's one of my biggest fears. "You're getting my clingy, obsessive, attached, insecure side that thinks you'll get tired of me or find someone better. So if I have to be open, you have to be okay with me being needy as fuck. I need constant reassurance that I'm not too much and you actually like me when my brain is telling me that I'm annoying and you're only with me because you feel bad for me or something equally as pathetic."

His eyes soften and he huffs a laugh. "That's it?"

"Don't laugh at me," I say quietly, hurt spiking in my chest at his cavalier response to spilling the rawest parts of myself.

"I'm not laughing, I'm relieved." He leans forward and kisses me before pulling back and capturing my face in his hands. "It's fucking music to my goddamn ears, Princess. Everything you just said makes you even more perfect for me. Give me all of your clinginess. I want you stuck to me like the cute little koala bear you are. Don't you ever let go and you better fucking come to me when you need attention, reassurance, love, hugs, food, coffee, and to hear what a good girl or a filthy slut you are."

"It's not too much?" I cup my hands over his and voice my most vulnerable thoughts.

"If anyone thinks you're too much, they can fucking go find less, because you're a dream come true to me. You're the other side of the coin to my desire to care for and see all of your needs met. You're the lighthouse that sets my course and tells me what's needed, whether it's full steam ahead or slow going. Right now it's time to fill you up. Lie back and spread your legs for me so I can show you just how much I want my favorite set of holes dripping with my cum."

I giggle, scooting to the head of the bed, lying against the pillows. Instead of coming for me, he goes to the dresser and opens a drawer. I immediately think of the paddle and the flogger from the last time he opened a drawer over there. He has toy hidey-holes all over this room that I really need to explore to take a full inventory. When he turns back around, he's holding a big pink vibrator. I blink and open my mouth, ready to object. This man is full of surprises and I'm not sure how I feel about this one.

"If you've used that on someone else you're not coming near my pussy with it," I warn, sitting up, instantly on edge.

"Relax, Spitfire, all of my toys are new and purchased just for you, that's why it's pink. You're the only one I've played with here, and it's been a long time since I've played at all. I'm going to fuck that tight ass and you're going to fuck yourself with this. When you come apart with both holes filled, it'll be out of this world."

My whole body flushes at his description and plans for me. He crawls onto the bed, reaching between my legs and tugging on the plug that I've forgotten about entirely at this point. It felt really good to have something to clench around when he was spanking me, and I felt fuller while he was fucking me, but I think I'm in for something entirely different, now.

"Breathe and relax for me, Princess."

I take a deep breath and let it out slowly, allowing my body to relax as instructed. He pulls the plug free, leaving me suddenly empty.

"Please, I need you," I whine and reach for him, the desire to feel him inside me taking over.

"You're such a good little whore, begging for my cock. I'll make it all better and fill your ass the way you need."

I toss my head back and moan, still not sure why his words set my pussy pulsing with need instead of infuriating me, but I embrace it and widen my knees in invitation. "Fuck me, Daddy, please."

A cool drizzle of liquid hits my pussy and drips down my slit. Payton's fingers work the lube through my center and into my ass, pressing in first one, then two fingers, and scissoring them as he spreads the lube where he needs it. He's stretching me, getting me ready to take him, and it's erotic as hell the way he preps me, praising me continuously with how good I'm taking him, how amazing I feel, and how badly he wants me. I'm going crazy with desire, my hips rocking against his hand, begging for him shamelessly. This is so far from the one time I've had any butt play, and I like it so much more.

"Use your words if you need to stop at any time. You'll feel pressure and it might be a little uncomfortable at first. I'm bigger than the plug and my fingers." He strokes his cock with a lubed hand, his fingers moving over the piercings I like so much.

"I don't care, fuck me, now," I beg.

He chuckles, handing me the vibrator and turning it on to a steady vibration setting. "Put that on your clit until I'm inside, then fuck yourself with it and see what you think."

I eagerly press the vibrator to my clit and jump slightly as his cock nudges against my ass. I relax, which lets him in. My eyes roll closed from the delicious pressure as he rocks into me, filling me inch by inch and stealing my breath. I feel each of his piercings stroking along my walls as my body hugs him tightly. When he moves, fireworks pop behind my lids. I'm so full and he's still pressing into me. I don't know if I can do this. I whine and shake, my eyes closing tightly as sweat beads on my forehead.

"I'm halfway, Princess. You can take me. Breathe, baby."

Halfway? Holy shit. He's going to split me in half. My toes are curling and I focus on the vibrator and what I like. It's not unpleasant, it's just different. I like giving Payton one more part of me, and it does feel good now that I've made it past the point where it feels like my body wants to push him out. Actually, oh yeah, that feels really fucking good now.

I cry out, my orgasm detonating unexpectedly from the vibrator stimulation and having my ass so impossibly full. He grips my hips, swearing as my body squeezes him over and over. I'm euphoric, my mind and body on another level, disconnected, and floaty. This is amazing, the best I've ever felt. I've fully surrendered my control and feel completely at peace.

"Yes baby, I'm proud of you. You feel so fucking good like this, stretching around my cock, taking every inch of me, and loving it like the dirty whore you are."

Payton moves my hand with the vibrator to my center and lines it up so I can press it inside as well. It's harder to take the vibrator now that Payton is filling my ass, but slowly I work it in and now I know the meaning of full. Jesus, fuck. I pant and whimper, looking up at him for guidance.

"You're such a good slut, letting me use both your holes any way I want. Fuck yourself, Princess, show me how you make yourself feel good."

My brain short circuits between the words and his commands, and I do it, fucking myself on the vibrator as he takes up an alternating pace. Oh God, this is too much, I can't handle it. There's so much stimulation, I'm so full, there are too many sensations. I consider telling him to stop, that I can't take it, when he shifts and hits a spot inside me that pushes me to the brink, I tip over, gasping.

"Fuck, Payton, oh my God, I can't stop, I'm coming!" I scream, clenching both him and the vibrator, my body locked up in ecstasy.

I writhe, my body no longer under my control. He roughly slams me onto his cock, and it prolongs the release, my cries continuing as he works me over. He lifts my hips and pumps into my ass, his balls slapping with the force.

"Come for me once more," he commands, his voice tight with restraint.

"I can't," I whimper, tears filling my eyes from the pleasure and stimulation. It feels so good but it's too much.

"You can take it. You're made for this. You're my personal cocksleeve and I love watching you come. Don't make me ask again. You're going to fall apart and this ass is going to siphon my cum so you can be full of me in all your beautiful holes." He moves a hand to my clit and presses down, circling with two fingers as he continues to fuck me.

His commanding tone and filthy words do it, sending me over the edge another time, screaming my pleasure to the ceiling as he groans and tumbles headfirst with me. Feeling him spill inside my ass as my core clenches around him and the vibrator is on another level of pleasure and it rockets another orgasm through me. I can't breathe through this one, it locks my limbs and holds me captive with rapture. My vision darkens and sparks ignite behind my tightly shut lids.

The next thing I know, warm water hits my back, rousing me. I blink and look up, cradled against Payton's chest. He's holding me like a baby in the shower and smiling down at me in the happiest way. The big, sappy man.

"There's my girl. You came so hard you passed out and almost took me with you. I don't think my cock has ever been gripped that hard before. If I wasn't already stupidly in love with you, I would be, now."

I laugh quietly and lean my head against his shoulder, exhausted and still feeling floaty. Between the emotional toll of the day, the margaritas, and the marathon sex, I'm ready to pass out for real. I feel light as a feather in his big arms and my head doesn't feel connected to my body at all. It's so nice to not think. My mouth doesn't have a filter for my thoughts that spill out.

"It's your magical ribbed-for-my-pleasure cock and that dirty mouth of yours. I'm so glad I took them off the bench after all."

Payton laughs, the sound rumbling against my ear. It's funny how something that annoyed me months ago now sounds like home. I sigh and snuggle into his chest, kissing his beautifully sculpted pec.

"I'm going to put you on your feet, but you're going to hold onto me. The amount of endorphins you're high on is enough to take down an elephant. Subspace is all sorts of fun, but let's get you back to baseline, Princess."

He gently sets my legs down and wraps my arms around his waist. I close my eyes and hold him as he runs water over my head and down my body. He shampoos my hair, taking time to massage my scalp until goosebumps line my skin and my knees weaken. He rinses it out and turns us so he can run conditioner through the long strands, his strong fingers combing through any knots he finds. While the conditioner sits in my hair, he soaps up a sponge with my vanilla body wash and gently scrubs my entire body. He takes extra care around my core, and I have half a thought that I should be embarrassed that a man is soaping up my pussy and ass. I giggle when I remember that he had his mouth, fingers, and cock in those holes not that long ago, and I was perfectly happy about it, so cleaning that area shouldn't bother me now.

He takes a moment to soap himself up and rinses us both off before turning off the water. I get lost in his stunning ocean-blue eyes and the water glistening against his golden skin. He seems to shimmer, cut like a sea god of ancient times, ready for worship from a mortal like me.

"I love you." I sigh, feeling drunk on the feeling. It's so strong there's no stopping the words that tumble out of me. "You're so gorgeous. And so nice. Why do you even like me?"

Payton frowns as he wraps me in a fluffy white towel and

begins to dry my hair with another. "You shouldn't be questioning my love, but I'll indulge you anyway." He kisses my nose as he picks me up and walks me out of the shower. "You're the most gorgeous woman I've ever seen, perfect for me in every way, and you didn't want anything to do with me."

He sets me on the vanity and opens the drawer where I keep my skincare, then pulls out the various bottles and jars of the steps I repeat nightly. He begins applying the serums and creams for me. I smile under his ministrations, not at all surprised by his actions. This is Payton Olsen at his happiest, a caregiver through and through. I'm a lucky bitch to be on the receiving end of his love, even if I don't fully understand why he'd choose me, a standoffish, prickly, mean woman who did everything in my power to push him away.

"You made me work for your affection. I had to earn your love, which makes it even better. You fit with me. Not just with my unique desires in the bedroom, or physically, but the way I want my life to be. You challenge me to do and be better, to think about things differently, to consider the way my intentions appear, and the reality of what my actions look like." He puts the bottles away and gets my brush out next, spraying a leave-in conditioner into my hair before he brushes it out because he's observant and knows every step I take and will follow them to the letter now.

"Oh, is that all?" I deadpan, overwhelmed by his sentiments despite asking for just that.

He boops me gently on the nose with the brush before scooping me up and taking me into the bedroom where he deposits me on the bed. He disappears into the closet. When he returns, he's in loose shorts and carries the super soft MIT T-shirt I love. It's perfectly worn in, fits me like a dress, and always smells like him even when it's been washed. He slips it over my head and tucks me into bed. I watch contentedly as he leaves the room, his back flexing and his incredible ass on display for a moment before he disappears. He comes back a few minutes later with a plate of food and bottles, crawls in beside me and pulls me close.

"You were so beautiful coming apart tonight. Drink this."

He untwists the cap from a bottle of blue Gatorade and hands it to me. I dutifully take it and realize how thirsty I am when it tastes like the most amazing thing ever.

"You weren't fighting me as much, letting me take you where you needed to go." He hands me a chocolate cupcake next and I laugh.

"Am I being rewarded with tasty treats for coming so hard I passed out?"

"Honey, this is aftercare, it's a necessary part of bringing you down from that fun, floaty subspace you drifted off to before you passed out and came back to me in the shower."

I've read about subspace—something that can be experienced as feeling floaty or high on endorphins from the pleasure of sex, the rush of a scene, or the pain of an impact session. I never thought I'd get there, but that's exactly what it felt like. Payton is bringing my endorphin levels back to baseline so I don't experience the negatives of too much oxytocin, endorphins, and adrenaline flooding my system only to be left depleted and feeling like shit later, which is subdrop. He's such a good Daddy.

I enjoy my cupcake and Gatorade while he massages my scalp and gently runs his fingers along the neck of my shirt. I'm not even surprised when the doorbell rings a short while later and he leaves me in bed to get the food delivery he ordered. Of course he did. He always considers all of my needs, sustenance beyond chocolate at the top of the list.

Forty-six

Payton

"What the actual fuck," Hayes growls, his eyes snapping to the screen that just went active on the wall of the boardroom at the push of a button from my laptop.

"Jesus, fuck, Pay, where the hell are you and why are you playing Big Brother with us?" Zander quips from across the room, taking a napkin from his assistant to clean the coffee he spilled over his hand when I scared the shit out of him.

"Good morning, dear brothers. I'm working from home today but didn't want to miss our morning meeting."

"You're...what?" Hayes asks, leaning onto the table toward the screen like he can intimidate me into materializing in the room.

"Working from home. There's no need for me to be in the

office all the time, and I wanted to give Ainsley extra support today, so here we are. Now, to get started with the status report—"

"You're shitting me," Zander cuts in. "You've never missed a day of work, always the first one into the office, and you're changing it now because of your girlfriend? Dude, you've got it so fucking bad."

"I don't see a problem here," I retort calmly. "This is exactly what *your wife* was trying to accomplish a few months ago but I managed to find on my own while avoiding her scheming. Ainsley's my girlfriend now, the love of my fucking life, and I'll eventually make her my wife if she'll let me, so expect my priorities to shift accordingly, work included." I pause for their reactions.

Their faces are priceless, both shocked into silence and staring at me like I've been abducted and this is my attempt to ask them for help. *Blink twice if you need help* kind of shit.

Hayes shakes his head slowly, an annoyed look replacing the shock. "It's not ideal *right now*, but it's about damn time." He was the first of us to fall and he's been deeply under the spell of his sweet debutante bride ever since. It doesn't surprise me that he'd be the most accepting of my decision to put Ainsley first.

"I can't fault you. Good pussy and a woman who keeps you coming back for more are hard to argue with," Zander says, predictably steering the conversation to a sexual avenue. "We can shift our priorities and the team's focus to better adjust for us all having home lives that are more important than work, now."

"Already done." I share my screen so they can see the new restructuring plan I've laid out and the timeline for our ongoing projects with who'll be running point, which SVPs will pick up the slack, and what teams will align as support. As COO, this is my job, so it was no problem to look at it as another puzzle to solve. "The only inconsistency with an unsure timeline is the sports complex and entertainment district the city put on hold due to the bad press we received with the implosion of the Atlanta Haute List."

Ainsley chooses that moment to enter my office with a fresh cup of coffee. When she hears the name of her website, she pauses and her face goes beet red. She lifts her head and swallows, taking tentative steps toward me, and sets the cup on the edge of my desk, then turns to leave. Before she can flee, I grab her by the hips and pull her into my lap. She's still in my MIT shirt and panties, but you can't see below her waist on camera, and I keep her tucked into my chest with a reassuring arm banded around her. This is why I wanted to be here with her.

Zander snickers. "I see why you wanted to work from home. You start this shit and we're all going to be calling in from the home with a woman in our lap." He shakes his head before allowing me to return to business.

"The city stalled our plans for the arena project after green-lighting everything leading up to this point because we've offered a lucrative deal. They're keeping us from starting the actual construction now, which will cause a huge delay and unnecessary backlog for the rest of our plans, and we'll hemorrhage funds if we can't get their approval to begin as expected. I'm working on a proposal that'll entice them to reenter favorable negotiations that will end with us breaking ground and beginning the build phase this fall as planned."

"They're hesitant to restart negotiations, and rightly so. We have a track record of bad publicity, with this latest fake dating scandal being the cherry on top. I don't see how we can come back from that and get them to move any faster," Hayes says. "We'll have to move the timeline back and take the financial hit."

Fuck. If Hayes, our CFO, is willing to take a hit to the bottom line, he really can't see a way out. This doesn't look good.

Ainsley's fingers trace a pattern along my thigh that feels too good as her teeth work over her bottom lip. I cup her chin and pull her lip free, tapping it as a reminder of what that does to me. She sticks her tongue out at me before she grows serious again, looking between me and the screen where my brothers are contemplatively looking at the project timeline.

"Your project is going to gentrify a portion of the city that's home to a ton of small, family-owned businesses that won't be able to afford increased rents, or be able to renovate to attract the same crowds as the fancy new bars and restaurants your project will lure in," Ainsley begins softly.

I nod, encouraging her to continue. If she has an idea, I want to hear it. She knows the area better than any of us. She spent two years reporting on those small local businesses, collecting stories from the people and area. She has a unique perspective as a journalist that we don't have from a development lens.

"Why don't you offer to retrofit the local businesses and utilities around the sports and entertainment complex so they'll benefit, and the city won't have to do any work to ensure the surrounding areas are up to par when your new project is complete?"

"What would that do?" Zander asks.

She shrugs a bare shoulder that's peeking out of my shirt and bats her lashes with an innocent smile that's anything but. "You'd be helping smaller businesses like Mama P's who would suffer from lost revenue. You'd get them on your side and have local support for the project before it starts, which is good for optics. By working with the local utilities to upgrade what comes into the area, you'll make sure they can handle the new user load of the condos and businesses of the entertainment district and arena, which takes a huge onus off the city to do it and saves taxpayer funds so it makes you look like heroes."

"That sounds expensive," Hayes grumbles, but he doesn't outright refuse, which is a positive.

"It's going to cost us millions of dollars, but it'll save our asses," I reply. I look down at Ainsley, perched in my lap where she belongs, solving our problems like it's the easiest thing in the world. "You incredible woman."

She huffs a laugh and leans her head on my shoulder. "I'm always happy to find ways to spend Olympus's money on bettering the community and making y'all give back instead of just getting richer."

"I'll be careful if we ever ask for your help again, but this is actually perfect. The city won't be able to deny us if we make that kind of offer," Zander says, stroking his jaw as he runs through the details.

"We don't have other options if we want to keep our original timeline. We add a few mil to the budget for the upgrades and pitch it to the city. I'll get a team to run an analysis and prepare a rough estimate for the scope of additional work and resources required before I draft the proposal and shoot it over later this morning. I bet we hear back by the end of the day. Hayes, do you approve increasing the budget as needed?"

Hayes growls, unhappy about the change, but finally relents. "Run the numbers by me before you send the proposal. As long as they're reasonable I don't see why we can't *adjust*."

"Good. Glad that's settled, thanks to Ainsley's genius ideas. What's next?" I rub her thigh, loving this easy access to her skin while in a morning meeting. I can get used to this.

"We have an update on the cyber attack," Hayes says from his place at the head of the conference room table where the Olympus side of the call is taking place.

I've been expecting this news. I released the video of Archer coding, and all of the information Ainsley provided, to our contacts and caseworkers at the FBI shortly after leaving New York yesterday.

"You don't say?" I don't hide the irritation in my voice. I'm ready for this saga with Archer to be over.

"It was that punk ass kid, Archer Donovan, like Rex said," Zander adds. "He was arrested this morning. He looked like a pulverized piece of meat as he was pulled out of his Manhattan penthouse. The piece of shit got what he deserved. Black eyes and a swollen face, his hands in casts, and he was limping as they shuffled him into a blacked-out SUV."

"Looks like someone got to him before the feds did, but if you ask me, they held back. He wouldn't have been walking if I'd gotten to the rat," Hayes adds.

"It's about fucking time. He deserves worse than what I did to him and what the justice system's likely to do."

Ainsley stiffens in my lap, her attention pinned on me. This is the first she's heard of what I've done with the information she provided. I run my hand up and down her back soothingly.

"So you're aware of this development and had a hand in how he looked?" Zander asks, leaning back and studying me.

"I told you, Ainsley saved our asses and had everything we needed to take him down. I gave that to the FBI. After I had a chat with Archer myself. Oh, and Rex may have helped. I think it's time we finally give him that board of directors seat he's been asking for. We can trust him." I direct my attention to Hayes. "The man has an incredible right hook. I can't believe you used to spar with him and never had your pretty nose broken."

"You resorted to physical violence instead of hacking him back?" Hayes asks, his brows drawing together knowing he's usually the brother we tap for that type of vengeance. "I'm impressed. Normally, you'd find a way to fuck with him virtually and not leave a trace, like he did."

"Oh, I did that, too, but some situations call for a personal, hands-on approach." I give Ainsley a quick glance, about to bring her into the family in a way that'll have my brothers just as protective of her as I am. "Archer is Ainsley's abusive ex. He's been cyberstalking her. I couldn't let that stand after he showed up in Atlanta and put his hands on her."

My brothers posture up, faces drawn into scowls, their shoulders expanding in outrage on her behalf. They nod in understanding, grunting their approval and taking in the little blonde spitfire in my lap in a whole new light. With that one revelation, she's now their family, too.

Ainsley turns to me, shock warring with fury for sharing her personal details that she holds so privately. It was worth it, seeing the instant change in Hayes and Zander toward her, accepting her as theirs to guard as part of our family, just like I knew they would. I know my brothers and what turns on their protective instincts. Sharing this small detail would do it faster than allowing Ainsley to slowly let them in and share herself on her own timeline. I'm pushing her on my terms, as usual, and she doesn't like it.

"I told you he wasn't worth it. I can't believe you went after him. Is this why you were in New York yesterday? For some fucked up version of a billionaire bar brawl?"

I kiss her nose with an affectionate smile and hold her tightly when she tries to get up.

"I was teaching Archer a lesson called *do unto others as you want done unto you*," I explain. Ainsley rolls her eyes. I continue. "He's a bully whose time had come. I'd given him a clear warning and he still came after you. He won't be harassing or putting his hands on anyone for a very long time, and he certainly won't be using his hacking skills. I have far too much dirt on him now. The FBI will take care of the rest, I presume. Ainsley's evidence links him to the signature he's used on countless cyber crimes, so he'll finally pay for his misdeeds. I have a feeling Archer and his dear old dad will have plenty of bonding time in the big house for the long, foreseeable future."

Zander laughs and rubs his hands together in pleasure. "I'm already working with legal on an injunction to stop Nephele Industries's jet engine production since we know they used the original Pegasus plans that were stolen from the cyber breach. That should help with our launch." He's smug now that his bungled project is back on track.

"I'll let Rex know he's finally getting what he wants," Hayes mutters, lacing his fingers on top of a stack of paper and staring down.

He has a history with Rex and they've been contentious ever since we bought out his family legacy, crushing the friendship the two had. Rex being beyond creepy and stalking Paige didn't help the matter, but his assistance during a rough time for our company—several times—put us in debt to him and made for an unsettled situation ever since. Hopefully giving Rex what he wants—a spot on the Olympus board of directors—will mean we are back on even ground.

This feels good.

Things are finally coming together the way they should. Challenges are being met with clever solutions that my gorgeous girl had a hand in. Nuisances like Archer are being dealt with. Unfinished projects like our jet engine are finding clo-sure. Debts are being paid. It's good to see so much of our effort over the last few years finding a natural conclusion or being rewarded after so much sacrifice.

"I've got a proposal to write for the city and you both have projects and tasks to manage. I think we're done with this meeting," I say.

"Get that deal restarted. We have a hockey team to bring to Atlanta," Zander says. "Ainsley, if you need anything I'm the brother to ask. Welcome to the family, blondie."

"He's an idiot who doesn't know a hook from a cross. If you have an enemy you want buried so no one finds him again, you come to me," Hayes adds.

Forty-seven

Ainsley

Payton's an asshole. I love him, but I don't agree with everything he does, and sharing my personal details, even with his family, without my explicit consent, really pisses me off.

Once he let me off his lap, I left his office and have been posted up at the kitchen table sending emails to every news outlet I can think of that may consider taking me on as a staff reporter. The Southern Sounder is still my only job offer and it's depressing as hell thinking I may have tanked my career for good.

All that hard work, and gossip is my only legacy and also what's keeping me from finding a legitimate job because no one wants to touch me with a ten-foot pole after the way I was publicly humiliated. Why did I even bother with the years of schooling, internships, and busting my ass at the Gazette? Why did I take the worst story topics and turn them into something worth reading time and again if I'm destined to be infamously known as the "Gossip Girl of Georgia" for the rest of my career? *If I even have a career left.*

I sigh and hit send on yet another email to a paper that takes freelance stories. I'll try to build up a portfolio as a freelance writer and reestablish my credibility that way. It's not ideal and the pay isn't guaranteed unless I sell a story, so I'll be hustling all the time, trying to find stories to write that are worth buying. It's something to do in the meantime to keep myself relevant and provide an income.

My email notification dings and I quickly scan my inbox. The new email is from John Buckman, the editor-in-chief of the Atlanta Free Press. I sent him the proposal for my human interest story on Payton yesterday. Maybe he's letting me know if they'll pick it up. I click it and my heart rate quickens as I read through the email.

From: "John Buckman" <jbuckman@atlfreepress.com>

To: "Ainsley Montgomery" <ainsmontgomery@memail.com>

Subject: Your Future with the Free Press

Dear Miss Montgomery.

Thank you for your story proposal. I've reviewed it and I'm intrigued. Your previous stories on Olympus International have been well thought out and your writing is excellent. You have a way with the craft and are a natural storyteller who has a confident grasp on the rules of journalism that you know just when to break to make your stories sing.

I also admire your tenacity in the face of adversity. I've heard from my peers that you have been diligently inquiring about staff reporter positions with local papers, yet turned down a position as a gossip columnist with the Southern Sounder. I was curious as to the possible reasons you would refuse such a position, so please forgive me for extrapolating from what little I know of you and the situation. I imagine it has to do with wanting to distance yourself from the gossip that brought you so much notoriety and wanting to legitimize your journalism career. This is a noble cause when you could so easily lean into the infamy instead.

While I may not know the whole story, I know your writing enough to understand you as a journalist, and with that, I'd like to have you on my team as a staff writer. If you're interested, there's a place for you at the Atlanta Free Press. You'll have to earn your spot like every reporter here, but you're already well on your way with the stories you've written for us and the proposal you've most recently provided. Should you accept, we'll assign you stories outside of the Olympus realm to test just how versatile your abilities are and let your talents truly shine.

I look forward to speaking with you soon. Regardless of your answer, we'd like to buy your story on Payton Olsen and his work at Olympus.

Regards,

John Buckman

I jump up from my chair and pace the length of the dining room and back, my hand over my mouth, eyeing my laptop like this is a trick. I purposely didn't reach out to the Atlanta Free Press, wanting to pitch my latest story first to test the waters, see if they're still amenable to working with me in a freelance capacity before I spring the idea on them of being a full-time reporter. John reaching out proactively and asking *me* to join their team is mind-blowing.

They want me on their team. I didn't completely wreck my career. There's still a future for me in journalism that doesn't involve gossip. Relief courses through my body and heady elation fills me.

Fuck yes!

I sit and quickly type a response, accepting John's offer. Minutes later, he replies with an invitation to stop by the Free Press office to finalize details. I slam my laptop shut and rush into the bedroom to shower and get ready. Holy shit, I have a job.

Payton walks into the bathroom while I'm putting on makeup and leans against the doorframe, watching me. "Care to tell me what you're up to?"

I put my mascara down and turn to him, fighting the smile that wants to take over my whole face. I give in and blurt out the news. "I accepted a staff reporter position with the Atlanta Free Press."

His eyebrows rise and he rushes in to scoop me in for a crushing hug. "I'm so fucking proud of you. I knew you'd come out on top and would find another paper."

I take his praise and affection without rebuffing it, which would've been my standard reaction before he asked me to trust him, to let him in, and let him care for me. It's an uncomfortable feeling, kind of like Velcro rubbing my brain, but I fight the urge to say something snarky or dismiss his confidence in me. I can grow and learn in this respect as much as I can from my gossip-mongering ways.

"I have to sign my contract. I shouldn't be gone long, but figured I'd put myself together and make a good impression.

"You'll be amazing, as usual. Take the Rover and stop for an iced coffee so you have your favorite drink to hype yourself up," he instructs. After kissing my head, he turns to the closet and retrieves an outfit. "Wear the navy pencil shirt and white sleeveless top I like so much. You look incredible and so professional. It'll give you an extra boost of confidence, and it'll make me want to fuck you even more when you get home."

Once I'm dressed, he even kneels and helps me into my favorite heels, doing up the ankle straps for me.

I smile and kiss him before taking the purse he holds out. "Thank you," I say simply, taking his help and letting him do the little things he likes so much that mean he's caring for me.

The Atlanta Free Press office is in a high-rise building downtown, the metal and glass structure intimidating as I walk behind John Buckman himself after signing my contract to join the staff as a reporter. My hand was shaking so badly I'm sure my signature is illegible, but it's the thought that counts.

The reality hit me while I was sitting in John's office that I'm finally achieving the dreams I put off years ago and thought I'd never have because of my failures and the part Archer played in fucking with me—both in grad school and most recently by hacking the Haute List and exposing me. But I'm as much to blame for my situation in life as any outside force, and I'm owning both of those situations. Archer wouldn't have been able to manipulate me if I hadn't been willing to write the article he gave me the information for, or expose me if I hadn't created an anonymous gossip site in the first place. I'm especially grateful for second and third chances as I look around the bullpen area full of cubicles and desks with busy people. It's such a shift from the mediocre and uninterested staff at the

Gazette, where writing was a job, not a passion. Here, you can feel the intensity, the drive, that fuels each person.

"You'll start out here with the rest of our staff reporters. It's not fancy, but it'll give you a spot to write and grow with the team," John says, pointing at an empty cubicle.

A tall, curvy, goddess of a woman with chestnut hair slicked back into a high ponytail pops up on the other side of the cubicle. She eyes me for a moment before grinning and walking around the half wall with her hand extended.

"Hey, I'm Lilah Williams, sports," she says as I take her hand. Her handshake is firm and she looks me directly in the eyes. She's all powerful energy and tenacity. No wonder she's writing for the sports section. She'll be able to handle the egos of the professional athletes in our city and get through the male-dominated segment of journalism without crumbling. It's an interesting contrast to her perfect, red-painted pout and cat eyeliner that's sharp enough to cut a man. She's a true *femme fatale*. A smokeshow.

"Ainsley Montgomery," I say, not sure what else to add.

"Ainsley will be covering the business beat as well as entertainment and lifestyle on occasion, if she'll deem us worthy of her critical eye," John supplies.

Lilah laughs. "I've heard about you and was an avid reader of the Haute List before I knew you were behind it. You're an amazing writer. You're going to be an asset to our team. I'm looking forward to getting to know you better."

"Actually, Lilah, can you show Ainsley around a bit more? I have a one o'clock meeting near Buckhead. I need to head out now or I'll be stuck in traffic for an hour."

Lilah nods and salutes John. "Of course. I give a better tour anyway. I'll show her where the best coffee shops within a four-block radius are, which cafés will cave and give her day-old pastries for free if she tells them she's a poor reporter, and all the best after-work drinks places."

"Could you at least start with the building and pretend to work, please?" John says with patient exasperation, like he's used to Lilah's humor and flippant ways.

Lilah crosses her arms over a generous chest that's covered by an Atlanta Condors football T-shirt tucked into wide-leg jeans and pristine white high-top sneakers. "Just leave, John. I'm fully capable of giving her a tour."

I like Lilah's assertive attitude. I can see us becoming work friends and maybe even real friends.

"Welcome to the team, Ainsley. I know I speak for everyone when I say we're looking forward to having you on staff." John shakes my hand and leaves, his meeting now his priority.

Lilah cranes her neck and watches him go, then unfolds her arms and beams at me. "Halle-freaking-lujah! I'm so happy to have another woman my age on staff. Everyone else is over thirty, which isn't bad, but I've needed a work buddy without kids and an ex-husband to complain about," she says, motioning for me to follow her as she starts power-walking past the cubicles in the bullpen. "This is where we work, blah blah. That's the supply closet you'll want to raid to steal pens and notebooks," she says, pointing to a door on the left. "That's the gross bathroom. Don't use it. Mike from legal eats gas station burritos every day and takes a massive shit around eleven that ruins it for everyone. Give yourself extra time to make it to the bathroom that's a slightly longer walk."

"Can you slow down? My legs are shorter than yours." I'm nearly jogging in my heels to keep up with her pace. Fuck being short. This sucks. It occurs to me that Payton always matches my pace, never making me stretch to keep up with him. I've never noticed that before, but it's just another way he's been quietly considerate of me from the beginning. I love that stupid man.

"Oh, shit, sorry, I'm not used to anyone dressing up in the office. John's super lax about the dress code, so feel free to wear sneakers and dress casually whenever you want. If you have a high-profile subject coming in for an interview or you're going to cover some big story, keep a blazer and heels in your car. That's what I do." She slows her strides and I'm able to stay by her side. I swipe my hair behind my ear, taking measured breaths.

"How long have you worked here?"

"Two years. I was in Seattle before this but moved home to be closer to my parents when my mom was diagnosed with MS. I grew up in Athens, so not too far away. My parents are still there."

"I'm sorry to hear about your mom. MS sucks." Damn, that's intense and so sad to see a loved one deteriorate to a disease like multiple sclerosis.

She shrugs, dismissing my comment, and points at a doorway. "That's the break room. Mark your food but expect it to disappear anyway. We have an office lunch thief and I've narrowed it down to Tammy from advertising or Cheryl from finance. Both of them are shady as hell and would absolutely steal your yogurt or eat your takeout. They even play pickleball together. What the fuck even is that? A stupid hybrid sport for lunch thieves who can't play real sports is what it is." She scrunches up her perfectly manicured brows and shakes her head, clearly disliking these women and their activities. "The nice bathrooms are just around the corner and have multiple stalls, so we don't have to share with the men. We can cry in peace when we need to if the patriarchy becomes too oppressive before we remember heads up, tits up, let's fuck shit up, because we rule the world, anyway."

"Sounds like my kind of bathroom," I deadpan.

She laughs as she whips around and starts marching us back the way we came. "That covers it for the office. Let's get out of here and I'll show you my favorite place to grab a coffee and breakfast sandwich. They make their own biscuits that are incredible and melt in your mouth. You can build your own sandwich, so it's fun to change up what you put on it."

"Yes, I need coffee. My adrenaline's dumped now that the anxiety has worn off and I'm dragging." I was too anxious and amped up to stop for a coffee like Payton suggested before coming to the Free Press.

We walk a few blocks from the office to Hestia's, a cute café that smells divine and is incredibly welcoming. The exposed brick walls and worn, wide plank wood floors are rustic, but the pink and white striped counter topped with gleaming white marble, the small tables and groups of pink chairs, and the pink accents everywhere are luxe and girly.

"This isn't really a place I imagined you would like from the very brief introduction I've had. I guess I need to slow my assumptions," I tell Lilah as she looks through the glass of the pastry case, checking out the sandwiches and desserts.

"Don't let my big attitude and job as a sports reporter fool you. I'm girly and love to indulge in the finest female things. If you ever want to go for a mani and pedi after work, I have the best place nearby." She wiggles her fingers, showing off her long, almond-shaped nails that are red and white with black designs and even sport the Condors's logo painted on a few. She's fully committed to the team, it seems.

"Noted." I laugh, looking at my short, natural nails that I don't bother to do much more than file semi-regularly. I've never made much money as a reporter, so I carefully budget my funds, and getting my nails done wasn't a splurge I wanted to make. Obviously, Lilah has different priorities, judging by the complicated design she's chosen and the really nice sneakers she's wearing. I shouldn't judge or assume I know anything about another person's finances, so I stop.

We order our coffee and biscuits, find a table in a corner, and sit with our food. I take in a breath, knowing it's about to be awkward like a first date where you have to learn about someone while eating, when Lilah speaks.

"You have one shitty ex. I'm sorry he did you dirty like that with the Haute List. I hope he gets what's coming to him. If not, let me know and I'll casually slip you some information for some enforcers I know who don't mind fucking up men who treat women badly."

I huff an unamused laugh. "Oh, don't worry, he got what he deserved. He was arrested this morning in connection with his other cyber crimes."

"Thank goodness karma or fate decided to work in this case."

Or Payton Olsen did. "Yeah, something like that. I'm just relieved it's behind me and I can move on from this whole situation." I'm keeping my cards close, not willing to open up completely to this relative stranger beyond what's common knowledge.

"At some point, I want the full story, but for now, cheers to seeing that motherfucker's tears!" She holds up her iced latte and I toast her with my sweet cream iced coffee and grin.

"I like that, and I'm way better off now. I'm finally happy."

She smiles at me. "That's adorable. Now if I can just find myself a hot athlete, I'd be set. Know any big dudes with bigger dicks that need a fine-ass honey to cheer at all their games? Because I'm available."

Yeah, I like Lilah Williams.

Forty-eight

Ainsley

Three Years Later

"Can you believe it's finally done?" I glance around the pristine promenade leading up to the arena in awe.

Payton looks at the brand-new mountain of glass and steel that is Olympus Arena, the new sports complex in downtown where the Atlanta Hydras will take the ice for the first time in their inaugural season. The project took years and millions of dollars to bring to fruition, but here it is in all its glory, people streaming in by the thousands to see our team.

"It's surreal, but I'm relieved the construction phase is done and we just have the team ownership to look forward to now," he replies, tucking me into his side as we enter a side door where security knows us by sight and usher us in quickly.

We head down a hallway toward the ice where we meet up with Hayes, Paige, Zander, Harlowe, and all the kids. Madelyn and Hana, both three, look freaking adorable bundled up in matching navy sweatshirts with the Hydras venom green logo on their chests, navy headbands holding back their hair. They're giggling together next to Hendricks. He's in a personalized Hydras jersey with Olsen and the number seven, his age, on the back. He's such a good kid, holding the girls' hands in his.

Zander waves. "Hey, blondie. Whoa there, buddy." His attention is quickly diverted to his two-year-old son, Axel, who's nonstop adrenaline and climbing the boards that separate us from the ice.

He captures the tiny terror in his arms and blows a raspberry on his tummy, causing the cute kid to giggle. That child is just like his father, looking for anything dangerous he can get into, giving his parents heart attacks regularly.

Harlowe sees me watching Zander and Axel. "Hey, girl. The offer to babysit still stands." She gives me a wicked grin, knowing I'll outright refuse every time because Axel scares the shit out of me. I don't want to take a kid to the emergency room with a split lip, or worse, because that's what Axel does. He's already had stitches in his chin and he's barely two.

She's holding her nine-month-old, Everly, the cuddliest, sweetest baby who sleeps most of the time. I joke that this was Harlowe's gift for having to deal with the hellion that is Axel. Ever's wearing a large bow on her head of dark hair, but her big gray eyes that match all her siblings blink sleepily at me when I hug Harlowe and kiss the baby's head. If all infants were as calm and lovely as Ever, I'd possibly consider my own. How Zander and Harlowe have four kids, three of them under three, is crazy to me.

Paige greets me with a hug, tugging at my jersey. "This is cute! I love it."

"Thanks! I like your outfit. I'll need to find one of those sweatshirts for another game."

She went with one of the team's classic crewnecks with a logo that looks like it's for a country club. She's perfectly preppy and so very Paige.

Hayes comes up behind her, one arm wrapping around her shoulders and bringing her close while he holds their one-year-old son, Zachary, in his other arm. Zachary looks like his older sister, Maddy, with bright green eyes and dark hair, but he has his father's intimidating scowl, whereas Maddy is angelic like her mama. I'm not fooled by it and come in close to tickle him, smiling as he erupts into giggles and squirms.

"Only you can get a full laugh like that. He's more reserved with everyone else," Hayes remarks, bouncing Zachary in his arm as the little boy ducks his face against his father's shoulder.

"We had a moment when I changed his diaper and he peed on me. I freaked out and tried to get the new diaper on him, tickling him in the process as I made all sorts of noise, and he started giggling. It made me laugh and that kept him going. We've bonded through a diaper change, unfortunately," I explain, reaching out and brushing Zachary's cheek, making him smile.

"Be careful, Pay, this little guy is gonna steal your girl if you're not careful." Hayes raises his eyebrows at Payton, who puts his arms around me and pulls me against his chest.

"I've got at least seventeen years until that kid is legal. I'm not worried." He kisses the top of my head and I melt against him.

"You might hear yourself called daddy sooner than that if she ends up with baby fever, though," Paige adds, winking at me.

I laugh. "I'm the only one who gets to call him Daddy. No babies necessary." I look up at Payton and he smiles proudly, reveling in my not-so-subtle acknowledgment of our dynamic.

"And it'll stay that way as long as you want it to, Princess." He traces the day collar necklace I still wear as he kisses me and gets groans from both of his brothers while Harlowe and Paige melt.

"You can talk about your kinky sex life all you want, just keep it PG in front of the kids," Zander says, holding Axel upside down over his shoulder as the toddler squirms. "Who knows, it might lead to another little one for us if it's hot enough." He pulls Harlowe in with his other arm and squeezes her ass.

Harlowe tips her head back and bellows a laugh, not at all embarrassed by her husband's overt sexuality. They're very open about their active sex life, whereas I tend to be very private and why I may have shocked them just now with my *Daddy* comment. It's taken years, but I'm opening up more with Payton's family.

The overhead lights dim and the spotlights start up a crazy dance as music booms over the speakers. The pre-game activities are starting. The Olsens, as the owners of the team, will play a role in the opening ceremony, and as the family, we get to join them. Harlowe and Paige open their bags to pull out ear muffs for the little kids, with only Axel fighting the hearing protection, as expected. Nothing is easy with that child. He makes everything a war. When Harlowe hands him a pack of fruit snacks, he finally stops fighting and forgets the earwear.

The door to the ice is opened and a carpet is rolled out to make it easy for the guys in their suits and leather shoes to walk on the slippery surface. The NHL commissioner, the team general manager, the coach, and the brothers, all walk onto the ice as the full team skates into place behind them. They welcome the fans to Olympus Arena, thank them for supporting the Hydras in their first season, and the commissioner officially recognizes the team as part of the NHL.

The GM, coach, and commissioner leave the ice, and we're beckoned on with the kids. I walk out between Harlowe and Paige, amidst the crowd of kids, feeling like part of a family. They set up the goal with our new goalie, Ryder Kingston, set to block the first shots that we get to shoot as the owners and family. The kids get to go first, and it's adorable to see them using mini sticks to shoot pucks at Ryder, who kindly lets them score.

When it's Axel's turn, he pushes the puck toward the goal and lets out a blood-curdling war cry as he throws the stick like a spear at Ryder, who uses his blocker to bat it away. Axel kicks the puck between Ryder's legs into the goal, then launches himself at Ryder's legs, clinging to his pads like a monkey as he howls in triumph.

The crowd erupts into cheers and laughter as Zander hurries across the ice to pull his deviant of a child off the unsuspecting goalie, who's trying to shake the kid off gently. Zander manages to unlatch Axel from Ryder's pads and they both laugh about it as Zander once again throws the toddler over his shoulder where he'll be out of trouble.

The brothers get to take their shots next, and Ryder easily blocks Zander's attempt in retribution for his child's recent attack. Hayes takes it a little too seriously, squaring up with the massive goalie and shooting the puck like he's been practicing but still not making it past Ryder. I'm laughing along with the girls when Ryder skates out of the goal and hands me his stick.

I take it, confused. This wasn't part of the plans we'd discussed. "What are you doing?" I've met all the players briefly but don't know Ryder well.

He lifts his mask. "Everyone's thinking that the Olsens aren't making their shots because I'm in the net. I think you need to give your man hell and stand in for me. Show all these fans it's not who's in the net that matters, it's their poor shooting skills keeping them from scoring." He winks at me and puts his blocker on my other hand and pushes me toward the goal. He flips a puck to Payton and skates after me, positioning me in the net and showing me how to stand and where to put the stick.

When he moves to the back of the net and clears my vision, Payton is facing me about fifteen feet away, holding a stick like it's the most natural thing in the world while I feel like this is the most awkward thing I've ever experienced. The blocker on my arm is warm and heavy, and the stick's too big for my hand.

And everyone is watching me. Oh, God, this is so embarrassing. My face is on fire and my knees are shaking. But I want to prove that Payton ain't shit when it comes to hockey and I can block his shot. I tap the stick on the ice and poke my tongue out at him. He throws his head back and laughs, taking his position and slapping the puck so it slides toward me.

Immediately, I notice something's off about the puck. It slowly slides toward me, and I stop it with the stick, dropping the blocker so I can pick it up. There's silver writing on the black puck that says *look up, Princess*, with a circle drawn in the middle with stars around it.

The crowd is screaming when I drop the stick and look up. Payton's there, on his knees in front of me, taking the puck from my hand so he can hold my fingers. "Breathe, baby," he coaxes, and I realize I haven't taken a breath since I realized something was off.

"What's happening?" I ask, though I'm pretty sure I know exactly what's going on. When he speaks, I realize he's been given a microphone and the whole arena can hear his words.

"Ainsley Montgomery, I've been yours since the moment you snarled at me for stopping you from ruining a perfectly good computer in the most heinous café. We've spent three amazing years together, but a lifetime with you wouldn't be enough. I'm so deeply in love with you I'll never be the same. I'll be yours until the oceans swallow the earth and then you'll still be the moon that controls my tides. Life has been so incredibly good with you, but I want it to be even more amazing, and the only way I see that happening is by you becoming my wife and making me the happiest man alive."

He pauses to pull out a velvet box and opens it to reveal a stunning diamond ring that has me gasping. Hot tears spill down my cheeks as he looks up at me with such ardent devotion and affection.

"Ainsley, my sassy Spitfire, beautiful Princess, and love of my life, will you marry me?"

No other answer even crosses my mind. "Yes." I quietly tack on *Daddy* after, just for him to hear.

I throw myself into his arms as his face splits into the stupid grin I love so much. He catches me but goes sprawling out on the ice as I cover his face with kisses and my happy tears. He holds me tight and murmurs into my hair until I stop crying. He sits us up, takes my left hand, and slides the beautiful ring onto my finger.

"How about we get off this cold ice and I take you up to our suite to enjoy the rest of our night?"

I sit up, pulling on his arm to bring him with me, and we return to our family, who are beaming at us. Payton pulls a mic out of his collar and hands it to one of the arena employees as we leave the ice. Paige and Harlowe pull me in for hugs while Hayes and Zander pound Payton on the back. My hand is stretched out to show off the ring and I get to admire the details along with everyone else.

It's stunning and so perfect. The large, pear-shaped diamond is the prettiest, delicate blush pink, haloed by round white diamonds, on a platinum band studded with pave diamonds. It's elegant and graceful and fits me perfectly.

We troop up to the family box, but Payton pulls on my hand to keep me from going inside with the rest. "We have our own box. I have plans for you."

Forty-nine

Payton

The owners' suites are midway up in the arena, with seats on outdoor balconies should we choose to view the game from there, but the large flat-screen TVs on the walls are playing everything that's happening below in high definition and it's easier to follow this way. Tonight, I don't plan on watching the game. I'm going to devote my full attention to my brand-new fiancée.

Ainsley's fingers tremble in my grip. "How are you feeling, Princess?"

"I'm so happy I don't know what to do. I'm kind of freaking out at how public that was and how many people just watched us get engaged. What's that going to mean with the news and gossip?" She worries her lower lip with her teeth.

We've kept our relationship as private as possible, but inevitably, there have been stories about us. The end of the Atlanta Haute List left a void that several new copycat sites filled. They don't do it quite as well as Ainsley did but still manage to post stories and get views.

I'm proud of her for expressing these emotions, but there's likely more she's not saying because that's the way my girl works. She can only voice so many feelings at once and stuffs down anything that overwhelms her instead of processing what she needs to.

"Feeling a bit overwhelmed?"

"So much," she says, eyes pleading for what she knows I'm offering.

"Do you need to stop overthinking?" I ask, ready to take on any burden she's carrying to help her in the way we've found works best. She likes a little pain and a lot of pleasure to get out of her spiral of anxiety that usually comes with new situations and overwhelming thoughts. She ends up processing her feelings just fine once her brain stops spinning. Otherwise, she'll stuff it down and dissociate. I want to avoid that with a happy new experience like our engagement causing her overwhelm.

"Please, Daddy, turn my brain off."

She leans into me, trusting me unequivocally to take care of every need as she surrenders her control. We've laid the foundation for this kind of trust through countless sessions where I've listened to her and shown her that while she submits to me, she's in control. A single word from her stops our play or changes the direction it takes. She has all the power in our scenes, dynamic, and relationship. Everything I do is for her pleasure, care, and protection.

"It's a good thing I brought this, isn't it?" I pull a butt plug and a tiny bottle of lube from my inside suit pocket and place them on the table next to her.

"What? Here? You can't be serious." Her eyes are wide in disbelief. To Ainsley, this suite is basically a public space. I'm pushing her boundaries by asking her to submit with strangers on the other side of a thin sheet of glass and in the suites next door.

"I'm quite serious. I want you to have something to clench around when I spank that perfect ass." She'll love the feeling just as much as she'll get off on the implied humiliation of someone looking inside and catching us in the middle of our scene. While she's not an exhibitionist, she loves to be degraded, and we've discovered it extends beyond just the dirty words that do it for her.

I take off my jacket and begin rolling up my sleeves, initiating the scene with the familiar action. She stills, entering her submissive headspace in preparation.

"Take off your panties, give them to me, and put that in your ass." I place a kiss against her temple, ready to watch.

"What about..." She gestures nervously at the floor-to-ceiling glass windows overlooking the arena and the hockey game below. There are seats right outside our balcony with fans cheering wildly, though our suite is soundproof and it's only a muffled roar in here.

"Don't you want to show off what a good fucktoy you are for me and how badly my slut wants my cum?" I ask with an amused chuckle.

She shakes her head and glares at me, the brat coming out when she was prepared to be such a good girl to get what she needs. "Yellow," she says, using her safe words before we've even begun, making me smile proudly. "We'll have security banging down the door when they hear me screaming from you turning my ass red. I don't want the embarrassment of having to explain what we're up to." She stands her ground, and I know this is a boundary she won't back down from. I cup her chin and smooth my thumb over her cheek, so in love with this feisty little spitfire.

"The glass is one-way. They can't see in, but we have a perfectly clear view of the ice. As much as I love your incredible body, I won't be sharing it with random strangers." I assure her. "It's also soundproof. Notice how we can barely hear the crowd out there even though they're insanely loud? No one is going to bang down our door because I'm banging you like a screen door in a hurricane."

The suite was designed with my needs in mind. As much as I'm an exhibitionist, I won't share a single intimate moment with my girl with anyone else. And I plan on having plenty of moments with her at games going forward.

She relaxes, realizing her privacy will be maintained. She smiles as she begins to strip, her fears alleviated.

I lean against the wall while she undresses, enjoying the view as her skin is revealed. Seeing Ainsley naked never gets old. She sends my desire flying with the briefest glimpse of her body.

She picks up the plug and pauses, holding up her left hand, my ring shining next to it. "My engagement ring matches my butt plug." She giggles and shakes her head. "You really think of everything. Only you would ensure all my jewelry is my favorite color." She pops the cap of the lube, coating the plug before bending over and pressing it against her ass, accepting it slowly while I watch.

Fuck me. I start naming every player on the Hydras roster to keep myself from getting too worked up from watching. She hands me her panties and I run the silky material under my nose while she watches. I'm intoxicated. Addicted to Ainsley, this little hit not nearly enough for me. I need *her*. I add the scrap of silk to my jacket pocket and turn back to her with a hungry look. I unfasten my belt and pull it off quickly with one hand, snapping the leather. Her mouth goes slack as she watches, eyes unfocused, entering subspace where she'll experience this session in a deliriously floaty state.

"Hands," I command.

She presents her wrists to me, and I wrap them with the belt. She's so beautiful, her wrists bound and my ring flashing on her finger. Fuck, that looks good. I step back and take in the sight. It's permanently rewiring my brain to experience an even deeper love for her I didn't know existed. I unknot my tie and slip the silk from my neck, walking around Ainsley as she trembles in anticipation, her nipples pebbled against the temperature in the room.

"Close your eyes, Princess."

She does, and I wrap it around her head, tying it into a blindfold. I lead her to the black leather sofa and bend her over the back, balanced on her tiptoes, her restrained arms stretched over the seat cushions.

"Did you drink more water than coffee today?" I ask patiently, my Daddy voice making her quiver.

She's quiet for a moment. "Not yet."

I bring my palm down across her bare ass, watching as she clenches around the plug and gasps. The first one is always a shock to the system. I tsk.

"What about your affirmations and meditation? Did you do those?" I ask, running through her short list of tasks I've assigned so she works through her biggest struggles and deals with her anxiety. It's part of our dynamic that extends outside of our play sessions and the bedroom. It's another way I'm able to care for her.

"I journaled for my meditation but not the affirmations,"

she says.

I slap her ass again, making her jump and wiggle against the couch. The wiggles help her overstimulated system deal with the pain, but she'll settle in soon enough.

"Telling yourself you're a strong, capable woman who kicks ass, is an incredible writer, and has a hot body shouldn't be difficult when it's all true," I remind her with a rumble to my tone that she loves, given the way her back arches and one knee pops, her foot coming off the ground and smoothing along my leg, needing connection. Normally, I position her on my lap in some manner so we're touching for intimacy during the pain, but tonight she needs to experience this on her own.

"It's hard to take myself seriously when I say those things," she protests.

I surprise her by tugging on the plug in her ass, getting a moan and quickly swatting a cheek when she relaxes. She yelps and grinds against the sofa, looking for friction. That's my good fucking girl.

"You'll do better next week or you won't get my cum, *and* I'll make you do the affirmations to me instead of by yourself," I threaten, rubbing my palm over the pink handprints blooming on her ass.

She whimpers, unhappy about the ultimatum. "Fine, I'll do them."

I bend down and bite her delicious cheek. She squeaks but quickly presses back against me when I stay low, pulling her open and lapping at her soaked core. I groan at the taste as I eat her from behind until she's squirming, teetering on the edge. I pull back, denying her the orgasm she's searching for because she didn't complete her tasks, but I'm willing to reward her for agreeing to work harder.

"Mmmm, that's my good girl," I growl against her. "Somehow, my fiancée tastes even better than my girlfriend did."

She's moaning and writhing, pushed up onto the back of the sofa with her arms so she can grind against my face. I stand and press her back down over the sofa and spank her ass again. Her cry is one of total pleasure and she widens her legs, looking for friction for her clit. I press the plug with my thumb and drive two fingers into her silky cunt, stroking her as I slap her ass again, feeling her clench around me. "There you go, baby, you're so close."

"More, please, Daddy," she whimpers.

"You're so sweet and obedient for me when you want something, Princess. But I want you dripping and pathetic. Make a mess and show me what my future wife looks like begging to come wrapped around my fat cock." I spank her again and she cries out, pleas for more and harder falling from her gorgeous lips in a beautiful chorus of passion while her pussy clutches my fingers as she loses control.

"Oh, fuck," Ainsley whimpers, her legs shaking as I stroke her through her release. She's dripping now, just like I told her, my hand coated in her mess. It takes everything not to drop to my knees for her again and lick her clean like a juicy Georgia peach.

I pull my fingers out of her spasming cunt and suck them clean. I wrap my arms around her and yank her against my chest, letting my hands roam along her warm skin. I trail my fingers up to her face and pull the blindfold from her eyes. She turns her face toward me, blinking as I remove the belt from her wrists.

"I want you free for what's next. Go stand in front of the glass and let me look at you." I step back to give her room to move away from the sofa and instantly miss the warmth of her against me. I'd attach this woman to me if I could. Let her sit on my lap and warm my cock through all my meetings, cling to me like a cute little koala bear, hold her in my arms so I can smell her neck or hair when I need a hit of her intoxicating scent. Fucking obsessed is what I am, and damn proud of it.

She takes wobbly steps to the window and turns to look at me with a devilish smile. There's my bratty baby girl. So much for the obedient good girl. She got off and now she's testing boundaries.

"Show your future wife how you crawl for her, Payton." She's confident, holding out her hands and beckoning me closer.

Oh, girl. She's waving a red flag in front of a bull with that request. I'd do anything for her. All she has to do is ask, but we haven't engaged in power exchanges much due to the demands of our dynamic and her comfort levels. I've always been the Dominant, the top, in our relationship because she needed it. But this? I can fucking do this.

I drop to my knees, feeling the hard floor beneath the fine wool of my trousers, keeping my eyes on her as I crawl to my fucking *queen* coming into her power now that she's wearing my ring and agreed to become my wife. It doesn't take me long to cross the space and end up at her feet, where I bow and kiss up her legs from her toes to that glorious pussy that has me so enraptured I'd do anything for her. I'm so fucking hard with this switch in our roles. I've known she's capable of topping, if she wanted to, since the night we went to Dionysus and she looked like my hot teacher fantasy, but she's always enjoyed bratting and submitting to me more.

I stay on my knees as I bury my face in her pussy and show her how I worship the single greatest thing in my life. She rocks back against the window and grips my hair, a moan escaping her as I spread her thighs wider and nudge one of her legs onto my shoulder for better access. I feast. I know her body so well at this point that each moan, every tensing of her muscles, and each intake of breath that she holds feels like my personal map to unlocking the pleasure chest waiting for me. Her legs go rigid, shaking as a release grips her and travels from her pointing toes to her center and goes off like the Fourth of July with her needy screams and bucking hips that grind into my face. I suck her clit and take her through the climax, easing her down with soft licks to her pussy, and wait for her hazy eyes to open and find mine with a shaky smile.

Now it's time to flip it back to what she needs and continue our work to get her out of that beautiful, busy brain of hers and help her let go so she can quietly experience the feelings, new situations, and emotions that are overwhelming her. I have to top the top that suddenly rose up in her. I stand and spin her, pressing her against the window, her wrists raised above her head in my fist. She gasps, the cold glass a shock to her flushed skin and sex-disoriented brain.

"You liked me worshiping at your feet, didn't you, my queen?" I ask, kissing her neck as she presses against me.

"Yes." She sighs, her warm breath fogging the icy window. "You're beautiful on your knees for me, my love."

I groan into her hair, my hands moving down to my pants. I unzip and push my boxer briefs down far enough to free my cock. "You know I'll get on my knees for you whenever you want, Princess, but I think you're desperate for my cock and you want me filling his greedy cunt more. I'm gonna fuck that pretty pussy and wreck you tonight."

She whimpers when I lift her up, holding her with one arm, and slowly pull her down onto my cock so she feels each of my piercings, a moan slipping from her lips when our hips meet. She leans her face against the glass and presses her hands at shoulder height as I wrap her legs around my hips for support so I can hold her waist and pump into her tight cunt with abandon. She's small enough for me to throw around and use like the fucktoy I love and I take full advantage. I angle her hips back, slamming into her before pulling out to the tip, her breath fogging up the glass around her face as she cries out with each thrust.

"Oh my God," she screams, her pussy clenching around me as I bottom out.

"Take it, baby, fucking own me with this tight pussy, my beautiful, filthy whore. You feel so good, my favorite set of holes." I'm holding it together by a thread, keeping up as much of the degradation and praise that makes her moan and grip me tighter, but I'm not going to last long the way she's strangling my cock. Seeing her pretty pink pussy stretching around my cock every time I slam into her and her engagement ring flashing when her hand moves is unraveling every thread of control I possess. This glorious woman is mine.

"Oh, Daddy, right there, please don't stop," she begs, her legs tightening around my hips in our contorted position.

I support her weight on my thighs and move a hand to her clit, circling as I continue to fuck her. Soon, she cries out and clamps down on me, her orgasm rolling over her like a tidal wave and dripping down my cock as she *squirts*. *Fuuuck*. The tight grip and the knowledge that I did that to her send me barreling over the edge. Pressing her against the window, I barely catch myself on one hand, burying myself balls deep as I come harder than I have in my life.

"Fuck," I swear, holding her tightly as my cock jerks and she squeezes me dry. When I can see straight, I carry her back to the sofa and fall back into it, Ainsley in my lap, still on my cock, with our cum spilling around our thighs. I love the way she wears it.

"I hope you pay the cleaning crew well," she quips dreamily, her breaths coming in fast pants as she leans into me. "We made an absolute mess out of that window and the floor. If that happens when we get engaged, I can't even imagine what the mess will be like when we get married and I'm your wife."

My wife. I want that. I laugh and hold her closer, stroking her hair and nuzzling her neck to start our aftercare. Of course she'd make jokes after the best sex and most explosive orgasms we've experienced in our three years together. That means I did my job. She's processing and no longer overwhelmed.

"Let's get married now. I want to call you my wife as soon as possible."

She sits up and turns to look at me, shock replacing the sex haze on her face. "*Right now,* when your cum is still sticky on my thighs?" she questions.

"Tonight, tomorrow, as soon as we can make it happen in a way you're happy with. I need you as my wife and I need to be your husband more than anything."

Talk about post-nut clarity. I came so hard I realized I don't want a fiancée. I need to start this chapter of our lives immediately.

"What about my family, the dress, and all the traditional things that weddings need?" She worries her lip until I pull it free.

"What about us is traditional?" I challenge. "Our relationship started out fake to appease my family. We have the kinkiest sex life and you're my collared sub, calling me Daddy while I use your perfect set of holes like the fucktoy you are. You wrote an anonymous gossip blog calling my family out on bullshit with our business for years before you were finally outed for it while dating me. None of that screams white chapel wedding with a reception at a country club where Meemaw leaves before the DJ starts playing Ludacris, but I'll do anything you want if it makes you happy."

She shakes her head. "I don't need any of that." Her lashes lower and she peeks up at me like she's sharing something secret. "I do want a pretty dress and a delicious cake and the location to be meaningful to us, though. What about at the lakehouse? Just our families and closest friends. A ceremony at sunset and a reception by the pool." She sounds wistful like she's thought about this.

"That's perfect." I can see the picture she's painted and I want that, knowing it'll make her happy. "What's our first dance song?" She's probably thought of that, also. She begins to shiver now that we've cooled down. I reach for my jacket and pull it over her like a blanket.

"'Never Let Me Go' by Florence and the Machine," she answers softly. I'm vaguely familiar with the song, but if she likes it, it's perfect. Hell, I'd dance with her to a banjo rendition of a Taylor Swift song if she asked me to.

"I like the way that sounds. A lakeside wedding with you in a beautiful dress in front of the people we love."

"And cake."

"Can't forget the cake. Chocolate, I assume?"

"Of course." She stiffens against me and I feel her hard-earned relaxation fleeing. "God, there are so many details and things to consider even if we do it quick and simple." Anxiety pitches her voice higher.

"Don't worry about a thing. I'll have a team on it tonight if you want. The only thing you need to do is make sure the dress you want to wear fits. I think Paige has a place she loves that does fast work."

"Haute Belle," Ainsley says absently, picking at her cuticles.

"We could do this fast and not worry about the details? It would be everything we wanted without the stress?"

"Yes, my love. I'd make your dreams come true. Say the word and you'll be my wife."

She looks up at me with eyes full of trust. "I want to be your wife. Let's do it."

And that's exactly what we do.

Fifty

Epilogue

Ainsley
One week later

The string quartet plays "Ocean Eyes" by Billie Eilish as I walk down the dock on my dad's arm toward Payton, standing in a charcoal suit silhouetted against the lake at sunset. I'm wearing a simple white, sweetheart neckline dress that hugs my curves and flares from my hips in a mermaid style without additional adornments. It's lightweight, soft, and feels divine on my skin. I knew it was perfect as soon as Angela at Haute Bride buttoned me into it. I feel beautiful, and the way Payton is looking at me, he thinks so. His deep blue eyes are shining with tears and happiness, and I can't look away.

We stop in front of the flower-covered arch as the music fades out. I can hear my mom sniffling behind me. My family is here, all four sisters included, which is a miracle given the short notice and everyone's busy schedules. Payton's family mixes in with mine, and a few of our friends are here—Luca and Della, of course, Javier from Olympus and his wife, Paloma, along with their two children, Diego from Olympus, and Octavius Rex, who keeps looking at my sister, Serena, like he's been smacked in the face for some reason. Lilah, who's become a great friend, just like I thought she would, is sitting with Knox Contraire, a football player from the Atlanta Condors who's a friend of Harlowe's and has become close with us over the years. It's an intimate crowd and exactly what I pictured for my wedding to the love of my life.

I pass my bouquet to Della, who squeezes my hand. I turn to Payton and sigh as I take him in. He looks amazing every day, but it's extra special today. The sunlight halos around him, giving him a burnished glow that sets his skin on fire and warms me from the inside out as the air cools around us. "I love you" he mouths to me, and I say it back. Suddenly, my dad passes my hand to Payton, having answered the officiant to begin the ceremony.

"Hello, my darling." Payton cups my cheek as he takes my hand and we face each other in front of the arch.

"This is happening, not a dream?" It doesn't feel real. Everything's in soft rose gold tones from the setting sun and the dock shifts softly under our feet. As excited as I am, there's anxiety creeping in, wanting to dull the glow and steal my happiness even now.

"It's as real as my love for you, Princess," he assures me. "Look at me, baby. Focus on me and the best thing to happen to us."

I suck in a shaky breath and nod, signaling the officiant to begin the ceremony. Payton rubs soft, comforting circles along the backs of my hands, becoming my anchor in the storm of my thoughts, mooring me to the moment and allowing me to be present. Soon, we're exchanging vows, and tears stream down my cheeks the moment he begins speaking.

"Ainsley, you're the love of my life, the compass that sets my course, and the wind that fills my sails. I've been in love with you from the day we met and patiently waited for you to catch up, knowing I only wanted to spend my life with you. You're precious to me, and I'm grateful every day that you chose me."

His smile is soft as I sob. I'm a complete mess, whereas he's composed and in control as ever. He reaches out and smooths the tears from my cheeks before he continues.

"I promise to love you as deeply as the ocean, with all its mystery, beauty, and power. Like the waves that crash against the shore, my love for you is unending and unstoppable. My love for you is like the sea, fathomless and infinite."

I hiccup and he pulls me into his chest, letting me hide my face against him while he whispers soothing words into my ear and smooths his hand along my back. The emotions are so raw, his words so beautiful and heartfelt. I feel each line branded onto my soul. I take a deep breath, his intoxicating sea salt and amber scent fortifying me like it always does, and pull away, grateful for waterproof makeup when his white shirt is streak-free. He gives me a questioning look, checking in. I nod to continue. Noses are blown from our group of family and friends, but I don't dare look. This is all about us.

"I promise to push your boundaries to help you grow, to believe in you ceaselessly when your faith in yourself is wavering, to champion your causes and make your dreams come true. I'll be the mirror that reflects your accomplishments, talents, and abilities to ensure you know how capable and amazing you are when doubts creep in. There won't be room for imposter syndrome with us. The storms of life may toss us on turbulent seas, but my love will not waver. I'll stand firm in my protection, guarding our love against all that rises up against us. You're my greatest treasure, and I'm your faithful servant forever."

I smile, knowing how true his words are. He's always been my biggest supporter, believing in my capability even when I didn't. He's the most wonderful man imaginable, and I'm incredibly lucky that he loves me this deeply and this well. He takes a ring from Zander and slides it onto my finger. He recites the vows we decided on together.

"I, Payton, choose you, Ainsley, to be my wife. I will respect you, care for you, and grow with you through good times and hard times, as your friend, companion, and partner, giving all that I can to fulfill our lives together."

The officiant turns to me and I gulp, knowing the heartfelt words I wrote now have to be spoken out loud, in front of more than just the person they're intended for. *Great.*

"Payton, I tried my best not to fall in love with you. I attempted to push you away and tell you I wasn't worth the effort. I wasn't ready for the kind of love you're so good at providing and didn't know what to do with an overly smiley man intent on talking to me even when I growled at him."

I hear teary giggles along with knowing chuckles from my family and Della. I'm not worried about that because it's all true.

"Instead of being deterred, you showed me with every action what true love, care, and affection is. You have become my calm before and after a storm. Your patience keeps me grounded when my world is spinning out of control. I promise to share myself with you in every way. To allow you into my thoughts when I'd rather stay silent. I promise to follow your lead, knowing you want the best for me in everything and will challenge me to be better. You've taught me to set aside my pride, to release my prejudices, and to accept that there is more to a person than meets the eye, and for that I'm eternally grateful."

Payton's eyes are bright, a tear tipping over his dark lashes as he blinks. I reach up and cup his cheek, his hand covering mine and moving it to his mouth to kiss my palm. When he releases my hand and I pull it back, he mouths, "Thank you, my love." I clear my throat and try not to get choked up. I swipe under my eyes and take another breath, determined to continue without completely losing it.

"I promise to give myself to you body, mind, heart, and soul, knowing I'm safe in your hands. I am yours and you are mine, and our love is a boundless ocean with currents we'll navigate together. I promise to trust you, to support you, to always keep you on your toes, and discover new things together."

I hear a snort that quickly turns into a cough that has to be from Zander. I smile mischievously at Payton and he returns the look. I absolutely meant it in a bedroom capacity to tease him, but I wasn't sly enough. I giggle to move past the silly moment and find my seriousness again with a reassuring squeeze of Payton's fingers. I give him a grateful look before turning to Della and taking the ring she hands me. I slip it onto Payton's hand. Holding it tightly, I look up at him with all the devotion in my heart as I recite my vows.

"I, Ainsley, choose you, Payton, to be my husband. I will respect you, care for you, and grow with you through good times and hard times, as your friend, companion, and partner, giving all that I can to fulfill our lives together."

The officiant closes out the ceremony with words that don't even register until he pronounces us husband and wife. Payton sweeps me back and kisses me, my hands coming to his face and holding on to kiss him back. This feels like a revelation, life-changing in the best way. With a few simple words, our lives are changed and we belong to each other forever.

The cheers from our family and friends erupt around us as Payton pulls me back to my feet and kisses me several more times. This man is a hands-on, deeply sentimental, sappy romantic, and he will take every opportunity for a public display of affection he can get. I'm laughing as Della hands me my bouquet and we walk back down the middle of the dock, starting our life together as Mr. and Mrs. Payton Olsen.

Thank you so much for reading The Southern Submission! If you enjoyed this book, I would be grateful if you could leave a review on the platform(s) of your choice. Reviews are so valuable to authors, and each one helps share our stories with others!

If you enjoyed seeing the other Olsens in this book and want to know more about them, you can read their stories! Hayes and Paige's story is told in books one and two, The Bourbon Bride and The Bourbon Bargain, and Zander and Harlowe's story is told in book three, The Southern Thirst Trap.

Interested in what's next? The Gods of the Ice series will follow the Atlanta Hydras, the Olsen brothers' new hockey team, with book one featuring the goalie, Ryder Kingston. Keep reading for a sneak peek!

Gods of the Ice Teaser

Ryder

"Kingsy, my man, I have news for you. It's good and bad, so I'll just rip the Band-Aid off. Boston traded you to Atlanta. You're going to that new team those billionaires bought."

My head swims at the worst news my agent could have given me. I squeeze the phone and pace across my living room, along the floor-to-ceiling windows that look out over Boston Harbor. How the fuck could this happen? I was named one of the best goalies in the league and we just came off a seven-game playoff run for the Stanley Cup. I was supposed to be signed for another eight years in Boston. I just fucking went through arbitration last year and spent this season showing the team why they needed to keep me. I've given seven years of my life to Boston, how could they do me dirty like this after I've given them everything?

"Tell me you're fucking joking, Mark, this isn't fucking funny," I growl, my mind still spinning down a dark tunnel of my personal hell.

"I'm shooting straight with you like I always do. They're in contract negotiations with Upton to keep him on instead. They couldn't have two number-one goalies forever, and unfortunately, you had the bigger target on your back with this series run and that devastating loss," Mark says.

His words burn like acid and remind me of my failures that are never far from my mind. We were so close to the cup, in the conference finals, game seven against Dallas, and the deciding factor if we would advance to the Stanley Cup finals. We lost, three to two, and those three goals were my fault. I let them past my glove and we lost our shot, again. The huge weight hanging on my shoulders and one of the biggest black marks against me in arbitration last year was not being trustworthy during playoffs. I proved them right again by not performing when it counted, and look where it got me, traded to a brand-new team in fucking Atlanta.

"I'm going to the hell hole of the South? Hot-fucking-lanta? This is a fucking nightmare."

"It's a thirty-three-million-dollar, three-year nightmare. That's the upside. We got you far more than Boston would've given you if they'd kept you. You're now the highest-paid goalie in the NHL. That should help make up for the trade at least a bit, and you get to help shape a brand-new team with an unlimited budget. These billionaires aren't sparing a single penny and are pulling in the best talent in the league for this team. I've heard rumors of their moves and it'll be good. They even got Connor Kennedy to coach. That man's a fucking legend. You'll be skating for someone with more cup runs and wins than any current coaching team can boast. This isn't what you had in mind, but it's not the worst that could have happened."

No shit. The worst is I could be done with hockey forever,

injured and unable to play, or so shitty no team wanted to pick me up. I see what Mark's doing, and I'm rational enough to understand this is a good fucking deal. But fuck, I don't want to be rational, I want to wallow and stick with my routine and the things I wanted for a change. Hockey isn't a sport you get your say in all that often, and I've been damn lucky to stick with the same team I was drafted to right out of college. Seven years is a lifetime to spend with one team, and I guess I was pushing my luck hoping they'd keep me longer. Knowing that doesn't make this loss any easier to swallow.

"So, what now?" I ask Mark, a note of despair in my tone I don't like the sound of. I need to know what's expected of me to establish my routine immediately. I know it's stupid to some people, but I need everything to be the same, and to know what to expect. I thrive in routine, knowing the rules and how to play by them—when to show up and where to be, what to eat, what my training plan is—all that fucking bullshit hockey players are told makes us superstitious sheep. And I know what they say about goalies being the worst. I just don't fucking care.

"You enjoy what little of your summer you can, settle up in Boston, and get your ass to Atlanta for training camp in September. And hey, another bright spot is Knox is in Atlanta, so at least you'll know a friendly face right off the bat and I'll finally have my two best clients in the same city."

That's the only upside I can see right now—living in the same city as my best friend for the first time since college. Knox Contraire is a tight end for the Atlanta Condors football team and the best dude I know. He'll have to save me from this nightmare one way or another because I don't have the option of turning down a trade this lucrative at the top of my career. I hope he's ready to be my knight in shining fucking armor.

The Gods of the Ice series is coming in 2025!

Acknowledgements

Acknowledgements

To my readers—thank you for joining me on this deliciously dirty journey through the Southern Gods series and sticking it out to get our favorite meddling middle brother's love story. Payton was a surprise from the first page and took me for a ride to get his happily ever after with the prickliest woman I've ever written. Cacti have nothing on Ainsley, but her spiky outside was protecting one of the most traumatized souls that just wanted to be loved I could have imagined. Payton saw that right away and knew how to love her, even when I was annoyed that she was making my life harder. I'm so grateful you have loved the Olsens and have grown attached to these morally gray billionaire businessmen brothers right along with me. It's hard to say goodbye – which is why I'm not! They will show up in the next series, Gods of the Ice, so we don't have to be done with them quite yet.

Many thanks to everyone who took the time to encourage, beta-read, edit, and provide feedback to help me create this novel. You're all the real MVPs!

Billy – I love you, always. Thank you for the princess treatment and for always supporting my dreams. I couldn't do this without you.

The amazing community I've built on Booksta – y'all are amazing, I love you all so very much and couldn't do this without you. I write for YOU and I'm so glad you found my stories. Whether it's shouting your love for my books and characters, making incredible edits, sharing reviews, or letting me into your DMs with my needy author ways and embracing me, you've all been so wonderful, caring, hilarious, and just so damn amazing! The internet is seriously the best for bringing your people together to create a community of some of the best ladies I know.

About the Author

About the Author

Adrian R. Hale is an enthusiastic lover of life who embraces big dreams, for herself and in her books. She writes new adult and contemporary romance featuring strong heroes with secret cinnamon roll sides, and dream-chasing heroines, with a little angst, a lot of swoon, and all the steam lovingly sprinkled in.

Adrian loves fast cars, baking sweet treats, hiking through Texas hill country, and is affectionately known as an agent of chaos to those closest to her. A self-professed caffeine addict, she loves a good vanilla oat latte, and will never turn down a tea party, especially in celebration of little milestones. When she's not writing or reading, Adrian can be found cuddling with her five dogs and husband, watching the 2005 Pride & Prejudice, DIY renovating her home near Austin, Texas, or listening to Taylor Swift.

Website: www.adrianrhale.com
Newsletter: https://bit.ly/AdrianHaleNL
Facebook facebook.com/adrianrhaleauthor
FB Group https://bit.ly/AdriansGoodGirls
Instagram: instagram.com/adrianrhale/
TikTok: tiktok.com/@adrianrhale
Goodreads: goodreads.com/adrianrhale

9 798991 871211